# Heart of My Seed

*"I will circumcise your heart and the heart of your seed to love the Lord thy God with all your heart, soul and mind."*
*~Deuteronomy 30:6*

# Heart of My Seed

Judi Charbonneau

This historical family saga is based on true events. It follows the hopes and dreams as well as the nightmares and demons of four generations. Dialogue and characters for certain events contained herein were created for the purpose of dramatization. The author tried to be honest and truthful without exposing others. Any offense toward cultural or religious groups is purely unintentional. The hope is that you will read it from start to finish so you do not miss any nuggets or surprises.

A portion of the proceeds from the sale of *Heart of My Seed* will go to support missions.

Cover photo *Rose on Wood*: © visi.stock/Fotolia
Author photo courtesy of: Judy Talent, JTeez Shotz Photography, Clovis, CA ©2013

Printed in United States of America,
United Kingdom, and Australia

**For**

*Rebecca*

*Morgan*

*Storm*

*Chyna*

*Madeline*

*Chase*

*Paige*

*Natalie*

# Acknowledgements

Steve, Gary, and Nicole: I am a blessed woman thanks to you, my dear children. Your dedication to your God and family, have exceeded my expectations. Your delightful personalities have brought me much joy. The eight grand-children you gave me bless me beyond words. Thank you for contributing to this book as you have to my life.

Robyn Meyers: Thank you my faithful friend for always being there for me. Checking up on me daily encouraged me more than you know. God used your love to lift me up when I felt inadequate. I'm forever grateful.

Julie Williams: This project could never have become a reality without you. Your constant input and inspiration kept me on track. You had a knack for interpreting my heart when I couldn't articulate what I wanted to say. You let me keep my voice and you never gave up on me. You have become a treasured friend. I look forward to reading the books you are working on. Thank you my friend.

# Introduction

**Judi Charbonneau**
**My Insignificant Journey with Significant Milestones**

My story does not start with myself—it goes back generations to those who laid a foundation of faith, those who deviated from it, and those who denied it. Nor will my story end with me—my legacy continues through my children, my grandchildren, and all who come to know me.

"I was not as good of a mother to your mom as she is to you," I told my granddaughter one day. "But then again, I was a far better mother than mine was."

"Good," Morgan said. "That means I'll be an even better mom than Mama."

As I recall this conversation, I'm overwhelmed by God's redemptive power. While it's true that I wasn't the best parent and missed the close relationship I hoped for with my children

*Mimi and Mo*

and grandchildren, I make no excuses. God would not allow it. Just as He doesn't let me boast in my accomplishments. Also, I get nowhere focusing on my mother's ills. He has called me to be responsible for my actions, some of which break my heart to this day. But in searching for His heart, I find people. Fallible people like me. Redeemed people like me.

# Heart of My Heritage

# Chapter 1

## Mary Falvey O'Niell

**Queenstown, Ireland ~ Winter 1879**

Even on tiptoes, Mary wouldn't be able to see over the crowd. She cast a fleeting look behind. If Mummy and Dadaí failed to catch up, she'd miss their final farewells, but in no way would she miss this ship. They should've left Nana at home.

*Mr. and Mrs. Henry O'Niell.* The name still brought a flush to her cheeks. She focused on the words painted across the trunk that bobbed its way through a sea of strangers—all their worldly possessions rode atop her husband's shoulder. All, save a few treasures she carried in the small bundle—and two tickets. She slipped her hand into her pocket, curled her fingers around the parchment, and pushed her way through dockworkers and pickpockets.

A great plume of steam bellowed from the ship's black smokestacks and melted into the storm-laden clouds. She gave them only a glance. If she lost sight of the trunk, she'd have a devil of a time finding Henry. Then what would become of her and their babe-to-be? The trunk dipped, then disappeared.

*Holy Mother!* All feeling went out of her legs. She skirted around a woman pushing a pram with half a dozen grubby children in tow, then circled back around to the right. Hadn't the trunk gone down that way? An old couple, hand in hand, blocked her path. Trying to avoid their shuffling steps, she slammed into a barrel-chested sailor. Her bundle hurled toward the cobblestones. She yanked her hand out of her pocket—tickets and all—and lunged, catching up her treasured bundle mere inches from shattering the jar of brambleberry jelly tucked within.

"Careful, Missy." The sailor righted her, but his grip on her elbow tightened.

"Pardon, Sir." She searched the crush of people separating her from Henry. She struggled to pull her arm away. The sailor's fingers bruised through her threadbare coat. His whiskery chin and rotten-toothed grin hovered close—greedy eyes sought her tickets. She clutched them so the ink threatened to blur in her palm and crossed herself. *St. Christopher, protect me!* The prayer lodged in her throat.

"Mary, love, over here." Back and to her left. Henry, bless him, stood on their trunk, waving her over.

She jerked her arm again and trod on the sailor's foot for good measure. This time the man loosed her. "Henry." She shoved the tickets back in her pocket, shouting his name with each faltering step.

People stopped to let her pass until she came to the foot of their trunk. Henry reached a hand down. "Come up and see the view from here. That's our ship." He pointed to the twin smokestacks.

Mary placed a trembling hand to her belly and shook her head. "We've enough excitement for one day."

Henry lowered himself onto the trunk and pulled her close. She melted into his embrace and shuddered a sob. "I thought I lost you."

"Never, my beauty." He stroked her raven hair for a moment, and then cleared his throat. "So, how'd you like being the body at the wake?"

She lifted her chin and gazed full in his face. His blue eyes were a bit bleary from last night's festivities. Who could blame him?

They'd been toasted in every roadside tavern they passed between home and Queenstown. "It's a strange thing indeed to be eulogized by family and friends—to be treated like life's ending…" The wind traced icy fingers down her spine. "…when it's just beginning."

A pensive look dulled his eyes. "We may never see any of 'em again." With a little shake of his head, the sparkle returned.

She nodded. "I guess you can't start a dream until you've said goodnight." Any minute they'd board the steamer for America and the real adventure would begin. It all felt so sudden. "I can't believe we're really here."

"Really going, you mean." Henry's freckles skipped across his face when he got excited. Today they danced a jig.

Mummy puffed to a stop at Mary's side, fanning herself with an open palm. "We were like to never catch you."

Mary turned and kissed Mummy's cheek. "Thank you for coming to see us off." She caught Dadaí's eye. "For the tickets to America. For everything."

Dadaí grinned. "Just don't forget to send for us when you get yourselves settled." With twinkling eyes, he dropped a small leather pouch in Henry's hand. "Your Daddy's clan gathered enough pounds and schillings to help you get settled. Too bad your folks' old bones couldn't come to see you off."

Nana poked her face between them and waggled a finger. "Don't go. You'll be scalped by Indians."

"Hush, Nana." Mummy edged her aside.

"No worse a fate than those staying behind will get from the land owners." Henry's chuckle tickled her ear.

Dadaí unclipped the watch from his vest and handed it to Henry. "May it bring you the prosperity it failed to bring me dad and granddad before me."

Henry sprang to his feet and whipped the cap off his head. "It can't fail to, sir." A single ray of sunlight lit his hair a fiery copper— like a sign from heaven.

Mary's heart leapt at the sight.

Mummy laid solid hands on either side of the small bulge of Mary's belly. "It breaks me heart to bid you go."

"Your grandchild will be born in America, Mummy! We can be grateful for that."

Mummy's face beamed. "Aye, we can." She untied her homespun scarf and wrapped it around Mary's shoulders.

Mary pressed her face into the soft folds. Peat smoke, soda bread, bog myrtle, and stout caught her up in a swirl of Ireland. Of Mummy.

"Have you nothing to send the young couple off to America with?" Mummy elbowed Nana.

"Haven't I given enough to those ungrateful shores?" Nana dug in her pocket and tugged out a hankie. "Three sons I gave during the years of the Great Hunger. Owen died of fever aboard a coffin ship. They buried him with the other unfortunates on Grosse Isle." Strangers stopped and stared. Hadn't they heard such rantings a thousand times? "John was killed in their war to free the Negroes, while our own Ireland—this Land of Tears—founders in British chains."

A few here-here's went up from the gathering crowd. Mary wanted to hide. She wasn't here for a lecture.

"And, me youngest, Sean." Nana wiped her eyes on the soiled hankie. "They worked 'im to death building their railways."

Mary searched for words of comfort—any means to quiet Nana. None came. Thirty years ago, the Potato Famine had been severe. Many more died in Ireland than those who went abroad. Now they stood on the brink of another such disaster. Mary squared her shoulders—she would take her chances in America.

With a great honking, Nana blew her nose into the hankie, emptying far more than anger or sorrow. "Take it." She held out the offending rag. "Bury a piece of me in America."

Mummy looked stricken. Had she no words when Mary needed them most?

"Take it." In Nana's withered hand, the hankie waved closer and closer to Mary's face. "Take it, child."

Henry snatched it from her and stuffed it into his back pocket. "It'll be our first duty when we set foot on land."

Mary gave her husband a grateful smile. His task perhaps. Hers would be to wash those trousers.

"What're you gawkin' at?" Nana thumped a sandy-haired stranger on the chest, sending the onlookers about their business.

"Never mind her outburst." Mummy drew Mary close again, cupping her hands to Mary's cheeks. "You're going to New York. Life will be better."

"We'll make it so." Dadaí laid one hand on Mary's shoulder, the other on Henry. "Mother of God, take care of me boy and girl here, for they belong to Your son Jesus. Help them find a proper home for a long and happy life."

Tears shone in Henry's Irish eyes. "It's time, love." He hoisted their trunk on his shoulder and plowed a course toward the narrow gangplank.

Mary fanned her eyes with the palm of her hand to keep her tears at bay. "I love you, Mummy. I love you, Dadaí." She bid her gaze to drink in every detail of her parents' faces. "I miss you already. We'll send for you soon. A year at most." She turned to follow Henry, but Mummy held her fast and kissed her forehead.

Silent torrents rolled down Mummy's weathered cheeks. "Until we meet again…"

Mary crossed herself, brushing her knuckles against Mummy's hand as she did the same. And whispered back the blessing. "May the hand of God protect you too, Mummy." Her heart ached to linger in her mother's warm gaze, to snatch Dadaí's hat and ruffle the down of his balding head, but the clomp-clomping of Henry's boots retreating down the dock tore her away. She hurried after him. By all the saints, she wouldn't lose her husband a second time in this throng.

A few yards from the gangplank, Henry slowed his steps. "Come around me and show the purser our tickets."

A squabbling family blocked her way, leaving only a foot of space for Mary to pass along the edge of the dock, without rope or railing for support. The steamship towered above her. A narrow gulf of icy water lapped the pilings below her. Her heart tried to speed up and stop all at the same time. "I can't make it."

His head swiveled left and right. "Make way," he bellowed and scooted the other family over, scarcely doubling her walkway.

One false step—one little jostle—would topple her into the ocean to be crushed between ship and dock. Determined not to let another *I can't* slip from her lips, she took a deep breath, forced her gaze ahead, and scooted around him.

"That's it, love." At Henry's words, she took a stuttering breath and her heartbeat slackened. She pulled the crumpled tickets from her pocket and held them out to the uniform-clad purser.

His white gloves reached for the tickets, then snapped back. "Sorry, Ma'am. This is the *City of Richmond*, of the Inman Line."

"But—"

His narrow nose wrinkled as if she'd offered him soured milk. "Those are for the *Chadwick*." He gave a single nod toward the tall masts further down the wharf.

"A sailing ship? But this is supposed to be a two week journey." Mary stared at the tickets. When she looked up, the purser busied himself with the other family.

Henry shoved his way forward. "You can't expect my wife to be on the ocean for three months. She's…she's…"

The bluster of his words scorched Mary's cheeks.

"…with child!"

The purser leveled his grey eyes on her belly. "Then buy the right tickets."

Henry's fingers curled. "I'll show you the right." The trunk almost slid from his shoulder.

*Saints preserve us!* If he clouted the purser, they'd lose more than the cost of their tickets. She forced her words through gritted teeth. "The *Chadwick* is fine." His eyes darted from the purser to her. She pasted a smile on her face and slipped trembling fingers through the crook of Henry's arm. "I can brave anything as long as we're together."

He searched her face in the way she loved. Like he would battle the very demons of hell to make her happy.

"Really." She touched his cheek, pleased her hands no longer shook. For an instant, the crowds disappeared. "A few extra weeks at sea will be nothing compared trying to board the ship."

The muscles under his sleeve relaxed. He cocked his head toward the purser. "You're lucky I married an angel." He spun on his heal, forcing the man to jump back to avoid being bashed by the trunk.

She held her chin high—this cretin would never see her cry—and marched to the clipper ship with her husband.

♥ ♥ ♥

*The departure*

Mary stood at the *Chadwick's* rail until her arm could wave no more, and her family, nay, the whole of Queenstown, melted into a distant lump. And still she stared—lest she forget to memorize the beautiful emerald green of her homeland. Lest she have to confess, the salt on her cheeks came from more than sea spray.

"A grand adventure." Henry breathed the words and looped

his arm around her shoulder. She snuggled into his side. A dream never began until one closed her eyes to the waking. She allowed herself to blink.

The *Chadwick* crested another swell and dipped, sending up a spray to match the misty night. The lantern light and shadows chased each other around the deck like so many rats. Huddled in a corner of the ship's deck, Mary squeezed her eyes shut to the dizziness and hung her head over a copper pot. This was not what she'd imagined on the dock only this morning. How could she survive three months in this rollicking ship? The two-week journey by steamer would've been worth any price. Something she couldn't admit to Henry just now. He knelt on one knee beside her and rubbed her back.

What little she'd eaten at supper had come up hours ago. "The rocking makes me sicker—" She gasped for air and another dry heave convulsed her chest. "—than it already is from the baby."

"I'll fetch you some water."

She gripped his hand and raised only her eyes to his face. Praying nothing but words would come out. "Don't leave me." She caught the concern etched around his eyes, and it threatened to break her heart.

Two bells sounded. A steward strode through the passengers still milling around on the deck. "No women on deck after 9 o'clock." The rustling of skirts that accompanied the exodus of ladies from deck made Mary's ears swim. She hugged the pot to her chest and gulped air to settle her stomach.

The steward turned a kindly face to Henry. "You need some help with your missus?"

Mary shook her head. Wasn't it embarrassing enough to be the last to obey the rule? She'd make it below by Henry's help alone.

He pulled Mary to her feet and spoke in comforting tones. "I found a berth next to a nice older couple. We will be safe there."

They stumbled over to the hatch labeled Emigrants. The sixteen-foot descent into steerage was half stairway, half ladder. The smell was not definable but sickening, cumbered with so many bundles of humanity crammed into a small space. The air grew darker the lower they went.

"Here we are Mary." Henry guided her to the married couples' berth, where layers of hammocks were strung, and curtained off by the tens. "Meet our neighbors, Mr. and Mrs. Kelly. We passed them on the road to Queenstown two days ago."

"Oh, yes." She had assumed at the time, from the lady's dress and bearing, the couple would be in a first class cabin aboard a steamer. Mary extended her hands in greeting, remembering all too late the filthy pot she clutched.

"Hello, dearie." Mrs. Kelly accepted the pot in delicate hands without even the bat of an eyelash.

Heat rose in Mary's cheeks as she tried to snatch it back. "I didn't mean—"

"We'll have no embarrassment, here." Mrs. Kelly set it on the floor. "I'm sure we'll be well acquainted by the end of this voyage."

Mr. Kelly peered at her through scratched up spectacles. "Yes, and if you need help with anything at all, I'll be happy to oblige."

Their kindly looks, so much like Mummy and Dadaí's, warmed her from the inside out. She was safe. "Thank you both." Mary managed a genuine smile. "If you could get me some fresh air that would be most helpful."

Mr. Kelly's laughing eyes winked. "No bottle of fresh air! I do have a bottle of juniper juice I'd be glad to share with ya."

"I think I better pass. Never been one for gin, and besides, I don't think it would be good for the baby."

"Oh! Your first?" Mrs. Kelly caught her by the hands. "You must be thrilled, but I guess this voyage will be that much harder for you."

Against her wishes to deny it, her head nodded.

"I've a treat of me own." Henry reached into an upper

hammock and retrieved the bundle Mary had brought. He untied the fabric and pulled out a bottle of whisky.

Mary poked her hand into the folds. Her fingers glided over prayer beads, baby booties, tiny christening gown, her copy of Jane Eyre. Her heart and mouth filled with sand, her whispered words croaked out. "Where's Mummy's jelly?"

A sheepish look came over his face. "I traded it at the last tavern."

"That's what I was protecting?"

"Sorry, Mary." He clinked the neck of his bottle against Mr. Kelly's. "Here's to the promise of new beginnings, and to new horizons. May we keep both before us." They each took a single gulp and recapped their drinks.

The scritching of cork and bottle set Mary's teeth on edge. Large tears rolled down her cheeks.

"You're tired, love, and I'm bushed." Henry kissed her forehead with soothing tenderness and wiped her tears with his clean handkerchief. He settled her onto the lower hammock. "My bunk is right above you in case you be needing anything."

She stifled one last sob. His trade made sense, considering the turmoil in her stomach. Better for him to have a bit of enjoyment. But for some unknown reason, now that the jelly was gone, brambleberry was all she could think of wanting.

Mary lay on her back in the swaying hammock pleading for sleep to overtake her. Every lace of her corset dug into her spine, but if she rolled over again, her legs would become hopelessly entangled in her petticoats. No matter which way she turned, the bunk was just short of positively uncomfortable. A dozen jars of jelly. That's what she'd give to be able to strip down to her shift, but with over two hundred folks aboard, their berth afforded no privacy. The ship rocked and rolled, and in the bunk to her left, a child cried out. Someone coughed. Another retched. Mary's stomach tried to answer back. *Oh, not here. Not now. I can't get out of this contraption.* She held Mummy's scarf over her nose and mouth and forced her mind to visions of Ireland.

From somewhere on deck, a tin whistle struck up a haunting tune. Henry caught up the rhythm, tapping its beat on the wooden board above his bunk, the way he'd done each time Dadaí played late into the night. If she closed her eyes, she could imagine home.

Home anew.

"Mary, my love." Henry's gentle touch nudged her awake. Daylight seeped into their berth, and with it a bit of freshness. She smiled into his adoring face. Perhaps she could endure this for another two months and twenty-nine days. He smiled. "The ship's bell will soon ring, calling us to breakfast. I hope you packed our tin ware at easy reach."

"It's right on top in the plaid linen cloth." She pushed up on one elbow. The slight movement sent her stomach spinning. "I don't think I can eat anything and keep it down."

He untangled her feet and helped her out of bed. "Please, Mary. For the sake of the baby—you need your strength."

"I'll try." Pools formed in her eyes again. She wiped them away while Henry fetched their tin ware from the trunk. "If weather permits, I'd like to stay on deck as long as possible. The air down here is too hard to breathe."

A length of twine strung through holes in the rims of their tableware bound tin mugs, plates, and utensils together. The mess jangled like sleigh bells as he swung it over his shoulder. He took her arm and escorted her down the narrow passageway.

"Someone coughed all night. Do you think ship fever is starting already?" She clawed at his arm. "Oh, Henry, I'm so scared."

He turned her to face him, crushed her against his chest, and whispered into her hair. "Mary, we labored over the decision to leave our families. You were determined to trust in your God. You encouraged me to take that step of faith."

"But typhus…"

His fingers brushed stray strands of hair from her forehead and he planted his lips there briefly. "I'm as scared as you are, but let's stay strong together." She nodded, pressing closer, drawing strength from his loving heart. With slow and shallow breaths, Mary entered the makeshift dining hall and took her place at the long table. The steward brought hunks of bread, and ladled porridge onto her plate. It slopped from one edge to the other with the motion of the ship. Mary pretended to eat, for Henry's sake. She pinched little pieces of bread and let them dissolve in her mouth— amazed at how they settled her frantic stomach. The weak coffee with a splash of milk, stayed down as well. Encouraged, she dipped her spoon in the porridge and licked a dollop off the bottom. It would better serve as paste. She slid her plate over to Henry, helped herself to a morsel of his remaining bread, and slipped it into her pocket to guard against future seasickness.

"That's my girl." He grinned at her and dropped the last of his bread into her other pocket.

By the time they reached the common pail to wash their tin ware, the water teamed with enough table scraps to look like the inside of her brass pot. Mary averted her eyes for fear of needing that vessel again so soon. "How much water is allotted us each day?" She choked out the question.

"Three quarts a piece."

"Do you suppose it's enough for drinking and washing, both? I'd rather not be getting a share of other people's disease."

"Aye, I thought of that me self."

## Atlantic Crossing ~ Spring 1880

And so it went, day in and day out for the next, what seemed like, unending weeks. When it rained, rivers ran fore and aft under Mary's bunk. Despite what little she ate, the baby inside her grew, leaving her in a constant state of wilt. Henry emptied his bottle and filled it twice from the purser's stock, using the coins from his little pouch. Water rations ran short and even those with the stoutest constitutions had trouble keeping their dinners down. Fever swept through all the berths. Children cried out in the night and mothers' wailed at the loss of little ones.

Each time a storm abated, Mary swathed herself in coat and blanket and huddled with Henry on deck for a welcomed breath of fresh air. The most recent deluge, rivaled Noah's flood, but lasted a mere ten days. Now, as evening fell, the sun threatened to burn a bright patch in the clouds, drawing a small crowd to the prow. "It feels good to be topside again, Henry." She placed one hand on the rail, looking out over the ocean and the other hand on her every growing tummy. "Ooh, the baby's kicking! Would you like to feel it?"

Henry's eyes darted left and right. A sheepish smile tugged his lips. "I won't hurt him will I?" His fingers hovered a hair's breadth above her bulge. Mary covered his hand and placed it on the spot the baby last moved. Henry grinned. "Do you think he knows it's me out here?" His Irish eyes were laughing!

Mary's heart melted at his playfulness. "Ahh, who said it's going to be a boy? Girls are ever so—"

"There's the Golden Door!" A tall man at the railing next to them shouted. His pointing finger bobbed up and down.

Evening lights twinkled in the distance. Beckoning. Winking and whispering, "Welcome to America." Footsteps pounded in the stairwell. The air bristled with activity as more and more people flocked to the deck.

"Papa, show me the Promise Land." A little girl giggled as her father swung her up on his broad shoulders.

A squat little man squeezed his way to the rail, grabbed Henry by the ears, and kissed him soundly on each cheek. "We make it, no?"

"No." Henry wiped his cheek and stammered back. "Er… Yes, we make it." Mary chuckled at the terrified look on her husband's face.

The tall man, lifted a woman off her feet, spun her around, set her down, and reached for Mary. She wrapped her arms across her belly and tried to back away from the nauseating spin she'd surely receive. Henry slapped the man's hands away and wrapped his arms around her. "I'll not let them trample you, love."

Mr. Kelly, arm in arm with his wife, bustled up. Mrs. Kelly's voice came out breathless. "I can't believe we will feel land beneath our feet once more."

"Dry land at that!" In the past ten days, Mary had come close to losing faith of seeing anything dry. All her pent up fears came out in a burst of laughter. She threw her arms around their necks and let her tears fall unbidden.

As sudden as the commotion began, it faded into a reverent silence, as one by one the emigrants faced their new homeland. Mary leaned her head against Henry's shoulder and stood statue-still as more and more lights came into view along the coast.

Mr. Kelly gripped the rail, his head and shoulders hung far out over the water. A quiet whistling sprang from his lips. Mrs. Kelly picked up the tune. "When sorrows like sea billows roll…" Her soft alto voice wafted over the shimmering waves and echoed back to the deck.

The chorus rippled in hushed tones from one person to the next, like the lighting of candles. "It is well. It is well with my soul." Then, sweet silence, as each seemed to be in his own world of thoughts about this new homeland.

Crowds pressed Mary to the railing as the clipper ship sailed into port at Castle Garden. All night the *Chadwick* had lay at anchor, but Mary refused to leave her post. With one glimpse of her home anew, exhaustion gave way to anticipation. First light dawned gray. Gray seas. Gray clouds. Gray smoke from a gray train, traveling into a gray city. A wondrous sight indeed.

Beside her, Henry shifted his weight from one foot to the

other. She put her hand on his arm. "You're pacing in place. Are you as nervous as I am?"

"A little. More excited, I guess." Still, he rocked side to side.

"If you keep it up, they'll mark you down as insane and send us back to Ireland on this infernal ship."

"Well, we can't have another three months of this." A smile eased the crinkles on his brow. "Are you ready to brave the immigration office?"

"As ready as I'll ever be, but please stay close to me. And whatever you do Henry, don't cough."

Once the crew lowered the gangplanks, he hoisted the trunk to his shoulder.

Mary was shoved to and fro, as so many people crowded to get off the ship and into the lines that would admit them to America. First one, then two people separated her from Henry. Numbness enveloped her, yet she fought her way forward. "Henry!" His name exploded from her lips.

He stopped and the two between them had to funnel around him. "Here, grab my hand, Mary." The trunk teetered, but he kept it balanced in one hand and reached for hers with the other. The warmth of his grip renewed her spirits. This ordeal wasn't nearly as frightening with him by her side. He smiled down at her as they inched forward together. "Your tag's getting crumpled."

Mary smoothed the document she'd pinned to her coat. The doctors would need to see her proof of immunization.

*Immigrants landing at Castle Garden*

The officers would need to know how to spell her name. With everything visible, maybe they'd get through the station faster. Someone shoved from behind, sending her stumbling forward. Only Henry's strong arm kept her from tumbling to the deck and getting trampled. "Jesus, Mary and Joseph," he bellowed. "Can't these rude passengers see we have a little extra bundle here?"

The man behind him mumbled a pardon.

Mary drew a deep breath and took her first faltering step onto the springy gangplank. Passengers pushed from behind. Passengers in front dug in their heels. She clutched Henry's hand until her fingers burned. The whole of the ship shuffled down the gangplank as one.

After what seemed like hours, Mary's feet went from plank, to dock, to solid ground. "We made it Henry." A sigh shuddered through her from head to toe. "We really made it. There's solid ground beneath my feet." Giddiness followed the same course as the sigh. "Thank the Holy Mother of God."

> These immigrants were among the last to be processed at Castle Garden. Soon after that, Ellis Island would be the destination of incoming immigrants.

# Chapter 2

## Henry O'Niell

**New York City, New York ~ Spring 1880**

Henry paused in the doorway of the stark apartment. "Wish me luck." He puckered up and tapped his cheek.

"You're Irish." Mary's lips hovered over the spot, her sweet breath teasing from jaw to temple. "You've all the luck you need."

"*You're* all the luck I need." He turned his head and captured her kiss. "Soon as I get a job, I'll buy you a fine table, chairs, a real bed, a—"

She pressed another kiss to his lips. "We've two rooms. Not everyone can boast of that on their second day in New York."

"I'm sorry I can't get you a window just yet."

"A window? And let that blustery wind whistle through? You got us a full ten by fourteen feet o' space. Perfect for when the baby comes." She removed an invisible speck of lint off his jacket. "Now get out of here, so I can do a bit of washing and mending."

The washbasin sat on the trunk, mounded with the clothes they'd worn for three months straight. Henry took a step toward them. "I'll toss these in the ash barrel on my way out."

Mary stepped between him and the basket, hands on her hips. "We'll just be keeping them until we have some money coming in."

"Then I'd better see to it." He slipped out the door, eased it closed, and bounced down the three flights of stairs. Wind tugged at Henry's coattails as he stepped onto the street, but it would not steal his excitement. Today, he'd get that job. And with his first pay he'd buy her a fancy dress—and maybe some shoes to fit her swelled up feet.

HELP WANTED. Broad letters scratched on a scrap of cardboard in the window of the first dry goods store he passed shouted to him. NINA. A name he'd never seen before—not surprising—he'd heard a dozen different languages spoken at Castle Garden alone. A man's ethnicity didn't matter. He'd welcome work from any source.

Henry straightened his cap, no, removed his cap, opened the door and stepped into his future.

A mild roar greeted his ears, voices melding together like an angry beehive, with one rising above them all. "Jake!" Down a narrow corridor that ran to the back of the store, the harried clerk hollered. "Where is that imbecile?" He dashed into, then out of the storeroom, his empty hands flailing.

The tightness in Henry's chest eased for the first time since leaving home. This job was his for the asking. He reached into the window display and snatched the sign, careful not to knock over the row of almanacs stacked on a roll top desk. He strode past bundles of blankets, stacks of cookware, racks of flannel shirts, bags of feed, tools, even a half-dozen bewildered customers.

"Pardon, sir." Henry looked the gentleman full in the eyes and held out the sign. "I'm here for the job."

A tomb-like silence robbed the room of noise. The women on either side of him fell back as if he were contagious. The balding clerk twisted his bony finger in his ear and pulled it out. "This here mick cain't read a lick."

Snickers sounded to his left and right. The cardboard sign

bowed in his hands. He took a steadying breath. "It says help wanted. I'm the right man for the job, let me speak with Nina and—"

"Nina?" The clerk's voice had a rusty hinge quality. "This guy wants to see Nina."

The woman to his left tittered. A man behind him guffawed. Red splotches broke out on the clerk's face and he brayed like an ass.

Tightness returned to Henry's chest, but he forced himself to join in their joke. He could be patient, despite what Mary thought.

When the clerk's laughter sputtered cut, he pulled a rag from his pocket, wiped a tear from the corner of his eye, and stepped toe to toe with Henry.

He held his ground and kept his voice steady. "I'm a hard worker, sir. I can read, do my sums—"

"Read this, N-I-N-A." The clerk tapped each letter with a force that reverberated to Henry's chest. "No Irish Need Apply."

A strangling sensation took hold of Henry. His feet lost all sense of the floorboards.

"Throw 'im out, Jake."

Henry swung, but his blow was useless against the mammoth that pinioned his arms behind his back and lifted him off the ground. He kicked over as many items as he could on his way back down the aisle, then was tumbled out onto the sidewalk to another bout of uproarious laughter.

A storm rolled in, gathering strength with every cardboard sign rebuffing his plea for work before he could ask. Weary, beat, soaked to the bone, Henry lit a candle stub from a kerosene lamp in the alcove of his tenement building. He trudged up the stairs, his news, rather the lack there of, turned his feet to lead. How could he face Mary without a job? He'd have to muster the confidence he'd felt this morning—for her sake. He blew out the tiny flame and set the stub on the doorframe.

He cracked the door open, hungry eyes seeking her comfortable form. Clothes festooned the room—draped over a line strung from one wall to the other. Next to his trousers hung Nana's lifeless hankie. He parted petticoat and dress to glimpse his wife. From the back, her slim figure looked unchanged. She turned, and the roundness of her belly brought a strained smile to his lips.

"How long have you been gawking?" A cute little smile curved her lips.

"Something smells good."

"Oh." She dropped the spoon and grabbed his hand, hauling him back through the laundry, and into the little room. "See what came." Her voice trembled like she was entering a royal bedchamber.

In the center of the room lay a narrow mattress. From the rippled look of their wedding quilt, they'd find as many lumps here as in Nana's mashed potatoes. He slipped his arms around her and stroked her belly. "Just don't roll over in the night, you'll kick me out of bed."

"Some ladies from St. Patrick's Church brought it over." Her musical laughter filled the tiny room. "You like it?"

"Fit for a king."

"Oh, and see this." She squirmed out of his arms and pushed him back into the main room, then pulled him through the curtain of clothes.

"So you've turned it into a three room apartment, I see." The trunk was now draped with a plaid cloth and set with their tin ware. "We've a kitchen."

Silver bells—the quality of her laughter, eased his weary mind. Her joy over such simplicity could almost make him forget his jobless state. He sank to his knees before the makeshift table.

The soft tread of Mary's stockinged feet marked her progression, as she came around the trunk. She set the kettle on the table, lifted the lid, and ladled out the stew. "You'll find a job tomorrow."

He kissed the back of her hand when she spooned a second

helping onto his plate. Mutton never looked so small, nor tasted so fine. He raised his glass. "To tomorrow."

## ~ Summer 1880 ~

Tomorrows came and went. Scores of them. The cold moisture that had once whistled up the stairwell and under the door turned to steam in the July sun. Mary never once complained about the lack of a window, but every bead of sweat on the back of her neck testified to her discomfort.

The few jobs Henry landed lasted but a day. He dragged his tired self home with no more than a dollar in his pocket, by way of the local tavern. One little drink, a chance to catch wind of another job from friends. Still, Dad's purse grew feather-light.

This morning, as usual, he reached for the doorknob and shot Mary a smile. With a little luck, he'd find something steady. "Wish me…"

Mary leaned against the back of their only chair—another church castoff—looking exhausted before her day began. It groaned and cracked.

"Wait." He dug into the pouch and fished out a penny. "Light a candle at St. Patrick's and pray for a blessing instead."

Her eyes grew rounder. "Candles are for the dead."

The dead? A laugh welled up in him. "Then I know God won't mind." He blew her a kiss. Today would be different. He felt it in the pricking of the hairs on his arms. Henry tucked his dinner, a boiled potato wrapped in a bit of cloth, under his arm and trotted down the street. Stench rose from the litter strewn around the ash barrel, and the sun was barely up. It'd be another scorcher of a day.

"O'Niell!" Jack stumbled out of the tavern door. "You hear about the work gang they're forming?"

"A new building going up?" He clapped his buddy on the back. "A tonic if ever I needed one." No harder work than construction, but a new project meant steady employment for the lucky few.

"Keep it down." Jack flapped his hands, but his whisper soared. "I been drinking with the foreman half the night. If word gets out, there'll be ten guys for every one they hire."

The tingling raced from Henry's arms to his legs as he set pace with Jack's long strides. "You think this guy will hire us, I mean, he won't be another one of those NINA types?"

"Naw. They're looking for bruisers. They won't care where we come from." Jack turned the corner and Henry fell in behind him to keep from ramming into a news cart.

"I've enough muscle grunt for that kind of work. Besides, I'd do anything to provide for my family." Henry's palms itched. "I tell you, if I see anyone putting one of those signs up, I…I'll bust their dial."

"Save your strength for the labor crew, Henry. And pump those stumps of yours faster. We gotta get there before they fill their quota." They jogged down the street, through the Fourth Ward slums and cut through an alley in the Bowery.

"Where do you think you're going? You white nigger." A whiskered man in rolled up shirtsleeves hollered from the doorway of a fifteen-cent lodging house.

The blood boiled in Henry's ears, but he refused to slow his pace. No foul-mouth was worth a lost job. "Hey, smart bullock! Eff off. Want your face smashed in, you ugly brute?" Henry threw the words over his shoulder as he passed.

Said brute started, picked up a chunk of wood, and stepped into the street. "You want ta try?"

This challenge couldn't go unanswered. Henry skidded to a stop and spun back. Several men flocked to the brute. Henry scanned the alley for a piece of pipe. With Jack's help, he'd teach 'em all some manners.

Jack yanked on the back of his collar. "Henry, keep your breeches on. We can't take those guys." The fabric dug into Henry's neck as he stormed forward. A button popped. "You come home, broken and bloody, with no job…" Jack's voice was like metal shavings. "What'll your wife say?"

Mary. Always his saving angel. He shot the bullies two fingers, turned and ran, ignoring their parting remarks. If things at the construction site didn't work out, he'd come back this way to work out his aggressions.

Henry raced after Jack a dozen more blocks. The ringing of pickaxe on cobble grew louder than his labored breathing. Carts of bricks and stacks of lumber choked the street in front of him. And men. Miles of men.

Every muscle in Henry's body ached from unloading cartloads of bricks, but he took the stairs two at a time. Mary would be thrilled at the way God answered her prayer. Now they could save enough for the baby—coming in only a month. A white flag fluttered ghost-like from the door across the hall. Another death in the tenement. The infant born last month no doubt. Every ounce of his being wanted to rip it from the tacks—pretend death didn't prey on the innocents in this hell.

He whipped his head back and forth. His neighbors might surrender, but not him. Not today. He burst through the door. "Mary, good news! You don't have to take in anymore washing."

She stood at the basin, her back straight as a plumb line. The agitation of clothes against washboard quickened. She'd have seen the flag by now—be fretting over the little one she carried. He crept close and softened his voice. "I started a new job today that'll last two months. Jack and me were the last two hires."

"Is that smoke and whisky I smell on you?" Mary's shoulders stiffened, but she kept the rags in the filthy water thudding up and down the board.

"It was just one, love." He slipped his arms around her and nuzzled her neck. "We had to celebrate—just a little."

She pushed him away with wet hands and a cross look.

"When I get my first pay I'm going to take you to an eating house."

Her lips disappeared into a pencil line. She turned back and plunged her hands into the brown water.

"I ain't letting on, Mary. Me and Jack were the last two hired. Why can't you be happy with me?" His words snapped. "It's for us. For our baby."

Her shoulders sagged and when she turned, her voice grew soft. Silent tears streamed down her face. "I didn't realize life would be so hard for us here in New York." Mary's sigh shook the paper-thin walls. "I mean, it's good, too. I just thought life would be better here, and it's just…different."

And there she was—her black hair tumbled over her shoulders, eyes red-rimmed, lower lip quivering. Like the first time they met and he played the hero. It was love at first grade. After he bloodied the biggest kid's nose, they left her lunch pail alone. He pulled her into his arms and let her weep out her frustrations.

"I feel like my belly is going to pop any day now. I don't see how I could get any bigger. And Mummy. How can I deliver this baby without her?" She pushed away from him. Her eyes skittered all around him. With the look of a wounded animal, she sank onto that rickety contraption.

He'd buy her a decent rocking chair by week's end. Before the baby came, at least. She pulled a foot into her lap and rubbed a puffy ankle.

"Mary, you've always been the patient one. Just a little longer and you'll see this job pan out. We'll have that better life." He reached over and patted her belly. "I promise."

"Oww!" Mary shoved his hand away. "Ooh, what was that?" Her fingers settled over the baby.

His blood ran ice cold, despite the sweltering room. "You ok?" He sank to his knees beside her.

Tiny lines etched her eyes and crinkled her fine brows. Her

breath came in short gasps as her hands flitted across her belly. "I'm scared Henry…the baby…it's not time."

He slid his hand to the small of her back. She winced. Her whole body went rigid. He jerked his hand away. "Wha—?" He cleared the shakiness from his voice. "Wha'do I do?"

Her eyes looked right through him.

*Jesus, Mary, and Joseph!* He wasn't cut out for this. *Water.* He stood up. *Don't leave.* He sank back to his knees, hands hovering, careful not to touch. *Don't cause more pain.*

After a moment, she let out her breath and great tears rolled down her cheeks. All he could see was that infernal fluttering of white on the neighbor's door. "I'm taking you to the hospital. We can't take any chances." Henry scrambled for the slippers under the chair and wedged them on her feet. Good thing the church ladies had brought them—he'd never be able to get her shoes over those swollen feet.

## ~ July 13,1880 ~

Henry paced the hallway of the small, dim hospital. If he hadn't stopped by the tavern… If he hadn't spoken harshly… If he…

A white-habited nurse poked her head out the door they'd just wheeled Mary into. "Your first?"

He nodded and started forward.

"First babies take hours." She placed firm hands on his chest and held him back. "You go on to the tavern around the corner. I'll send for you when the wee one comes."

"Leave Mary?" Never! Her moaning called to him. He tried to push his way inside. She needed him.

The old bat was stronger than she looked. She backed him right into the wall opposite the door. "This is woman's work in here. Go have a drink." She retreated back into the room and closed the door in his face.

He slid down the wall and sat, eyes boring into the door. Ears straining. Fingers twitching. He should go back for Mary's prayer beads—if not for her, for himself—but an invisible hand pressed him to the floor.

The doctor went in.

Mary screamed, too many times to count.

A tiny squall—that made his heart skip.

When the doctor came out, Henry staggered to his feet, head spinning with questions his mouth was too dry to ask.

"You have a son." Beneath a wiry mustache, the doctor's grin slipped a bit. "He's a little small, from being so early. Your wife and baby will have to stay here a week or so."

"When can I see them?" He raked his hand through his hair, toppling his hat to the floor.

"No need to worry. The nurse will come for you soon. Everything is fine. Just fine." The doctor walked away, whistling a happy tune.

*Fine.* Henry breathed in the word. *At what cost?* His breath exploded out. How was he going to pay for a weeklong hospital stay for wife and child? He gulped in another breath. He was a papa. Cost didn't matter.

The white door creaked open. "Mr. O'Niell, you may come in to see your family now."

He nearly bowled her over getting to Mary's side. The baby— his baby—lay at her breast. His cheeks hurt from all the grinning. "He has your black hair. He's beautiful."

She met his gaze, and for the first time since he'd brought her to America, her tired face boasted a radiant smile. "Yes, and your smiling eyes, Henry. Do you want to name him Harry, after your father?"

Henry nodded. His eyes teared as he kissed the top of her head.

Mary ran her cheek across baby Harry's downy hair. "May God give you…" She played with his ten little fingers. "For every storm, a rainbow…For every tear, a smile." She wiggled his tiny toes. "For every care, a promise…And a blessing in each trial."

Henry sank on the bed and slipped his arms around his little family. No, life in America wasn't better—it was perfect.

She lifted her gaze and smiled into his eyes, then bent her head over their most precious bundle, her voice a lilting lullaby. "For every problem life sends…A faithful friend to share…For every sigh, a sweet song… And an answer for each prayer."

So, their little family was growing and it didn't take long before Mary was with child again. Bessie came into the world the following year. Life was still a struggle, but they were happy just the same.

## ~ Fall 1884 ~

"Brain fever." A grim-faced doctor dropped his stethoscope into the black leather case. "Keep him cool. Get him to drink something. It has to run its course."

Henry walked with him to the door. "Will Harry be alright?"

"Only time will tell." The doctor surveyed the room one last time. "And, for heaven's sake, keep him away from that little girl of yours."

Henry closed the door and sprang into action. There'd be no white flag hung from his door, not if he could help it. He pulled the mattress from the bedroom into the main room.

"What are you about, Henry?" Mary rang out a clean rag and bathed Harry's neck and forehead.

"I'm keeping you and Bessie safe." He picked up Harry, mat, and all and strode into the bedroom. "I'll stay with the boy here until he's over the worst."

"But, you've work in the morning."

"I'll miss a hundred days if…" A sob threatened to choke out his words. No matter, Mary would understand. He placed the mat on the floor and dropped to his knees.

"He's my son, too." Lamplight reflected the tears in her eyes.

"Aye. I see your beauty in him every day." He stroked the black hair from Harry's forehead. Gobs of it came out in his hand. Even more reason to shut his darling wife out. "Fetch me the water and close the door. I'll not risk my ladies."

Mary nodded and crossed herself. She placed the bowl of water inside the bedroom, scooped Bessie into her arms, and swung the door shut. The soft click did not drown out her lilting voice lifted in prayer.

The fever lasted two days and slowly Harry recovered. When his hair grew back, it was silvery white.

## ~ Summer 1885 ~

Henry snuffed out his cigar, a well-deserved treat after another endless day of backbreaking labor for pennies. If anyone said there was no hell, let him haul bricks in a New York summer. A brief stop at the corner tavern did little to drown the taste of dirt, sweat, and sawdust. At least Mary didn't grumble about that anymore.

The gas lamp at the bottom of the stairwell to his tenement was out again. No need lighting it. After five years of treading this path, his feet knew the way. He trudged up the three rickety flights, slipped through their door, and slumped onto a chair to untie his boots.

Mary's chapped hands plunged up and down in the washbasin, her eyes squinting under the kerosene light. As usual. "I got excited over seeing a green, living thing today. I didn't even care it was a weed in the crack of the sidewalk. It got me thinking, Henry. How can we give our children what we never had—" Mary swallowed her disappointment. "We've less now than then."

"Not so." Henry forced a happy note into his voice. How long would he have to play the cheer-up-the-wife role? He'd seen enough of 'em go insane—he couldn't risk her losing heart. "We have two beautiful children. Bread on the table. A roof over our heads."

"A roof, yes." Her whole body shivered. "How long will we have to live in this windowless room like so many cockroaches?"

The same motion echoed within him, head to foot. How had they come so far and gotten nowhere? A great vice squeezed his ribs. Some provider he'd turned out to be.

She must have sensed it—her ashen face swept his way. "I'm sorry." She rushed to him, fell to her knees, and laid her head in his lap. "I didn't mean to complain."

He stroked her raven hair, damp with the steam from the washbasin. "Hush now. You're tired, and the sun beating down like the Sahara doesn't help. Once it goes down, we'll sneak up to the roof, spread a blanket, and catch a fresh breeze."

"Us and the two-hundred other cakes baking in this oven."

Her quiet words stabbed his heart. He'd find a way to get them a real house, or he'd die trying. "All my volunteering with the fire department will pay off. Captain Bradshaw says a job'll open up any day now." A spasm of coughing wracked his body. He gulped in air to get it under control. If this kept up, he'd hack up a lung.

Mary shot to her feet. The concern in her red-rimmed eyes hurt his chest worse than the coughing fit. "I'll get a doctor to check you—"

The door flew open.

"Look what I found in the street." Harry, with the newspaper tucked under one arm, ushered a sopping-wet Bessie through the door with his other. "She found a leaky fire hydrant to play in."

Bessie beamed and held up an armful of tattered cloth. "Looky, Mama. I got 'em from the ash barrel." Her red curls bounced around her face. "I'm helping."

From the depths of Henry's stomach, anger welled—not at his darling daughter. No, it accused him directly. What kind of father couldn't make enough money to support his own? Mary scooped the rags from Bessie's arms and whisked them into the washtub.

She stripped Bessie's filthy dress and tossed it in as well. Tears lodged in Henry's throat. Only the destitute were rag pickers. No one in Ireland ever spoke of the American nightmare. Somehow he should have known?

"Father," Harry tugged on his sleeve, held up the newspaper, and puffed out his scrawny chest. "I can read the headline."

Henry's chest tightened, further. He could count every rib through his son's thin shirt. "You should be in school."

"$100,000 Raised in US for Pedestal for Statue of Liberty." The words spilled out as he picked up his cigar box full of clippings and started to trim the article from the paper. "See, Papa. I don't need school. I'm gonna be a newsy."

"Because you can memorize a headline? No, son. I won't let you become a Street Arab."

Harry tucked his chin to chest, then set down the scissors and crept close. He cupped his hands around Henry's ear, but his whisper filled the room. "Papa, I uhh…met a crippled boy today. I asked him what happened."

Mary gasped. "Bessie, go get ready for bed." She stepped to her son's side and rubbed his back. "Go on, Harry."

"His pa did it to him so he'd get more money begging. I'd rather be a newsy than have my bones broken!"

Too young. His son shouldn't be privy to the horrors of the slums. Yet there he stood like a man, lips pressed tight, fighting back the tears. No papa could be prouder. Henry met Mary's doleful eyes—a silent prayer surely on her lips. He pulled Harry into his arms and softened his voice. "You have the promise of me, and your Mama, and the good Lord that what you saw today will never happen to you. You get your schooling and you can be a doctor, a lawyer, or run the whole newspaper. Do you hear me, Harry?"

"Yes, Papa." He buried his face in Henry's chest and a sob echoed off his ribs. Harry's small hand wormed its way between them, collecting each hard beat of Henry's heart.

It took a moment before Henry could find his voice. "Then

we'll not speak of it again." He struggled to his feet and the coughing fit struck again.

Mary patted his back, only worsening his hacking. "Let me help you to bed. Harry, run fetch the doctor."

"Stay…Harry." He caught the last cough with a great throat clearing. "It's nothing a little dinner and reading the paper won't cure."

"A full plate of Irish stew and few less of those smokes wouldn't hurt, either."

"Now, Mary, I only have a cigar now and then when I'm out and about with the fellas." He gave her a little snicker.

"I think they're stealing your appetite. That, and working sunup to sundown." She gave him one of her stern looks. "I've got eyes enough to see you've been losing weight."

What price to return his home to peace? He leaned down and kissed her on the neck. With a trembling sigh, she turned and melted into his arms. He mumbled into her hair. "Mary, my love, things will change soon as I get that job at the fire station. I'll slow down then…get more rest…you'll see."

She tilted her face up and looked him in the eyes "You better promise me Mr. O'Niell." She thumped him playfully on the chest. "I don't want to be left alone to raise two small children." Her voice turned husky soft." Besides, I'd die without you!"

"I promise you, Mrs. O'Niell."

## ~ March 1888 ~

Henry sat bolt upright in bed. His ears were accustomed to the sound—quiet as a kitten's mewing—here in the bowels of the tenement building. His body responded to it without direction from his mind. What time was it, day or night? He cursed the windowless room as he pulled on his trousers.

"What's the matter?" Mary's sleepy voice called from the other side of the mattress.

"Fire alarm's sounding in the street."

"Come back to bed. It poured all day yesterday, what could be burning in this weather?"

"It's my job to find out."

"It'll be yours next week. Today you're a volunteer and you need your rest."

He pounced back on the bed. His lips fumbled for the sound of her voice and he stifled her complaint with a kiss. "I'll be back in time for breakfast." Off the bed and out the door he trotted before

*Great White Hurricane*

she could issue any demands. He tugged his hat over his ears and jogged down the stairwell, buttoning his coat as he went. He pulled the door open.

An arctic chill whistled through him—harsher than any March he could remember. A good three feet of snow had drifted against the doorstep. He turned back for his scarf and mittens. No. What Mary didn't know, Mary couldn't fret about. He scrambled over the mound on hands and knees—into a glistening new world.

Gone, the grey New York he'd known from the day they disembarked the *Chadwick* eight years ago. In its place, a sparkling city without soot or sludge. What he wouldn't give to share this moment with Mary—to gaze upon this wonderland—to wrap her in his arms and let her feel the hope and peace this blanket of white whispered under the gas lampposts.

The fire alarm blared again and obediently, he trudged into

the street, sinking up to his boot tops with every step. With each breath, the blustery wind filled his lungs with ice crystals.

A snarling sputter sounded overhead—with sizzle and spark, a power-line snapped. Henry dodged the end nearest him. The siren echoed into silence. The other end slapped the snow mere feet from the lamppost. Electricity and gas—mortal enemies. One arc from the wire, one faulty valve, and the whole thing could become the devil's torch. He ran back to the stairwell, snatched up a shovel, and used the wooden handle to move the wire as far from danger as possible.

By daybreak, he met up with Captain Bradshaw and some of the fire crew at the East River Waterfront. Flames licked a warehouse and filled the already blackened sky with ash. "The water lines are frozen and we can't get the engine through these drifts." Captain Bradshaw shouted to his crew. "We'll fight the blaze with what we got." The shovel proved to be man's best friend, yet for every shovelful of snow Henry threw onto the fire, the greedy flames spread fast under the whipping wind.

At nightfall Henry trudged home with aching lungs. The hope he'd seen in the pristine snow was trampled back to dingy grey.

"Henry! You're half froze." Mary fumbled with his coat buttons and pulled it from him. "Harry, fetch your Papa that bowl of soup I've been keeping hot for him." She rambled on while she untied his boots, helped him to bed, and poured broth down his throat.

Too exhausted to ward off her fussing, Henry closed his eyes and listened to Harry's proud voice read a full news article about the Great White Hurricane.

> Some two hundred New York City lives were lost in this snowstorm. An estimated $25 million was caused in property damage from fires alone. The storm ravaged the entire eastern seaboard, but New York City was hit hardest of all.

# Chapter 3

# Mrs. Henry O'Niell

**New York City, New York ~ March 1888**

"God…what were you thinking?" The words fell with barely a sound from Mary's lips as she dropped to her knees at Henry's bedside. She gently rubbed his arm, turning cold faster than she wanted. She couldn't let him go—any more than she had the power to keep him from slipping away.

She needn't lay an ear to his chest to hear the rattle—needn't hold the lantern closer to know the painful truth. One look into his face told all. His Irish eyes were dying while her Irish eyes were crying. After all they endured—how could she be losing her husband…her life? She had trusted God for her future, had she not? But this was not the time to dwell in the should-have-beens. She reared up, sucked in a shaky breath, and wiped her eyes. The need to be strong overpowered all else. "Harry, fetch Father O'Reilly."

"At St. Patrick's?" Harry's drowsy voice sounded behind her.

Everything in her wanted to scream for the doctor, but Henry's slight nod, confirmed her fears. "Get Father O'Reilly."

In a shot, Harry was out the door and Bessie stood trembling by her side. "Can I help Papa?"

Mary stroked her daughter's red curls. "Go back to bed, honey.

Papa's going to be fine." A lie. Her heart knew it the minute it came from her lips—impossible to take back now. She gave Bessie a little push toward her bed without taking her gaze off Henry's face. If she looked anywhere else, she'd melt.

In a weak voice, so small she had to put her ear to Henry's lips. "Mary, promise me our children will get an education…whatever it takes…to have a better life."

"Henry, please." She choked on tears. "Don't leave me, you're the only man I ever loved. Everything will be okay. Shush now and rest."

"Mary…I'll always love you. Promise me…" He gasped a breath. Then was silent.

Tears filled her eyes. Still she rubbed his arm, if she could bring back the warmth, she could bring back the life. Her jet-black hair draped onto his chest. She'd give anything to hear his rattling cough again.

Bessie nestled into her side, her little body wracked with sobs, but Mary couldn't pull her hands away from Henry's lifeless limbs, not even to comfort her darling girl.

Mary rocked. She pulled his hand to her lips and kissed it over and over. "I loved you from ever I saw you, Henry O'Niell. First grade, it was. Do you remember? How me, little Mary Falvey ever turned your head, I'll never know. You were a rowdy kid, always making the other's laugh."

She raised up and kissed his forehead. "I loved your red hair and ruddy complexion. It matched that wild personality of yours. And oh, your blue eyes, how they danced when you were happy or playing a prank. I'll hide those memories in my heart." She pressed her lips against his, but he was gone.

She sank back to her knees, wrapped an arm around Bessie and clutched his beloved hand in farewell. The prayer tumbled out of a sobbing heart and broken spirit. "Hail Mary, full of grace, the Lord is with thee. Blessed art thou amongst women, and blessed is the fruit of thy womb, Jesus. Holy Mary Mother of God, pray for us sinners now and the hour of our death… Amen."

Mary stood for the final prayer of Mass and smoothed her black skirt. She held Harry and Bessie on each side of her. The words of Father O'Reilly's prayer flew around the vaulted ceiling, but refused to alight in her mind. In the hush that followed, she turned to leave. She looked into the sea of faces and her knees buckled. Never had St. Patrick's seen so many parishioners at one time. The whole church turned out for the remembering of her Henry. Captain Bradshaw and his family sat in the pew behind her. And Jack, who swore the roof would cave in if ever he visited a church, stood in the back.

Captain Bradshaw shook her hand. "Our condolences, Mrs. O'Niell. Your Henry was a h…heck of a man, ma'am. Everyone thought so. He knew his business right well and never hesitated to help a bloke in need. He'll be missed."

"Thank you." The words came automatically—more times that she could count on her way down the aisle.

"Mama, you're hurting me." Bessie's small voice broke through her daze.

Mary looked down at their hands. Bessie's red fingers poked out from her white fist. "I'm so sorry, honey." She raised the little fingers and kissed them. "Harry, take your sister out to the courtyard to play. I need to talk to Father O'Reilly."

At the large arching doorway, his massive hand hovered above her head. "Bless you, my child."

"Thank you for everything. I don't know what I'd do without the support of our church family." Or what she'd do, period. With two children to raise and a promise to fulfill. Her heart could break no more.

"Mary, I know you have a lot of decisions to make. Be assured

I'll be here to help and advise you anyway I can. You do have some options we can discuss."

"Can a rag picker have options?" The part of her that died with Henry now wanted to live for her children's sake.

"This may not be the best time, but one of our parishioners needs a domestic servant. If you're interested…" He handed her a slip of paper. "Here's her name and address."

"Thank you Father." This time her heart broke with gratitude.

Captain Bradshaw sounded the fire engine bell. In the street below, men stood, ready to run the engine through the streets in tribute to her husband. Behind it, Jack and five other men from his construction crew shouldered Henry's coffin.

"Come children, it's time to say good-bye."

*Funeral Procession*

Father O'Reilly walked her down the steps, to her place behind the pallbearers. "Go with God, Mary. May He bless and keep you and yours. God be with you."

"And with you, Father."

She took hold of Harry and Bessie's hands and followed Henry one final time through the crowded streets.

Mary bundled her children in their coats and set out to meet with her potential employer. She glanced at the address in her hand, then up at the beautiful brick house at the other end of a walkway lined with stately trees. Stepping onto the porch, she was taken aback by the handsome brass doorknob. *Well, here goes!* Mary reached up and struck the knocker two times.

Miss Helen, did not keep her waiting long. The door swung open and a tall woman, with hair pulled into a tight bun, gave Mary an emotionless smile.

Mary stood tall and proper, mirroring the woman's posture, but her voice came out shaky. "Good afternoon. My name is Mary O'Niell." She swallowed and managed a steady voice "And these are my children, Harry and Bessie."

"Yes Mary, I've been expecting you. Father O'Reilly told me all about your situation. I'm so sorry for your loss. Please come in."

As Mary stepped in she glanced around the beautifully decorated room. All the cushions were perfectly angled and not a speck of dust could be seen.

"Oh, Winnie, come and meet our visitors." A little girl, about Harry's age but much taller, came bouncing into the room. Not a hair out of place and dressed as proper as her mother. "This is my daughter Winnie. Sweetie, why don't you show Harry and Bessie what you planted on the porch." The children followed the little girl out onto the veranda. Bessie looked back at Mary several times on the way out the door, then clung to Harry's coat sleeve.

Turning to Mary, Helen continued. "Father told me you needed employment. We have something in common, you know, I too, am a widow."

"Oh, I don't think Father told me that. Then again, I was in such a fog at the time. We also need a place to live. Harry is eight and Bessie is seven. They're good children."

"Well, Mary, I would like to hire you as soon as you can start. However, I only have a room for you and your daughter. She would be a lot of company for my Winnie. I couldn't have any boys live here. I'm very strict about that, and besides a boy needs a father. Can I make a suggestion?"

Mary hung her head then looked back up. "Yes, please." Could giving up her son actually fulfill her promise to Henry? She was going to choke on the lump stuck in her throat.

"I'm not suggesting your son live on the streets. I'm a member of the Children's Aid Society. I know you're aware of the orphan trains. We have one scheduled to leave next week, and can make room for Harry on it."

Mary peered at Miss Helen through misty eyes. "I need to talk to my children first."

"Of course, just let me know and I shall make the arrangements. And Mary, I'm sure you and your daughter will be very happy here. You will be paid at the end of each week."

Back in their little apartment, Mary collapsed into the rickety old chair and stared into space, numb in her being! "Harry and Bessie aren't able to know their precious grandparents, and now they're without their papa." Her heart felt heavy. *Now Harry without his mama, too!* "Oh how I will miss him."

A warm, little hand touched her arm and she jumped. Had she spoken aloud?

"Don't worry Mama, I can take care of you." He looked up at her, his hazel eyes smiling just like his Papa's used to.

Mary patted the seat beside her and Harry snuggled close to her side. She tilted his head up to look into his innocent face. "Harry, I can't earn enough money doing other people's wash for us to stay here together." Tears filled her eyes. "To give you the life your papa wanted, I need to send you to a place where that will be possible. My dear son, it would mean we would have to be separated, maybe for a long time."

Harry looked hard and long into his mother's eyes. "Mama, I will do whatever Papa would have wanted. I will go wherever I need to go. I will come back to you when I can."

His words melted her heart. She kissed the top of his head, then held him by his shoulders and looked into his sweet face. She whispered, as she brushed the hair out of his eyes. "What a handsome young man you've turned out to be. How I wish you still had my black hair to remember me by. I know you'll make us proud." She smiled, with quivering lips, as tears rolled down her cheeks.

As she stroked his white hair, Mary prayed as she did many times since the first day of his life. "May God give you…For every storm a rainbow…For every tear, a smile…For every care a promise and a blessing in each trial…For every problem life sends…A faithful friend to share…" Her voice broke as she choked on a tear.

Harry took his mama's hand. "For every sigh, a sweet song… And an answer for each prayer."

*Historic Photo of Rag Picker*

# Chapter 4

## Harry C. O'Niell

### New York ~ Spring 1888

After visiting the House of Refuge, all the necessary arrangements were made for Harry to board the Orphan Train. Here the little family stood at Grand Central Station. Harry tucked his cigar box of newspaper clippings under his arm. It held his greatest treasures, every article he'd shared with his papa. Bessie clung to his sleeve, her big eyes watching the throng of people bustling here and there. He glanced up at Mama. Never had he seen her so downcast, except when he lost his papa.

She bent down to his level and raised her voice just above the clacking of a train rolling into the station. "Harry, my dear son, I have something to give you. I know your papa would want you to have this pocket watch that your grandfather gave him." Her voice quivered as she gently put it in his hand. "Keep it and remember us every time you look at it."

He threw his shoulders back. He was a man now. Like Papa. No tears would stain his face. "I will always remember where I came from Mama. And, I will think about you and Bessie often."

"You are older beyond your years, Harry."

Harry gave a playful tug to one of Bessie's pigtails. "I will miss you, little rag-doll."

Bessie's lips opened and closed, but no words came out of her mouth.

He stooped and gave her a big hug then turned and wrapped his arms around his mama's waist. They all held each other tight.

"Children, children." Miss Helen, Mama's new employer marched through the crowd in a fancy dress and huge purple hat with fat paper roses. She clapped her hands as she herded a group of tattered boys up the steep steps into the railcar.

Harry fought to give his face a brave look, but the tears came anyway. It was time! He had to let go.

A nun in somber black patted Mama's hand. "Don't worry ma'am. I'll be with your little boy. We'll make several stops where advertisements have been posted in churches and various other places along our route. We have about forty children this time, but rest assured, we'll find a proper home for each of them."

Harry climbed up the narrow steps into the train. He shuffled down the aisle where kids, nearly all boys, of all ages and sizes, knelt or stood on the hard benches on his left. They hung their heads out the windows, waving their arms, shouting to the crowds. The kids on the side away from the platform sat in their seats looking scared and hopeless.

Harry pushed his way onto a seat on the left. Just one last look at Mama and Bessie, one last chance to wave goodbye, but he was too small, too short to see anything. Being crowded on every side, he stood on the seat on the other side of the aisle. The door shut with a clang. The train whistled and

*Orphan Train*

lurched forward. He clutched the back of the seat to keep from falling over. On the other side of the car, boys toppled into their seats and scrambled back up, blocking his view again. He and forty other children were northbound for their future destiny.

"Hey Shorty." Someone tapped on his shoulder. "What's your name?"

Harry plopped down on the seat. He couldn't see anyway.

Next to him, a tall, lanky kid with a kind of smirk or confidence on his face—but friendly just the same—stuck out his hand. "I'm Thomas, but if you want to be my friend, you can call me Tommy."

"I'm Harry, but you can call me Shorty if you want. I don't mind." He shook the boy's hand. "I guess I am short for my age. I'm eight."

"You got awful funny hair for a kid."

"That's what happens when you get brain fever and live."

"Well, I'm twelve and a half." Tommy measured Harry with an arc of his hand, from the top of Harry's head, back over to his own chest. He frowned. "You might have a hard time finding someone to take you in, since you're so small."

Harry stretched as tall as he could. "I might be small, but I'm smart and strong, just like my papa…" The word stuck in his throat for a second. "…was."

"What do you mean *was*? Is he dead?"

Harry hung his head. "That's why I'm on this train."

"My dad's in jail…I think." Tommy looked down and blew out a sigh. When he met Harry's eyes, his voice was happy again. "Well, lots'a luck. Hey, I got some marbles. Maybe we can find a small corner and play with them."

"Sure Tommy, anything to pass the time. I think it's going to get boring here. I've got some news clippings if you want to read them."

"Uhh…maybe you can read them to me sometime."

The train picked up speed and the boys closed their windows to keep the cold air from whistling through and stealing their hats.

Harry followed Tommy to the back of the car and crouched down in a corner to play marbles.

Three hours passed with laughter filling the railcar from boys shoving this way and that. Hot, sticky moisture trickled down Harry's back in the narrow quarters.

The nun made her way through the crowd and tapped several of the boy's shoulders. "We'll be at our first stop soon." She placed one hand on Harry and the other on Tommy. "Stand up, boys, and tuck in your shirts. You want to look decent for the ladies and gentlemen waiting to greet you." The brakes screeched, the train slowed and rolled into a new station. Tommy shoved the marbles into his pockets. "Quickly now, boys. We haven't much time." The nun ushered them onto the platform, down a cobbled street, and into an opera house.

Harry stood on the stage without flinching, as one by one, men in flannel shirts and overalls pinched his muscles. He watched Tommy out of the corner of his eye.

A big man with bulging arms leaned close to his friend's face. "Show me your teeth, boy." He pulled down on Tommy's chin.

When the man moved away, Tommy whispered to Harry. "I feel like we're being paraded like livestock." The man glared back at them. Harry shifted his eyes straight ahead and didn't say a word. About nine boys were chosen. Harry, Tommy, and the rest of the boys were hustled back to the train depot. Harry's chest hurt and his eyes blurred as he stumbled up the train steps and into his seat. Tommy patted his shoulder. "You alright?"

"I hoped for some Irish luck." Harry shrugged. "I wanted to get picked at this stop, so I'd be closer to my family."

"Maybe you got lucky. If those boys got a good home—only time will tell. Why…we should be glad we weren't picked. I hear some kids get abused or treated like animals. Here, I found this in the street for you." He reached inside his vest and pulled out a newspaper. "Read me something."

Under the heading *Orphan Train Soon to Arrive,* Harry read,

"Those who desire to take children on trial are requested to meet them at the train depot at the time above specified." Harry looked up. "On trial? You mean they can send us back?"

"Sure. Also, because you're small, you might not be picked at all."

"What will happen to me then?" Harry's stomach got a sick feeling inside. He couldn't be sent back—couldn't not be picked. That would make Mama worry too much.

Harry was shuffled off and on the train, and inspected like cattle more times than he bothered to count. With each stop the ritual drained him. By the time they reached Albany, half the boys, and one of the girls had found homes. Even though there was an empty bench in front of Tommy, Harry slipped into the seat with his friend. "You know what Tommy? I'm scared of being picked and scared of not being picked."

"Well, I'm glad we're still together." The usual look of self-confidence on Tommy's face turned to one of sadness. "I thought I'd be picked by now."

"Not me." Harry shook his head.

The nun, fully dressed in her habit, carried a large basket down the aisle. She paused at each seat of children. When she got to Harry she tipped the basket toward him. "Here you go boys, you have your choice of a chunk of bread or an apple."

Harry looked over at Tommy. "I'll take the bread." Harry held out his hand.

"And, I'll take the apple." Tommy snatched one from her basket.

The nun gave them a knowing smile. She dug in the bottom of the basket and handed Harry the largest chunk of bread.

Harry tore the bread into two pieces. "I thought maybe we could share."

"Hey, that's what I was thinking." Tommy pulled out his

pocketknife and cut the apple into two perfect halves. "We must be kindred spirits, me and you."

Harry took a bite of his measly meal. Maybe tomorrow he'd get picked. He and Tommy both. "Think we'll get to live in the same town?"

"We made it through this many days together. Why wouldn't we? Hey, let's share our meal again tomorrow."

"You bet. That was a great idea we had." Harry chuckled.

"Yeah, we're pretty clever." Tommy joined in the laughter.

After eating, Harry's eyes grew heavy. Next to him, Tommy's head bobbed a couple of times. Harry scooted to the seat in front of him, curled up, and slept.

The sun rose behind and to the left, the way it always did. The train clacked its way though farmland and forest, over creeks and a large muddy river. The nun came to their seat and tapped Tommy on the shoulder. Harry stood up to go with him, and she placed a hand on his shoulder, too. This time, it returned him to his seat, instead of calling him forward. "I'm sorry, little man." She looked at Harry while she ran a comb through Tommy's hair. "You don't need to come out this morning."

"I won't be long, Shorty." Tommy dug into his pocket and pulled out a handful of marbles. "Watch these for me."

"Okay, Tommy." The marbles trickled into his palms and he caught every one. He studied them while Tommy was gone—pretty and smooth. Bessie would like them. He practiced shooting them. *How does Tommy make them spin so fast? I'll ask him to show me how to hold them when he gets back.*

But, Thomas never came back to the train. Harry felt more alone than ever! He leaned his head against the window and stared at the hills and trees and grasslands that rolled past. His mind wandered into daydreams of running back to Mama and Bessie.

Over the next few days, Harry marched with the remaining kids to more station platforms. Other boys and girls got picked. Harry crept back on the train to be carried farther and farther

*New York's Orphans*

from his friend and family, until only a little girl about Bessie's age, and a boy his age, huddled in the very back seat. Were they brother and sister? Tears stung his eyes hoping they could stay together.

The scenery outside the train slowed and buildings came into sight. The nun tapped Harry on the shoulder. "We're in Buffalo. There are only three of you left, so this will be our final stop." She handed him a chunk of bread. "Go on, eat."

Harry pinched off a tiny piece and put it between his lips. It tasted like sawdust. *I'm scared. What will happen if I'm not chosen today?* He started to ask, but the bread made his mouth so dry the words wouldn't budge.

The nun moved down the aisle to the other boy and girl. She led them once again onto a platform, this time in a church. Harry stood with eyes straight and hands behind his back, like he'd been taught to do. Were the other two as tired as he? He didn't have the heart to find out.

A beefy man walked in the door at the back of the church. "That's all what's left? I wasted a day coming into town for nothing." He stormed out and the door banged shut.

At the edge of Harry's sight, an older couple stared at him—not through him like people did when they squeezed his scrawny arms. The woman laid her hand on the nun's sleeve. "Sister, we have no children of our own."

"Feel free to look them over. Talk to them if you like."

The couple walked right up to Harry. They didn't inspect his muscles. Didn't look at his teeth. They just smiled. The woman brushed his hair off his forehead, with a touch as soft as Mama's. Did she like him? He liked her—just because of the way she looked at him.

She bent down and met him face to face. "What is your name, young man?"

He swallowed hard, but his words came out soft. "I am Harry Charles O'Niell, ma'am."

"Well Harry, I am Mrs. Gerlach and this is my husband Mr. Gerlach."

"Nobody ever picks me." Oh, why did he say that, now they would pick the other boy, or the little girl?

Mr. Gerlach let out a big belly laugh. Mrs. Gerlach, covered her mouth with a gloved hand. When she pulled it away, a pretty smile spread over her face and up into her eyes. "Do you know why you haven't been chosen, yet?"

Harry shook his head. He was too little, but no way would he tell them that.

"You are just the boy we were hoping to find today. I didn't know your name, Harry, but I've been praying God wouldn't let anyone else get you."

"Even if I'm small for my age?"

Mr. Gerlach's bushy mustache bounced up and down in time to his laughter. Mrs. Gerlach cupped her hands onto Harry's shoulders. "You're perfect the way God made you. We want a son young enough to grow up to be a fine gentleman and old enough to help on the farm. What do you say, Harry?"

Harry gave a sheepish grin and held out his hand. "You can call me Shorty if you want to."

Mr. Gerlach shook Harry's hand and laughed even louder. "It's a deal. I'll go sign the papers so we can skedaddle."

The horse and buggy ride to the farm seemed as long as the train trip from New York City. Harry sat between his new mother and father. He folded his hands in his lap, chewed the inside of his cheek, and watched them out of the corners of his eyes. Mr. and Mrs. Gerlach looked down at him, over to each other, and back at him again and again. Little smiles flitted across their faces making him feel shyer than if they'd pinched his muscles. His new parents seemed very kind and were God-fearing like Mama. Still, he didn't know what to say or how to act.

Mr. Gerlach filled in the quiet spaces. "We have a hundred acres south of here, in a little corner of God's heaven, called Orchard Park. Besides corn and cattle, our farm produces butter, milk and apples for extra income. It's a lot of hard work. Especially since most of the young folks moved west and so many blacks are getting better jobs. I'm always looking for extra help." He placed a hand on Harry's shoulder. "I know you'll be a big help on the farm, but that's secondary to you getting an education. A man needs both hard work and book learning to get ahead. Would you like that?"

Mr. Gerlach sounded just like Papa, without the Irish accent. Harry nodded. Maybe he'd be able to fulfill his parent's dream for him.

They turned down one dusty road and up another. Little green sprouts decorated freshly plowed fields on both sides of the rutted road. A beautiful house, larger than any Harry had seen stood at the end of the drive. Where New York City had been gray, Orchard Park was all green and brown with a sky so blue it made his eyes ache for all the staring. Mama would love this place. Mr. Gerlach stopped the buggy in front of a big red barn and helped Mrs. Gerlach and him down.

"Come along, Harry," Mrs. Gerlach said. "I want to show you to your very own room."

Own room? He followed Mrs. Gerlach through his new home—his eyes feeling like they might pop out of his head at any moment, he was staring so hard. There was a sofa, and plump leather chairs, paintings on the walls, a lamp with a lacy shade... The smell of fresh baked bread came from the kitchen. He climbed the stairs behind her, his hand gliding over the polished banister. *I could slide down this!* When she showed him his room, he had to blink, or his eyes really would fall out. It was larger than the main room in the apartment back in New York City.

"Let me show you the washroom." She led him down the hall and filled up a claw-foot tub. "Here's a towel and some clean clothes. I'll just let you be, Harry." She started to walk away, then turned back and smiled at Harry once again.

He held up the checkered shirt. "How'd you know my size?"

"I told you. I've been praying for you, Harry."

His eyes grew moist.

Mrs. Gerlach stooped down and lifted his chin. "God will take care of you Harry and we will give you the best we have to offer. I hope you will be very happy." With that, she smoothed his hair and walked out.

Harry washed and dressed quickly, then went in search of his new family. He stopped in the parlor, just outside the kitchen door and peeked in.

Mr. and Mrs. Gerlach spoke in low tones as she cooked a huge fried chicken dinner. Pots steamed over the stove and the table was laden with all the trimmings. "My heart hurts for our new son, John. I hope we can bring some happiness to his little soul."

"Don't worry Claudine. Trust in the Lord with all your heart and lean not unto your own understanding."

She gave her husband a little smiling sigh, as she sat down.

Harry's heart beat faster. She wanted to make him happy. He walked into the kitchen all fresh and clean.

Mrs. Gerlach beamed. Mr. Gerlach motioned to him with kind eyes. "Sit yourself down here, son, I'm sure you must be ready to feed your face."

"Yes sir, I'm hungry and it smells so good."

"Alright then, let's say grace." Mr. Gerlach took Harry's and Mrs. Gerlach's hands in his big calloused paws. "Bless us, Lord, and these thy gifts, which we are about to receive. And bless our new friend…" His voice broke a little. "…and son, Harry."

Harry looked up at Mr. Gerlach, a lump of *thank you's* stuck in his throat. No one had ever given him so much. They exchanged a smile then he proceeded to eat like a pig.

Every time he looked up, Mrs. Gerlach grinned at him and spooned another helping of mashed potatoes or green beans onto his plate. "It does my heart good when people enjoy my cooking."

"Well…" Mr. Gerlach cleared his throat. "This is a new day for us, and a new life for Harry."

After eating big helpings and two pieces of apple pie, Harry set his fork down. "May I be excused…uh…sir? I'm very tired and would like to sleep in my new bed.

"Of course, son." Mr. Gerlach said with approval in his voice. "You've had quite a trip. Have a good night."

"There are clean pajamas under your pillow." Mrs. Gerlach started to rise.

"Now, Mother." Mr. Gerlach waved her back. "Harry's a big boy. He doesn't need you fussing over him his first night. Come, I'll help you with the dishes."

Harry scooted his chair back and walked to the doorway. Then turning around again, he looked at Mr. and Mrs. Gerlach with those big Irish eyes. "Thank you both…for picking me."

In his new room, Harry took out Papa's pocket watch, wound it, and placed it on the stand next to his bed. He slid the cigar box of newspaper clippings into the top dresser drawer and slipped into bed. From the downy mattress, he could view the night sky through his window. The days it took to get to Buffalo seemed like a lifetime. As he pulled the decorative spread onto his tired body, he gazed at the shining stars that splashed across the sky. A sad spirit washed over him as he thought about Mama and Bessie, still in New York City. *I wonder if they are looking at the same stars.* He said his prayers, drifted into a deep, sound sleep, and dreamed of his family.

Harry had gone through many emotional experiences for his

tender young age. Even so, when he woke up to a rooster crowing the next morning, he surprisingly felt like he was home. It must have been Mama's prayers that kept him.

Harry didn't know it till later that he was being adopted that day and would be treated like the son the Gerlach's never had. He would be their only child. Harry was one lucky little boy!

> An estimated 200,000 children were removed from the city streets on the east coast and sent on orphan trains to rural farms. Many of these children were never adopted by the families who took them in and received no right of inheritance.

# Chapter 5

## Harry C. Gerlach

### Orchard Park, New York ~ Spring 1895

Harry settled well into his new family. Mr. and Mrs. Gerlach became real parents to him. He was growing into a fine intelligent young man. A hard worker like his father, Henry. He gained respect from friends and neighbors. Harry was still small of stature—took after his mother's side of the family in that regard.

"Good morning, Harry." Charley called out with that weird clucking sound he made every time he started to talk. As a neighbor, Harry liked him. He was rough around the edges, but always made Harry feel like one of the guys. Charley pulled his horse and buggy to a stop in the road. "I've been wanting to talk to you."

Harry strolled to the edge of his property. "Good morning, Charley. What's on your mind?"

"Well…I've noticed how good you are with the animals."

"Yes, sir. I enjoy working with them. I think I understand them more than people sometimes." He gave a sideways grin.

"The county fair is just around the corner."

"My parents always take me. It's one of our favorite outings. Ma always wins the blue ribbon for her boysenberry jam."

"I was wondering, if your parents allow it, would you be interested in riding my horse in the races at the fair? You're just the right size and if you win with my horse, it would mean some extra money in your pocket. You would have to train for it though."

"Really, Charley? That would be so much fun." His heart started to race. "I can't wait to talk to my parents. I'll get back to you soon. Thanks again." Harry ran down the drive, back toward the house to find his parents.

"Okay, Harry," Charley called after him, "come on over after you talk to your folks."

Harry barged into the house. Father set his empty coffee cup on the table. Ma looked up from the bacon she was frying at the stove. "There you are, son. You were out early this morning, what have you been up to? You look out of breath."

"Charley came by to talk to me about something. Umm…he asked me…uhh. He wanted to know if I'd…uhh.

"Spit it out." Father sounded gruff, but his mustache lifted with his smile.

"If I'd be interested in racing his horse at the Erie County Fair. He wanted me to get your permission, of course."

His parents looked at each other for a long time. How they communicated, just by looking each other in the eyes was a mystery. Father stared at Harry over his spectacles. "Son, I'm not sure that's such a good idea. You have your chores and studies—not to mention it might be unsafe."

"Please, Father. I promise to get all my chores and studies done. Charley says I'm real good with animals, especially the horses."

Father looked at Ma again. "Your mother and I will discuss it alone and have an answer for you at supper tonight."

"Yes, sir." Harry grabbed a biscuit and scooted out the door and back to work. He was on pins and needles the rest of the day.

Suppertime couldn't come fast enough. When the sun finally dipped low in the sky, Harry ran back to the house, stepped through the back door and looked over at his parents. If only he could read their faces. Ma wiped her hands on her apron as she turned to set the table. Father waved him into a kitchen chair. "Well, Harry, after much thought we finally came to an agreement. We will grant your request, although your mother was a little more reluctant."

Harry jumped straight out of his seat.

"Hold your *horses*." Father half-laughed at his little joke. "If you leave one chore undone, or fall behind in your studies, it will all come to a halt."

"You will not be disappointed and I won't disappoint Charley."

"We will hold you to it, son." Father clapped him on the shoulder. "And one more thing, you'll be making a *fair*—" He chortled again. "—bit of money. You'll put that in the bank for college."

And with that, Harry ran for the door. Charley needed to hear the good news. He stopped, then turned and walked over to his mother giving her a quick kiss on the cheek. "I'll be right back, Ma!" She cupped her hand over the spot where he'd kissed her. A gentle smile curved her lips and her eyes shown with tears. Harry looked at her closer. "You okay, Ma?"

"Ah…go on with you." She snapped the dishtowel at him. "Charley will bust a seam waiting to hear your news."

"Hey Charley…they said I can do it. I can be your jockey! I'm so excited."

"Hog diggity! Let's go into the barn, partner. "Gomer Jones, meet your new rider, Harry, or Shorty for short. Shorty, meet your new horse, Gomer. When can you start training."

"As soon as I finish my chores. I'll be over."

So, Harry started training to be a jockey. Sometimes, it wouldn't be till dusk that he would mount Gomer. He would ride far into the evening after a hard day's work. *Dusk is my favorite part of the day. It's so peaceful.* As he rode with the breeze in his face, Harry would often reflect on how different his life was here from his life in New

York City with his family and his hard working father. He was oh so grateful for his life now, but his heart still ached for his sister and the touch of his mama's arms.

"You're working too hard." Ma's voice carried through the open window, when Harry came home for lunch. He paused to listen. If Father needed more help, he needed to know.

"It's nearly the end of summer and with the fair approaching, I'm glad to give the boy some leeway regarding his chores." Father let out a low whistle. "Harry and Gomer Jones ride as one. It's a sight to see."

"Does Harry know you've been sneaking over to Charley's to watch him train?"

So, Harry had a fan. He almost laughed aloud.

"Our son's the finest jockey I've ever seen. I'm going to go to the races. Maybe even bet on him and Gomer." A wooden spoon clattered against the stovetop. "Claudine, you should come and see him at work. Tonight is going to be an exciting race."

"Alright, but just one time."

Harry's excitement doubled—not only would he get to race, his parents would be there to cheer him on. He pasted a casual look on his face and walked in the door. "I'm heading to the racetrack. Anyone want to come with me?"

Ma stripped off her apron, tossed it onto the table, and grabbed her purse before Father pushed his way out of his chair.

At the track, Ma, pulled a crisp dollar bill out of her purse. "This goes against my better judgment, John, but I'm going to bet on Harry's horse. Maybe it's not really gambling since we are just here to support our son."

"That's exactly what I thought, Claud.

Harry pushed Gomer to his limits that night and, low and behold, Gomer Jones came in first.

With the odds high, Ma won $150.00 on her dollar bet. "Oh

my! Since I won money, I guess I have to admit to gambling." The look on her face was a combination of guilt and giddiness. "What will I say to the Ladies Guild at church?"

"Don't worry Claud, His mercies are new every morning." A roar of laughter left his lips.

At the fair the next year, spirits were high for Charley, Gomer and the Gerlach's. Harry rarely lost a race in Orchard Park or Buffalo, so how could he miss the winner's circle at the Hamburg Fairgrounds. Before the beginning of each race the horses trotted around the track. Harry mounted his horse and looked into the stands. He held onto the reigns with one hand and patted Gomer with the other. *Let's do it again o'boy.*

"There he is, John!" Ma chimed so loud her voice carried to the track. "I love those green and yellow colors on him, though they're looking a little tight."

He gave his parents a wave, and trotted Gomer up to the starting line where Charley waited for him.

"Good luck, Shorty. Make sure you battle for that inside lane."

"Will do, boss." He nudged Gomer to the chalk line where the other horses waited. He tucked in his elbows and leaned forward watching the starter's flag. At the whoosh of the flag, he dug his heels in. Gomer jumped off the line and took the early lead, but rounding the first turn, Midnight Madness overtook him. By the time he reached the finish line, five other horses had crossed.

He jumped from Gomer's back and walked him to his stall. He curried Gomer's brown coat until his boss showed up. "I don't know what happened, Charley. He just sort of gave out after the first lap."

"The problem isn't with Gomer." Charley slapped him across the belly. "Your ma's good cooking's what happened. You got to cut back on the biscuits and jam."

This was all he needed to bring his adventure to an end.

Harry took the disappointment gracefully. He was like his mother, Mary, in that respect. "Well." He smiled up at Charley. "It was fun while it lasted."

## ~ **Summer 1898** ~

Graduation Day! As Harry sat listening to the speakers he couldn't help thinking how fast time had passed since he came to live with Mr. and Mrs. Gerlach. He had done very well in school. *I wish Mama and Papa could have shared this special occasion with me.* However, he was thankful to have the Gerlach's in his life. They'd been so good to him. When the dean called his name, he looked over at his parents sitting straight-backed, their eyes following his every step. Harry walked onto the makeshift stage at Orchard Park High School.

Once the ceremony was over, he made his way through the families sharing in this mutual celebration, past the punch bowl, to where his parents waited for him in a quiet corner.

"He looks so handsome in his graduation suit." Ma smiled as he approached.

"I agree." Father clapped Harry on the back. "We did good."

"And, we have a surprise for you." Ma elbowed Father.

Father put his hand on Harry's right shoulder. "Your mother and I couldn't be more proud of you, Harry. We prayed about what would be an appropriate graduation gift."

"Father, the life you've given me is gift enough."

He reached down and picked up a brown, leather valise.

Surprised, Harry broke into a wide grin. "It's very handsome and it'll come in handy when I go off to college. I couldn't be happier."

"Open it." Ma had an impatient little girl look on her face.

"What? Here in this crowd?" Harry laughed and unbuckled the bag in slow motion.

"Harry Charles, I'm going to take it back if you don't hurry it up."

"Okay, okay, Ma." Inside was an envelope. He flipped it over and silently read the note on the outside.

*Hope you have a good visit with your mother and sister in New York City.*

"You mean…" Harry's thoughts refused to come out as he fumbled to open the envelope. Staring at him was a round trip ticket to Grand Central Station. He looked up at his parents. Satisfaction and joy radiated from their faces.

His eyes got blurry and with gratitude, he put his arms around his parents. He couldn't speak.

The following week, Harry packed his valise for his venture to New York City. He was about to board a train for the second time in his life. This train was not like the one he knew ten years earlier. Instead of a broken down railcar, with hard benches, he climbed the steps into a first-class passenger train. *What a blessing and what a difference, traveling as a passenger instead of a peasant!*

"Help you with your bag, sir." A Pullman Porter, in a crisp white jacket and black pants, took the valise and stowed it in the cabinet above Harry's plush seat.

Harry fished in his pocket and handed the man a tip.

"Thank you, sir."

"The name's Harry." He held out his hand in greeting.

"Wesley." The porter shook his hand in a dignified manner.

"Do you like your job, Wesley?"

"Yessir, I do." Wesley gave him an easy smile. "It's the best job for a Negro. I can feed my family and put a nice roof over their heads. Not many black folk are as lucky as me."

"That's swell, Wesley! I read that Mr. George Pullman died last year."

"Yessir, and President Lincoln's son, Robert Todd, is our president now. I hope he doesn't cut back on our wages like Mr.

Pullman did." He flipped the coin in the air and caught it. "Good thing I got me some tips to make up the difference."

"How many hours do you travel in a month?"

"Ya see, that's the hard part. I work four-hundred hours a month and get paid $27.00. My brotherhood complains about it but I'm just glad to have a job."

"Wait a minute." Harry jotted down the numbers. "That's only seven cents an hour. Most men earn twenty. Are there benefits to make up the difference?"

"Sure. I especially like traveling north where folks treat us like we're real people. You know when George Pullman was alive everyone called us all George! Well, when they called me that, I always pointed to my nametag and told them…my name is Wesley. You know the saying: When Lincoln freed the slaves, George Pullman hired them."

Harry nodded, it was good they had a job, but oh, the injustice of not getting paid for the value of their service. "Thank you for sharing that with me. It makes me want to get involved in helping citizens who are treated unfairly, like yourself. My Papa was dealt harshly with when he first came to America."

"Well, I just thank the good Lord for what I have. And what I don't have, He'll make up the difference. Can I get you a pillow, Mister Harry, or will you be heading for the sleeping car."

"A pillow would be great, Wesley. I think I'll read a little before I head that way. *I just hope I'm not too excited to get some shut-eye.*

Harry jumped from the train as soon as it arrived in New York City. He went straight to his old parish, St. Patrick's church. Someone there just had to know where his mother was living. Memories flooded back as he entered the church. He crossed himself with the holy water and genuflected. Turning to his left, he found his old priest hanging out in the church parlor. *I think that's him. He looks older.* "Father O'Rielly?"

"Yes, young man, what can I do for you?"

"You probably don't remember me, but my name is…uh… was Harry O'Niell." My parents and I used to come here every Sunday for church."

"You're Mary's son? Of course, your mother and sister still belong to this parish." He shook Harry's hand warmly. "You look well, Harry. How are you doing?"

"Yes, Father, I have been blessed with a caring family. Can you tell me where my mother and sister are now? They were going to stay with some parishioners after I left, but only till Mama started her new job as a domestic servant."

"Of course, follow me." They took the long walk down the side of the sanctuary and into the church office. Father O'Rielly, sat down slowly and pulled out his address ledger. He thumbed through it. Harry's heart beat faster with each page turned.

"Ahh, here it is." He copied Mary's address on a piece of paper. "She has been here for ten years now. Can I offer you a cup of tea before you leave."

"No thank you, Father. I'm anxious to see my family. I don't have a lot of time in New York." They shook hands once more before Harry turned and rushed out the door. With the piece of paper in hand, he sped down the congested streets. Soon he would see Mama and Bessie.

With no trouble at all, Harry found the address. The large house stood back from the street in a prominent neighborhood. The sprawling lawn and walkway rested in the shade of large sycamores. Mama loved green, and she always wanted to live in a brick house. This was a place she and Bessie could be happy. He felt good about that. He wiped his palms on his slacks and walked up the steps. He reached for the brass knocker, then stopped to smooth out his hair and clothes. With a deep breath, he struck the knocker twice. Would he recognize her? Would she—

The door opened and a lovely lady stood before him.

Harry had to catch his breath. Mama. Older than he remembered, but more beautiful than he ever realized, even with a few strands of grey through her raven black hair.

He swallowed. "Mama, it's me, Harry."

Her Irish eyes went wide. She placed her hand on the door casing and sagged against it. "Harry…is it really you?" He pulled his papa's watch out of his pocket and held it up for only a second, then opened his arms to her. She fell against his chest and hugged him tight. The years faded away. Her embrace was as comforting as it had been ten years ago.

"My beloved son! You've lost your Irish brogue."

A beautiful redheaded girl ran to the door. "Mama?" She stared at Harry, a curious look on her face.

"Bessie, it's your brother." Mama's voice was choked with tears. "You're brother's come home."

"Harry! I didn't recognize you." She grabbed his hands.

"Well, I'd recognize you anywhere with that curly red hair like our papa's and those blue eyes." Harry grinned. She was still a tiny thing. "What, no pigtails?"

Bessie jumped into his arms. "Oh, Harry, how I've missed my big brother!"

They spent the next few glorious days catching up on each other's lives. They walked the long city blocks and had lunch in Central Park as they talked and laughed together. Harry found comfort holding Mama and Bessie's hands at the cemetery, with no need for words to pass between them. Sometimes they cried, reminiscing about times past. "It seems like we've never been apart, Mama."

"Yes and the days fade faster than seems fair." Mama looped her arm through his and walked with him to the train station. Bessie took his other arm and matched his steps.

"Work is waiting for me on the farm. I have to get back."

"It was so nice for Mr. and Mrs. Gerlach to give us this blessing. Please thank them for me." Mama's voice sounded close to tears. Bessie bit her lower lip and nodded.

Steam from the train bellowed, inking out the sky. Somehow, saying farewell was harder this time. "God keep you, Harry." Mama rose up on her toes and kissed his cheek.

Bessie tapped the brim of his hat. "Don't forget your little rag doll."

He playfully tugged on one of her red curls. "How could I…?" He'd never been short on words, but today, they failed him.

Mama grabbed Bessie's arm, circling them up. She bowed her head as she'd done so many times and prayed over her children and he prayed over his mama and sister. Three hearts embraced. Mama squeezed his hand and looked at him with tear-stained eyes. "Please come back when you can, my son."

Harry's heart ached. *I need to be strong; I'm not going to cry.* But, he couldn't stop the tear that ran down his face. It took every ounce of willpower to pull away from them and board the train. He jumped onto the first step as it began to chug forward. He looked back one last time to keep a picture of the women he loved in his mind's eye.

Mary clutched Bessie's arm to keep from toppling over when Harry let go. She felt like she was in mourning once more. Her heart ached with each step Harry took.

The train belched and rolled forward. Harry waved. Then he was gone!

*How many times must the cord be cut from me Lord.* I must let go of my first-born once more.

"It's okay, Mama," Bessie whispered. "He'll come back again."

For Harry, the ride home left him lonely. With that far away look in his eyes, he was deep in thought. *At least I have a happy memory to hold on to for now.* He was grateful for that, but his Irish heart was breaking.

## ~ **Fall 1898** ~

Another chapter in Harry's life would prepare him for the future his papa, Henry, had dared to dream for him. Mr. and Mrs. Gerlach showed they had a lot of faith in their only son as they made plans for him to go to the University at Buffalo. "John, God has filled the void in our hearts for a child we could never bear. Harry has brought much joy to our life."

"I know Claud, but it is time to let him find his own way. We've prepared him well."

Harry dipped into his savings and enrolled in the School of Medicine. He always had a soft spot for the poor and for those discriminated against. He remembered every story his papa told him about being an emigrant—about scraping to get by during those early days in New York. And, mostly about the night his papa died. If they had been able to afford a doctor, would things have been different?

Harry noticed how the blacks, like Wesley, were treated the way his papa had been–having to work extra hours with less wages. He didn't like it one bit. He was always finding himself on a political wagon for one thing or another. Harry kept busy with his studies. In his spare time, he enjoyed making up stories. Only occasionally would Harry go out drinking with the guys. And, like his papa, he loved his cigars. They only cost a nickel each, cheaper than cigarettes, and besides that, they lasted longer. Oh, Harry thought of every detail.

## ~ **Summer 1899** ~

Harry drove home to help on the farm. The physical labor would be a welcome change to all the studying. A For Sale sign hung from the fence, next to the entrance of the gravel road that led home. He stepped on the gas. Bouncing along the potholes and ruts, and came to a screeching stop in a cloud of dust at the rear of the house.

Ma met him at the back door. "You're home a day early."

"It was supposed to be a surprise for you, but I got the shock."

"I meant to write." Ma lowered her voice. "Your father fell into poor health. If we sell the farm now, we'll get plenty of money to retire."

"Father's always worked as hard as two men." Harry nodded. "I think that's the best decision you could make."

## ~ **Fall 1899** ~

Harry headed back to University at Buffalo. He wasn't the smartest in his class, but he studied even harder than when in high school. Harry had his Papa's Irish heart for lending a helping hand to whoever was in need. And, thankfully, because of the Gerlach's, he could be generous when needed.

## ~ **Spring 1900** ~

"This year's going by fast, but not without some major events." Harry told his roommate when he walked in the door. "Listen to this, *US Navy's 1st Submarine Makes its Debut* and this one, *US Post Office Issues 1st Books of Postage Stamps.*"

Harry clipped the headlines from the newspaper and added them to the growing collection in his cigar box.

"That's nothing." His roommate hitched his thumb toward the door. "The dean wants to see you in his office."

Harry walked the long hall to the dean's office. Whatever the news, it couldn't be as bad as the last time he was there.

"Harry, have a seat." The dean motioned to the wooden chair in front of his desk. "I want to offer my condolences."

Harry gave him a puzzled look. "You already have, sir."

The dean cleared his throat. "No, Harry. It's your mother. She's passed on, too."

He sank into the seat. How could he lose both of his beloved adopted parents in the same year?

"Besides being friends of mine, your parents were great contributors to this school and other causes, close to their heart."

"Yes sir." He fought to keep his voice steady. "These wonderful people took me into their lives and hearts." *They asked so little in return.*

"One other thing Harry, last time I visited your mother, she asked me to hold on to this scrapbook she started for you. I think it's time you have it for your own purposes."

"Thank you for everything, sir, and for the friendship you had with my parents. I am determined to honor the family name I carry with me."

Harry signed one last check to pay off the medical bills his parents had accumulated during their years of declining health. He stuffed it in the envelope addressed to the hospital, and with that, his inheritance was gone. As much as his heart ached to see them again, it felt good to take care of their final business.

He looked around his dorm room, picked up his guitar, and strummed a few cords.

Matt, from down the hall, strutted into his room. "What are you up to, Harry? Wanna go out? No more finals!"

*Why do all my friends have to be six feet tall or more.* "I don't think so, Matt. I'm in the middle of writing a song."

"Really! What's it called?"

*"Through the Mire."*

"Oh, that's funny. Or maybe not." He plopped onto the edge of Harry's bed and gave him a studious look. "Is that how you're feeling? Losing your folks and all."

"Naw, but I know a lot of others feel that way and I empathize with them. I'm a happy man. I've been blessed to have parents who loved me and did all they could for me. I guess I should tell you that I'm not going to continue school in the fall. My money is almost gone and so is my ambition to practice medicine."

"Well, that makes three of us."

"You're kidding! Who else?"

"Jason. Actually, he convinced me to join him in a traveling medicine show. That guy has a good head on his shoulders. Hey, we need some entertainment and you're a funny guy. You want to join us as the comedian?"

"Hmm! Did you hear the one about the two drunks who were walking upgrade between the railroad tracks?"

Matt shook his head, and a grin spread across his face.

"One of them said, 'This is the longest shtairway I've ever been on.' His buddy replied, 'It's not the shtairs that bother me, it's the low banishter.'"

"That's a good one, Shorty! You're hired."

He shook Matt's hand with an enthusiastic grip. "I can't pass up a chance to see the country."

For more than two years, he traveled with the show and visited every state of the union.

## Covington, Kentucky ~ 1902

"Well guys, it was fun while it lasted, but our time as traveling medicine men has come to an end. I don't know about you, but I don't have a dollar to my name. I've never been so flat strapped."

Matt scratched his head, then perked up. "I'm going home to

my folks. I'm sure they can find something for me to do. What about you Jason?"

"Well, I have enough money to get to Grand Rapids, Michigan. The Pere Marquette Railroad is hiring. You should try to make it up there, Shorty."

"Life as a railroad man? Sounds like a plan. Maybe I can put on a show tomorrow and raise enough money for the trip."

"Tomorrow is Sunday!"

"Yeah, so I'll have a crowd of church-goers."

Quite a crowd attended him the next morning. Every one of those church people showed up late for services, but in high spirits.

## Ft. Worth, Texas ~ 1912

"Mr. Gerlach? I'm Martin McCain, the reporter with the Ft. Worth Weekly."

"Yes, I've been expecting you. Please, have a seat. And help yourself to one of my fine cigars."

"Thank you, maybe later." Mr. McCain sat down with pen and tablet in hand. "It's gracious of you to give me this time, knowing how busy you are."

"No problem. I can relate to you guys, since I myself worked as a reporter while in Milwaukee. Not an easy job."

"Our readers would be very interested in how you got to this place in your career. You're well respected and quite popular. My readers want to know what would make you give up a career as Chief Car Inspector."

"Well, Martin, if you can write as fast as I can talk, I'd be glad to oblige." Harry swirled his cigar around his mouth before taking a puff.

"I have worked on nearly every big railroad in the country but came to Fort Worth to carry out what I have chosen as my lifework—the solution to the problem of capital and labor. I am going to devote the remainder of my life to solving the evil strike and with this idea in view I have been studying law for two years. I expect to be admitted to the bar in the fall. When I passed through several strikes and saw the deplorable condition that prevailed in such times, my life purpose was changed. I resolved to work out some means by which strikes could be averted."

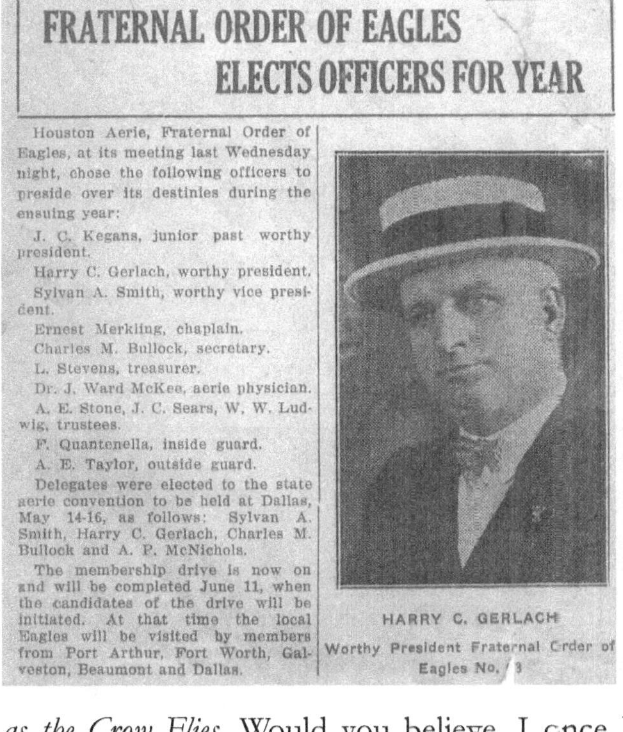

**FRATERNAL ORDER OF EAGLES ELECTS OFFICERS FOR YEAR**

Houston Aerie, Fraternal Order of Eagles, at its meeting last Wednesday night, chose the following officers to preside over its destinies during the ensuing year:

J. C. Kegans, junior past worthy president.

Harry C. Gerlach, worthy president.

Sylvan A. Smith, worthy vice president.

Ernest Merkling, chaplain.

Charles M. Bullock, secretary.

L. Stevens, treasurer.

Dr. J. Ward McKee, aerie physician.

A. E. Stone, J. C. Sears, W. W. Ludwig, trustees.

F. Quantenella, inside guard.

A. E. Taylor, outside guard.

Delegates were elected to the state aerie convention to be held at Dallas, May 14-16, as follows: Sylvan A. Smith, Harry C. Gerlach, Charles M. Bullock and A. P. McNichols.

The membership drive is now on and will be completed June 11, when the candidates of the drive will be initiated. At that time the local Eagles will be visited by members from Port Arthur, Fort Worth, Galveston, Beaumont and Dallas.

HARRY C. GERLACH
Worthy President Fraternal Order of Eagles No. 3

"My readers will be glad to hear there's someone on their side of the labor issue." His pen scratched a few more lines in his tablet. "Say, is it true you've taken up literature during your wanderings?"

"Sure enough. I've written two books, *The Merry Christmas of Dirk Bernard* and *Straight as the Crow Flies*. Would you believe, I once had an ambition to become a playwright? While in New York City I wrote, *Lead and Oil*, a romance in the life of a painter. It dealt with economic conditions and was produced in Gotham and other nearby cities with a fair degree of success."

"When do you have time for all this?"

"My brain never stops spinning and since I travel so much, I use that time to let my creative juices flow."

"Just a couple of more items, Mr. Gerlach. About your invention of the new and improved switch chain. I understand you secured a patent and could reap rich rewards since several railroads are contemplating using it. What will you do with that handsome sum of money?"

"I long for money only to further my plans, and surely if it comes, that is the way it will be applied."

"And lastly, your fans would like to know if you miss or plan on returning to your birthplace of New York."

"Mr. McCain, you can tell them for me that I had rather be in a box car in Texas than a Pullman palace sleeper in New York City."

"That's a great quote to end on Mr. Gerlach and will make the Texans here very happy. Now if you would allow us to shoot a picture of you…" He waved his cameraman in. "This will conclude our time together."

"Just let me put my hat on so I can appear a little taller." Harry replied with a smile in his Irish eyes.

## Houston, Texas ~ 1914-1915

After passing the bar, Harry looked for employment at a Texas law firm. With handsome credentials and his experience as a rep for the Pullman Porters, not to mention his charm, he landed a job at Hume & Hume Law Firm. With Houston being the largest city in Texas, there would be no shortage of clients.

Jef knocked on the doorjamb of F Charles Hume's office and waited. Sure, the man was blood relation, but the illustrious attorney only hired the best, and being a nephew hadn't automatically earned Jef the job.

"Enter." His uncle looked up from his files and handed Jef a sheet of paper. "As you know, we have a new attorney coming in tomorrow."

Jef stared at the typed parchment. "What's this?"

"Well, if we were in France, I'd call it a *résumé*. Let's just say it's a summary of the man. I'm counting on you to show him the ropes."

"Got it, boss." Jef gave his uncle a little salute and rushed down the hall to his office to read over the notes and collect his thoughts. How was he going to teach the new guy anything when he'd only been at the firm a week himself?

```
             Harry C. Gerlach
  208 Park Hill Drive, Fort Worth, Texas


Work Ethic:
I'm applying to be part of your firm
because I have a heart for the Negro
clientele that have a need to be served in
your firm. I'm intelligent, experienced
and have leadership qualities it takes
to stand up for those who cannot defend
themselves.


Work Experience and Education:
State of New York
   School of Medicine, University Buffalo
   Police Judge


Fort Worth, Texas
   Brotherhood of Railway Carmen America
   Frisco Chief Car Inspector
   Worked with Robert Todd Lincoln
   Pullman Porter Representative
   Intimate connection to Labor movements
   Legal training
   Admitted to the State Bar of Texas


Selected Skills and Abilities
   Can do well with people
   Listen to the people
   Energetic
   Hard worker
```

Harry approached the law firm in the business district of Houston with a sense of pride. Nice and close to downtown, it was a modern office building and quite impressive. After walking through the big double doors, Harry headed straight for the stairs. Elevators were for lazy people. And that was one word no one ever used to describe him. On the 7th floor, above an office door, a plaque read: HARRY C. GERLACH, Attorney at Law. He rather preferred the title, Police Judge, he'd earned working in New York, but this was fine. Real fine.

Across the hall from his office hung another sign: JEFERY HUME, Attorney at Law. *Nephew to the head of the firm.*

A tall, young man with blond hair and pale blue eyes stood in the hallway. "Mr. Gerlach. I hoped I'd beat you here this morning to welcome you!" He seemed quite sophisticated in a double-breasted, dark sharkskin suit. His hand shot out. "I'm Mr. Hume."

Harry shook his hand with a firm grip. "Call me Harry. Thanks for the welcome." Harry removed the hat. The one he always wore in an attempt to increase his stature.

"And you can call me Jef. Hey, there's coffee at the end of the hall there. Just help yourself."

"Thanks Jef, I'll do that. I have a lot of organizing to do, so if you'll excuse me, I'll talk to you later."

"No problem. Maybe we can go out for a drink after work. See ya."

Harry walked into his office and closed the door. For a moment, he felt a little overwhelmed as he looked around the room. *Now this is the nicest office I've had so far. I'll always have the Gerlachs to thank for everything I've accomplished. Although, they could never replace my Mama, I have loved them as parents just the same. How could I not?*

With the last of his things in place, Harry opened his door to get himself a cup of coffee. Somehow, in that half-hour, the hallway had filled with waiting clients. Some were young, some were old, most of them were of color, and all looked like they had needs. Adrenaline coursed through his veins. Here, he could make a difference, he'd found his place in the world.

"Well good morning everyone! I'm Mr. Gerlach, and if you'll be patient, I promise I will talk to each one of you." So the day began and there was no rest for Harry. This suited him just fine. *I love this job.*

As Harry was locking his office door at the end of the day, Jef came by. "How'd your first day go? Are you up for that drink? I know a nice quiet club just two blocks west of here where some of my friends hang out. It's called the Green Room."

"Sure, I'm always up for a nightcap. How'd the place get its name? They want all our money?"

Jef raised one eyebrow. "Was that a joke?"

"Sometimes they're funnier before I tell 'em." Harry laughed as hard as he worked.

Inside the club, Jef introduced Harry to some other attorneys. Harry liked Michael. He had a fun nature and didn't care what anyone thought of him. He was just—himself.

"Well, if you two don't make quite a pair from Hume & Hume Law Firm. How tall are you Jef? 6'2"? Harry, do you mind if I call you Shorty?" He busted up laughing.

"I can't seem to get away from that nickname. Can I call you Mikie?" He grinned.

"Touché," Michael lifted his drink as everyone joined in the laughter. "Just so we don't disclose our nick names in open court.

Someone else proposed a toast. "I think we'll refer to the newest members of Hume & Hume Law Firm as Mutt and Jef."

"Why not, that's my favorite cartoon." Harry liked all the guys and thought they were pleasant enough. He glanced in the mirror behind the counter. Even though he was only 5'5', he was quite the looker. And his silver-white hair? It only made him look more distinguished.

A platinum blond stared at him in the mirror. She winked. Must be his Irish smiling eyes that made it hard for the ladies not to notice him. Harry made sure he stayed on the stool as long as possible so she wouldn't notice how short he was. *I think I'm going to like this lifestyle.*

He tore his gaze away from her. "Hey guys, anyone interested in going to the movie house this weekend? I can take a couple of you in my new Model T."

"I'm in." Jef tipped back his glass and polished it off. "I think Charlie Chaplin is playing. I love that guy."

"Count me in too," said Michael. "Sounds like fun."

Jef elbowed Harry. "If you play as hard on the weekends as you worked today, we're in for a wild good time."

Harry had more clients than he could handle. They thought he was the best and that he really cared for them. In truth, he did. As usual, Jef beat him to the office, cup of coffee in one hand and the Houston Chronicle in the other. Harry never read the paper until he got home at night. "Listen to this Shorty, more articles written about you: 'Another case won by Harry C. Gerlach. After joining the firm of Hume & Hume, only a few months ago, Mr. Gerlach has worked relentlessly for his mostly black clientele. He is gaining quite the reputation for his cleverness. In court he is known for getting things thrown out on technicalities.'"

"Thanks for sharing that Jef, I'd like to cut that out for my scrapbook."

"Really? I thought only women did that sort of thing."

"It was a woman, my mother, who started it. It just makes me feel like I'm honoring her by keeping it up. If it wasn't for my parents adopting me, I wouldn't be here."

"Oh that's swell, Shorty. I'm sure she'd be proud of you. Hey, I better get busy. I need to work harder so I can get an article written about me."

"Ha, see ya later. Oh, by the way, I hear there's going to be a Big Band at that new hotel Friday night."

"Let's go. Sounds fun even though I can't dance. I like to watch the girls and I sure do like those new dress styles with skirts above the ankles."

Harry had to admit he liked them, too, and thought they were quite sexy.

## ~ 1915 ~

"Finally, a Saturday with nothing pressing to take care of." Can a guy go insane, talking to himself? "I think I'll catch up with my scrapbook." There I go again! Life was flying by and the times were changing fast. If Harry wasn't working or playing, his nose was in the newspaper. He pulled out his bottle of rubber cement and leafed through the stack of clippings waiting to be pasted in his scrapbook.

```
August  15,  1914:
The Panama Canal offi-
cially  opens  only  a
few  days  after  the
outbreak of World War
I. The project took 32
years to construct and
caused  an  estimated
28,000 worker deaths.
```

```
October  21,  1915:
The first transatlan-
tic    radiotelephone
communication is made
from  Arlington,  Vir-
ginia,  to  the  Eiffel
Tower in Paris.
```

```
December 10, 1915:
The    one    millionth
Model   T   automobile
rolls   off   the   Ford
Motor Company's assem-
bly  line  in  Detroit,
Michigan.
```

```
1915:    The    taxi-
cab  makes   its  first
appearance in American
cities. Service costs
a nickel, and the pop-
ularity  of  the  cabs
leads to the develop-
ment of intercity bus
lines.
```

**Met Agnes Toups**—That was the biggest news for Harry, even though it never appeared in the newspaper.

He had to talk to someone about this girl. Thank God for the telephone! *I should know Jef's number by heart.* Harry reached for the telephone directory. *Unlisted?* He picked up the phone. "Operator, please connect me to Jef Hume."

"One moment please."

"Hello."

"Jef, its Harry. I need to talk. Can you come over?"

"Uh, sure Shorty. I can be there, say, about an hour?

"That would be great." He hung up without remembering to say goodbye. *Oops.*

As he waited, he daydreamed about the moment he laid eyes on her: He went right up to her, introduced himself, and asked her to dance. With the slightest flutter of eyelashes, she turned away for a moment to get her coat ticket, then looked into his eyes and said, *"Oui, monsieur."* That turned him on!

A knock sounded at the door. "Come in, Jef. Want some coffee?"

"Okay. What's up?"

"I can't stop thinking of her."

"Who, Shorty?

"Her name is Agnes. That petite gal cutting the rug last night."

"Oh yeah, I saw how she strutted into the club like she owned it. Her calves even showed just below that sheer black dress."

"Yes, I noticed, Jef. I also noticed that she is shorter than I am. You know how many women I can say that of?"

"You made quite a pair on the dance floor, Shorty. She looked like quite the party girl."

"Yeah, she's fifteen years my junior, but the cutest thing I ever laid eyes on. Did you see that adorable little turned up nose on that cute little face? Not at all hard to look at."

"Ha! Sounds like you've got it bad, and that ain't good. Is she the kind of girl you'd bring home to your parents…if they were still alive?"

"Boy, our upbringing was as different as night and day. I'm smitten with her just the same. There's a dance contest tonight. She asked if I was going and "yes" just popped out of my mouth. I can't wait to find out more about this Agnes girl."

Not only did Harry meet Agnes at the dance again. He managed to get a picnic date with her. When he pulled up in front of her house, she sashayed down the walkway with a baby on her hip.

*Huh?* Harry trotted around to the passenger side of the car and tried not to look surprised as he opened the door for her. "And who is this?"

"Roy meet Mr. Harry. Harry, meet my son, Roy. He's six months old." She gave Harry a heart-melting grin. Not the least bit shy about it. She explained her situation as much as she wanted to, and Harry filled in the blanks as much as he could. Agnes was an unwed mother.

She tickled the baby under his chubby chin. "We're going to have a good time, little Roy.

Harry helped them into the Model T, took his seat, and hit the road. "Agnes, tell me your story. I want to know all about you."

"There's not much to tell. I was born in the French Quarter of Louisiana, west of the Bayou. I have no idea who my father was, so my siblings and I grew up poor. Even as a young girl, I could cook and sew up a storm. Those skills got me hired out to contribute money for our family. I'm a great cook! Everyone says so." Agnes looked at Harry with those penetrating eyes on her pretty little face. "Then there's Roy. No excuses. I got mixed up with the wrong guy. He never hung around long enough to find out I was going to have a baby. That's what I get for partying too much. I'm sorry I did that, but I'm not sorry I have little Roy. We live with my brother and mother. They help me out with Roy."

Harry liked her honesty.

She shrugged out of her sweater, revealing a tight, v-necked blouse and tattoos—a rose on her upper right arm and an anchor on the other. "Agnes, can I ask how you got those tattoos? I never noticed them when we met at the dance."

"Oh, those things? Well, when I was twelve, two of my uncles had just got out of the Service. They dared me to get a tattoo of an anchor. They were Navy guys. I showed them! I got two instead of one. I wanted a rose."

*She is a feisty thing. I kinda like it and I'm falling hard.* So their short courtship began.

A couple of weeks later, Agnes invited Harry to meet her family. She also showed off her good cooking with all that Jambalaya, Chicken Gumbo, and Shrimp Creole. "Very tasty." Harry always complimented her even though it was different from what he was used to. He started going over to eat many times after that. One afternoon when dinner was over, Harry took Agnes outside to sit on the porch. "Agnes, I love your cooking, and I think I love you."

Agnes tossed her head and her pretty turned up nose. "You better more than think you love me, or you won't continue to be blessed by my cooking." That contagious smile spread across her face again.

As soon as Harry got home from work the next day, he went for the telephone. "Hey, Agnes, can you get a babysitter tonight? I know you love to dance and I love dancing with you so what do you say we do that tonight?"

"Sure, Charles and *ma mère* are both home tonight." Pick me up at 7:00 p.m. sharp!

Next he rang his friend. "Hey, Jef, it's me. Agnes and I are going to the dance tonight. Thought you might like to join us."

"Why Shorty? Do you want to dance with me?"

"Very funny! I'm thinking of popping the big question to Agnes tonight. Assuming she says yes, I'd like you to be there to help us celebrate."

"Shorty! This is kind of fast isn't it? Are you sure this is what you want?"

"I just don't think I can live without her. I've never felt this way before about any other woman. I'm already thirty-five and not getting any younger. I think she will keep me young.

"Alright then, what time should I meet you?"

"I'm picking Agnes up at 7:00, so any time after that. And Jef, if Agnes says yes, I'd like you to be my second Best Man"

"I'm all yours, Shorty. Who's the first Best Man?"

Harry's eyes smiled at Jef through the phone. "You're talking to him."

# Chapter 6

## Agnes Toups

### Houston, Texas ~ 1915

"Mama, Harry is taking me dancing tonight." Agnes swayed to the Big Band tune playing in her mind. "I'm sure you don't mind watching Roy for me, and Charles will be home to help you."

"Agnes, you've been seeing a lot of that Monsieur Gerlach. It is serious, no?"

"It is if I have any say in the matter. And call him Harry, please, Mama. Or you can call him Judge. That's what I call him now. Just think, I might have my very own Judge."

When the Model T rumbled up to the house, Agnes gave Roy a quick kiss and ran out the door in her new, red dress.

The sun was setting, but judging from the gleam in his eyes, he could see every seam she'd sewn—every perfect dart she'd tucked. A foolish grin spread across his handsome face. "Agnes, as usual, you are as cute as a button. This is going to be a special night."

"Judge, as usual, you are full of compliments, and for that I wouldn't mind sewing some buttons on your shirt, if you ever have the need." She smiled to herself. *I know how to get what I want.*

"I just might, Aggie. Oh, Jef is waiting for us at the club, so we best get going."

Agnes threw the front door open and waltzed into the house. Her feet were still dancing and her heart was bursting with the news.

"Mama! Charles! I'm getting married. I'm going to sew me the prettiest dress I ever wore. I can sew you something too, Mama."

The two of them looked at her with sleepy eyes and opened mouths.

"Well, does the cat got your tongue? Say something!"

"Ooh la la, when is the big date, *ma fille?*

"Three weeks from Sunday. Harry's friend is a judge, too, and he will perform the ceremony for us at his home."

Charles, quiet man that he was, sat in his favorite chair tapping his fingers.

"Say something." Agnes stared him down.

"I don't know if I would feel comfortable there, Aggie."

Agnes rolled her eyes and shook her head. "Charles, don't you give me no guff…aren't you happy for me? The judge is even going to adopt Roy so he will have a real father."

"*Oui, ma petite soeur*, you know I am! Monsieur Gerlach seems like a wonderful man. He's very educated and is quite older than you, no?"

"*Oui,* Charles. That doesn't bother me one bit, and besides, I need someone who can take care of me and Roy. Plus, Harry likes going dancing just like I do, so I can still have my fun."

"Aggie, you seem to get along with the down-and-outers and the up-and-outers just the same. I admire you for that.

"*Oui,* Charles. I think that's another thing Harry and I have in common. He knows what it is like to be poor.

"In that case, you have my blessings, *ma petite soeur.*"

"Mama?"

Mama winked. "*Oui ma fille, moi aussi.*"

Agnes's heart soared. Harry loved her and she had a blessing from the two people who's opinion she valued most.

**December 31, 1915:** Harry C. Gerlach takes a wife at the culmination of their romance. The wedding took place in the home of a friend and Honorable Judge C. J. Robertson. Standing up for Harry C. Gerlach was his friend and colleague, Jef Hume. Miss Toupe's brother gave her away and the mother of the bride was matron of honor. Also in attendance was the bride's young son, Roy. The couple have left for New York State where they will tour by automobile. Following their trip they will return to their new home at 3902 Leeland Avenue in Houston.

# Chapter 7

# Mrs. Harry Gerlach

### Houston, Texas ~ 1916-1923

"Judge, will you be coming right home tonight? We need to sit down together and make a list of guests for the party next weekend."

"I think so, Aggie! Oh, don't forget your interview with a gal from that maid service. I don't want you working so hard with the baby coming."

"*Merci* Judge. *Je t'aime.* I can't believe you bought me this beautiful brick home—a two-story at that. You've been so good to me, but I must admit, it's getting harder climbing those stairs when I'm running after little Roy. I will welcome the help."

"All I want you to worry about is that good creole cooking of yours and a few French words on the side. Now, give me some sugar, so I can go to work."

"There's the door bell, little Roy. We have a visitor." She shifted Roy to her other hip and opened the door.

"Hello, Miz Gerlach." A slender, colored lady held out a calling card. "My name is Ruthie May. The Maid in the Shade Agency sent me over."

"Come in Ruthie, I've been expecting you. This is my son Roy. Let's go in the kitchen and have some coffee. I made a lemon meringue pie, too."

"Yumm, that sounds good. Smells good, too! Miz Gerlach, how much cooking is required, if I should get the position?"

"Unless I'm sick or dying, you won't be taking over that chore for me. I love working my magic in the kitchen. My husband loves my French-Creole cuisine, and no one can do it better. No offense."

"None taken, Miz Gerlach."

"You can call me Agnes. I never had a maid before. As you can see, I'm going to have another little one and this is a big house to keep up. Also, my husband is a busy, important man, and we entertain a lot. You would need to help clean up after those occasions, plus the daily chores."

"I think I would enjoy working for you, Miz Agnes." She held out her arms. "Can I hold your boy?"

"Please, I cain't hardly carry him anymore." Roy smiled at Ruthie as Agnes handed him over. "He seems to like you already, when can you start? I need someone as soon as possible."

Ruthie reached into her purse. "If you would sign these papers, I will bring them to the agency this afternoon and I can start tomorrow first thing."

"That's wonderful. Let me show you the room that will be yours. I just need to finish the curtains."

They climbed the stairs together, with Roy still in Ruthie's arms, playing with her wiry hair. "There are five bedrooms and yours is here, in the middle."

"Oh, Miz Agnes, this is beautiful. I ain't never had a room to myself before. Hope it's not too much trouble to sew those curtains."

"If you start tomorrow and watch Roy, I'll have them done in no time at all. It's another one of my specialties." Agnes, pleased with herself, was bursting with pride.

"Judge, is that you?" Agnes ran to meet him at the door and threw her arms around his neck. "I hired a nice, colored girl today. I really like her and I think she liked me, too."

"Who wouldn't like you, Aggie?" His eyes smiled back at her. "When can she start?"

"Right away! Her name is Ruthie and she starts tomorrow. We will have no trouble at all pulling your party off. It's going to be great having the help. Thank you so much, Judge. You're the bee's knees."

Bernice came into the world a few months later, then Cornelia three years after that. Harry, Jr. made his appearance the following year, and just before he turned two, Agnes delivered Martha. With five children to look after, Ruthie became more like a member of the family than a maid.

## Gerlach Home ~ 1924

"Ruthie, can you get the door bell? I'm changing Martha."

"Yes Miz Agnes. I'm right here."

"Good morning, my name is Madeline Meyers, a reporter from the Houston Press." The lady's shrill voice carried all the way up the stairs. "Is the lady of the house in?"

"Yes ma'am, won't you come in. I'll go get Miz Gerlach."

"I'm coming, Ruthie! *Oh, Lordy! The judge told me a reporter might come.* Agnes scurried down the stairs and handed Martha into Ruthie's waiting arms. "Put her down for a nap."

Madeline looked around at the simple, but nicely furnished

room. She pulled off her gloves as she bent down and picked up a baby doll.

Agnes brushed her hair out of her eyes as she met the reporter in the entryway. "Hello, I'm Agnes Gerlach, my husband told me a reporter might come by. I didn't expect a woman, but I'm glad you are." *She's so cute and petite.*

"Nice to meet you Mrs. Gerlach, I'm Madeline Meyers from the Houston Press. You can call me Maddy."

"And you can call me Agnes. Oh, I'll take that doll off your hands." They exchanged a knowing smile. "Can I offer you some coffee or tea?"

"Tea would be nice for a change."

"Ruthie, can you fix some tea for Miss Meyers and me? We'll, be in the sitting room."

"Yes, ma'am."

Agnes directed Madeline to the velvet chairs, the ones Harry had bought for *his Aggie.* Madeline took a seat facing her, crossed her ankles, and took a notepad out of her purse. "Agnes, I'd like to interview you about your life with Judge Gerlach, if I may? Your husband's had quite a career so far and is very popular. We'd just like to give the people an inside view of his life outside the courtroom."

"*Life* is the word. We have a lot of life and love to go around in the Gerlach household."

Miss Meyers asked many questions, scribbling every word Agnes shared. "Can you tell me the names and ages of your children?"

"Yes, I don't have too many yet that I cain't keep tract of them." The rattle of little feet sounded through the house. "Roy is nine, Bernice is eight, Connie is five, little Harry is four, and Martha is almost two. As you can see, I also have one in the oven."

"Needless to say you keep busy. I don't know how you do it. Do you have any hobbies? Does the Judge have any hobbies?"

"I stay busy with everyone wanting my attention at once, but I have Ruthie to help me out. I love to cook, so the kitchen is my domain. Ruthie does almost everything else. Judge's hobby is his work. He loves it. He does like to scrapbook but he's kind of turned that over to me lately."

"Well, you have a lovely home, Mrs. Gerlach. Oh, by the way, are you aware of the nickname Judge Gerlach has had pinned on him?"

"Silver Shorty? Of course. I think his friends started that. Some of them have called him Shorty for years and with his white hair, since childhood, it seems to fit."

"Does it bother you or the Judge, that his height is made reference to like that, Mrs. Gerlach?"

"Are you kidding? I think that's why he picked me, because I'm shorter than him." She broke out in a wide contagious grin.

"I like that. Thank you for taking time and allowing me this interview. I'm sure my readers will be pleased and our competitors jealous."

"Thank you Maddy. It was my pleasure."

"Honey, I'm home. Where are you? Where are the children?"

"The kids are in the backyard with their friends. I'm in your office working on *your* scrapbook. There is hardly a negative article about you, Judge. You sure have made something of yourself. I'm proud of you and I know your folks would have been."

"It's because of where I came from. My mama's prayers, learning from my papa's hard work, and the Gerlach's who gave me all the advantages as their son. Are you clipping the other articles of history?"

**March 17, 1924:** Five Douglas World Cruiser's were built, for the US Army Air Service, for an around-the-world flight.

**May 10, 1924:** J. Edgar Hoover Named Head of the FBI

**June 26, 1924:** US troops leave Dominican Republic after 8 years of occupation.

"Yes, Judge. You ask me that all the time. I know what you want. Here, look for yourself."

Agnes dropped the scissors onto the desk and eased the rolling chair back. "Oh…Judge. I…I'm glad you're home early. I think I just wet my pants."

"Why did you do that?" His smile faded into wide-eyed alarm. "Oh, you mean the baby's coming?"

"Yes, now help me upstairs. Go outside and tell Ruthie to come help me deliver this little one while you watch the kids."

His shoulders went tense. "Shouldn't we get you to the hospital?"

"Harry, just do what I say and don't give me no guff."

"Okay, okay! Ruthie! We have a situation here. Aggie needs you right now!"

## ~ July 1924 ~

Agnes flopped back in the bed. Baby number six was out and wailing, but she was too tired to watch as Ruthie cleaned and dressed the newest little Gerlach.

"Miz Agnes, look at your beautiful baby girl." Ruthie brought her to the side of the bed. "She is perfect. Warms my heart just looking at her."

"I hope the Judge isn't disappointed. He kinda wanted another boy to even it out a little—you know—another little lawyer. Will you tell him he can come in now? And Ruthie, try to keep the kids quiet. I'm real tired."

"Yes ma'am, and my friend Buela is comin' to help me out. Where is that girl? The house's run amuck with chillins while I'm midwifing."

"Lordy, Ruthie, stop muttering. You're acting like you've done all the hard work here."

The doorbell rang and Ruthie jumped. "That must be Buela, now. At least Judge is home to let her in." She waltzed to the doorway with the baby in her arms. "Buela, trot on out to the yard and check on the chillins. Judge, Miz Agnes would like you to come up now."

"Thank you, Ruthie. How's she doing?" His footsteps sounded on the stairs.

"They both do just fine, Judge. This one's the easiest I delivered so far. See for yourself." She pulled the blanket away from the baby's face when he approached. "Little Autumn, meet your daddy."

Judge Harry peeked his head in the doorway and smiled at Agnes. "Can I hold her?" His eyes got a tender look as he reached for the baby. Her husband never looked so melancholy before.

Ruthie handed her over. "You okay, Judge? Are you disappointed it's another girl?"

"No, Ruthie, not at all." Harry rocked Autumn in his arms. "I can't help notice how much, even as a baby, she resembles my mama. Look at all that jet-black hair and she has Mama's Irish eyes. She even has freckles!"

"Why Judge, as many chillins you already have, you seem really taken with this little girl baby."

He kissed her forehead and whispered, "I shouldn't feel this way little Autumn, but you are Daddy's favorite little girl."

"Judge," Agnes piped up. "Do you think we're done having kids yet?"

"I don't know Aggie, we only have six and my lucky number is seven."

"Did you hear that, Ruthie? Are you going to stay with us if we keep having kids for you to chase around?"

"Oh, Miz Agnes, you know I love these chillins. I'm not going anywhere, anytime soon. I love this family more than I can ever hope to. I wanta be the only mammy these chillins ever know. Of that I'm grateful."

"Do me one more favor Ruthie. Clip out the announcement of little Autumn when the judge gets his paper."

"Of course, Miz Agnes. I'd be happy to. I'd do anything for my, Miz Agnes."

## Houston, Texas ~ Winter 1925

Agnes stirred the jambalaya and gave it a little taste. Perfect. Maybe she could find a minute of peace to sit down before the newest baby woke up and needed fed. Cooking and chasing kids all day was tiresome work, even with Ruthie May's help.

Harry's car pulled into the driveway and she glanced out the window. How long had it been since they did something fun? She'd beg him to take her out tonight if her dogs weren't barking. She smiled when he walked through the door. "Judge, you got your lucky number seven so I hope you're done getting me pregnant."

"Ha, I think I had a little help in the bed business, Aggie. Joseph Chappel Hutchison Gerlach will grow up to be a fine lawyer."

"*Oui*, with all his namesakes, he has every chance."

"Speaking of which, his last name may give him the greatest edge. I've decided to run for Congress. You know how Jef and others have been hounding, or encouraging me. Well, I think it's time. So after the holidays we'll be busy." He covered his mouth and stifled a cough.

"Now that women are allowed to vote, you're guaranteed mine. But, Harry I'm starting to worry about you. You've been working so hard, you're losing weight. Isn't my cooking good enough for you anymore?"

Harry made a little frown. "Don't be silly, I love your cooking, Aggie."

"And, what's that cough all about? Maybe you should lay off those cigars. And by the way, I'm out of my Camels so if you could pick me up a pack, I'd appreciate it. What was I saying…oh yeah… lay off those cigars and don't work so hard."

"I work too hard and you worry too much. Say, do you think you could come with me when I make my announcement?"

"I'll be by your side Harry. I'm proud of you and there's nothing I'd like more. Except for you to start taking better care of yourself."

## Joe's Barber Shop ~ Spring 1926

Agnes cradled Joseph in her arms and looked down at her children, all pressed and polished, lined up along the storefront of Joe's Barber Shop. How Ruthie got them all ready for their papa's big day, she'd never know.

A news camera flashed when Harry stepped up to the microphone. The press waited to report the announcement, and a hundred or more constituents, crowded the sidewalk. Agnes's heart fluttered when she saw their excited faces.

Her judge seemed ten feet tall.

**HARRY C. GERLACH ANNOUNCES FOR CONGRESS**

DEFENDS STATE'S RIGHTS AND RAPS PROHIBITION. CHILD LABOR CONTROL AND INHERITANCE TAX IN OPENING ANNOUNCEMENT

"Good day everyone. Thank you for joining me as I officially declare my candidacy for United States Congress. As you know I am not a professional politician and maybe a little unconventional and unusual. But, I love it that way and it would be my honor to serve the people of Texas. It will be my task, between now and November to earn that honor. I'd like you to meet my first love and helpmate, Mrs. Agnes Gerlach. She keeps me on my toes along with our seven little Gerlach's. I appreciate your vote in June and together, we will get the work done for the benefit of you and yours. Thanks again!"

Harry spent the better of an hour answering questions from the press. He shook hands with every constituent on the way to the car.

Agnes's fingers were numb from all the well-wishing shakes and her face hurt from the continual smile. "There sure were a lot of people there, Judge. I didn't expect that. Oh, and I saw that reporter Madeline Meyers."

"I saw a couple of reporters I know, too. I hope they get all the quotes right. You know how those guys can be."

"Judge, I know the people love you but do you really think you have a chance to win?" *I wish I was as confident as my husband.*

"Well, I'm not a hundred percent sure, running against the incumbent and all, but if I make it past the primaries, I have the black vote. I've done so much for them—gladly, I might add. And I guess I made it pretty obvious I'm running on a *wet ticket*—backing the repeal of prohibition. That can't hurt." He winked at her.

"Ruthie, I don't know what I'd do without you. You've become my friend and righthand woman. I love that I have someone close I can confide in." Agnes kept rocking back and forth with baby Joseph on her breast. "I gotta tell ya, it really bothers me that the Judge is losing so much weight and coughing more than normal."

Ruthie, as usual, was folding little clothes. "I know, Miz Agnes. You told me how his father died and I'm sure you don't want that for Judge."

"I sure don't and I myself am getting tired caring for all these youngins! If it wasn't for you, I couldn't do it, with all that entertaining expected of us. It's a little more than I imagined life would be married to Judge. And, he's too busy to worry about anything but campaigning for Congressman. The man has only two outlets—cigars and making babies!"

"Oh, Miz Agnes! I wish there was something more I could do to make you feel better about things."

"Don't worry about it Ruthie. I think lucky number seven is just wearing me out. We need to put him on the bottle soon. That should help. Can you take him so I can get a little nap?"

"Of course, Miz Agnes. You just rest your pretty little head."

## ~ Fall 1926 ~

*I've never seen my husband so down trodden.* "Judge, I know you're disappointed you lost the election, but I'm not. Now, maybe you'll take time to go to the doctor. Your health is declining and you know you need the rest.

"As a matter of fact, I'm going to take the rest of the week off, so that should make you happy."

Agnes could hear the letdown sound in his voice. He looked so tired. "Of course it makes me happy, Harry. I wish it made you happy, too."

"Ruthie, you need to call Doc Porter. Ask him to come to the house and check on Judge. He's too sick to get out of bed."

"Yes, Miz Agnes." She ran to the telephone and dialed with shaking fingers.

"Miz Agnes, he'll be here shortly."

"Thank you, Ruthie. Now, if you can get the children to bed, I'll put a pot of coffee on for the doctor." Agnes fumbled with the coffee pot and set it to perking. *O Lordy, I'm getting scared*

The knock at the door finally came. Agnes ran to the entryway. "Come in Doc. I'll show you to his room."

"I'm glad you called, Agnes. I've seen Harry from time to time and been trying to get him to come in for a visit." They climbed the stairs together. At the bedroom doorway, Doc Porter looked in then turned to Agnes. "I'll meet you downstairs when I'm done, Agnes."

Agnes moved away with her shoulders slumped. She took the steps slowly and held the rail tight as she made her way back to the kitchen. She poured a cup of coffee, pushed it aside, and lit a cigarette. Her insides churned. *How can a house full of kids be so quiet? They must sense how sick their daddy is.*

A soft step sounded behind her, and she jumped out of the chair.

"Agnes, I didn't mean to startle you."

"What is it, Doc?"

"It appears Judge has Pneumonia. Keep him in bed. Your husband is a sick man. I can check on him every day after my other appointments at the office."

Her heart sank. "I appreciate that Doc. Do you want some coffee before you go?"

"I better not, Agnes. I gotta get home to the missus. I'll see myself out."

"Okay, thanks. See ya tomorrow." Agnes pulled her rosary beads out of her pocket and prayed the rest of the evening.

## ~ November 1926 ~

"Miz Agnes, it's quite a chore for me to keep the chillins quiet and out of the way. They keep peeking, creeping, and crawling into their daddy's room. He don't even seem to notice. I'll try to keep them downstairs."

"Whew, I'm still drained, but I haven't heard the Judge coughing for a while. I'm thankful he's finally able to rest." Agnes climbed the stairs and entered his room, careful not to wake him as she sat on the bed. She rubbed his cool arm, unlike the feverish skin she had felt over the past few days. A chill ran through her body.

"Judge?" She rubbed a little harder. "Harry!" She grabbed his shoulders and shook him with rough, jerking movements. This couldn't be happening. "Ruthie, come in here and shut the door."

"Oh, Miz Agnes. Is Judge gone? I'm so sorry! What do you want me to do?"

Agnes couldn't think. Her body shook with emotion. Then she slowly straightened her back and spoke in a calm voice. "Get me a basin of water, wash rag, shaving razor, and a comb." *I will clean up my husband.* "Then go call Doc Porter, gather the children, and read their favorite story. Close the door behind you."

Agnes entered one last article into the judge's scrapbook, with Ruthie by her side, rocking baby Joseph.

# HARRY GERLACH DIES AT HOME AFTER ILLNESS

### Widely Known Attorney Succumbs to Attack of Pneumonia; Was Candidate for Congress on Wet Platform

Harry C. Gerlach, 46, widely known Houston attorney, died at his home, 3902 Leeland, at 5:25 p. m. Sunday after an illness of five days. Mr. Gerlach was stricken with pneumonia Tuesday and was confined to his bed. He took a turn for the worse Sunday and died unexpectedly, with members of his family and a trained nurse at the bedside.

[He was] a candidate for congress against Daniel E. Garrett in the July primaries. He made the race on a "light wines and beer" platform, and was defeated.

He had practiced law in Houston for the past 16 years and prior to that time practiced in Fort Worth. He was born in New York in 1880 and received his legal training in New York City and Buffalo. He was admitted to the Texas bar in 1900.

When Mr. Gerlach lived in Fort Worth he was general counsel for the Brotherhood of Railway Carmen and since has been connected intimately with labor movements in Texas. He was at the time of his death general counsel for the Musicians' Protective association.

He was a member of the Eagles, Houston lodge No. 151, B. P. O. E., and the Sons of Hermann. He was at one time a police judge in New York.

He is survived by his wife, Mrs. Agnes Gerlach; three sons, Harry C., Jr., Roy and Joseph Chappel Hutcheson Gerlach; four daughters, Bernice, Martha, Cornelia and Autumn Gerlach, and a sister, Mrs. Bessie M. Finch of New York.

Funeral arrangements will be announced by the Earthman company, who are holding the body pending the arrival of Mrs. Finch.

"Ruthie, this turn of events has upended my world. I'm still full of life and here I sit home alone with seven kids. It was the judge who wanted so many children, not me. Thank God for you and the radio. I love that Louis Armstrong." Agnes started dancing around the room.

"My friends call him the King of Jazz. I like him, too, Miz Agnes."

"You know I heard on the radio they're starting to make talkies. Can you imagine going to the movie house and hearing what the actors are saying?"

"I cain't imagine, Miz Agnes."

"Oh, but most of all I would so love to go to one of those dance marathons! They're doing dances called the Charleston, Fox-trot, and the Shimmy. You know I could do all those dances. People dance till they drop. I think they hold them at the Speakeasies. I would like to own one of those, then I could dance every night. But I cain't do it with all the chillins at my feet.

"You should get out, Miz Agnes. You're still young and shouldn't have to be stuck in the house all the time. It's the roaring twenties after all. I heard a couple from Galveston holds a record of dancing for three weeks."

Agnes stopped in place. She stared through her wedding picture hanging on the wall as she contemplated her next move. "You are so right Ruthie, but there's something I have to take care of first. Will you help me pack up some clothes for me and the kids? We are going to take a little trip."

"Sure, Miz Agnes. Will you be needing me to go along?"

"No, Ruthie. Why don't you make a visit to your relatives? And Ruthie, thanks for everything you've done for our family. I love you like a sister." Agnes turned away so Ruthie wouldn't see her eyes fill with tears.

*Our Daddy*

# Chapter 8

## Martha Gerlach

**Galveston, Texas ~ January 1927**

Martha gripped her little sister's hand and followed Mommy down the sidewalk. Her toes were still numb from sitting in the car for such a long drive. "Hurry, Autumn, Mommy's getting too far ahead of us."

"But, I'm cold."

"Then run." A raindrop splashed Martha's face and she pulled Autumn faster, catching up with her family.

Mommy went up some steps and knocked on a big door. "Stand up straight, Roy. Martha, for heaven sakes, don't let go of Autumn's hand. Oh, why aren't they answering?" Roy slouched, baby Joseph fussed, and Mommy bounced him on her hip and straightened her pretty hat three times before the big wooden door opened.

"Hello. May I help you?" A lady in a black, flowing dress with a white bib peeked out the door. She wore a funny hat with a stiff, white band that came down on each side with black material that covered all her hair and hung down her back. She carried a bucket in one hand and had a rag thrown over her shoulder. Martha pinched her nose.

"My…that smell of disinfectant is strong. You must keep this place very clean." Mommy stepped back and took a breath. "I have an appointment with Mother Superior. Please tell her Agnes Gerlach is waiting."

"Yes ma'am. I'm Sister Mary Bridgett. I'll tell her you're here." The door shut and that was that.

Roy made a face. "I can't believe she just left us standing here on the steps. It's starting to rain."

Harry Jr. hopped up and down, pointing at the closed door. "That lady was dressed like a penguin!" Everyone giggled, even Mommy, who hadn't smiled since Daddy died.

Sister Mary Bridgett opened the door again and scooted aside as a stout woman appeared. She was dressed like a penguin, too. "Hello Mrs. Gerlach, I'm Mother Superior. Won't you come this way?" She turned and waddled down the hall. They followed the Mother Superior through the huge building without saying a word. Doors lined each side of the hallway and the click, click, clicking of their shoes echoed on the shiny floor.

When they got near the end of the hall, the mother penguin stopped. "Children, you may sit on these benches while I speak with your mother."

Martha sat across from the door so she could watch Mommy.

"Mrs. Gerlach, why don't you take a seat in my office?" Mother Superior sat at her desk and pointed to the single, metal chair in front of her tidy desk. "The baby must be heavy in your arms."

"Yes, not a baby anymore, but not a toddler either." Mommy sat down. "Do you think this will take long? I'm in a bit of a hurry to get going."

Mother Superior raised her eyebrows and looked over her glasses at Mommy. She tapped her pen on the desk. "Mrs. Gerlach, you look like a capable woman." Her voice was sharp. "The least you can do is fill out these papers. We need this information for the upcoming census."

Mommy took the papers from her hand. She stood up and walked to the door, a sad look in her eyes. "Be good."

"Yes, Mommy." Martha said at the same time everyone else did.

They giggled, all except Mommy, this time. She stepped back and closed the door.

The clock on the white wall ticked and ticked, hundreds of times. "When's Mommy coming out?" Martha swung her feet back and forth as fast as her little legs would pump.

"Stop fidgeting." Connie thumped her hard on the top of the leg. "If you don't stop it, they'll put us on an orphan train, just like they done with Daddy." She scrunched her face close to Martha. "It'll be your fault."

Martha stopped swinging her feet. "You think you my Mommy?" She sucked in her breath and stuck out her lower lip.

Bernice held Autumn in her lap and leaned around Connie. "Martha, they don't do that anymore. Connie's just being her mean self."

"See Connie, Bernice is older, so she knows." Martha sat back against the cool wall. She blew out a little puff of air with a sigh of relief.

The little hand on the clock ticked a hundred more times, then the doorknob turned and Mother Superior marched out—alone. No Mommy. No baby Joseph. "Come children, it's time for bed." She clapped her meaty hands twice and a tall woman rushed down the hall. "This is Sister Mary Joseph. You boys will go with her to your ward. Girls, you will come with me."

Martha followed her sisters and Mother Superior down the narrow hallway and up some stairs. She tugged on Connie's sleeve. "My tummy's grumbling."

Connie pulled her into line. "Shhh…don't start complaining."

"When's Mommy coming? When are we going home?"

The look on Connie's face was more scared than cross. "I think this is our home, now."

At the top of the stairs, Mother Superior led them into a big room with little beds lined up on each side and girls on most of them. "Girls, these are the Gerlach children. Bernice, Cornelia, Martha, and Autumn." Martha stared at the girls in the room. The girls stared back. She squeezed Autumn's hand. Autumn squeezed back. This was nothing like home.

Bernice whispered to Connie. "What the heck was Mommy thinking?"

Sister Bridgett came in and gave them each a blanket and nightgown. She patted each one on the head. "Such a pity," she mumbled. "Lord, take care of these new little inmates." And with that, she hurried out of the room.

> Agnes's flesh won over her spirit. She did what she felt she needed for her sanity. She signed the last paper, walked out the door, and bought a speakeasy in Louisiana. She never looked back.
>
> Autumn was the youngest child ever to enter this orphanage.

## St. Mary's Orphanage ~ 1929

Martha wrapped her arms around her little sister, Autumn, to protect her from the gusty wind. Another visiting day was leaving fast, along with the priest. He patted Martha's head as he padded down the steps beside her. The other kids stopped looking for Mommy ages ago. *I only waits here 'cause Autumn's sure Mommy will show up this time.* And well, how many times could she be wrong?

"Is that her?" Autumn bounced on her bottom and pointed to where a tall woman chased her runaway hat down the street.

Martha shook her head and reminded her again. "Mommy has black hair, silly." Autumn sank further into Martha's side and her thumb popped into her mouth, as she pouted. Martha pulled it out for her. "Autumn, you're getting too old to suck your thumb. Now listen to me. Mommy has to work 'cause we have no Daddy. She does important things. Why I bet, on the way here after her job, she had to run into a burning building to save someone's little girl, like you."

"I never heard a fire truck." Her other thumb got sucked into her mouth, but Martha left it there this time. *Big sisters don't make good mommies.*

"Tell you what. I'll take you to Aunt Bertha's for dinner in a couple of days." Martha tenderly brushed the bangs out of her little sister's eyes. "You like that."

Autumn's head bobbed and she smiled around her thumb.

When Sunday came, Martha bundled Autumn into her coat and walked her to the two-story house, nearly a mile away. Dried leaves danced around Autumn's feet as she pulled Martha along the street and to the steps of Aunt Bertha's house.

"Autumn, you go up by yourself. You know how Aunt Bertha loves you. I'll wait right here on the steps for you."

"K." Autumn climbed up the steps and balled her fist. She knocked four times. The door swung open on quiet hinges and Aunt Bertha smiled at Autumn. "Ah, my pretty pet has come to Sunday supper! We're having your favorite, chicken and dumplings." Autumn beamed up at her aunt. She glanced back at Martha and smiled. Aunt Bertha took Autumn's little hand in her dimpled one and pulled her inside. The door clicked shut and the finest smells in the world disappeared back into the house.

Martha plunked herself down on the bottom step and scooted up step by step to hear the music on the radio. *I wonder why Aunt Bertha doesn't like me.* Al Jolson sang, and then Mommy's favorite, Louis Armstrong. Martha drew her knees up to her chin and wrapped her itchy skirt around them to keep her ankles warm as she tried to sing along to some new songs like: *My Mammy, I Ain't Got Nobody,* and *Someone To Watch Over Me*

When the sound clicked off, Martha knew supper was being served, so she squeezed her belly till it's button was nearly inside out and turned her mind to other thoughts.

The sun was just going down when Autumn darted out with

the biggest sugar cookie Martha had ever seen. Autumn waved goodbye to Aunt Bertha and plunged down the steps, leaving a Hansel-and-Gretel-like trail behind her. Martha's stiff legs took a while to catch up. "Can I have a nibble?"

Autumn shook her head. Sugar crystals sparkled like diamonds on her lips. "Auntie says it's for me only."

Martha looked back at the house, Aunt Bertha was already drawing the shades. *I guess aunts don't make good mommies, either.*

Martha pulled the oversized apron on and pushed a wood chair up to the big stove. "Autumn, Sally, come on. It's our morning to make the breakfast." The girls each grabbed a handle of the metal pot and managed to drag it over to Martha.

As usual, she laughed out loud. "It's almost as big as the two of you." She helped them lift it, and all together, they worked to center it over the burner. "Now bring me the pitchers of water to fill the pot half way up." Martha struck a long match and lit the gas stove.

*Poof.* Martha jumped off the chair so the fire wouldn't get her. She almost slipped in the trail of water the little girls left on the white floor. When the water was boiling hard, Martha climbed back up and poured the oats in. The long wooden spoon barely reached the bottom of the pot.

"Let me do it." Autumn crowded onto the chair and grabbed the top of the spoon.

"Be careful." Martha tried to help her stir it, but she pushed Martha off the chair.

Autumn gripped the spoon with both hands and swirled it through the bubbling mush. She gave Martha a big grin. "See, I'm a big girl."

"Keep it stirring. I'll get the bowls."

Autumn gave her a little I-know-what-I'm-doing huff. Sally scrambled up on the chair beside Autumn, brandishing a second spoon.

"It's lumpy." She punched the spoon straight down, over and over.

"It always is, but my brothers like it this way. They say it's like having dumplings for breakfast."

Martha's arms were loaded with a stack of bowls when Autumn let out the loudest scream. *If anyone's still asleep, they aren't now.* The bowls tumbled away from her, *a whipping for sure*, and she whirled back to the stove.

Autumn's arms flapped like a baby bird and the chair went topsy-turvy. Sally jumped free, but somehow pulled the pot over, as Autumn and the chair toppled to the ground. The pot thunked to the floor, spewing lumpy oatmeal as it rolled across the linoleum.

Harry Jr. poked his head in the kitchen and his eyes got big and round when he spied the mess.

"Go get some of the boys to help us clean up, or we'll all be in trouble." Martha was close to tears herself. He darted out and Martha slumped down beside Autumn. She thrust her hand over her sister's mouth. "You got to be quiet or you'll bring the whole house in there with your wailing." Then she saw Autumn's arm—coated in scalding oatmeal.

"Put some—" Autumn spoke in gasps. "—butter on it."

Martha shook her head and a tear rolled down her cheek. "We'll get hurt worse for wasting it." She wiped the mush off with the apron, hugged her sister tight, and blew on her arm until the door opened again.

Harry, Roy and three of their friends bounded in, laughing and pointing. Bobby slipped and slid in the mush. A big grin spread across his freckled face. "It's just like being in the snow." Harry took three fast steps, spread his arms, and glided across the oatmeal. Soon all the boys were running, slipping, sliding. Autumn was crying and Sally was hiding under the sink.

The door flew open again and everyone froze in place. Even Autumn held her sobs. The familiar handclaps of Mother Superior stopped the boys in their tracks. She stood in the doorway—with a scowl on her face.

*Autumn in the orphanage*

Roy whispered in Harry's ear. "You know what this means, we'll all be kneeling in rice for our punishment."

Sure enough, after everything was cleaned up, all the children were put in a line and ordered to kneel in rice. All, but Autumn, who escaped punishment because of her burned arm. That day was not to be forgotten by anyone in the room, and Autumn had a *forever scar*.

Over the remaining eight years, Autumn enjoyed being the favored child at the orphanage.

# Chapter 9

## Autumn Florence Gerlach

### Galveston, Texas ~ 1936

Autumn clutched the handle of her little suitcase and stepped up to the large front doors of Ursuline Convent. Too old for the orphanage. Too young for the world. An emptiness spread through her heart—too great to explain.

*I'm not a bad girl, but where else can I go. Some girls make a vow when they enter the convent. But no way will I let them make a nun out of me. Okay here goes, after all, what other choice do I have? I can't just live on the street."* Autumn threw her arms across her chest and felt the familiar *forever scar* on her arm. Ugly, distorted, painful, she tugged her sleeve down to hide its hideousness. She crossed to herself, and muttered, "I'll never eat oatmeal again." With that, she stepped over the threshold, ignoring the real danger—a scar built up on the inside of her soul.

"Autumn? I'm Sister Mary Gertrude." A round little woman met her at the door. "Welcome to your new home."

"Thank you, Sister." She gripped her suitcase tighter. "May I have my own room?"

"Don't be silly, novices and boarders share the large dormitories. The Great Depression might be over for some, dear, but not for all and certainly not for you! Now, come along and let me show you to your ward." She led Autumn into a small room. "First thing you need to do is put on this gown. The doctor will be here any minute now to examine you."

When Sister Mary Gertrude returned, Autumn wiped her eyes and ducked her head. Doctors had come to the orphanage and checked her ears, and eyes, and throat, even listen to her chest before. But this exam was terrifying and humiliating. Had the doctor checked for diseases or her virginity? She didn't know and would never ask. *I wish Martha was here to hold my hand. She's been most like a mother to me. Why did they have to send us to different convents?*

Nine and a half years she'd waited for her real mother to come back—mailed hundreds of letters without one in return. She'd send one more, telling Mommy about this horrid place, where she hadn't any of her brothers or sisters to turn to.

Autumn unpacked her clothes and sat down to write the letter. A group of girls laughed and giggled on one side of the room. At the opposite side, another group glanced at her and whispered behind their hands. *I'll just keep to myself. The girls here are either goodie-two-shoes—groomed to become nuns—or pregnant and promiscuous.*

*How will I ever get out of here?*

## Ursuline Convent ~ 1941

The big doorbell rang, but no one paid attention. Typical. Autumn curled her feet up in the chair and continued reading. Scarlett had just landed her second husband.

The bell rang twice more before Sister Mary Gertrude bustled past the reading room to answer it. Voices floated down the hall, but Autumn didn't care. No one important ever came. "Hello, may I help you?"

"Lordy, what took you so long. I'm here to see my daughter. I'm Agnes…"

Autumn's ears perked up. She put her finger at the stopping spot and listened.

"…Olsen."

*Right first name, wrong last name.*

"Please come in." Sister Mary Gertrude said to the stranger.

"Thank you, Sister. Nice place."

"Follow me, Mrs. Olsen." High heels clicked down the hallway. "You can wait in the parlor. I'll go find your daughter and send her in."

*See, no one important.* Autumn flipped her book open and escaped back into a happier place. Something brushed her shoulder and she jumped, nearly losing her place in the book. Sister Mary Gertrude chuckled. "Well, aren't we the jumpy one? You have a visitor! Your mother is waiting in the parlor for you."

"Are you sure? *Uhh*, okay. Thanks." Autumn placed her bookmark and got up. If this was real, she'd be running to the parlor, but her feet barely moved.

Ninety-one times, she'd made Martha sit on the orphanage steps on visiting day. She'd waited alone twenty-seven more times after Mother Superior sent her best sister to St. Peter's Convent. Autumn hadn't bothered to count the months since she'd come to Ursuline. She peeked around the parlor door. The woman in the chair wore a smart skirt and tailored jacket. Her petite hands fluttered as she stared into a silver compact mirror and applied more lipstick. Same dark hair. Same dark eyes. She'd come. Autumn took a deep breath and stepped into the parlor. "Hello, Mommy! It's good to see you. Is everything okay?"

"Of course, Autumn. Can't a mother visit her daughter just because? Well, you sure are growing up—and filling out—I may add."

"Thanks, I guess. You look good, Mommy."

"Well, after your father died I bought a speakeasy in Louisiana…" She wiggled her ring finger on the left hand. "…then sold it when I remarried. You have another little brother."

*No wonder I didn't recognize the name. And her new family must have kept her away all these years.*

"Oh, don't get all pouty." Mother reached beside her and held out a package wrapped in brown paper. "I brought you something."

Autumn's pulse raced as she unwrapped the present. "*Ooh,* it's pretty. Looks like something out of one of those Harper Magazines."

"I sewed it myself."

Autumn held the flowy, green dress up to her shoulders. The hemline fell mid-calf and the v-neck—wow—the nun's wouldn't approve. "I don't think I'll be able to wear this in here."

Mommy winked. "I made plans with Mother Superior to take you out for a visit in two weeks so you can wear it. I hope it fits you."

"I'll make it fit, Mommy. What's the occasion?"

"I met a nice young man that I'd like to introduce you to. You know how in every letter you send me, you beg me to get you out of here?"

Autumn nodded.

"Well, he's looking for a wife, so I told him about you. If you two hit it off, you could get out and be taken care of. Lord knows I can't support you. I still have to take care of your half-brother, John. He's eleven now. You can meet him once you're out of here."

Bitterness crept into Autumn's heart once again. *Where were you when I was eleven?* "Whatever you think best, Mommy dearest."

"Are you getting smart with me, Autumn? Don't be getting your panties all in a wad, girl. Now, I must get going, I left little John at your Aunt Pauline's. Can you walk me to the door?"

The *click-clicking* of Mommy's high heels was the only sound Autumn heard when she walked her mother down the hall. Every click grated on her nerves—the sound of being left behind—again. Mommy stopped at the front door and gave Autumn a peck on the cheek. "So, I'll see you in two weeks."

"Goodbye, Mommy."

## ~ **March 1941** ~

For two weeks, Autumn found it hard to concentrate, even on her favorite book. Her head jerked up every time the doorbell rang. And, how many times had she read the same paragraph?

Sister Mary Gertrude trotted down the hall, again. "Oh, hello Mrs. Olsen. Autumn is expecting you and…?"

Autumn shut her book and crept to the door where she could hear better.

"This is John Marshall. A new friend of Autumn's."

"Hello, Mr. Marshall."

"Nice to meet you, Sister."

Autumn backed to the far corner of the room, that guy sounded Rhett-Butler suave.

"You can wait in the parlor. I'll go get your daughter."

Autumn couldn't wait, she ran from the reading room, but stopped when she came around the corner and saw Mommy and *that guy! Oh boy!* She walked as gracefully as she could the rest of the way.

He was tall and handsome with a roguish smile.

In a shy voice, she greeted them. "Hi, Mommy."

"Hello, Autumn. I want you to meet John Marshall."

"Hello, John."

"*Bonjour*, Autumn, it's nice to finally meet you. You're prettier than *votre mere* told me. You have a pretty name, too." John spoke with confidence in his voice. "And please, call me Johnny."

"Thank you, Johnny."

Mommy elbowed Johnny. "Well, the way my daughter is looking at you all moon-eyed, you'll have a wife before you get shipped off to war after all."

Autumn's cheeks flamed and she glared at Mommy. "We should go now. I only have two hours before afternoon rosary."

"Okay, I'll hold my tongue and allow you two time to get better acquainted."

"How old are you, Johnny?"

"I'm twenty-two. Only six years older than you. I joined the Navy to get out of the slums of Louisiana, just in case that's on your mind."

"Of course, I'm interested in knowing more about you. So, please, tell all."

Johnny visited Autumn sporadically over the next two months, but only for a couple of hours at a time. Autumn eyed the brown paper package he carried under his arm when he showed up one afternoon in May. He held out the present, but didn't let go when she grabbed it. "You have to wait until we're outside."

"We're going out? Just the two of us?"

"Mother Superior finally granted us permission. Come on, before she changes her mind."

Autumn scooted out the door and tucked her arm into Johnny's. She lifted her chin high and imagined all the inmates staring out the windows with jealousy in their eyes.

When they'd gone several blocks, he handed her the package. "Autumn, *votre mere* sent this dress with me for you to get married in. She's already signed the consent forms. That's if you want to marry me. We can go to

*Autumn escapes the convent*

the justice of peace right now and you don't have to go back to that place anymore."

Autumn's heart raced. He hadn't gone down on one knee or showed her a ring, but surely that was a proposal. He stared at her with an expectant look and she met his gaze squarely. "Johnny, do you know that song, by Frank Sinatra? I think it's *Someone to Watch Over Me*. Maybe that's my song."

"Is that a *yes*, Autumn?"

"That's a yes, Johnny. I'd like that, but where would we live?"

"Right here in Galveston. I got a room for us at a boarding house. It's not much and we have to share kitchen privies, but it will be our own little place."

"Okay. It'll be nice not to sleep in a ward full of girls. Maybe I could get a job and then we can get a place with a kitchen."

"That would be fine. You will soon be Mrs. John H. Marshall.

# Chapter 10

## Mrs. John H. Marshall

### Galveston, Texas ~ December 1941

Soldiers crowded the train station, all heading off to fight Hitler and Mussolini, and the Japanese. The world was still reeling from the attack on Pearl Harbor. Autumn bit the inside of her lip and hurried to keep up with her husband. Johnny walked with a spring in his step, looking confident and handsome as always. He was leaving her, but she wouldn't cry, not in front of all these strangers. He touched her on the shoulder. "Don't worry, Autumn. Now that America's in the war, it won't last long. I'll be home before you know it."

"I hoped we'd get out of that apartment before you left. I'm scared living at that boarding house."

"You need to get over that.

*Autumn and John Marshall*

You're going to have a baby in a couple months. You have to be a big girl."

She went quiet again. *He's right. And, the last thing he needs is to be worrying about me.* She looked up at her husband. "How does that song go? You gotta ac-cent-chu-ate…the positive and e-lim-in-ate…the negative. Latch on to the affirmative…and don't mess with mister in between."

"That's right Autumn, keep that thought."

"All aboard…" yelled the conductor. "All Aboard!"

"Autumn, you be good now you hear."

"And you be careful, Johnny."

He gave her a short and sweet kiss. And, just like that he was gone.

And even with the crowd pressing around her, once again, she was alone.

Autumn walked away, looked over her shoulder, and whispered. "Maybe I shouldn't mess with the mister…Marshall."

## John Sealy Clinic, Galveston TX ~ February 1942

"Well, little one, it's just you and me." Autumn stared down at her little baby girl, her little *war baby* as everyone called this new generation. "I'm going to name you Judy after the singer, Judy Garland. Maybe someday we'll find that rainbow she sings about. I'm going to hate to leave you when I go back to work at the diner. It's going to be real hard."

She ran her finger along Judy's soft cheek. Tears formed in her eyes and she blinked them back. *Mommy once held me like this. How could she have thrown me away?* A new kind of vow formed on her lips and she kissed the top of Judy's head. "I'm going to be a good Mommy. I'm going to keep you always."

"Hi, Autumn." Wilma's weathered face peeked around the curtain. "Congratulations! You up for a visit?"

"Hi, Wilma! It's good to see a familiar face. Please come sit down."

"My sister and the others at the diner said to tell you hello and if you need anything let them know."

"Tell them *hi* right back. I heard they got a new cook."

"Yes, and I'm helping out till you get back. Although they won't let me wait on anyone, being colored and all. They really like you there."

"Wilma, if you need a job, would you like to babysit for my little Judy? I might even need you some evenings. I heard there are dance halls where the girls get paid a quarter a dance."

"I'd love to. Can I hold that little bundle of joy?"

"Yeah, you might as well get acquainted. Wilma, meet Judy. Judy, meet Wilma."

"You're a right pretty baby." Wilma held Judy close and crooned. "For Thou has formed my inward parts; Thou hast weaved me in my mother's womb. That's my favorite Scripture, little one. He made you right fine, too."

Judy turned her head and tried to suck on Wilma's face.

"Oh honey, you don't want to kiss my ol' black face!" She started laughing.

Autumn joined in. It felt good to laugh.

## ~ Summer 1942 ~

Autumn picked up Judy from Wilma's house and walked the two blocks to the rooming house where they resided. *I dread going home. I detest climbing these stairs with a baby in my arms. I hate—* She stumbled over a bum in the stairway, let out a little gasp, and ran the rest of the way to the safety of their little room.

Nights were the worse. To warm a bottle, Autumn had to go out into the dim hallway and walk five doors down to the community kitchen. Judy fussed again and Autumn rolled over. "Not tonight, baby. I just can't go out there. You'll have to cry it out. I don't want to run into another bum, on the way to the kitchen." She covered her ears with a pillow. All she could think of was getting out of this place. *Maybe I should do what my big brother Roy did. Move to San Francisco, California.*

*Someday. Somewhere over the rainbow.*

*Wilma takes Judy to see Santa*

# Heart of My Life

# Chapter 11

## Judy Ann Marshall

As it turned out, my Mother's *somewhere over the rainbow* moment filled my life with storms. No one knows what a little girl is thinking, and if the sorrow in my eyes told of the hurt in my soul, no one seemed to notice. I learned to swallow all complaint, in fear of Mother's harsh punishment. Leaving Wilma "Ma" was my first heartbreak, but her faithful prayers would one day reach me from a distance.

### Galveston, Texas ~ 1945

"Come here." Mother held out her hands, but her face wasn't happy. "Now!"

"No. I want my Ma." Judy threw her arms around Ma's neck and hid her face in the clean dress smell.

"Wilma is not your ma." Mother's voice snapped and crackled. "She's the help."

Giant sobs shook Ma's round body. "Bye…"

Judy pushed straight up in Ma's arms. If the squeeze got tighter, her stuffing was gonna come out.

"Bye…my…girl." Ma's words were whispery and jiggled as much as her body.

"Don't cry, Ma." Judy patted her wrinkled brown cheeks with both hands. "Come wit us to San Fan-isco."

"I wish I could, sugar." She took a big breath. "But I can't. You need to go on a long trip with your Uncle Harry and your mamma."

Judy stuck out her lower lip. It quivered all by itself.

"You gotta promise me to say your prayers like I taught you." Ma gave her a little bounce. "Okay?"

Judy looked to Uncle Harry, standing with the taxi man, to Ma's pretty, little house, then up into the sky, where the sun danced behind fat green leaves. She had to promise. She did everything Ma said to do. "Okay, Ma." Judy flopped her head against Ma's shoulder. "I wov you."

"You're like to break my soul with all your loving, sugar." Ma's eyes made wet spots on the front of her dress.

"Give me Judy." Mother's fingers pushed in between Ma's hug and dug into Judy's sides.

Ma held her tight for just a bit more. Her whisper tickled Judy's hair. "Lord. I'll not see my sweet girl again, this side of Heaven. She's been like a daughter to me these past three years." Her eyes looked up. "You watch over Judy as I pray for her from a distance."

"Wilma!" Mother said her name like a bomb and tugged harder. Her nails bit through Judy's dress and ripped her out of Ma's arms.

"Yes, Miss Autumn." Ma's hands flapped empty in the air, then she spun around, and ran into her house. The click of her door was loud as a scream.

Mother put Judy down so hard her eyes got watery. "Get in the cab."

Judy walked backward to the taxi, keeping her eyes on the closed door the whole way.

## California here we come

At the train station, Mother pulled Judy out of the Busy Bee Taxi and made her way through the Galveston Terminal Railroad Station. There were many bodies moving toward the Sante Fe "all aboard" call. Judy hung tight to her mother's skirt, her head turning in all directions as she tried to take in all the new sights. Once on the train, each mile put space between who she left behind and the new that lay ahead. She had never seen so many people and men in service uniforms. She was told her father wore the same kind of clothes and she would meet him one day.

"Help! I'm stuck." Judy pounded on the inside of the bathroom stall door. "Mutter…help!" She looked back at the toilet, she'd just peed, but might wet her panties any second.

"Yoo-hoo." A happy voice—not Mother's growl—sang out. "Little girl."

Judy sucked in another sob and listened. Was the voice calling her?

Fingers with pretty polish and a sparkly ring waved under the door.

Judy waved back.

"Just crawl under the door, honey. There's plenty of room."

"Okay." Judy squished flat on her belly and wiggled out of the stall.

The nice lady with red cheeks and a big smile helped Judy to her feet. "You're a brave little girl." Her yellow curls bounced with every clack of the train. "Let's wash your hands and I'll walk you back to your seat."

"Thank you, ma'am." Judy stretched up on tiptoes, but couldn't reach the sink.

"Let me help you." The lady wrapped her arms around Judy's middle and lifted her up. A smile jumped back on Judy's face. With feet dangling, she ran her hands under the cold water. The lady whisked the gritty soap powder into a soft foam. Judy could stay here and play all day with her new friend making soap bubbles on all ten fingers. The lady dried Judy's hands on the towel and set her down. "There you go, honey."

"Come to where I sit." Judy grabbed her hand and pulled her through the car. The jiggly train bumped her into someone's seat.

"Hey, watch it." A grumpy man shuffled his newspaper, but Judy didn't stop.

"Mutter…Mutter…"

"Where have you been? I told you—" Mother's scoldy face turned smiley when she saw the lady.

"I found a new Ma!"

The lady's eyebrows scrunched together then smoothed out. "Oh honey, I'll be your friend. I'd never presume to—"

"She wasn't talking about replacing me." Mother scowled at Judy, but gave a little laugh. "Wil-ma was just the babysitter." The frown returned to her voice. "What took you so long?"

The lady answered before Judy could think up the words. "Your little girl was stuck in the bathroom. I guess the stall door got jammed."

"Oh, thank you! I guess I should've gone in with her. My name is Autumn and this is my brother Harry."

"Can ya see the family resemblance?" Uncle Harry squished his cheek up against Mother's, grinned like a lion, and pulled down on her lower lip. They both had the same crooked teeth.

Mother slapped his hand away.

"Same southern drawl, too." The lady giggled. "It looks like we're traveling companions." She slid into the seat behind Mother and smiled at the man in white. "I'm Annie and this is my husband, Jimmy."

Mother turned in her seat. "Jimmy, I see you're in the Navy. Judy's father is a sailor also. She's never met him. We're hoping he'll be out in a few months and will meet us in San Francisco." The more Mother talked, the more Judy's new friend forgot about her.

Judy stood in the aisle as tall as she could and raised her voice. "I'm Judy."

Mother gave her the squinty-eye, but kept talking.

"That's swell." Jimmy leaned across Annie and held out a coin. "Judy, this is a lucky penny. When you get to San Francisco, you make a wish in the first fountain you see."

"Thank you, mister." She clutched the shiny golden coin in her hand. *No one ever gave me a penny before. I must be rich.* "Can I sit with you and your mutter."

Jimmy laughed and patted the seat between him and Annie. "Sure Judy, but this is my wife, not my mother."

She scrambled into his lap. "Oh. Does she have a penny too?"

Annie bathed her with another smile. "No Judy, but I have a piece of candy in my purse." She turned back to Mother. "May I?"

Mother nodded and for a moment she looked happy.

Annie held out a handful of lemon drops. "Would you like one?"

Water splashed around Judy's tongue at the sight. Never had she seen so much candy at once. "Yes, ma'am." She popped one into her mouth.

"She's so cute." Jimmy whispered above her head. "I want a little girl like this someday."

Judy stood on the seat and threw an arm around each of these new friends.

When the train could bounce along no further, Judy and her family took a ferry ride into San Francisco, then hopped into a yellow taxicab that drove up and down the winding streets. She pressed her face to the window, until the man called out, "Here we are—700 Arkansas Street." A tall gray house stood on the hill. No yard to play in. No big tree. She dragged her little suitcase up stairs, stairs, and more stairs.

Mother smoothed her skirt as Uncle Harry knocked on the big door. He ran his hand through his hair. At the sound of footsteps approaching the door, Judy hid behind her mother's skirt as the door swung open. A man with a mustache the color of midnight grabbed Mother in a big bear hug. "Autumn! Harry! Come in. Come in." He slapped Uncle Harry on the back.

"Hello, Bubba. You look like a regular Clark Gable" Mother gripped Judy's arm and pulled her into the house. "Judy, this is your Uncle Roy."

He bent his face down to Judy. "Uncle Bubba, to you." His huge mustache skipped with every word. "And this is your Aunt Flossy."

A very pretty lady, taller than Uncle Bubba and with hair the color of the moon, elbowed him out of the way. "Well hello, Judy. We're so glad to finally meet you." Her voice was as kind as her smile. "We are going to get well acquainted."

The only thing bigger than Uncle Bubba's mustache was Aunt Flossy's tummy. Judy pointed at it. "What'd you eat?"

"Judy!" Mother snarled her name, but looked like she might smile. Uncle

*Aunt Flossy and Uncle Bubba*

Bubba stood off to the side. His mustache quivered and his eyes were laughing, but no sound came out.

One by one, three boys ran into the room. Aunt Flossy cleared her throat. "Judy, these are your cousins. Buddy just turned six." Buddy looked just like Uncle Bubba, but smaller and with no mustache. "Ray Wayne is five." Aunt Flossy ruffled his moonlight hair. "And Jimmy's four."

Judy threw her arms around her littlest cousin. "I have a sailorman friend named Jimmy!"

He squeezed back. "We're going to be friends, too."

"And soon you'll have another cousin." Aunt Flossy rubbed her belly.

Buddy patted Judy's head. "You get to stay with us for a couple of months."

"Yeah." Wayne Ray dropped to his knees and put his hands on her shoulders. "We'll teach you all kinds of good things."

It didn't take long for Mother to get a job. Aunt Flossy ran around the house, picking up toys, cooking dinners, and washing clothes, while the grownups were at work. Judy followed Jimmy everywhere. In the boy's room, Jimmy shoved a beat up dump truck out of the way and flopped down on the wood floor. "I'm bored."

Judy plopped down next to him. "Me, too."

Buddy and Ray Wayne looked at each other and grins broke out on their faces. "Hey Mom," they hollered at the same time. "Can we go outside to play?"

Aunt Flossy poked her head in the room. "Just for a little while, your dad will be home from work soon and dinner is almost ready."

The big cousins raced to the door, but Aunt Flossy grabbed them by their collars. "You boys look after Jimmy and Judy. Ya'll hear?"

Ray Wayne spun back around and pulled Judy to her feet. "C'mon Judy, we have to go down the steps on the side of the hill. My dad built those steps. There are one-hundred of them, if you can count."

She held tight to Jimmy's hand as they climbed down the steps and followed the other boys.

"Hurry up!" Ray Wayne yelled from the sidewalk. "We need to cross the street before a car comes."

Judy ran her fastest. A car blasted its horn as they reached the far sidewalk.

"Over here." Buddy waved Judy and Jimmy over to where he and Ray Wayne were standing, just up the street. High above their heads was a red box with big letters. Buddy socked his brother in the arm. "Ray Wayne, you're the tallest, you pull it."

He stretched real tall, "I can't reach it." He jumped, but his fingers barely touch the bottom of the box.

"Awe…" Buddy took a step toward the park. "This ain't no fun."

*Old fire alarm*

"Wait. I got a plan." Ray Wayne sounded excited. "Judy, come over here. Buddy and I will lift you up and you pull that handle there."

She looked from one cousin to the other. "Okay."

Sirens screamed even before she climbed down off the big boys' shoulders. Buddy got bug-eyed. Ray Wayne's ears looked all twitchy. He gave Judy a little shove from behind. "Quick run as fast as you can or the firemen will get us in trouble." The boys raced across the street, without even looking for cars.

Judy ran behind them, her heart pumping as hard as her feet.

Up, up, up the boys went to the top of the stairs. They stamped their feet and waved their arms. "Hurry, Judy. Hurry."

For every step up, she slid down two. Falling, scrambling, scraping her knees. She started crying. *Do firemen whip kids? With their belts?* Even if they didn't, mothers did.

Judy sat quiet at the dinner table. So did her cousins.

Only Aunt Flossy did the talking. "Autumn, we had a little excitement today." Mother raised her eyebrows, and took another bite of fried chicken. "Firemen came to our door and we didn't even have a fire." Aunt Flossy looked at each of her boys, one at a time. "Judy got her knees all scratched and bloody." Aunt Flossy's eyes looked right at Judy.

She pulled her dress over her hurt knees.

When the telling of the *big ordeal* was done, all the adults had stern looks on their faces. Then Uncle Bubba's mustache started to twitch like it did the first time Judy met him. Aunt Flossy's lips curled up, and even Mother looked like she was going to spit out a chuckle.

Judy leaned back in her chair. *Whew, no whipping this time!*

Aunt Martha came for a short visit and the house was more crowded than usual, but Judy didn't care. She seemed to be the favorite of Nannan, as she called her aunt. During the day when everyone was busy, Nannan would play with her, dance with her, even take her shopping.

*Judy and Nannan*

Nannan scooped Judy up in her arms and danced around the room like she'd done the last few days. "I've got to go now." She hugged Judy tighter, then set her down by the front door. "I'll miss you, little darling." She picked up her suitcase and disappeared down the stairs.

Tears stung Judy's eyes and a cry rose in her throat. She ran onto the porch. "Wait, Nannan, I want to go with you."

"Stop that." Mother swatted

her from behind. "If you make a scene, your Aunt Martha will never come back."

*Life without Nannan.* That hurt worse than a spanking. Judy tried to obey, but the tears came harder and the cry came louder.

"Stop your blubbering." Mother scooped Judy up around the middle and walked to the kitchen sink. She turned the cold water on full blast. Judy remembered the game she played with her friend on the train. She sucked in her last sob and held out her hands to play in the water.

Instead of making soap bubbles, Mother shoved her face under the faucet.

Judy kept quiet for several days so her mother wouldn't get mad again. But with the adults at work and the cousins at school, loneliness got more powerful than fear. "Aunt Flossy, may I go outside."

"Yes, Judy, but don't go past the empty lot. Since the boys are in school, they can't watch after you." Aunt Flossy mumbled under her breath. "As if that did any good."

Two kids were playing in the empty lot. "Hey, what's your name," yelled the boy. He looked like he'd been playing in the dirt and his sand colored hair was all scrappy looking. "I'm Joey."

"My name is Judy."

"Why do you talk funny?"

"I don't know. Why do you talk funny?"

The little girl piped up. "Hi Judy, my name is Margaret and I think I know why you talk funny." Margaret was very pretty with blond hair and sky blue eyes. She seemed nice.

"Why?"

"Where were you born?"

"Gal-was-ton, Texas."

"Okay, that's why, Joey. They talk different from us in the south."

Judy liked having new friends. They played and argued every day. Joey was always teasing her. "Judy, I'm going to take your chalk home with me."

"NO, Joey or I'm going to tell my Aunt Flossy on you." She used the same threat every day.

Margaret loved Joey and made sure her friend knew it. "Judy, I'm going to marry Joey when I grow up."

"Na-uh, I'm going to marry Joey." So they proclaimed Joey on a daily basis.

One evening at suppertime, Mother tapped her fork against her glass and gave everyone a big smile. "Bubba, I really appreciate you and Flossy letting us stay here. I finally got a little apartment about eight blocks from here at 743 Rhode Island Street. Plus, Pacific Telephone & Telegraph Company said they will keep me on. I passed the probation period. Have you noticed I dropped my southern accent?" Mother started dressing very nice and looked real pretty.

Uncle Bubba never said much but his kind eyes and smiles had a way of talking for him. "Yes, and my sister has become very stylish."

Aunt Flossy passed the potatoes, smashed to perfection, around the table. "I like the way you do your hair now. It compliments your pretty face. What about Judy, Autumn? Will you be bringing her over every day?"

"No, that's another thing. The landlady, Lorraine Federoff, has three children close to her age and offered to babysit. How convenient that they live just upstairs. Our apartment is in the basement. We have to go into the garage to get to our bathroom, but it'll be affordable till Johnny gets home and finds a job. Again, I hope you both know how grateful I am for all your help."

Autumn fixed the little apartment up with her first couple of paychecks. Her new neighbor, landlady, and babysitter came downstairs. Lorraine was a strong looking woman with salt and pepper hair. She even looked pretty without a lot of make-up. "I brought a hammer, Autumn, in case you need some help."

"Thanks Lorraine, I didn't know how I was going to pound the nails in the wall. I'm having some girls from work over tonight." Together they hung up what few pictures Autumn had.

One was a face—only black—and turned to the side. The shape of the nose and chin looked just like Mother's shadow.

Judy kept staring at it, studying it. "Mother, is that you when you were a Negro?"

Mother's hand flew with her words, smacking Judy right across her cheek. "What a stupid question. It's a silhouette cameo portrait—a profile of my head cut out of a piece of black paper."

*Mother's silhouette*

Lorraine's eyes got big, but she stayed quiet, not like her usual loud self.

Judy hung her head and held back her tears.

"Get in the kitchen. Your dinner's on the stove. I can't visit with Lorraine with you pestering me. And you better eat every pea on your plate tonight. I don't want you taking two hours to do it like last time."

"Yes ma'am." *Yuk! I hate peas.*

As hard as she tried, Judy gagged on the peas and as the sun went down, she was sitting in the dark kitchen.

Mother rushed in and flipped on the light. Without saying a word, she grabbed Judy by her long black hair and dragged her to the sink. Mother lifted her up and put her face under the faucet.

Judy tried to cover her head with her hands, but Mother pinned her arms to her chest.

*Huuh huuh.* Judy gasped even before the water clogged her nose and mouth. She kicked. She tried to scream. Water rushed up her nose and down her throat, making her eyes burn. *I can't breathe. Am I going to die this time?* Finally, Mother dropped her to the floor. It was over and she was still alive.

Mother dried her hands on the dishtowel. "My company will be here soon, so put your pretty dress on."

Later that evening, Mother, acting so hoity-toity, served her friends glasses of wine. "Judy, why don't you dance for the girls?"

Judy's face lit up, smiling from ear to ear. Mother took a few short steps to her new phonograph and put on her favorite album by Doris Day. She delicately put the needle on the vinyl record and it played *Sentimental Journey.*

Judy swayed and spun her little dance. *I wish my boyfriend, Nat King Cole, was singing instead.* She twirled around a few times and noticed she was getting a lot of attention from the ladies. *I love doing this.*

When the song was over, Mother propped her nylon

*Autumn Marshall*

stockinged feet up on the ottoman. "Judy, tell the ladies who my boyfriend is."

"Fanka Noka"

Everyone laughed, but one of the ladies said, "I love Frank Sinatra, too.

Autumn sipped on her wine. "Watch this, girls! Come over here, Judy. Kiss my feet." Judy's stomach felt sick inside. She felt her face go red, but as usual, she obeyed. Mother had a good laugh. The ladies followed with a small laugh, but they looked uncomfortable. "You should go to bed now, Judy. Tell everyone goodnight."

"Yes ma'am. She could barely look into the faces around the room. "Good bye." With head bent and body numb, she went into her room, closed the door, and shut away her embarrassment.

## ~ 1946 ~

*"Dance ballerina dance,"* Nat King Cole was singing on the radio. Sitting on the floor, Judy jumped up and started dancing. *I'm going to be a ballerina when I grow up.*

"Judy, stop dancing and get your dress on. I told you your father is coming home today and you're going to meet him for the first time." Mother's right hand was on her hip and that meant she meant business.

"Okay, but my boyfriend is on the radio."

"Turn it off, since you can't seem to stop dancing every time his songs come on!"

With a pout on her face, she obeyed and got dressed. Before long, there was a knock. Mother flung the door open and greeted her husband with a hug and a kiss. Then he stepped further into the kitchen and looked at Judy for the first time. She was scared and shy at the sight of him. He seemed so tall but looked handsome in his Navy uniform. He had dark brown hair, brown eyes and was slightly tanner looking than Judy and her mother.

"Hello Judy, I'm your father. I finally get to meet you."

"I know you're my father, Mother told me about you."

"Well, we'll get to know each other in time. I'll even

*Johnny Marshall*

take you to baseball games." He looked at Mother. "The Seals Stadium is close by."

"Well, lawdy daw," The sound of irritation in Mother's voice echoed through the kitchen.

Judy looked at her mother then back to her father. "I don't know about baseball games. I like to dance."

"I know, your mother wrote me about that so why don't you go turn on the radio. You can dance while your mother and I visit with a little drink."

"Yes, sir. Thank you."

♥ ♥ ♥

If only walls could talk. For the next three years, Judy danced, Johnny drank, and Autumn screamed. This could go on from sun up to sun down. Together her parents fueled fights and threw furniture at each other.

*Nat King Cole*

With every battle, a new boil would manifest on Judy's little bottom, at least a half dozen now, causing pain and bleeding. *I hope I don't get in trouble for my pants being all bloody.* She crouched in the corner and hid her face on her knees. Closing her eyes, she tried to escape into the words Nat King Cole sang on the radio.

"Well, if you don't like it here, Johnny-boy, you can leave." Mother's words screeched above *That Old Black Magic.* "And by the way, you can take Judy with you. I raised her alone the first four years and you've been nothing but useless since you came back. It's high time you did your part."

"What do I need with a girl? She don't like baseball and can't carry on my name. If you don't want her, drop her in the nearest orphanage."

"That's a low blow and you know it." Mother slammed a kitchen chair against the table, sending a glass crashing to the floor.

The shards exploded around the room and Judy scrunched further into the corner and pressed her burning face deeper into her knees. If Mother noticed her wet cheeks, she'd only get madder.

## ~ 1948 ~

"Judy, run faster so we don't miss *Howdy Doody Time*." Donna, the oldest of the Federoff children, urged her on. Their family had just gotten their first television. What a new experience for all! The kids rushed home from school and once inside the door,

*Judy and the Federoff children*

climbed the steps and flung their coats and things aside. They all laid down on their stomachs in front of the *one-eyed* monster, propping their heads on their little fists. Giggles rang through the house.

"Boy, this beats playing on the roof," one of the twins piped up. Things were so much better for Judy now. The twins, Karen and Daniel no longer beat up on her. She was happy to have them as friends.

"Judy, your mother's downstairs, here to pick you up." Mrs. Federoff helped Judy gather her things. "I'll see you tomorrow after school."

"Okay, bye."

"Where're we going, Mother?"

"To see our new apartment. We're moving just two blocks away so you can still go to Mrs. Federoff's after school. Also I need to tell you that your father won't be living with us anymore, but you will still see him sometimes. He said he wants to take you to a baseball game."

"Oh, okay." *Not my favorite thing to do!*

"You'll still be able to go to the store for me too. It will actually be closer to our new place. And, by the way, I asked the Greeks at the store why it takes so long for you to pick up just one or two items for me. You know what they told me? They see you dancing in front of all the trees along the sidewalk. Why do you do that?"

"I dunno. I guess I think they're my friends."

"Is that so? Well do your *friends* have names?"

"Yes, Mother. I named some of them Jesus, Mary and Joseph."

"I see, well when I send you to the store, I don't want you lollygagging, ya hear?"

"Yes ma'am. Can I ask you a question Mother?"

"That depends on what it is."

"Am I ugly?"

"Well, you might not be smart but you aren't ugly either. Why?"

"Oh, there's a boy at school I kinda like, and I always smile at him. Today he turned to me, looked right in my face and said, 'you sure do have big eyes and buck teeth. You are UGLY.'"

"Come here, let's cut you some bangs, then you will look prettier." With some dull scissors, Mother whacked off the hair hanging from Judy's forehead.

*Judy's sixth birthday*

"There, that ought to do it. Now run to the store and get me a Mars candy bar."

"But it's already dark outside."

"Well, ask your tree friends to protect you. And no dawdling, I'm hungry for chocolate and almonds."

"Okay." Judy put her coat on and stepped into the night. Why did Mother have to be so afraid of the dark? Two ways led to the store. The sidewalk was a scary, long, three blocks. Judy chose the shortcut through the empty lot. She stuffed her hands into her coat pockets and walked as fast as she could without streetlights. Weeds snagged her stockings and the uneven ground tried to trip her. This way was just as frightening, but if she could get to the store and home faster, it was worth taking. The wind brushed her bangs off her forehead. *I hope that boy likes my new haircut.*

Judy never told her mother but at school the next day, a nun told her she looked stupid with short bangs. *Gosh, now I think I'm ugly and stupid.*

At 872 Kansas Street, Judy met new friends. She learned to play hopscotch and kick the can. Roxanne taught her how to steal from the vegetable truck. But Judy never could do that. She still had guilt over steeling that apricot off the neighbor's tree when she lived on Rhode Island Street. She did however eat the fruit that Roxanne stole. They played *real life* situations in Roxanne's basement. Judy pretended to be a grown woman who lost her husband and she would uncontrollably cry real tears.

"Are you okay, Judy?" Roxanne knelt beside her and put her arm around Judy's shoulder. "Yeah, but I don't think we should play this. It makes me sad. Let's pretend we're ballerinas."

I BECAME A LATCHKEY KID for the next few years and saw very little of John Marshall. Autumn was busy with her daily job, dating and dancing. In my loneliness, I had no idea of the truth of God's word. "Though Father and Mother forsake me, God will lift me up." ~Psalm 27:10

# Chapter 12

# Robert Wagner

WHEN A FATHER GIVES UP HIS DAUGHTER, at age ten, it leaves a scar in her spirit. Why would any man want me when my own father didn't? However, God had not abandoned me, and to prove it, he sent a nice man to take me as his own.

## ~ 1950 ~

Bob pulled up to 872 Kansas Street, in what he had described to Autumn as his shiny black *limo*—except in reality it was a 1936 Plymouth Sedan. He saw two little girls playing hopscotch. One looked over at Bob and smiled with her big brown eyes. *That's Judy! I recognize her before I even meet her.* He grabbed the bag off the front seat and hopped out of his car, smiling at Judy on his way up to the house.

"It's your turn, Judy," her friend huffed.

"Okay, hold your pants on." Judy gripped her favorite charm and tossed it to square number seven.

Just then, Autumn opened the door. She wore her pretty apron and had her hair done up just so, except for a little string of it hanging over her left eye. "Hi Bob, come on in and I'll get Judy. What's that you got there?"

"Oh, you told me Judy liked Seven Up so I brought her some."

"That was nice of you." She leaned out the door and raised her voice. "Judy, tell Roxanne good-bye for now. Our company is here."

"Can you play tomorrow, Roxanne? Maybe we can play kick-the-can with some of the other kids."

"Sure, see ya later."

Judy skipped up the walkway to their small, cottage-style house. Autumn had it fixed up real cozy. Judy slowly pushed the door a little wider and looked up at Bob, then at Autumn. "Judy, I'd like you to meet Mr. Wagner, the gentleman I told you about."

"Hello, Mr. Wagner." She was a tiny thing like her mom, with big brown eyes that made Bob's heart melt.

He knelt down to her level. "Can you please call me Bob? I'm hoping we can be friends, not just formal acquaintances."

Judy looked at her mother, and with an approving nod, turned back to Bob. "Okay, sure Mr. Wagner, I mean Bob."

"Judy, you get cleaned up for dinner. Bob is taking us to the movie house later to see *Cinderella*."

"Oh goodie! Thanks, Bob."

"I got some Seven Up for you, Judy. I'll put it in the icebox to keep it cold while you get ready."

Judy skipped happily to the sink to wash up and Bob walked over to the icebox. He pulled the latch to open it and while putting the Seven Up on the shelf, he noticed something strange. "What's this, Autumn?"

Autumn rolled her eyes as she snatched the dirty socks from his outstretched hand. "That girl is always putting things in the wrong place. Sometimes I find the garbage in the clothes hamper. It drives me crazy. She's always daydreaming."

"I think it's funny and kinda cute."

Judy turned from the sink, dribbling water on the floor. The look on her face was priceless as it went from surprise to a shy smile.

Autumn slapped a towel in Judy's hands and turned the water off. "Bob, it's real nice of you to include Judy in our date today."

"I'm looking forward to enjoying time with both of you."


## ~ 1952 ~

For the next two years, Bob dated Autumn every time his ship was in port. He grew to love Judy, too, so after proposing to her mother, he had an idea. "Autumn, I would like to be a dad to Judy. What do you think?" He held Autumn's slender hands in his.

"I would love to be a family, Bob." Autumn's brown eyes sparkled.

"Do you think John Marshall would be willing to give her up?"

"Well, he doesn't see much of her anyway. Let's see. You know he complains about having to pay $40.00 a month child support because he has a car payment for that amount."

"Then, maybe this will relieve him of that problem. Can you approach him with the idea?"

"Sure Bob, I'll deal with him."

Autumn got off at her bus stop and met Judy halfway down the block. "Hi, Mother." Judy was out of breath from jump rope. "Can I still play outside?"

"Yes, of course. I have some things to do before dinner. I'll call you when I need you."

Autumn walked into her house and kicked off her stiletto, pointed shoes. She flopped down on the sofa and rubbed her poor sore feet through her nylon stockings. Placing the phone on her lap, she dialed JUniper7-5013. "Oh, that's not it." She hung up and dialed JUniper7-5103. *How am I going to remember more digits when the telephone company changes our numbers over from five to seven digits?*

"Hello?"

"Oh, hello, Ann?"

"Yes, this is Ann."

"Hi Ann, this is Autumn, is Bob home yet?"

"Hello Autumn, yes just one moment please I'll get him." *Bob's mother is always so formal. I guess because she's a business woman.*

"Hi, Autumn. I was just about to phone you. What's going on?"

"Well, good news. I talked to my Ex and he's willing to give up Judy so you can adopt her. I guess he'd rather have a car than a kid."

Bob's voice got raspy. "I'm going to be husband and dad. A readymade family. I'm very happy, Autumn, and I want to make you happy, too."

"You already have, Bob. Should I tell Judy?"

"No, I want that to be special. I'll talk to her myself."

"Well, you do know how to do things right." Autumn's eyes were misty. *No one has ever treated me so good.* She smiled into the phone. *Having a man in the house means I won't have to count on Judy to stay awake and listen for burglars at night. And if we have more children, we'll have a built-in babysitter.*

The following weekend, Bob took Autumn and Judy on a picnic at Golden Gate Park. He knew Judy loved it there with ponds filled with swans, and the colorful gardens. The aroma in the air touched the senses. In some places, they could hear music playing in the distance. There was always something going on at Golden Gate. Bob helped Autumn spread out their blankets and set the basket of food on it. They were right next to the Japanese Tea Garden. "Judy, I'd like to talk to you about something."

"Okay, Bob." She placed her chin on her hands and looked serious. "What do you want to talk about?"

"I'll give you two some privacy." Autumn sauntered over to the fountain.

"Judy, you know I love your mother and we're getting married in a couple months."

"Yes, and we're having my dress made to match Mother's. It's made of yellow *taffeeta?*"

"Ha, I think you mean taffeta. I know you will look real pretty in that. What I want to know is would you like me to be your dad? Because, I would like you to be my daughter."

"How can you do that? John Marshall is my father."

"Well, I would adopt you and you could call me Dad."

"Yes Bob, I want you to be my dad. I think I love you and I like you, too." Judy threw her arms around him.

"I love you too, Judy." Bob got all choked up. *I will always love my new daughter, Judy.*

*Agnes and Autumn*

*Bob, Judy, and Autumn*

# Chapter 13

## Judy Ann Wagner

### ~ 1955 ~

"I'm in big trouble, Joanie!" Judy caught up with her friend after school. "I really goofed this time. I was sterilizing the baby bottles late last night and let them boil too long—they burned. I'm scared to go home. My mother's going to be frosted."

Joanie was a triplet but she was Judy's favorite, much taller and slimmer than Judy, with chestnut hair and pale brown eyes. The smile in her voice was always comforting. "Maybe I should go home with you, huh?"

"No, that'll just make her even angrier. I don't know when I started being so afraid of my mother." It wasn't the first time

*Triplets with Judy's Sisters*

she wondered if that was normal. She lowered her voice to a whisper. "Are you afraid of your mom?"

"Not at all, Judiann." *I love it when she calls me that.* "My mom's not as strict as yours. You're always babysitting for little Autie and Denise or cleaning house."

"Yeah, my mother calls me her maid. Guess I am at that."

Joanie looked horrified. "Does she ever…beat you?"

"Well, she has beaten me with the belt when I needed it. But that's not near as bad as when she used to put my face under the faucet."

"That's awful!"

"Yeah…it feels like you're drowning."

"Why did she do that?"

"I always cried when my Nannan would leave after a visit. I wanted her to take me with her because I love her so much and she's always been so kind to me. I wish she was my mother. You know it's not so bad when my dad's home. When he's gone I have to sleep with my mother."

"No way."

"Yeah. She's scared at night and keeps me awake. If I fall asleep, she pinches me. That's why I'm so tired in school."

"Oh brother, I guess if you fall asleep in school I better pinch you on one of your cheeks. Ha-ha, just kidding."

"Gosh, Joanie, sometimes I change so many diapers I think I smell like pee. Will you please tell me if you ever think I do?"

"I promise. Well, call me later if your mother lets you."

"Okay. Oh, Joanie, don't talk on the horn while you're in the bathtub. I heard you could get electrocuted."

"Ha, you're such a worry wart. See you later alligator."

"After while, crocodile. Hey Joanie, you're my best friend."


"Joanie, it's me." Judy squeezed into the corner, cupped her hand around the mouthpiece of the phone, and whispered." Just called to tell you I can't talk on the phone because I got in trouble for burning the baby bottles."

"Okay, Judiann, I'll see you tomorrow in French class. And let's wear our poodle skirts."

Mother stormed into the kitchen with angry eyes and spat her words out. "Judy, get off the phone. I swear, you don't know how good you have it around here."

Judy avoided her eyes. "Yes, ma'am." *I wish Daddy was home.*

"Mother, can I go to confession now? I did all my chores."

"Why do you have to go to confession every Saturday? You always confess the same sin." Mother mumbled in a whiny tone. "'*I stole an apricot when I was five years old.*' That poor priest must be bored of hearing the same thing week after week! Okay, but no lollygagging on the way home. You need to babysit so I can go out with some friends."

"Yes, ma'am! I'll light a candle for Daddy to come home soon." *Gosh, I can never keep track of what ship he's on. He changes so often.* Judy put a comb through her hair and a little Aqua Net hair spray, then skedaddled out the door and down the street before Mother could change her mind.

## Church of Epiphany

Judy skipped and ran the eight blocks to her parish church. As she climbed the steps, she started feeling warm inside. She dipped her finger into the holy water and made the sign of the cross. *I love being in here. It's so peaceful and I wish I could stay all night. Oh good, there's no line at the confessional.* Judy walked down the side isle and stepped into the confessional. She closed the door and eased onto the kneeler. Again she crossed herself as the priest slid the confessional window open. *I'm so glad it's dark in here and hopefully he can't see me. I can only see that he has glasses on but I think its Father O'Connor.* "Bless me Father, for I have sinned. It has been a week since my last confession."

"What are your sins, my daughter."

"When I was a little girl I disobeyed my mother and stole an apricot from my neighbor's yard."

His voice was easygoing. "Hmm, anything else child?"

"I can't think of anything, Father."

"Very well then, for your penance say one Our Father and three Hail Mary's. Now go and sin no more." He blessed Judy with the sign of the cross. "In the Name of the Father, the Son and Holy Ghost."

"Thank you, Father." Judy made the sign of the cross, too. She stepped out, slipped into a pew, knelt down and said her penance. Then quietly walked over to light a candle for Daddy. *Oops, I forgot to bring my nickel to light a candle.* She looked around to make sure no one was looking, then took a candle and lit it from another one. *I wonder if I need to go back into confession for this!* She hesitated before walking back up the aisle. *I don't want to go back to my unhappy dwelling place.* Judy noticed a prayer card on the floor. She snatched it up and read the verse. *Matt. 11:28 Come unto me, all ye that labor and are heavy laden, and I will give you rest.* Was the verse meant for her? She labored and if heavy laden meant what it sounded like, she was that, too. The part about getting rest sounded good, but how could that happen in a house with a demanding mom and two crying babies? No, the card must belong to someone else. She crossed herself one last time as she walked out the doors of the church.

## Russian River ~ Summer 1956

After many summers at Russian River with the Federoff's, Judy's family now stayed at Uncle Harry's cabin. He bought it so the Wagner's would have a place to go. It wasn't that far from the Federoff's, so Judy and Karen were allowed to take on a little job for spending money. They used it to buy lunch on the river and go roller-skating in the evening.

Mrs. Federoff poured Autumn another glass of wine and leaned back in her chaise lounge by the river. "Autumn, more than any of the other kids, Karen and Judy are like two peas in a pod. They both do the silliest things."

"Yeah, how fitting that they're going bean picking together tomorrow." The ladies laughed.

Judy stood shivering in the cold grey morning. "Karen, are Tim and Larry going to meet us here at the river?" She shifted from side to side.

Karen was a sweet kid and very attractive with her blond hair and blue, German eyes. "They sure are. Should be here anytime now. They said they would carry us across so we won't get wet."

"Hot diggity dog." *I hope Timmy will carry me.*

"Hey, Judy, let's make sure we keep our feedbags close to us today."

"Good idea." Judy clutched her purse to her chest. "The boys have filled them with crawdads more times than is funny. Here they come, and here comes the sun. I hate walking down here when it's still dark."

"Me, too! Hi, Tim. Hi, Larry." Karen's eyes danced at the sight of the boys.

"Hi, girls. Ready to cross the river?" Larry bent down and folded up his pant legs.

"Yep," Judy and Karen answered together.

Larry looked at Judy, then at Karen, then back at Judy. "Okay, this is how it's going to go. Since Judy is smaller, I'll carry her and Tim can carry you across, Karen."

"Works for me," Karen said with a happy voice.

"Me, too." Timmy grinned at Karen.

Judy stood with her feet firmly planted in the sand and a sinking heart. *So much for my hope!* As usual of course, Judy kept her wishes to herself and went along with the plan.

The river looked like steam was coming off its surface as Judy clung to Larry's back. They crossed without incident. It felt warmer over the river than it had standing on the land. "You guys did good—didn't drop us once. Thanks!"

"You're welcome, Judy. Now for the hard work of picking those green beans. We work in twos and get 50 cents per basket. It takes a long time so don't waste any. Try to fill up two baskets so we will all make one dollar each today. It'll probably take four hours then we'll go to the beach afterwards." *Timmy is so smart.* "Come on Karen, you'll be my partner."

Judy and Larry picked up a large bushel basket that looked like a hamper with handles on it. The farmer showed them how to snap the beans off the vine. When they filled the first basket, they yelled "hamper" and a carrier brought them an empty basket and gave them a ticket to turn in when they were done for the day.

"Judy, your hands are blue, are they cold?" Larry blew into his cupped hands. "I know mine are."

"They sure are, Lar. I can hardly feel them. This is hard work, but it'll be worth getting some spending money."

"I agree. Will you be going roller skating tonight?"

"I hope so, I love roller skating. It's almost like dancing."

"Well, save me a dance tonight, okay?"

"Sure, Larry."

When it got close to noon, the sun was high and hot. "Now I'm sweating."

"So am I." Larry laughed. "What a difference from being cold this morning and now."

"Hey you guys!" Tim hollered over to them from the scale section. "You ready to cross back over and get some lunch."

Judy walked over to them wiping the sweat off her brow. "For sure. I brought 50 cents from home but I'm saving the dollar I made today for skating tonight." *I wonder if Timmy will save me a dance!*

"Cool," said Tim. "Hey, Karen, save me a dance tonight."

They made their way down the river to Maribel Beach and crossed the river.

"There's my mom," Karen waved to Mrs. Federoff with that sweet smile of hers. "She's going to drive us home later so we don't have to walk. I'm so tired."

"Oh goodie. Looks like she brought my mother and sisters down to the river, too." *I'm so glad Mrs. Federoff is here to help Mother with the girls.*

Judy and her friends wandered to the far end of the beach. They ate lunch and swam for a couple of hours.

"Okay everyone! It's time to hit the road." Mrs. Federoff called to them as she folded the blankets.

"Bye, boys." Judy and Karen picked up their belongings. "See you at the rink tonight." They ran down the beach, squeezed into Mrs. Federoff's 1956 Pontiac Bonneville and rolled down the windows to enjoy the afternoon Russian River breeze. Judy and Karen held the girls on their laps on the way home.

Judy pulled a piece of gum out of her pocket along with the dollar she'd earned. She tossed the wrapping out of the car, then suddenly screamed in horror.

"What is wrong with you," Mother snapped.

"I just threw my hard earned dollar out the window."

"Huh, why did you do that?"

"I meant to throw my gum wrapping out but threw my dollar out instead."

Mrs. Federoff laughed. "Karen and Judy—definitely two peas in a pod." Now everyone was laughing—except Judy.


## ~ **Summer 1957** ~

Judy popped a 45 record in her new Phillips record player. *You Ain't Nothin' But a Hound Dog* started blasting and Autumn started yelling. "Judy, you better be packed and ready to go when Uncle Harry and your grandmother get here, or you'll miss your bus trip."

"Yes ma'am, I'm ready." Judy couldn't sit still, so excited to be going on her first trip back to Galveston, Texas where she was born and best of all to be going with her Mimi, her grandmother Agnes. *Just one more song.* She took the record off and put in another 45. *Shake Rattle and Roll* rattled the windows. *I'm all set.* She looked around the room one more time to make sure it was all clean, even though Uncle Harry would sleep, smoke, and stink it up. *When I come back it will smell like a pig's fart.* Uncle Harry, being a Merchant Marine needed a place to stay when he was in port. *If only my room was my own.* She ran up the stairs and into the kitchen. "Mother, can I have that babysitting money I earned the other night from our neighbors, Mr. & Mrs. Russo?"

Mother held a stubborn pose. "H**L no! You'd probably just lose it anyway. Your grandmother has enough for both of you. Now don't be pouting or I'll cancel your precious little trip."

Judy kept an emotional distance from her mother as that familiar resentment and bitterness came upon her. "Yes ma'am." She held further comment. *I can't wait to get out of here for a couple of weeks. I better tread carefully.* The front door opened, bringing in Mimi and Uncle Harry. Judy almost laughed—Mimi looked like the little tea pot—short and stout. Her once dark hair was now blue grey. Good thing her daughter, Martha, had a beauty shop to keep her looking good. All the same, grandmother was so cute. *I love the way she always adjusts her glasses on her turned up nose. We get along great, maybe because Mother dislikes both of us.*

Uncle Harry walked down the hall with Mimi behind him. "Are you ready, Judy" I'm driving you and Mimi to the bus station in my brand new car."

Autie and Denise came running around the corner into the hallway. "Hi, Mimi." They didn't like Uncle Harry much so they ignored him. Uncle Harry carried Judy's suitcase out to the car.

"Hello, darlin's. We have to get going so say good-bye to your big sister."

"Bye, Cissy." Denise reached up and gave Judy a big hug.

"Who's going to take care of us, Cissy?" Autie asked in her whiny voice.

"Well Mother, of course, silly. But when I get back we'll go to church together again, okay?"

"K…bye Cissy."

"See you in two weeks, girls. Love you. Goodbye, Mother. See you."

"Be good, young lady." Mother wagged her fingers at both Judy and Mimi, dusting the floor with ashes from her cigarette.

The door shut and Judy followed Mimi to Uncle Harry's shiny, red and white Chevy Bel Air. "Nice car, Uncle Harry. Can I drive it sometime, now that I have my driving permit?"

"Yeah, you need to practice for your license and I don't think you want to practice in your dad's 49 Army pickup."

"Cool." Uncle Harry pulled away from 320 Winding Way, down the hill to Geneva Avenue, passing the Cow Palace along the way. "Mimi, have you ever seen that guy named Billy Graham on television? He holds these big meetings here at the Cow Palace sometimes. People go *ape* over him. After he finishes speaking, hundreds of people get out of their seats and walk towards the stage to *receive Jesus*. I think it's so weird."

"No, cain't say that I have."

Uncle Harry hopped on the 101 Freeway to downtown. The closer they got to the Greyhound Bus Station, the more Judy got butterflies in her stomach. They said their good-byes and hurried to the ticket counter. Agnes always walked so fast—no one could keep up with her. *When is she ever going to slow down?* Judy settled into her seat on the bus and smiled over at her grandmother.

Mimi grinned back. "Judy, it's going to be three long days, with lots of stops in between. Stick close whenever we get off to get a bite to eat or go to the restroom."

"You got it, Mimi. I'm sticking with you." Her brown eyes were smiling! "Can't wait to meet my Aunt Connie and cousins in Galveston!"

## A couple of days later

"Judy, wake up! We're at a little stop."

"Where are we, Mimi?" Judy's voice was sleepy.

"El Paso, Texas. We're getting close to our destination."

Judy followed Mimi off the bus and walked into a wall of warm air. "Yikes, Mimi, look at all those black beetles! How can we walk to the building with all these things on the ground?"

"Shush girl, just follow me." With reluctance, Judy followed her grandmother, shirking and sweating every step of the way, squeezing Mimi's hand, not willing to let go. After what seemed forever, they reached the doorway. Once inside there was another surprise for Judy. There were two ladies' washrooms side by side. One said COLORED ONLY, the other said WHITE ONLY. She followed her grandmother to the WHITE ONLY washroom. In front of them, standing at the washbasin, a tall black lady washed her hands with her back to them. She wore a black suit and white hat. Someone started screaming at her! To Judy's surprise it was her *sweet* grandmother!

"Who do you think you are? Get the #@%#! out of here or I'll throw you out." Agnes wagged her finger at the woman. Others entered into the washroom and started ganging up on that poor woman. Agnes wouldn't stop yelling at her till the lady, slowly but surely, strutted out with her head held high. *She's making her own statement.* All the ladies muttered their disapproval to each other. Judy's heart sank as she stood with her mouth open and her mind confused. She was horrified and couldn't understand how her very own Mimi could treat someone like that. That scene pretty much put a damper on the rest of the trip for Judy. She stayed very quiet back on the bus and in her seat. Judy had never seen that side of Agnes and it took a long time before she could look at her grandmother in the same way as before!

## ~ Fall 1957 ~

Judy's intentions on this fine September morning were to look sharp and be sharp in her new school. She would be neither if her home life never changed. She stepped into the kitchen, seeing Mother, six months pregnant, sitting with a cup of coffee and a cigarette hanging out of her mouth. "Judy, make sure you come straight home after school. You need to watch the girls for me while I go to my doctor appointment."

"Yes, Mother." *The only thing good about coming home to babysit is that I get to watch the Mickey Mouse Club with the girls.* She and her sisters would sing along to M-I-C-K-E-Y M-O-U-S-E.

San Francisco was having one of her beautiful Indian summer days. Judy was excited to start her first day at Balboa High School. With Pee-Chee in hand, she ran out the door and around the corner to catch the #28 bus. It's tail lights blinked from halfway down the block. *Oh Poop! I just missed it.* "Hi Vickie, looks like we both missed the bus. Wanna walk or wait for the next one?"

"Oh, let's just walk. We've got plenty of time. What homeroom are you in? I'm in 219."

"I'm in 302. It sure is a big school. Hope we don't get lost." Judy and Vickie got to school in just enough time to get to class before the bell rang. "See you after school, Vickie. I'm going to take a short cut to my class."

"See ya."

Judy bounced up the steps, with her pony tail swishing back and forth, through big double wood doors, crossed the hall and through one of the back doors that led to the quad. She nonchalantly slowed down so she didn't look like a *newbie* as she crossed the square to the back building. There were lots of other students doing the same thing. *Umm, that boy sure looks like that Joey kid I used to play with when*

*I was four years old staying at Aunt Flossy's.* He looked at Judy as they approached each other. After she passed him, Judy turned to look back at him to see if he was looking back at her, looking back at him. He stopped and grinned. "I'm going to tell my Aunt Flossy on you."

"Joey! Is that really you?"

"It's me in the flesh. I can't believe we're going to the same high school after all this time."

"Well, it's good to know another person in a school of three-thousand students. I just moved to this area so most of my friends from Aptos Junior High are going to Lincoln." The first bell rang so they both scurried off. "Maybe I'll see you around, Joey. Bye."

Judy found out later that Joey was using drugs, so they did not reunite their childhood friendship and she would not be marrying Joey. *I wonder where Margaret is going to high school? She probably won't be marrying Joey, either.*

## ~ Spring 1958 ~

"Mother, I got a job at S. H. Kress five and ten cent store. I work on Wednesdays and Fridays after school and on Saturdays." Judy was excited and proud of herself.

"That's fine, but you still need to do your chores. I can't take care of these kids and clean the house all by myself." Judy had a little brother now so that made three to take care of. "And, you have to buy your own clothes now you know."

"I know, Mother. Don't worry." *I wish I got paid for all the chores I do around here.*

## ~ Fall 1958 ~

"You *have* to do this, Judy!" Rita was nearly jumping out of her skin with excitement. "I've never met anybody who was on television. You can be the first."

"Yes and you're such a good dancer you could win the contest." Sharon chimed in. Judy's friends were coaxing her to go on *Dance Party*, which was a San Francisco KPIX television program with Dick Stewart. It was a version of American Bandstand held in Philadelphia.

*It doesn't matter what I want, it's what Mother will allow.* Judy just kept walking, looking at the ground till she walked right into a telephone pole. "Ouch.!"

Both girls laughed at her. "You better watch where you're going, Judy or you won't be able to do anything." Sharon got right back to the subject. "Whata ya say Jude, will you do it?"

"Only if it's not on a day I have to work."

Rita did her little happy dance. "Cool… It's on a Thursday and you're off that day right?"

"Yep. Now I just need to make sure my grandmother will come over and help my mother with the kids."

"Right on!" Sharon grabbed Judy's hand and spun her around. "You're sure to win."

So it was settled. Agnes helped Autumn so Judy could go to *Dance Party* at KPIX. Agnes with the girls, Autie and Denise, sat in front of the television to see if they could get a glimpse of their Cissy among all the other teenage dancers. "I see her. She's wearing her plaid skirt and black & white saddle shoes with her new bobby socks." Autie said proudly.

"Me, too. Hi, Cissy!" Denise jumped up and waved at the television.

"Lordy, that girl isn't very stylish, but look at her go," Agnes said. "She reminds me of myself, just the dances are different." Judy was dancing the jitterbug with her partner to Jerry Lee Lewis singing *Whole Lot of Shaking Going On*.

Autumn peeked around the corner but didn't say anything. *I never had it as good as my daughter.*

At the end of the program they announce the winner of the dance. "Lordy, if that don't beat all, Autumn. Judy and her partner won the contest, just like I did in my day. Autumn, you hear me?"

A couple of hours later, Judy came in the door. "Hi, Mimi. Did you see me on television? I can't believe I won."

"Don't be silly, you are your grandmother's granddaughter!" They both laughed. Autumn put her hand on her hip and mumbled out loud. "Well, I'm the mother."

Judy looked back at her mother. "Thanks for letting me go, Mother. It was real fun." She turned back to Mimi. "They want my partner and me to come back for the dance off. Problem is, I work on the Saturday they're filming it. What am I going to do?"

Autumn stepped further into the living room. "You're going to do the right thing, Judy. Work comes first."

"Yes, Mother, that's exactly what I was thinking." So that was the end of Judy's television career. She settled on dancing in her bedroom to Bill Haley's *Rock Around the Clock*.

## ~ Spring 1959 ~

"Judy, what are you doing up so late when the electricity's out. It's midnight."

"That's why I lit the candles, Mother. I've been studying ever since I got home from work. I just can't get this stuff into my head."

"Why try so hard, it's not like you're smart enough or rich enough to go to college."

"Really? You're probably right. One of my teachers gave me a 'D' in her class and she said the only reason she didn't give me an 'F' was because I tried so hard. I feel like I need to keep trying. It's just in my nature I guess. Also, if my grades aren't good enough I can't join all the sports, like Fencing."

"Why do you want to do all that? You aren't good at any sport. You're not like me in that way. I've always been athletic, learning in the orphanage."

"Well, to be honest, Mother, I do it to get pins to decorate my Senior Sweater next year. As soon as I get my pin, I quit that sport and go on to another. But, more than anything in the world, I want to become a song girl in the fall. Try outs are next month. There are sixty girls trying out, but they only choose six."

"Lots of luck with that, young lady."

Judy rose early every morning and practiced every day till tryouts. As fate would have it, she came in seventh place. Devastated, she walked into the house with shoulders slumped and a sad voice. "Hi Mother. Hi, Daddy. I didn't get it. I think I made a fool of myself because I cried when my name wasn't called. I feel so stupid." Judy went to her room and played one of her favorite Johnnie Ray songs, *The Little White Cloud That Cried*. She danced to the song with movements that told the story. Judy became quite good at pantomiming these songs.

In the mean time, Daddy went right out and bought her a gift. He knocked on her door and handed her a ceramic donkey. "Here's a souvenir to remind you of the day you made a jackass of yourself." He was always trying to be funny so Judy forced herself to laugh out loud, not wanting to disappoint him. Still, her heart was bruised.

## ~ 1960 ~

Pretty girl she was not, kinda plain she was. Judy didn't know how to be stylish and with a limited budget, she dressed very plain and conservative. So it was a surprise to her that she was somewhat popular in her senior year. That was in big part due to one particular boy who took a liking to her. Denny Dennison asked Judy to go to all the gigs he and his band played. He was cute and talented with a great personality. Denny was not very tall but neither was Judy.

*I think he likes me because I'm vertically challenged.* While Denny sang, she danced her heart away. It was the first time in her life she felt *significant.* "Denny, it's getting late and you know I have to be home by midnight."

"Hurry up, George. Judy, has to get home or her mother will go ape and she won't be able to go out next weekend." Denny didn't have a car, so they had to rely on George to get them places.

"Chill out, Denny. We'll get your Cinderella home on time. You should be glad you didn't have to take the bus tonight."

"I am. That's how we go on most of our dates, right Woman?"

"That's right, Denny. I don't know why you call me that. Let's get going."

In the car, on the way home Denny turned to Judy. "Woman, will you go to the prom with me?"

"I thought you'd never ask. I turned down Dennis because I wanted to go with you. I want to fix him up with my friend. Can we invite them to go with us?"

"Sure, I'll put them on our reservation list for the restaurant."

## ~ June 1960 ~

Autumn loved to entertain and in the past, Judy would work all the next day cleaning the after party mess. It was a disgusting, stinky job. However, it seemed like all those good deeds were going to pay off for Judy on this night—this special occasion. Autumn did one of the nicest things for her daughter on Prom night. All the couples were invited to meet at the Wagner house for a cocktail party—not real cocktails of course. They would take pictures and eat hors d'oeuvres before going out for the big gala. "I feel like a princess, Mother." *I hope I look pretty enough.* Judy wore a strapless white chiffon dress. It was ankle length with petticoats underneath. She bought it with her own money. Nannan bought her a simple necklace that was the perfect touch.

"I think your prince is walking up the steps now." Mother gave her a genuine smile.

At 5:30 p.m. the doorbell rang. *Let the fun begin.* Judy opened the door with her little sisters in tow. Denny, looking so handsome, stood on the threshold with a pretty wrist corsage in his hands. "Judy, you look beautiful."

Denise piped up, "Are you going to marry my Cissy?"

Judy's cheeks grew hot. "Shush, go get some punch."

Then little Autie chimed in. "She asks all of Cissy's boyfriends that." Judy's face burned even hotter.

"Well, I don't blame her." Denny laughed.

*Denny is so hip.* Judy sighed to herself. *I really dig him.*

The rest of the night was one to remember. And no curfew! After they took pictures, all eight couples gathered while the boys helped the girls put on their capes. Everyone looked more like adults than ever before. They were all so grown-up but secretly no one really wanted to be. Judy didn't want this experience to end. *I've had a good senior year and it's almost over.* They all journeyed on their way to dine at Place Pigalle. After an elegant French meal, they arrived at the Ball in the Mural Room of St. Francis Hotel, meeting up with more friends.

The band was playing *Primrose Lane.* "Judy, we're not wasting anytime. I never get to dance with you so let's get started."

They danced the night away. Judy was in heaven with Denny by her side instead of on the stage performing. "Denny, since I don't have a curfew tonight, I want to have a drink."

"Are you sure? You are always the only one that never drinks."

"I'm sure. I'm tired of being a wet rag. This is a special night and I want to be like everyone else." The last song of the night was one of Judy's favorites, *In the Still of the Night. How appropriate.* As they stepped out into the night air, it seemed to be made for this special occasion. The new moon was still hanging from the sky.

"George, where are we heading? We want to have a drink somewhere."

"We can try my place first. If my parents are home then we'll have to go to Al's or Eddie's."

As fate would have it, the kids couldn't find a drink anywhere in San Francisco. However, it was still the best night of Judy's life thus far.

## ~ Summer 1960 ~

Ready or not, the day had arrived. It didn't dawn on Judy at the time, but she was doing something her mother, Autumn and father, Johnny Marshall had never done. She was graduating from High School. "Mother, is Mimi going to meet us there? Is Nannan coming?"

"Yes, Judy, You asked me that two times already." She answered in that sharp tone of hers.

"Oh yeah, sorry. Are you ready, Mother? Uncle Harry's waiting outside to drive us. Let's go."

"Hi, Uncle Harry. Thanks for picking us up. Here comes Mother, we better get going."

"We have plenty of time, Judy. Don't worry."

"Well, I have to be there early to get lined up with everyone else. See my cap and gown?" Judy twirled in a circle to give him the full effect.

"Now who's making us late?" Mother hopped into the front seat. She and Uncle Harry chit-chatted with each other all the way down to the San Francisco Opera House where 750 students would be graduating. Judy sat

*Judy and Denny at graduation*

quietly reminiscing her senior year at Balboa High. The highlights were performing at the Senior Jinx to *Hey Mr. Flattop* in front of the whole school and being Denny's girlfriend. Uncle Harry dropped Judy off before finding a parking place.

"Hi, Denny! Is your mom and sister here?"

"Yep, they're always early. I've been waiting for you before going inside." He grabbed Judy's hand.

"Thanks. I'm so nervous. I'm sitting in the front row but at least you're right behind me. I'm so happy we've been going steady. I hope we'll stay that way."

"Of course, Woman. Let's go in."

Once inside, and with all the graduates seated on stage, Judy looked for her family. The Opera House was full to the ceiling. Finally, Aunt Martha walked down the aisle so Judy could see her. When they caught each other's gaze, tears spilled out of Judy's eyes. She loved her Nannan. That made her graduation more special than anything. Aunt Martha had never graduated from high school, either.

Since college was out of the question, more than anything, Judy considered another vocation, one that would get her out of the house. "Mother, I want to join the service." Her voice was excited at the thought.

"Forget it. Only two kinds of girls join the service: round heels and queers."

Judy's face fell as disappointment crushed her latest dream. "Oh, then I guess I'll take that job at Pacific Telephone & Telegraph Company."

"Yes, that would be best. You can still help me around the house and with the kids." Mother patted her swollen belly, another baby was expected in October.

"But Mother, my friends Sharon and Rhonda asked me to move into an apartment with them."

Staring at Judy, Mother shed big tears. "You can't leave me here to do all the work."

"Alright, Mother, don't cry. But I'm eighteen and plan to go dancing whenever and wherever there is one."

"Fine, you do that. Just so you bathe the kids before you go and come home at a decent hour."

"Sure, no problem." *I guess I'll have to get a married to get out of here.*

Having a fulltime job allowed Judy to do things she liked to do. After taking the bus home from work, she changed into her leotards and caught a bus to the dance studio across town, once a week. She took jazz dance lessons with a group of twelve-year-olds and performed with them. Then a step up from that, the teachers asked her to join a dance group to perform at the Marc Hopkins

*Judy at the Marc Hopkins Hotel Performance*

Hotel. And finally, Judy took modeling classes but, being too short to model on the runway, she was asked to model shoes. She would have to go to Las Vegas, but Mother said it wasn't a good idea. She was probably right about that. Still, Judy always wished she could have done that.

## ~ 1962 ~

Judy and Denny remained friends for the next couple of years. However, Denny started dating other men, so Judy did too. She took a bus to wherever there was a dance. There was almost always dancing at the USO and no shortage of men to dance with. She didn't drink and always came home alone but tired the next day for staying up so late. It never failed that Judy would fall asleep in her bus seat on the way to work. Her head would bump against the window. Other passengers would be kind enough to wake her. "Miss, we just passed your bus stop." *How embarrassing! Now I have to run back to my stop so I'm not late. Not easy in three-inch heels.*

On the weekend, she would go out with some of the girls from work. Her friends liked going to the coffee houses and listening to jazz in the outside cafés where they served espresso. Judy didn't like jazz or espresso but sat there puffing on a cigarette, without inhaling, trying to look cool. *Why am I doing this? I don't like espresso, jazz, or cigs. I'd rather be dancing somewhere.*

If she wasn't working or dancing, she was cleaning house and babysitting. Judy was lonely but never alone. Mother always had something to say about Judy's choices.

*The Wagner Family*

"What the heck are you looking for, Judy? You're too picky and I think the kind of guy you want will just end up leaving you." As Mimi had done for Mother, Mother fixed Judy up with dates. One guy was actually married and from another state. "Maybe you should go out with Bob's cousin, Norrell. He's a good man and he has a house and everything."

"He also has a daughter, Mother."

"So. I had a daughter and Bob married me."

♥ ♥ ♥

Judy dated her adopted dad's cousin. He treated her good and got her out of the house more than she could on her own. He did a lot of things around the house for her mother so that made Autumn happy.

"Mother, Norrell asked me to marry him. I guess I'll accept his proposal."

"That's a great idea! I can't wait to plan a big wedding!"

*Judy "Cissy" Wagner*

"Mother, we don't want a big wedding. Since Norrell's been married before, we just want a small wedding." Secretly, Judy was not in love with Norrell and just wanted to get out of the house. Mother and daughter never saw eye to eye with each other on anything and Judy was tired of it.

"Well, if I can't plan the kind of wedding I want, then I'm not going to do anything for you."

"Have it your way, Mother."

"Hey, don't get smart with me. You're still under my roof, young lady"

Weakened by her mother's cold eyes and voice, she dropped her gaze. "Yes, ma'am." *I don't deserve a wedding anyway, I'm just using poor Norrell to get out of this house.*

## ~ **January 1963** ~

Autumn answered the phone on the third ring. "Helloooo?"
"Hello. Is this Mrs. Wagner?"

"Yes, who's this?

"This is Sandy. I work with your daughter, Judy. The girls in the office want to have a surprise shower for her at a restaurant. She keeps saying she has to babysit. Can you help us?"

"No. I need her to help me out before her dad comes home. His ship comes in the day she's leaving for Las Vegas. It was her choice to get married there."

"Uh, okay then, thanks."

The girls gave Judy a shower at work. Sandy pulled Judy aside. "Judy, I just want you to know that we had planned a special surprise dinner shower for you at a restaurant but your mother said she needed you to babysit. I'm so sorry."

"That's okay, Sandy. My Aunt Flossy wanted to give me a shower, too, but my mother absolutely forbade it. I don't know what her problem is. Well this is the last week I'll have to babysit for my controlling mother."

# Chapter 14

# Mrs. Judy Charbonneau

I THOUGHT I WAS MAKING MY GREAT ESCAPE, but without the Lord, there was no peace. Moreover, can a woman love if she's never been loved? I discovered a truth greater than myself—joy came with the entrance into my world of my three beautiful children.

## Las Vegas, Nevada ~ January 1963

"I now pronounce you man and wife." The priest then blessed them. Uncle Frank and his wife stood by the newlyweds. Judy's body felt numb and her eyes filled with tears. Her new husband whispered in her ear, "I hope those are tears of happiness." Her sadness filled up too much space—she could barely put a smile on her face.

Poor Norrell—using a good man like him to get away from Mother. *This is not how I imagined my marriage to start.* Being a good Catholic girl, Judy had kept her virginity for someone she hoped to fall in love with and then have a beautiful wedding like her friends did. *Norrell is a good man. He will take care of me and I won't be under Mother's control anymore.*

They walked out into the cold Las Vegas night air. "Uncle Frank, thank you for standing up for us and getting us a place to stay."

"No trouble at all. I made sure they didn't give you twin beds." He winked at Norrell.

Judy felt her face turning red hot. *I will lose my virginity tonight.*

Norrell and Uncle Frank laughed. "Oh, and you kids can go to any show on the strip. Just mention my name, Frank Ivey, and they will bring you to the front of the line. But, first let's go get a bite to eat. I have reservations at the Sands Hotel."

"Sounds great, Uncle Frank, I'm starved." *I want to stay out as late as possible.*

*Judy and Norrell Charbonneau*

Now, fifty miles away from her mother, Judy settled down to the life of a suburban housewife in Warm Springs, California. Since Norrell had custody of his five-year-old daughter, Susie became Judy's responsibility. Not only did she feel guilty for using Norrell to get away from her mother, she now felt guilty for not loving his little daughter. *I guess I can't control how things affect me.*

Dinner table cleared now, and cloth in hand, she washed each dish methodically as she stayed deep in thought. *Maybe if I adopt her, my feelings will change.* That will also earn me points to get to heaven. Her eyes continued to gaze far away into the dusk of night through the kitchen window. Looking back at her husband with his nose in the news, she picked up a towel to dry her hands. "Norrell, I want to adopt Susie so she will have a mother."

Out of character, he put the paper down and looked up with a question mark in his eyes! "Really? Gee, that would be great. Let me think, I'll call my attorney and see what we need to do to get things rolling. What a great idea, Judy." Norrell's face lit up.

Judy gave a weak smile as she turned her face away. Slowly she walked back to the kitchen sink. *I hope I'm doing the right thing.*


## Alameda, California ~ November 1963

Norrell and Judy followed their attorney into his fourth floor office. "Mr. Charbonneau, your ex-wife has requested to see Susie before she agrees to this adoption."

"What? She hasn't seen her in over three years!"

"Well, she said she didn't know where you were and she has been clean for about a year and a half."

He turned to Judy. "What do you think?"

She stared back at him with a blank look, this might harm her plans, but she had to be honest about how she felt, at least on this occasion. "I think a mother should be able to see her daughter."

"Okay then, make the arrangements, Mr. Janzen."

The Nimitz Freeway was busy as usual from Alameda back to Fremont. Being lunchtime made it worse. The only sound inside their black Chevy Impala, was the radio playing the top-forty hits. Judy was selfishly getting lost in the music and a silent hope that maybe Susie's mother would take her. Elvis Presley was singing one of his songs, "return to sender…address unknown…no such number…no such zone—"

"We interrupt our regular programming," came the voice of Walter Cronkite. "From Dallas, three shots, as earlier reported, were fired at President Kennedy's motorcade today near the downtown section. We have just received a report from Dan Rather that the president is dead… It has been confirmed that President Kennedy died at 2:00 P.M. EST." Mr. Cronkite's voice cracked as he ended his announcement. Then all was silent, except Mr. Cronkite trying to clear the emotion in his throat to no avail.

Judy bit her lips to fight back the tears, but could not hold them in. Emotion gave way as she cried all the way home for the first president she had hoped to vote for in his re-election. That evening they watched the historic, sad incident unfold on television.

Little Susie had her nose pressed up against the window waiting for her mother to arrive for their first meeting since she was a baby. Her face was set in concentration and in her deep voice for such a little girl, she announced. "There she is!"

"Susie, stand aside while I open the door," Norrell said with a serious voice. He opened the door wide and nodded to his ex-wife, Cindy, with no smile on his face. "Susie, this is your mother."

Cindy was a medium height gal and a little chunky. She had short blond curly hair, blue eyes, and a button nose. It was hard to ignore the resemblance. Susie was just a miniature picture of her mom. Cindy bent down and placed her hand lovingly on her daughter's face, looking into her eyes. "Hello, Susie." It was like watching a scene in a movie. The two seemed lost in each other's presence. How could two people have such a connection when separated for so long?

It wasn't long after that visit that Norrell agreed to let Susie go live with her mother. That made Judy happy and relieved but oh so guilty that she hadn't been a better mother to Susie. She had done everything right but couldn't give her the love a little girl needed and deserved.

## Fremont, California ~ Summer 1964

"It's a boy!" Dr. Reschke called out as he passed the big guy to the nurse. "I think he is worth all your hard work."

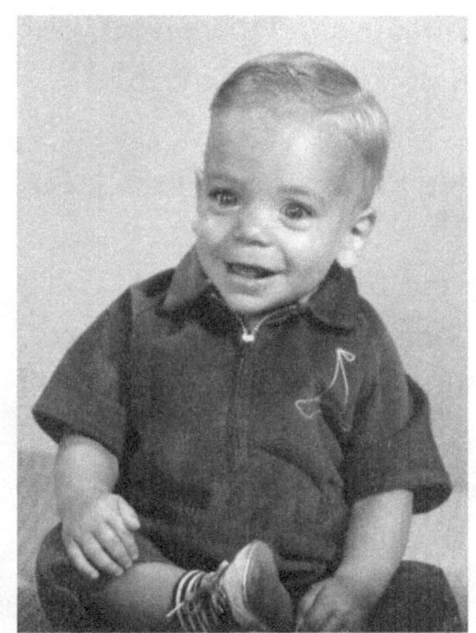

*Steve Charbonneau*

"Wow, he's 8 ½ pounds." Nurse Barbara turned from the scales. "Being three weeks late, he probably put on a little more weight."

Judy lay back, exhausted after a long and hard labor. In those days, doctors did not readily do cesareans. "His name is Steve." Judy reached out for her newborn. Her heart overflowed. *I didn't know I could love someone so much.* "You are my first love, little Steve," she whispered in his little ear.

Norrell appeared in a matter of minutes. "You did it, Judy. Wow! Could his blue eyes be any bigger?"

"I guess they have to match his big head." Judy was surprised she could still laugh as tired as she was. "Norrell, thank you for giving me a son."

## ~ 1965 ~

*Ding…dong.* "What's that Steve-o? Let's see who's at the door. Oh, hi Bev."

"Hi, Jude. Have the coffee pot on?" Her neighbor walked right into the house.

"Come on in and I'll have it perking in no time at all."

"Wow! You're looking good. What did you do to get back in shape?"

"Weight Watchers and Jack LaLanne. A lot of good it does me. I'm pregnant again."

"Oh, didn't you want another one?"

"Oh sure, I want a girl. It's just that it took me a year to get back in shape and now I'm going to get fat again. How about you? Are you going to have another one?" Judy poured their coffee.

"Well, that's why I came over. I'm expecting twins."

"Congratulations! I've always wanted to have twins. I think I'm jealous."

"Isn't it funny? I don't want twins and I'm having them. You'd like to have twins and you don't. Too bad we can't change places, especially since Don isn't that helpful and he has a roving eye. Still, I'm madly in love with him."

"Oh no! Here Norrell is the perfect husband and I'm not happy. I feel so guilty, Bev. I have no joy when I face each morning, except what I feel for my son. What's wrong with this picture?"

"Not sure, Jude. I'm so sorry. I wish I could stay longer to cheer you up but I better go. Two cups of java is my limit. Besides, Don's watching little Donny while he's home for lunch, but he has to get back to work. Come over anytime and we can talk some more. Keep your chin up."

## ~ **Summer 1966** ~

"Dr. Reschke, I keep wetting my pants!" Judy gasps into the phone, while Norrell helps her sit on the kitchen stool.

"That means your water broke. Get to the hospital immediately. You're three weeks early! I'll head on over there now."

Gary was born ten minutes after they arrived at Washington Township Hospital. *What a difference from my first delivery.*

"He's kinda ugly, Norrell. I wonder if we got the right baby."

"Don't be silly, he looks just like you."

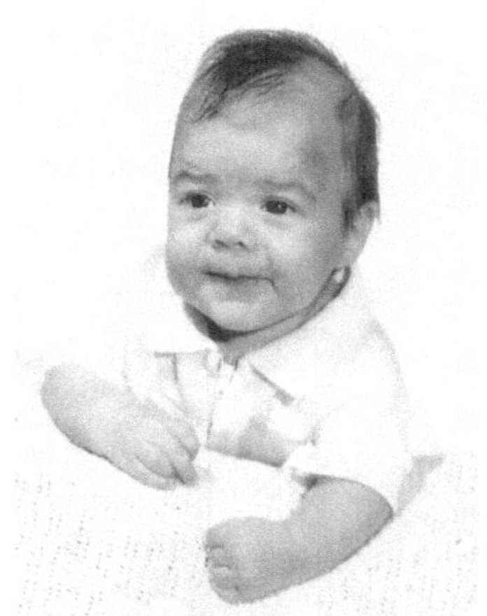

*Baby Gary Charbonneau*

"Oh great…a pair of uglies. I guess you're right, but maybe I should ask the nurse just in case."

The nurse peeked from around the curtain. "Honey, he is your child and like your husband said, he looks just like you!"

"I think my ears are turning red."

"I'm sure she's right." Norrell laughed.

"Norrell, you know I wanted a girl so bad and when they told me he was a boy I was so disappointed. Funny thing is, about two seconds later, I got so excited that I have two sons. Thank you, Norrell."

*Gary and Steve Charbonneau*

"Uh…no problem."

Judy picked up the phone next to the bed. "Hi Nannan, my baby came early. Can you still come stay with me?"

"Well of course, darlin'. I'll come the day after tomorrow. How are you doing?"

"I didn't think I could love anyone as much as little Steve. But, I soon found that my heart is big enough to be flooded with just as much love for my little Gary."

"That's great, Poopsi. I can't wait to see him."

"Nannan, I gained fifty pounds again and only lost seven after the delivery. Will you help me get started on another diet?"

Of course, honey, see you soon. I love you"

"I love you too, Nannan."

"Judy, I'm so excited about this business trip to Saudi Arabia and St. Croix." Norrell rolled another pair of socks and tucked them into his suitcase.

"That's great. I'm excited for you, too. Where is St. Croix? And, how long will you be gone?"

"It's an island in the Caribbean Sea. I'll be gone from four to six weeks, depending how long it takes to get those centrifugal pumps going."

"You must be smart to be able to handle a task like that. I'm proud of you." She meant her words. She liked Norrell, respected him, so why couldn't she love him? Maybe, absence would make the heart grow fonder. Unfortunately, it didn't.

"I'm going to run away from home." Steve didn't want to go to bed yet, so walked out the door into the still warm, October night. How many times had Judy wanted to do that very thing?

"Okay Steve, I love you." She watched out the window to see what he would do. He looked up and down the street, turned, ran back up the sidewalk, and knocked on the door. Judy sang out in a cheery voice. "Who is it?"

"It Teve! I forgot my PJs."

As Judy opened the door, Steve ran past her into his bedroom and jumped onto his bed. "Mom…can you read dis book to me?"

"Oh yes! Good old Dr. Seuss. I do not like green eggs and ham. Sam I am…"

Sleep took over for Steve no matter how hard he fought it. With both boys tucked away, Judy sat in the dark with a candle lit and her glass of red wine. *So this is what it's like to be a single mom.*

A soft knock at the door jolted her out of her downhearted mood. "Who is it," she called in a low voice.

"It's me, Don."

She cautiously opened the door to find her neighbor's husband standing there with his tall, strong frame, curly black hair, and distinguished glasses on his handsome face. "Hi, Don! Is everything okay?"

"Oh sure, I just thought I would make sure you're doing okay, alone and all. Can I come in?"

"Yes, of course. Can I pour you a glass of wine?"

"That would be great."

Judy reached for a goblet out of the cupboard, then she realized Don's arm was around her waist. "What are you doing? You have a wife and kids at home!"

Just as he turned her to grab a kiss, Bev switched on the light and was standing in the doorway! "Yes, Don! Like Judy says, you have a wife and kids at home."

Don let go of Judy and stomped out the door with his wife close on his heels. Judy was left feeling awkward, confused, and embarrassed. Poor Bev! *I hope this doesn't ruin our friendship.* Judy sat back down again feeling more lonely and sad for herself and her friend.

## ~ Fall 1967 ~

"Hey Bev." Judy held the phone to her ear and hoped Bev would still want to be her friend. She needed someone more than ever to talk to. "Wanna come over for a cup of coffee before the kids go down for a nap?"

"Sure, the twins like playing with Steve and Gary. Be right over."

Judy set down the phone and opened the door to her friend. She poured the coffee and slumped into a chair. "Bev, I'm pregnant again, and I don't know how I feel about it. There seems to be such a void in my heart and life. It makes me feel guilty. I love my boys so much, I should be content."

"Well, maybe you'll get your girl this time."

"I hate to admit this but I tried to abort my pregnancy and it's against my religion."

"What do you mean you tried? How?"

"I slid down the stairs on my stomach. It hurt me but I don't think it hurt the baby." *It's probably going to be a stubborn one.*

"You are a silly girl."

"Speaking of girls, I'm almost hoping I get another boy. That way if I decide to leave Norrell it will be easier and cheaper. You know with hand-me-downs and all."

"Don't you love your husband?"

"I care about Norrell but I was never *in love* with him. I used him to get away from my mother. Shame on me! I feel like the life is being choked out of me. I can't even wear turtle necks." Judy poured Bev another cup of coffee since the children were playing without a lot of commotion. "Thanks for being my friend, Bev."

"I don't know what to say but anytime you need to talk I'm just two doors down. When is the baby due?

"Well, if it doesn't come three weeks early or three weeks late like the boys did, it should be around mid-August. Time will tell."

## ~ Summer 1968 ~

"Hi Nannan." We got our girl. Nicole Denée. Can you come down and help me?"

"What do you think, Poopsie? Be there as soon as you get home from the hospital. How did your delivery go this time?"

"I can hardly believe she came right on time. I wasn't in labor near as long as with Steve and she didn't come fast like Gary. She didn't weigh as

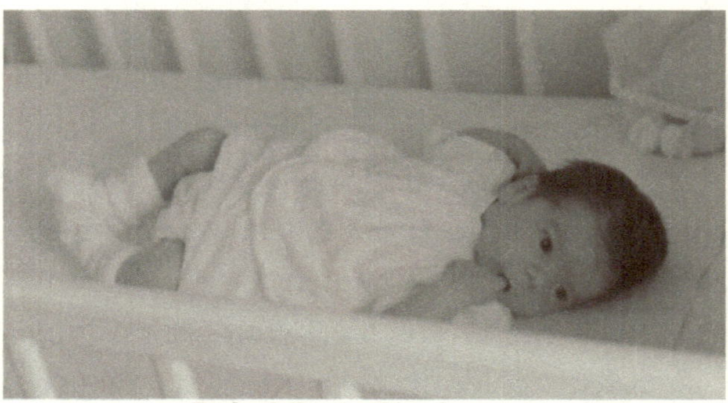

*Baby Nicole Charbonneau*

much as Steve but she weighed more than Gary. I think she's just perfect and so cute."

"Good, can't wait to see her. And we'll get you on another diet, right?"

"You know it. Seems like it takes me a year to get the weight off, then I get pregnant again. But this is my last."

*My three babies: Gary, Nicole, and Steve*

## ~ 1969 ~

Even with her three precious children, Judy struggled with boredom, loneliness, and guilt. *I shouldn't feel this way. What is wrong with me? My family is better off without…* She could hear that thought throughout the day. That night when everyone was in bed, she took a bunch of pills and downed a bottle of cold medicine. She crept into bed to let the meds take their course. *I hope this does the trick.* As she lay there, a funny feeling came over her. *I feel like I am a blob of gross nothing.* She felt her body turning inside out. It wasn't a pretty sight and she sensed she better say a prayer. *Our Father, who art in heaven, hallowed be Thy name; Thy kingdom come; Thy will be done on earth as it is in...* She just melted away till morning. Judy woke up as she usually did. *I seem to fail at everything. I will go to plan two!*

It was eight o'clock and the kids were bathed and bedded. Judy was fidgety, knowing what was coming. Finally, the knock at the door. "Norrell, can you get that?"

Norrell opened the screen door. "Yes, can I help you?"

"Are you Norrell Charbonneau?"

"Yes."

The stranger handed Norrell an envelope. "Please sign for these papers." Norrell looked at the bundle for some time before signing, leaving the door hanging wide open. His jaw and body tightened as he made a fist.

Judy just stood there to take it—a blow would be less painful than the guilt consuming her heart—but he stopped just short of hitting her. "Judy, you are a self-centered, selfish woman."

His words should have stung, but she was too numb to feel them. "I know, Norrell, but I am a miserable woman. I'm so sorry." *I guess I've become my mother's daughter. Selfish and self-centered.*

"You will live to regret your decision."

"Maybe you're right, Norrell, but I can't go on like this."

His expression softened and so did his voice. "Is there someone else, Judy?"

"Not at all. I would never think of cheating on you. You're a nice man and I hope you find someone someday who will really love you."

The hardness returned to his voice. "Well, don't think you are going to get the house and don't think I'm going to be babysitting for you."

"The house is too big for me anyway. Why do I need a five bedroom, three bath house to take care of? But Norrell, I hope you will still be a father to these kids. If you don't someone else might take your place."

"Whatever." Norrell slammed the door, and in the distance, one of her children cried.

> NORRELL WAS RIGHT. I regretted everything just like he said I would. The words *selfish* and *self-centered* rang in my ears for years to come. Saddest of all, the bitterness I saw in his eyes that day, kept him from his kids.

It was fun at first. Judy always had her bags packed with things for her kids and herself. They would take trips to Petaluma, where her cousin lived with his family. "Hi, Michael, are you and Janet up for company again this weekend? And is my Nannan going to be there."

"Yes, Mom's coming tomorrow, so come on up. We'll have a gas!"

"Whoopee! See you soon."

"Come on kids, we're going to visit our cousins."

They jumped into their little 1969 Datsun, good on gas at 25 cents per gallon. They blasted the radio and sang to *Jeremiah was a Bullfrog*. Their favorite song. So, up 101, over the Golden Gate Bridge, through Marin County and finally—Petaluma. No one fought or fussed. These were happy times. But, would they last?

# Chapter 15

# Mrs. Judy Duvall

OUT OF THE FRYING PAN AND INTO THE FIRE. I had made a huge mistake! God was trying to get my attention but I was deaf to His call. And even though I was blind to Him, God was watching us from a distance.

## ~ 1970 ~

On the way home from Reno, Judy and Bill stopped off in San Francisco to see her family. "Hi, Mother. I want you to meet my new husband, Bill Duvall. We just got married in Reno yesterday. Bill, this is my mother, Autumn."

"Hi Bill, glad you stopped by. Where are you guys going to live?"

"We'll live in Milpitas for now." He stuffed his hands in his pockets.

"Hi, Autie. This my new husband."

"Hey, Cissy. What's that in your panty hose? It looks like a piece of toilet paper."

"Oh my God, I must have had that in there since I went to the bathroom at the last gas station. How embarrassing?"

Everyone laughed. "You haven't changed much, daughter. Umm, can I talk to you a minute."

"Uh, yeah I guess so. Autie, you and Bill can get acquainted."

Mother dragged Judy into the kitchen and shut the hallway door. "That guy is so ugly. What the heck do you see in him?"

"Well, I like his blue eyes and…he has a good personality."

"And, what the heck are you wearing?"

"Oh, they call these hot pants and my white go-go boots. Remember that song *These Boots Were Made for Walking?* Well, I don't think these boots were made for walking 'cause I keep tripping."

"Well, I don't like them and I don't have a good feeling about that guy."

"His name is Bill and it is my choice, Mother."

I HATED TO ADMIT IT but Mother turned out to be right about this one. Bill used my money to buy himself a truck, cheated on me, and worst of all, he didn't treat my boys very good. That was *not* okay! In the still of the night, I decided to divorce number two. I walked away from the condo bought with the settlement money from my last divorce.

My poor children were uprooted once again.

# Chapter 16

# Judy Charbonneau

My children were my strength, but men were my weakness. I wanted to be a good mom for the children I so loved, but I wanted my fun, too. Dancing was still in my blood.

## San Jose, CA ~ 1971

"Mom, why are your hands all bloody?"

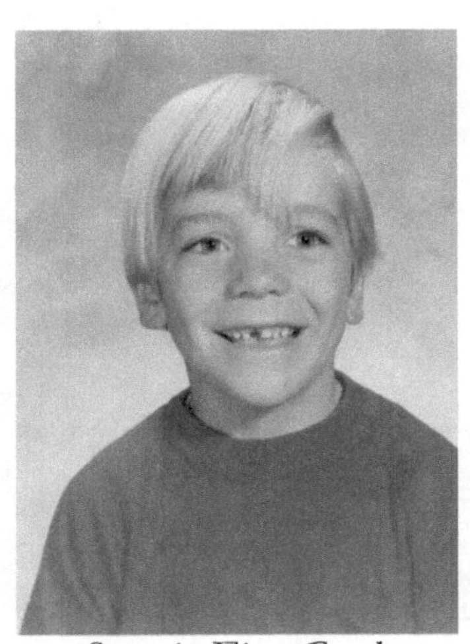

*Steve in First Grade*

"Oh, Steve honey, they hurt so bad. It's from the fiberglass I build the boats with. Remember I told you about my job?"

Steve shook his head. "My poor, crazy mother."

"You know how to put a smile on my face, sweetie. But, I won't be doing this long because I'm going to go to school just like you do. I'm going to get a degree in Dental Assisting."

"Whoop-de-do, Mom."

189

"I don't know where you learn this stuff but I love it. Now go play so I can talk to Jerry on the phone."

"Is he your boyfriend now?"

"I think so, Steve. But only if you approve."

Jerry was a nice looking man with blue eyes and sandy brown hair. He seemed to love kids and they seemed to enjoy him. Judy reached for the phone and dialed Jerry's number. "Hi, Jerr! I just called to tell you I took your advice and signed up to start school in the fall."

"Cool. I know you can do it."

"I hope you're right. I told you that I had a hard time in school. I never thought I could go to college.

"Judy, anyone can go to college. Hey, why don't we go on a picnic tomorrow? I'll get the charcoal if you can bring something to bar-b-que."

"I have hot dogs, buns, and all the fixings."

"Great, I'll pick up some chips and drinks. See you around 11:00."

"The kids will be thrilled. See ya."


"Hurry up Steve, you're so slow. Mom wants you to bring her some towels." Gary, even though younger, was always the first one organized and ready to get going. Just like their births: Steve was always three weeks late and Gary was three weeks early.

"Come on kids, Jerry's here. Gary, help your sister get her shoes on."

"Hello! Is everyone ready?"

"Yeah!" "Yeah!" "Yeah!"

"Here Jerr, I have everything in this cooler. Let's roll." It was about a forty-five-minute drive to Coyote Creek.

"This is my favorite spot. The kids and I come here at least once a week in warm weather. I love creeks." *I could sit here and watch the kids playing all day.*

"Is everyone hungry?" Jerry hoisted the bag of charcoals onto the picnic table. "I better get these going, while the kids are playing."

"Yeah. The kids had an early breakfast. They never let me sleep in." Judy turned at the sound of the boys crashing through the brush. "You kids stay right where I can see you. Boys, watch your sister."

It only took thirty minutes for the coals to get hot enough for the hot dogs. As Judy looked on, Jerry started getting things out of the cooler. He pulled out the mustard and catsup and… "Hey Jude, where are the hot dogs?"

She stepped over to the cooler to look inside. "Uh, I guess I forgot them. Oh brother, I feel my ears turning red."

"Umm, do you think the kids will notice?"

"Well, they'll be disappointed but we've had to eat catsup sandwiches before. My boss doesn't always pay me my earnings and I've had to scrimp."

"Hey kids, come get your catsup sandwiches." Jerry called out.

"What? I wanted hot dogs," cried Gary.

"Well, if you don't complain, I'll get us some milkshakes on the way home."

Jerry got three "Okay's."

Jerry dropped the family off after a fun day for all. Judy got the kids all cleaned up and turned on a horror movie. The boys and Judy loved them but little Nicole frequently hid her face in Judy's neck when the scary parts came on. *This is my favorite time being alone with the kids.* Steve lay on the floor, his head propped up with a pillow. On the couch, Nicole sat on one side of Judy and Gary on the other. As she was combing through Gary's hair with her fingers, Judy noticed a bump. *Oh God, it's a tick.* "Kids, we need to go to the emergency room."

"Why, Mom?" Steve didn't even take his eyes off the movie.

"Gary has something on his head and I just want to get it checked out." *I don't want to tell them what it is.*

"Oh, bummer." Steve moaned.

So off to the emergency they went. After an hour wait they all marched into the room directed by the nurse. "Hello everyone. I'm Dr. Gomez. What do we have here?"

"Will you look at his head doctor?"

Dr. Gomez washed his hands and stepped over to Gary. "Jump up here young fellow." Dr. Gomez probed around his head and saw the tick. He quietly walked over for some kind of tweezer instrument and started digging out the tick. Gary sat very still and quiet but his eyes were wide and started to water. "What a brave young man you are, Gary." He showed us all the tick.

"Ewww!" Everyone joined in the chorus. Then Dr. Gomez looked over at Steve and asked. "Son, what is that brown stuff coming out of your nose?"

Steve started to cry, "I put a chocolate covered peanut in my nose just for fun."

"Gary, jump down so your brother can get on the table. Nothing like killing two birds with one stone." Dr. Gomez got another long tweezer kind of instrument and pulled the peanut out of Steve's nose.

"Thank you, Doctor. Kids, let's go home and try to watch another horror movie."

"Can we make popcorn, Mom?"

"You bet, Steve."

## ~ Fall 1971 ~

"Jerry, look at this. I got all D's on my tests!"

"Maybe college isn't for you, Judy." He didn't even look up from his newspaper.

"But you said anyone could get through college."

"Well, I guess I didn't know you that well."

"Huh? I told you I had a difficult time learning in high school. You know what? I can get a tutor. It doesn't cost anything."

"What subject?"

"History, Health Education, and Psych. Oh, and Biology. I guess all of them."

"Good luck with that."

"Thanks, I'll need it."

Judy got herself a couple of tutors. One in particular, John, was dedicated to helping her pass her classes. John was just out of the service and had a wife and baby. One day after their studies, John asked if they could talk awhile. "Judy, I don't want to offend you but I want to tell you that I love you."

Not knowing what to say, she just stared at him with eyes wide.

After an uncomfortable moment, he looked back at her more intently and said, "and, Jesus loves you."

She didn't quite understand what he was saying but answered. "Thank you, John. And thanks for all your help." What he said was nice, but she didn't know what to do with it, so left it at that. She just didn't *get it.*

> GOD WAS TRYING TO GET MY ATTENTION, but I was unaware of His leading and slow to learn of His ways. So, He reached down and saved my children.

## ~ Spring 1972 ~

Judy and her kids lived in a small apartment in East San Jose. They were practically the only white family living in the projects. Once while Steve was sitting on a slide in the play area, he witnessed several, tattooed gang members break into an apartment and stab a guy to death. It didn't stop him from playing outside and being adventurous. One bright Saturday morning the kids were playing a few doors down when Judy heard footsteps outside. *Who could be at my door?* She put down her psychology book and opened the door just a crack. "Yes?"

"Hi, my name is Janet from South Hills Baptist Church. Can I have a moment of your time?"

"I guess so. Do you want to come in?"

"Yes, thank you." She had a Bible in her garden worn hands and seemed a little nervous and a lot pregnant.

"My name is Judy. What do you want to talk about?"

"Well Judy, a couple of things. I want to invite you to our church."

"No thank you, I'm not Baptist—I'm Catholic."

"Oh, that's okay. You know, I just want to share with you that since I've been reading my Bible and going to church, my life has changed. Before, I couldn't even handle my crying one-year-old, but now I have the peace of the Lord."

"Oh, that's nice." *What is she rambling about? I need to get back to my studying.*

"Do you have children?"

"Yes, I have three children, four, six, and eight."

"Well…another thing…I want to tell you about our bus ministry. If you would allow your children to go to church, we would pick them up about 8:00 on Sunday morning. We would feed them lunch and bring them back about 2:00 p.m."

"Is it free?"

Janet smiled and nodded.

"Oh, I'd like that. I could sleep with my boyfriend while they're gone. I never have a babysitter and their dad only sees them about four times a year."

Her mouth dropped open and her eyes got wide. "O-o-okay then. We'll take good care of them and I'll leave you this pamphlet with all the information about our church if you ever want to come."

"That's really nice of you. Thanks, Janet. I'll have them ready tomorrow at 8:00."

She walked Janet to the door with a joyful heart. *I have a babysitter every Sunday now.* The church lady was barely down the walkway when Jerry came strolling in. Judy smiled. "Well, I'm popular today. I can't even get to my studying."

"I'll leave if you want, Jude."

"No way! Guess what. The Baptist church is going to pick my kids up every Sunday morning and keep them till after lunch."

"Cool. Hey Jude, I was wondering why we don't ever visit your parents."

"Well that's a thorny subject. My mother is mad at me and I don't much feel like dealing with her. I'm happy without her in my life. Daddy is usually out at sea. He's a Merchant Marine."

"Why is she mad at you?"

"Oh, I went to visit my mother's sister Martha, my Nannan, who's a beautician and cuts my hair. It was a weeknight so I came right back. When my mother found out I was in the city without visiting her, she called and started yelling at me, then hung up. I hope I never have to talk to her again."

"I don't think that's right, Jude. We should plan a visit, so why don't you call her and make arrangements."

Judy felt heat coming to her face. "I'll think about it." *Oh brother! I wish people would leave me be.*

"Hello Mother, how are you?" *I can't believe I'm doing this.* Judy wrapped the phone cord around her finger and stared at the clock.

"I'm fine."

"Mother, I have a new boyfriend and he wants to meet you."

"Well, you know where I live. Just call before you come."

"Okay. Thanks, Mother." *I'm not looking forward to this. But, whatever will be, will be.*

Judy had hoped Jerry's charm and good looks would win Mother over—and in a way they did. Trying herself to make a good impression, Mother paid attention to him and ignored her daughter, as usual. At least, Judy had Daddy's attention. He was always happy to see her and make her laugh.

## ~ Fall 1972 ~

"Jerry, my friend Peggy from Chicago is coming over tonight. Can you pick up a bottle of wine?" Peggy was a classy gal. Just the opposite of Judy who was described as a little bit country, a little bit hippy, and a little bit rock and roll.

"Sure, I'll come over about 7:00."

"Good, she'll be here by then."

Jerry and Peggy really hit it off. Too good for Judy's liking. Peggy was a tall, beautiful redhead with an air of confidence that Judy knew nothing about. *All I want to do is put her in a cab and send her back to her hotel. I hate it when I get jealous.* They all drank a little too much and Jerry kept flirting with Peggy. Late into the night, Peggy got up to go to the bathroom. A loud thump was heard and both Jerry and Judy ran into the bathroom. Peggy had fallen into the bathtub.

"Oh my God, Peggy. Are you alright?"

"Yeah, I think so."

Compassion won out over jealousy, as Judy helped her friend out of the tub. "Jerry, I think you better go now. I'm fixing the couch for Peggy to sleep on."

Reluctantly Jerry grabbed his jacket and headed for the door. "Good night girls, it was nice meeting you, Peggy."

## ~ Spring 1973 ~

"Hey Jude, when this job is over, I will be transferred to Southern California. I will actually be moving in May."

"Wow, that's just around the corner. I graduate in June. Can you believe I made the Dean's List?"

"I know and I'm proud of you. I guess staying up late at night when the kids were in bed paid off. Do you want to get married?"

"Wow! What? Really? I didn't know you cared. I need to think about it. Okay, when?"

"How about right after your finals? I'll have a place for us by then. And, I'd like you to ask your parents if we can get married in their house." The Wagner house on Winding Way had a lot of character. The original owners who built it were high society. It was told that they entertained Mrs. Bess Truman more than once. The house wasn't huge but elegant enough for its time, built in 1929. It stood on a large lot for San Francisco with windows all around. The kitchen gave a view of downtown with twin peaks to the west. The best part was hearing the church bells at certain times of the day. "And I want you to wear a white dress."

"Really? You mean like a real wedding? I usually get married in Nevada."

"Yes. I never had a wedding with my first wife either. So, this will be a first for both of us. We'll go shopping for a ring tomorrow. Oh, and another thing. I think we should go to church like a family."

"You mean before we get married?"

"Yes, this weekend. I want to do things the right way."

Judy got all the kids up and dressed. "You guys are going with Jerry and me to the church around the corner, today."

"What about the bus, Mom? What about lunch?" Steve and Gary took turns with their questions.

"I already told them you wouldn't be going. And don't worry about lunch. I won't let you starve, sillies."

Judy was kind of nervous and excited all at the same time. She'd never been to a Lutheran church before. As they got out of the car, an usher directed them to the children's church. A nice middle-aged lady wearing a floral dress and a name tag that said JANE was there to greet them. She asked the names and the ages of the children. Jerry took charge. "This is Steve who is eight."

"I'm almost nine."

"Okay. This is Gary who is six."

"I'm six and a half."

"Okay. And this is Nicole who is four." Nicole just smiled with her big brown eyes. "My name is Jerry and this is my wife, Patty."

Judy's eyes went wide with shock and her heart raced a little. "Oh, Jane, my name is Judy, not Patty. I don't know why he said that." *I can't believe he called me his ex-wife's name.*

"Ha, I bet that's his pet name for you." Jane said politely.

*Some pet name!*

The children were taken to their Sunday school classes. As Jerry and Judy walked toward the church, Judy nudged Jerry and whispered, "Why did you call me Patty?"

"I guess it's just a habit."

That was the first and last time they went to church as a family.

For the next three months, Judy was busy with finals, finding a wedding dress for herself and outfits for the kids for their up and coming wedding. Nicole thought she was getting married, too. "Mom, what color is my dress going to be?"

"Oh, I have a nice yellow dress picked out for you. We'll go this afternoon to try it on. And you boys are going to have nice matching suits."

"Far out." Steve laughed out loud.

*Steve, Nicole, and Gary Charbonneau*

## ~ June 1973 ~

"This is our last date as an unmarried couple, Jerry. I can't believe I'm done with school, getting married and moving all in one week."

"Yup." Jerry slurred his word and ordered another drink. "Too bad my mother couldn't make it down from Montana. We'll have to plan a vacation next year so you can meet her and my kids."

"That'll be fun. And, since your kids are the same age as mine, they should get along good. It's funny that your two oldest are boys and youngest a girl, just like mine."

"Uh huh. You know my family will be a little surprised when they meet you."

"Why is that?"

"Oh, they always thought I'd bring home someone who looked like the typical, beautiful California girl." Jerry had a silly grin on his face.

"What are you saying? Do you mean they are expecting someone like my friend Peggy?"

"Yeah, like her."

"Sorry I'll disappoint them." Judy clutched onto her purse and felt her eyes burn. *I feel like a wounded turtle.* That pretty much put a damper on the rest of the evening and on her up and coming wedding.

---

I DIDN'T ATTEND MY COLLEGE GRADUATION. I got married that day instead. It was a short and sweet ceremony at my mother's house, performed by a Unitarian minister. He didn't mention God at all.

---

*This is Judy not attending her graduation*

# Heart of My Faith

# Chapter 17


# Mrs. Judy Wood


THERE WERE VALLEYS AND MOUNTAIN TOPS in the summer of my life. I held on to precious Scriptures such as, "Behold, old things are passed away, and all things are new."


## Garden Grove, California ~ 1973

"Jerry, do you still want to start going to church as a family?"

"No, not really. I actually don't believe in a supreme being."

"I guess I don't either, but the neighbors offered to take the kids, so we can still have Sunday mornings to ourselves." The Henderson's faithfully took the kids to church, even on Wednesday evenings sometimes.


## ~ Fall 1973 ~

Employed as a Dental Assistant in Huntington Beach, Judy liked her job but the babysitter made more than she did. $45.00 of her paycheck went to the sitter while Judy only ended up with $40.00 a week. At that time an oil crises left a shortage of gas, long lines and high prices—55 cents a gallon at the gas stations. As she moved around the kitchen, fixing dinner Judy discussed the situation with her husband. While she was talking, she kept sampling the spaghetti sauce simmering on the stove. "Jerry, I'm bummed out about this gas shortage and it makes my blood boil. The line was all the way around the block when I went to fill up your gas tank. You know what I'm going to do tomorrow. I'm going to ride one of the kid's bikes to work. It's only nine miles so it shouldn't take that long on a bike and there are no hills here. Plus I won't have to go through the line again to fill up my car."

"More power to ya, thanks for filling up my car," he said in his nonchalant tone.

"I'll call Dr. Jamison and tell him just in case I get into trouble along the way."

Jerry came over to the stove to be a taster. "Hey Jude, there's not much sauce in the pot."

Her face turned red as she looked into the pot and realized she'd eaten most of the sauce. "Uh, I guess we'll have a little bit of spaghetti and a little bit of mac and cheese. Yeah, that'll work. Jerr—can you run to the store and pick up some cheese?"

With a firm grip on the handlebars of Steve's bike, Judy set out early in the morning. A blanket of fog engulfed her as she left their driveway and her body tightened to the cold. His bike had a wide seat on it and at 104 pounds it seemed to be just the right size for her. She took in the ocean air along the way. *This isn't that bad, my legs are holding up just fine.*

Dr. Jamison was waiting for her at the back door of the office. "You're late."

"It took me longer than I thought, is our first patient here yet?"

"No, you're good. I was just worried about you, knowing you were changing your mode of transportation."

"You know what? I didn't think there were any hills but on a bike, you see hills that weren't there the day before."

Dr. Jamieson laughed. "Hey, did you know I race bikes in competition?" He was younger than Judy and more physically fit. "Maybe we can duke it out sometime."

"No way! I just want to get to work and back without waiting in those long gas lines."

"Oh, by the way—" He chuckled. "If we have a break today, I want you to fill my car up for me so I don't have to wait in one of those lines."

"You're the boss." *Oh brother!*

She changed into her uniform and sterilized the instruments for their first patient, feeling quite energized.

Five o'clock came and Judy changed back into her biking clothes for the long ride home. At one intersection, a lady was turning the corner and almost ran over Judy. She couldn't restrain her mouth and hollered at the driver. "You stupid lady, I hope you run out of gas."

Huffing and puffing, she finally turned the corner onto Vanguard Avenue where the neighbors were standing around waiting for the big arrival. Surprised, she waved her hand. "Hi, everyone."

"How was it Jude?" Mel called out.

"I'm not at all tired but boy is my butt ever sore."

Jerry walked out of the garage. "Hey Jude, the seat on that bike is too wide, that's why your butt's sore. We're going to buy you a new bike tonight." For the next few months, weather permitting, she got to work quicker and with a lot less soreness riding her new yellow Schwinn 10-speed.


"Hey Jude, you better take your car tomorrow, we're invited to my boss's house for dinner so you can't be late." His brow wrinkled and disapproval grated in his voice. "And, by the way, you need to get yourself an outfit. You spend all your money on the kids and you look like a ragamuffin."

"Okay, I get off early tomorrow, so I can hit the mall afterwards to find something."

After a stressful day at the office, Judy rushed to the mall and literally ran from one end to the other in search for the perfect outfit. More winded with every step, she finally found just the right one. It was a yellow floral bell-bottom cotton pant suit. *I think it looks real good on me but it's four inches too long. I'll look for some tall shoes.* She ran back to the other end of the mall, found, and bought her first pair of platform shoes. Even with everything on sale, there was barely enough money in her coin purse. *Whew, just made it.* With the last purchase finalized, she ran back through the mall to the parking lot, her stomach a little clenched.

As she pulled up the driveway, everyone was standing before her, dressed and ready to go. "Hi, guys, I'll be ready in a minute."

"Hurry, Jude, we're running late."

Beads of sweat gathered on her nose as she tripped down the hallway toward her room, then stopped short. Gary was at it again! He had emptied everything he could out of the bedroom he and his brother shared. Gary liked his bedroom organized and this was always his solution. Take everything out, put everything back in, and draw a line down the middle of the room. *But now, Gary? Really? Just wait till we get home!* Scurrying into her room, she threw on her new duds and rushed right back out. "Okay, let's go."

They arrived at Tom and Fran's fashionably late. Jerry made the introductions. The kids ran off to play with their girls and wine was offered to the adults. "Oh, yes thank you."

Everyone, more than ready to relax, sat down around the table for a grown-up conversation. Tom was a tall, handsome man with eyes that twinkled. Fran was quite short, had a tiny voice, and a round face. They seemed so formal to Judy, but like her grandmother, she had the ability to be with the down-and-outers and the up-and-outers.

With a funny expression, Fran looked over at Judy. "What's that hanging underneath your arm?"

Judy looked down and then up at Jerry, who had an uncomfortable look on his face. *Oh my God—I can't believe it.* She pulled on the string, trying to act nonchalant. "Oh, it's just a price tag!"

Tom and Fran chuckled and Jerry joined in. Judy's ears turned red but that moment broke the ice and the rest of the evening was an enjoyable one. Fran chattered her way through the evening. They would share more good times as long as Tom & Jerry worked together.

Everyone was in a good mood when they piled into the car and took their places for the twenty minute ride home. Judy turned to her middle son. "Hey Gar Bear, I know you like to keep your room neat and organized, but I really hated tripping over all the things you put in the hallway."

"I know Mom, but that's the only way I can clean up Steve's mess. I wish I had my own room."

The age-old complaint. Judy felt his frustration. Well, maybe she could come up with a solution that didn't involve contractors and building permits. "Okay—everyone listen up. From now on when anyone leaves something out, I will put it in a box. In order for you to get it back, you'll have to pay a nickel for small toys and up to a quarter for bigger items."

Steve groaned and Nicole's head popped up in surprise. "Does that mean me and Dad, too?"

Dear Mrs. Room Fairy

Have a nice day. And my floor is vaccumed. Don't leave any candy please, if my room is fit to your qualifications. Pray that me and Steve will be able to go to mt. I love you Mom.

Gary

"Uh, yeah, but for you only a penny...or a nickel at the most."

"Ha ha. Nic-ole ain't worth a dime." Steve cracked up laughing.

Judy shot him a don't-torment-your-sister look. "And, if you keep your room clean..." She smiled at Gary. "Or your side of the room—the Room Fairy will leave you a little surprise."

Jerry gave a thumbs-up to Judy's idea. "We're home. Hope everyone has everything in its right place!

## ~ Spring 1974 ~

Three pairs of eyes were staring at their mom, waiting for her to wake up. "Mom, will you please come to church with us this Sunday?" Steve asked with his piercing blue eyes shining with hopefulness.

"We've been praying for you." Gary crawled up on the bed next to Judy.

Steve poked Gary in the arm. "*Shhh.*"

"Please, Mom," Nicole begged. *Who could resist those big brown eyes?*

A smiled tugged at Judy's lips. "Okay you guys! But just one time and don't ask again. Maybe I'll ask Patsy if she wants to come with her boys."

"Yea!" "Yea!" "Yea!" They all jumped up and down.

Judy hopped out of bed and picked up the phone to call her friend, Patsy, who worked at the corner drug store where they first met. She was a very attractive and classy lady with short blond hair and blue-green eyes. But, most of

*Those Big Brown Eyes*

all, Patsy exuded love. She made everyone feel special. She and Judy hit it off and on her day off Patsy would come over to Judy's for lunch. "Hey Robby, can you put your mom on the phone?"

The receiver clunked down on the other end of the line and Judy heard Robby running and hollering for his mom. Seconds later, she came on the line. "Hey Jude, what's up?"

"Hey, thought I'd ask if you and the boys would want to come to church with me and my kids this Sunday?"

"Oh, are you into that? I've been wanting to try it because my sister-in-law has been talking to me about her church." Patsy's voice rose with excitement.

"I'm not really into anything. I'm just going because the kids asked me."

"You bet I'll go with you. Just let me know what time."

"I'll ask my neighbor and call you later."


## ~ Sunday ~

"Well hello, an elderly lady greeted them with a warm smile. My name is Evelyn."

"This is my friend, Patsy, and my name is Judy. We're here for Sunday school."

"Well, you're in the right place. Please help yourself to some coffee and have a seat."

Everyone extended warm friendly smiles as they came up to introduce themselves. With Evelyn on the piano, Sunday school got started with a song. She was also the teacher. Judy was all ears and Patsy's eyes were wide with wonder. It was the start of something big for both of them.

After church, while Judy was fixing lunch, Steve came up from behind and wrapped his arms around her. "Hey mom, how did you like church, will you go again?"

"Well, to tell the truth, Steve, I really liked Sunday school but not the church service."

"Why not, Mom?"

"Because, when that man standing on the stage was praying, it made me cry! I don't know why but I think that's weird. I will go to Sunday School though."

"That's great mom. I love you."

"Me too, Steve."

## A couple of months later

"You know Patsy?" Judy poured her friend another cup of coffee. "It's strange that I've gone to Catholic school and church almost all my life but never knew that much about Jesus until now. It's exciting."

"Same here. I wish we knew someone we could talk to about our unanswered questions."

"Hey, next time you come over for lunch, I'll invite my neighbor, Mel, and we can ask her some questions about Jesus."

The following Thursday the three of them sat down at the small kitchen table. Patsy and Judy were so excited to have a real live Christian eating lunch with them. However, they didn't seem to know what questions to ask. They didn't even say a blessing. Mel was a quiet soft-spoken woman. Maybe she was shy!

When she left, Patsy leaned across the table, her eyes shining. "Hey Jude, I think we should get baptized. My sister-in-law said that's how you get filled with the Holy Spirit."

"I was baptized as a baby so I don't see why I should do it again."

## ~ July 1974 ~

Judy admired Patsy and wanted to be like her, so she decided to get baptized just because Patsy was doing it. Neither one of their husbands wanted anything to do with church. However, they came to their baptism, which was at the Sunday Evening service. Since it was Jerry's birthday, their two families planned on going to Farrell's Ice Cream Parlor for a Pig's Trough afterwards.

All those being baptized had to go in the back room that led to the baptismal. When the pastor's wife gave out the gowns, she asked everyone to say something when they reached the baptismal before getting dunked. Judy wanted no part of speaking in front of all those people. "If I have to say something then I don't want to get baptized."

"You don't *have* to Judy, but it would be nice for the congregation to know what the Lord means to you."

"Okay then." *Oh brother, I guess I'll make something up.* She practiced in her mind what to say and it sounded pretty good, considering that beads of sweat were breaking out on her nose. "My name is Judy, I'm very happy to say that the Lord has made a difference in our family. I just want to be filled with His Holy Spirit." The pastor said a prayer before dunking her. Well, nothing seemed to happen, like Patsy said it would. She just came up all wet.

In bed that night, for the first time ever, Judy talked to God. "Lord, I meant what I said tonight. I do want You in my life. Please forgive me of all my selfish wrong doings and help me be a better mother." In that quiet moment, her body went feathery light and she felt His touch. *Is that an earthquake?* But wait. *I grew up in earthquake land so no, that's not what it is.* Someone gently laid His hand on her head and then placed it on her heart. It wasn't her husband, he was asleep. It was Jesus and He filled the void that was in her soul from her early beginnings. *I will hang on to this for a lifetime. Tomorrow my life changes forever!*

# Chapter 18

# Judy Wood

WOW! WHAT A DIFFERENCE A DAY MAKES. I didn't make a 180 degree turnaround like I hoped. I still screamed at my kids, used the belt on them, and said things I shouldn't have said. Struggling with guilt and shame, I asked my kids' forgiveness over and over again. When they got into their teens, I was still asking forgiveness for my past shortcomings. Their response amazed me. "Mom, God let us forget all that."

## ~ Spring 1975 ~

Judy walked up the path that led to the elementary school office. Memories of her own experience in Catholic grammar school surged to the forefront of her mind. *I never remember my mother coming to my school. I hope the teachers are nicer than some of the nuns were.* And why had Nicole's teacher called her to come instead of sending a note? Judy took a deep breath and walked into the office. "Hi, I'm Judy Wood and I'm here to meet with my daughter's teacher, Mrs. Ware."

The secretary glanced at the oversized wall clock. "Mrs. Ware is on her lunch break. Have a seat, Mrs. Wood. I'll call her."

Judy sat in a red, plastic chair. She pulled on her ear out of nervousness—always timid around authority.

Within minutes, a pleasant looking woman in a blue pantsuit entered the office. She held out her hand and gave Judy a reassuring smile. "Mrs. Wood. It's nice of you to come. I wanted to tell you about Nicole's reading skills. Sadly, she's not up to par with the class and we might have to hold her back."

"Mrs. Ware, I noticed the books she brings home do have some very hard words for a first grader. Whatever happened to *Run Spot Run?*"

Mrs. Ware gave a little laugh. "We're a MAGNET school. We're a little more accelerated than the other elementary schools, so we must hold our students to a higher standard. Please be assured, Mrs. Wood, we only want what's best for your daughter."

Judy wanted the best for Nicole too, but having to tell her the bad news was going to be painful.

Judy's little first grader waltzed into the house at the end of her school day. With heavy heart, Judy greeted her at the door. *She appears not to have a care in the world. How do I tell her?* "Nicole, come sit down with me, sweetie. I have something to tell you."

"Okay Mom! Let's talk." She plunked her books on the coffee table and hopped up on the couch next to Judy.

"I was called to your school today and had a meeting with your teacher. And…"

Nicole's big brown eyes held on to her mother's with expectation. "And what, Mom?"

"Well, Mrs. Ware told me that because of your reading level you might have to be held back. She said because you're so tiny, that it shouldn't be a problem for you."

Tears filled Nicole's eyes. She turned her face away for a moment, then turning back, she spoke with a sad voice. "Well, it is a problem for me, Mom. I don't want to be held back so I'm going to cry to God and ask Him for help."

"That's great, honey. I'll be praying for you, too." *I sure hope our God comes through. Lord, she has the faith of a child. Please answer her prayer.*

Every night tender prayers could be heard from little Nicole's bedroom, sometimes crying followed.

A couple of weeks later, she came home with a flyer that announced a reading contest at her school. "Mom, I'm going to participate and read lots of books! I'm sure this is God's way of helping me become a better reader."

*Wow, what courage my daughter has.* "Nicole, you never cease to amaze me."

So the journey began. Every day Judy took Nicole to the library where she checked out book after book and read them aloud night after night. "Nicole, are you sure you can read this many books?"

"I have to, Mom. And you know what? I love reading now."

Spring came to an end and the contest was over. It just so happened that the day they announced the winner, Judy was at the school office, getting transfers for their next move. She could see the kids gathering in the yard but didn't know what was going on. Then, the principal's voice echoed over the loudspeaker, "Congratulations to Nicole Wood, winner of the reading contest." Then, a little later, "Nicole Wood, Most Improved Student."

Nicole ran into the house that afternoon. "Mom! I did it. God helped me! I won the contest." Her eyes sparkled and that smile was contagious.

"I know Nicole. I'm so proud of you. And, I have something else to tell you."

"Oh no!" She froze in place. "What now?"

"You won't have to be held back. You are moving on to the second grade!"

"Really? I hoped I could change what was going to happen to me, but I didn't know if I could."

"You sure did. Hope is a powerful thing."

"Then you should have named me Hope."

Judy didn't let her daughter's innocent words hurt their celebration. "I didn't know what hope was until long after you were born." She grabbed Nicole's hands and they did a little happy dance.

"I know what it means, so if I have a little girl, I can name her Hope."

Mother and daughter laughed, embraced and thanked their God with another dance.

Gary ran into the living room and screeched to a stop. He rolled his eyes in an exaggerated manner. "Oh, brother."

*Nicole and Gary Wood*

## Move to Antioch ~ 1975

"Hey guys, the movers are here. Get your things together. We're going to get on the road. Ask Dad if he needs any help."

"How far is Antioch, Dad?" Nicole tucked another book under her arm.

Jerry was just finishing loading the station wagon. "It's about a five hour drive but we can't move in till tomorrow so we'll spend the night half way there."

"Hey, Dad." Steve rushed out of the house. "Do you need any help?"

"No, but someone has to be in charge of the cat and the bird."

Before Steve could answer, Gary ran out the door. "I will,

Dad." And in no time at all, the Wood family headed to their new home in Antioch.

"We'll be spending the night in Gorman," Jerry announced.

"Oh, isn't that near Six Flags, Jerr? Can we take the kids there?"

"We'll see." Jerry gave a little shake of his head, which meant there would be no opportunity.

*I feel bad for the kids.* "Hey you guys can go swimming! I brought your swimming suits."

"Whoo-hoo! Yippee!" the boys shouted. "Thanks, Mom."

"Mom, I don't want to go swimming." A pout hovered on Nicole's lower lip.

"Why not? You like to swim."

"Because Jaws might be in there!"

"What a scaredy cat." Gary made a face at his sister.

"Stop it, Gar Bear." Judy gave him a stern look.

After their swim, the family had a bite to eat before heading to their rooms. "By the way boys, we aren't supposed to have animals in the motel, so don't tell anyone and keep Oscar quiet. We'll be right next door if you need anything tonight, but don't stay up too late 'cause we're leaving early in the morning."

## The next morning

"Jerry, I'm going to play a trick on the boys. Nicole, you be real quiet and just listen."

*Ringgg. Ringgg.* "Hell...o." Gary's sleepy voice answered the phone.

Judy disguised her voice with a high pitch. "Hell-o, this is the manager. Do you have any pets in your room?"

"Uhh, just a minute… Steve, the lady wants to know if we have any pets in our room." His voice quivered as he spoke in a low voice.

"Well, you have to tell the truth."

"Uhh, yes we do," Gary confessed.

"Well, you are going to get in trouble because it's against the rules."

"Uhh, okay!" Gary hung up the phone and came running into his parents' room. His eyes were wide and his face was white as he told them what happened. Jerry and Judy couldn't hold it in any longer and burst out laughing.

"Mom! That wasn't very nice. It really scared me."

"I'm sorry, Gar Bear, I couldn't help myself." It took a while before they could gain his trust after that.

## Antioch, California ~ 1975-1977

Antioch was a good town for the short time the Woods' lived there. They found a good church. Judy and her kids were growing in the Lord together. Judy learned to pray for her children and had devotions with them every morning. Wednesday was church night for the kids. Gary's teacher was Gloria Short. He came home one night all impressed. "Mom, my teacher told us a story about a thirty-one year old man that was a bed wetter. It really touched me, because, you know—my problem—and now that I'm nine, it's really embarrassing. Well, in the story, people prayed for the man and he got healed." Gary heaved a heavy sigh. "No one ever prays for me, Mom."

"Well, Gar Bear, I'll pray for you. We'll pray before you go to bed tonight and every night till you get healed." And so the ritual began. It lasted two months before his healing took place. Then one night, as Judy had been recently taught, she prayed a scripture. "Lord, by your stripes, Gary is healed."

When she finished praying, Gary looked into her face with his

*My Little Crew*

big brown eyes, smiling. "Mom, when you said, 'by your stripes Gary is healed,' I felt something inside me. I don't think I will ever wet the bed again." And so it was as Gary said.

Judy was so excited she decided to share this with her mother, hoping to glorify God. However, true to form, Autumn asked sarcastically, "If it was God, then why did it take two months?" That gave Judy an uncomfortable feeling in the pit of her stomach. *She always has to pierce me with her knife of words.*

Being bothered by it, she later asked Gary why he thought it took so long for God to heal him. "Well, Mom, we have grown closer these last two months praying together every night."

"Oh yes. Why didn't I think of that?" Judy smiled. Gary had always been a little more distant to her than her other children. When he was eighteen months old he had to be left in the hospital due to dehydration. In those days, they didn't accommodate parents to stay the night and when he was brought back home, he would scream every time Judy tried to sit at the dinner table. He punished her for the longest time. *Lord, thank you for bringing us closer. You get so much mileage in every situation.*

"Good morning, Gloria. How's Claude doing? Is he coming to church?"

"Yes, thanks. He had a bad spat of the flu but he's fine now. Glad my girls didn't get sick."

"Gloria, I've been meaning to thank you for sharing a story with your Wednesday night class. Gary told me about the man that was a bed wetter and got healed through prayer. It caused us to pray for Gary and he doesn't wet the bed anymore."

Gloria looked confused as she wrinkled up her nose. "I don't remember telling a story about that... Wait—I told a story about a thirty-one year old man that was bedridden! I think Gary misunderstood."

"Oh, that's funny! I thought it was odd that a grown man would still wet the bed." They both laughed out loud. "Well, God can use anything and I think He has a sense of humor."

"Another thing, Gloria. My daughter, Nicole, tells me she wants to change her name to Julie. What the heck is that about?"

"Kids are so funny. Maybe she saw someone on TV that really impressed her. And, I have noticed her brothers tease her by saying: Nickel ain't worth a dime."

"Yes, I've heard that, too. Well, I'm going to tell her she can use her middle name, Denée, but definitely not Julie. Just so you know when you see her. And maybe you're next lesson should include the sin of lies."

"I always try to include that in every lesson. Why?"

"Nicole took something that didn't belong to her and then lied about it."

"What'd you do?"

"I told her she better go to her room and talk to Jesus about it. She wandered off and a couple of minutes later, strolled back into the kitchen, looking all innocent. So, I asked her if she talked to Jesus."

"Yes, Mom!"

"Well… What did He say?"

"He said He forgives me."

Gloria smiled big. "I like that."

## Huntington Beach, California ~ 1977-1978

On the road again, to Southern California. Because of Jerry's job, the Wood family moved on the average, every one and a half years. Judy took a job delivering lunches for Maid

*Denée, Gary, and Steve*

Fresh to several law firms and like businesses. Following a weekend the family spent in Tijuana, she came home with the Montezuma's revenge. Gary, the nurturing one in the family, volunteered to skip school and help her with the route. Judy was literally bending over with pain while Gary carried the heavy basket of sandwiches and salads. He was very helpful and comforting. *My special angel got me through the day!*

*Gary Wood*

When little league came around that year, and Judy had the opportunity to reward Gary, all she could think of was the long drives back and forth to practice and games. Regretfully, she didn't allow him to participate. But, like his great-grandfather of old, Gary didn't let that keep him down. He joined his brother in ministering at the convalescent home. They didn't tell their parents till much later what they were doing. They read the Bible to an old man who had never talked or had any expression on his face. After many visits, the nurses were amazed, for the first time, a smile formed on this little old man's lips when the boys went into his room.

> MY KIDS ARE AMAZING! Even when I mess up and let my selfishness have its way. Through the blessings that happened in that convalescent home, God may have redeemed my hasty decision. Yet, to this day, I regret not letting Gary play ball.

MOVING TIME CAME AROUND AGAIN. Destination—Montana, where Jerry would work for his brother-in-law. Montana turned out to be a trial that would shake my faith, plunging me into a spiritual desert that would threaten my hope and my marriage.

## ~ **January 1979** ~

"Jerry, I sure hope this works out for us. Am I going to be taking care of six kids? Yours and mine?" *I sound so selfish.*

"Don't worry, Jude. My kids live out of town on a farm. We'll probably hardly ever see them. Hey, I'm glad we bought this maxi van. It will be a comfortable trip for us. And when we do have all our kids together there'll be plenty of room."

"Well, I don't want to be driving it around. It's too big for me." *I can't believe we bought this big horse.*

That *big horse* proved to be helpful while in a snowstorm on Montana highway I-15 between Boulder and Helena. Huge flakes of white blew so thick Judy could barely see the taillights in front of them. "Jerry, slow down. Why are you going so fast when you can't even see through all that snow?"

"I'm only going 20 mph, Jude. It just looks like we're going fast because of the snow blowing against the car." Fear showed on everyone's faces.

Gary's knuckles were white as he gripped the seats from behind. He kept telling the other kids to be quiet, as if he was the one doing the driving. "Follow that big truck, Dad."

"What do you think I'm doing? I'm pretty sure he's trying to guide us through the storm. This is the worst I've ever driven in."

Needless to say, Judy was praying Scripture in her spirit. "Every valley shall be exalted, and every mountain and hill brought low; the crooked places shall be made straight, and the rough places smooth. ~ Isaiah 40:4"

And so, with God's help, Jerry and the truck driver got them through the snowstorm. They thanked the truck driver with a honk and a wave. Judy and the kids praised their God. The road would continue to be rough-living in Montana.

## Harve, Montana

After only two weeks and settled in their new home, Jerry popped in for lunch. "Judy, because of today's storm, my kids can't get home so they'll be staying with us. Hope you have enough to feed four extra kids."

"What do you mean four extra?"

"Their little sister, Angie, will also be staying here."

"Oh." *So much for not having to take care of three extra kids. Now I have four plus my three. Seven kids! Yikes!*

As it turned out, they were all good kids and Judy didn't mind at all. She was cooking and cleaning after four extra bodies. She even learned how to bake bread. *If only Jerry liked my cooking.* And guess who taught her? Jerry's ex-wife! Judy and Patty became friends.

All of Jerry's family lived in this eastern town of Montana. He was one successful, educated, and popular guy among them. He spent a lot of his time going out with his nieces, leaving Judy home alone with the kids. Steve and Gary felt like they lost favor with him running out of their lives. If they ever wanted permission to do something, they would have Jerry's boys ask because he always said yes to them. Steve and Curtis were the same age. Opposite in their looks, Steve had blond hair and blue eyes and Curtis had dark hair and dark eyes. Gary and Gerald were the same age. Gary was small for his age and Gerald was tall and lanky, he looked a lot like his Dad. Tiffany and Nicole Denée were close to the same age. Tiffany had blond hair with blue eyes while Denée had dark hair and big brown eyes. They all had a great time together.

But not all was good in the Wood household. Steve was struggling and Judy felt his pain. While putting clothes away one day she found a note in his drawer. This proved her concern for her first born. She eased herself onto the edge of his bed to read it.

> I don't like going to school, the kids pick on me every day. Dad doesn't pay any attention to us kids, only his kids. No one understands me. I needed shoes to run a marathon and Mom buys me some from the grocery store. I'm not very happy.
> Steve Wood

Judy's body went limp as she slid to her knees and put her head in her hands, trying to brush overwhelming sadness away. After a few moments passed, she continued with the chores at hand. That night when all the kids were in bed, Judy sat by the window and watched the lightning in the sky. It was like natural fireworks. This really was "Big Sky Country" in Montana. *I need to get a job Lord, so I have spending money for me and the kids. I want them to be able to go to camp with the church and pay for extra things the kids need. Help me!* Judy opened her bible and read a Scripture that spoke to her. She claimed it for her family. "I will circumcise your heart and the **heart of your seed** to love the Lord thy God with all your heart, soul and mind." ~ Deut. 30:6

"Oh wait, I think circumcision might hurt. *Duh…*"

## ~ **Spring 1979** ~

Not only did Judy get to pay for the boys to go to camp, she was able to pay for another young man who didn't have the money. The morning they went to camp with the church, left Nicole Denée and Judy home alone, while Jerry was visiting his kids on their farm *with their mother!* Oh, that left her with a jealous heart. *I hate pity parties for one.* Her eyes stung with hurt. She didn't know what to do about it, and then about noon a thought came to her. "Denée, get your PJs. We're going to find the camp where the boys are and spend the night there." Denée was all up for that and they were on their way in twenty minutes.

By now they had traded the maxi van in for a smaller car. Judy had driven that *horse* into the ditch too many times and it was too big to dig out. Black ice was a devil in disguise. And with snow on the banks, it was impossible to know where the road ended and the ditch began. Even though Judy was a taxi driver for all seven kids, she only had two to four at a time. Never, all seven at once.

They were only on the road for forty-five minutes when Denée pointed out the window. "Mom, I think that's it."

"Hurray! I think you're right." And she was. They walked right in to the camp like they belonged. A couple of ladies came towards them with a welcome hello. Judy threw her shoulders back. "I came to help."

"That's great. Would you like to peel some potatoes?" the older one said.

"Sure, anything. I just want to be here."

"Well, do you know the Lord sent you?"

Judy was really confused. "No, I never heard anything like that before. What do you mean?"

"Our other helper had to leave because of a family emergency." The older lady with the soiled apron on, tucked a strand of hair back into her hairnet. "So you and your daughter can have her bed."

"Oh my gosh, I never even thought of where we would sleep. I guess I wasn't thinking at all." So Judy and Denée helped in the kitchen which was in the back of the large meeting room. The speakers and musicians could be seen and heard while they prepared the meal. The boys were surprised to see their mom and sister there but didn't mind at all. God got Judy through an otherwise difficult weekend.

Still she spent many nights alone while her husband was out and about. Judy was becoming jealous, angry, bitter, and depressed. Every morning she talked to God while fixing her hair. "Lord, I don't want to pray to You anymore but for the first time ever I'm afraid if I die I'll go to Hell, so please keep me in the palm of Your hand." She would flip open her Bible and read one verse, just to cover all the bases. But it still wasn't enough to drown out the one thing that always convicted her.

A self-proclaimed wimp, Judy was disgusted with herself. Feeling like an outcast and hearing comments regarding her faith, she had made a request of her husband—in a desire to fit into this new place, she actually asked, "Jerry I want you to tell your family that I am not a Christian." Oh my God. *Lord, I can't believe I did that. I never meant it in my heart. I feel so much like Peter. Please forgive me. I'm so ashamed.*

## ~ Fall 1979 ~

Curled up in her bed in the middle of the day, soft footsteps crept into her room. "Mom, are you okay? I'm worried about you." Gary sat on the edge of Judy's bed.

"Yes, Gar Bear. Thanks for asking."

"But Mom, you don't seem yourself. You seem so sad all the time!"

"Well, I guess you're right. I haven't been myself."

"What is it, Mom? Mental, physical, or spiritual?"

"Oh Gary, I guess it's all three. Mentally, I'm confused. Physically, I'm tired all the time, and spiritually, I'm not where I should be with the Lord."

He put his hand on hers. "Then I'm going to be praying for you, Mom, just like you've always prayed for me." Kneeling by the bed, he bent his head and his little prayer touched her soul. "Dear Lord, please help my mom be happy again. Give her back her energy, and most of all, help her feel Your love. And mine too, Lord."

"I appreciate that, Gar Bear," she whispered. Her eyes filled with tears but there was a smile in her heart.

Gary would see his prayers answered rather quickly. The next day someone handed Judy a book, for no reason really. It was called,

"How to Be the Wife of a Happy Husband." *Hmm, he already seems happy, what about me?* She read it anyway and started applying things learned in the book regarding her actions and reactions. As Judy changed, Jerry stopped going out with his nieces and stayed closer to home. He even took her on an overnight date into the *big city* of Great Falls. Judy always hated leaving the kids home alone but Jerry insisted.

Coming home from their date, they found Gerald and Gary sitting in the dark kitchen eating cereal. It was about 8:00 p.m. "What's up with you guys?" Judy immediately sensed something wasn't right. They looked at each other but no one answered.

"Gary?" Jerry walked to the table.

"You tell them, Gerald." Gary kept nibbling at his cereal.

"Okay, I taught Gary how to drive the truck. Uhh, your turn, Gary."

"Well, we just stayed in the driveway. Umm, your turn, Gerald."

Jerry placed his hands on the table and leaned toward them. "Someone better spit it out—now."

Gary stood up. "We have something to show you. Come on, Gerald."

The parents followed the boys out the door onto the snow-covered driveway. They both stood in front of the garage door and pointed. They finally told the story. Turns out, they didn't just *stay in the driveway.* After young farm boy, Gerald, had driven through the fields around the house, Gary wanted his turn. As a thirteen-year-old from California, Gary had yet to drive. To make matters more challenging this was a manual 4-speed. Gladly, Gerald taught Gary how to drive the truck. Unfortunately, they approached the house a little too fast. From the beginning of the lesson, Gary was responsible for the clutch and Gerald was responsible for the gas. The brake responsibility had yet to be discussed. So, as the story went, when Gerald yelled at Gary to stop the truck, Gary stepped on the clutch as the truck coasted right through the garage door and almost into the back yard. The bricks busted and flew everywhere.

They had gone to the contractor neighbor and borrowed some cement to attempt fixing it before the parents got home. Not good. It was a job for a professional and they ended up surrendering a good amount of allowance to help pay for it. Of course, that was just to teach them a lesson. All was forgiven and became a funny memory.

Steve struggled with a lack of self-worth and confidence. His feelings of inadequacy got the best of him as he tried to figure himself out. He so wanted to be accepted. His faith was also shaken. Now, it was mom's turn to be the prayer warrior. When he left for school, she would get a baby picture of him, put it on the bed and get on bended knees. Judy prayed Psalm 23 for him every day he was at school. *When my kids hurt, Lord, I hurt.*

One morning, Judy sensed the Lord speaking to her heart. *Go look in Steve's bedroom.* Obeying immediately, she walked down the steps to the basement and opened his door. Her eyes scanned his bedroom. *What am I looking for? Is it another note like I found before?* She scrambled around his wastepaper basket. Nothing there. Then, she opened his dresser drawers one by one. No notes or letters. With her hands, she felt under his mattress. Bingo—six bottles of wine! *Oh, no! God, how could you let this happen?*

When Jerry got home, she told him what she'd found. Even though Jerry did not share their faith, when the chips were down, he supported Judy in the important areas. After dinner that evening, they sat Steve down for a little chat. "Steve, your mom found these bottles of wine under your mattress today! What's up with that?"

"Oh, those belong to my friend."

"What friend is that?"

"I can't tell you."

Jerry frowned. "Why is your bedroom window unlocked?"

"Oh, so I can go to the bathroom during the night."

Judy's eyes bore into his. "What? You've got to be kidding. It's been eighteen degrees at night. Does your pee freeze?"

"You're grounded for two weeks," Jerry proclaimed.

Later while they were discussing Steve's behavior, Judy thought she'd get her husband's opinion on something. "Jerry, when Steve is in church he's not paying attention and he doesn't want to be there anymore. Do you think I should just let him stay home with you if he wants to?"

"No, at age fifteen, he's not old enough to make that decision."

"Okay then." *Lord, thank you for speaking through Jerry.*

## Leaving Montana ~ Summer 1980

The sun had not come up yet, when Judy and the kids prepared for their trip—returning to California! "Are we all set, kids?"

"Yeah, Mom! Hey Denée, do you have to take Grover everywhere? You've had that thing since we left Antioch."

"He's my favorite and I don't want the movers to lose him."

"Oh, brother." Gary rolled his eyes. "He looks pretty raggedy."

"Steve." Judy tossed her keys to her oldest. "Now that you have your driver's license, you can help me drive back to California. Dad has a house waiting for us."

"Cool. How many places will we stop on the way?"

"We'll probably stay one night in Great Falls and then stop one or two more nights after that. I guess we're set. Let's pray before we take off."

"I'll pray," Gary volunteered. "Lord, please protect us while we travel back to California. Help Steve not get us in an

*Gary, Denée, and Steve—What a team!*

accident. Help us not fight and help us find a good place to sleep for the night. In Jesus name!"

## Great Falls, MT

"This is the Christian Bed and Breakfast I heard about. We'll stay here."

"Oh goodie," Denée unbuckled her seatbelt.

Exiting the car, Judy's clothes felt sticky and the warm air did little to eliminate the feeling. Gary reached the door first and rang the bell. A tall, dark-haired woman in her forties opened the blue door with white trim. "Hello."

"Hi, my name is Judy. I called ahead of time about getting two rooms for the night?"

"Oh, let me get my mother." She spoke without emotion, her sober face held no expression. "Mom, there's a family here to stay for the night."

A friendly face came from around the doorway. "Hi, I'm Lois and this is my daughter, Becky. Please come in and welcome!" She was much friendlier than her daughter.

Judy stepped into the livingroom. "Oh, this is charming."

"Yes, we…I love it. My husband passed away a few months ago, we both loved the place. Your rooms are upstairs. The first one on the right is for you and your daughter…?"

"Oh, I'm sorry, this is Nicole, I mean Denée and my sons, Steve and Gary."

"Nice to meet you. Your rooms are right next to your mom's. I have some snacks for you in the kitchen, this way. Breakfast will be served at seven o'clock sharp. Becky is in charge of that and she doesn't want anyone to be late. Oh, and this is our dog, Ginger."

The kids petted Ginger as she lazily moved to them and smiled with her tail. She was a golden retriever-mixed breed dog. After a nice snack, they checked out the bedrooms. Steve flopped onto the nearest bed. "Did you notice how cold Becky is, compared to Lois, who is so warm and friendly?"

"Yeah. How could you not?" Gary dove onto the other bed.

"I didn't notice." Denée proclaimed.

"What world are you in," the boys teased.

"I think it's nice she didn't notice, but I think we should pray for Becky. She's obviously not a happy woman. Lois just lost her husband and maybe Becky is taking it hard. You know they say, a situation like that can make you either bitter or better. Let's pray."

## The next morning

Judy and her kids rushed to get to breakfast on time so Becky wouldn't get upset with them. She cooked bacon, eggs, potatoes, and toast. "*Umm*, this is good." Steve shoveled another forkful of eggs into his mouth.

Denée scooped more jam on her toast. "I like this boysenberry jam, Mom."

Gary, being the picky eater, didn't want his eggs. He shyly looked at Becky who was in the kitchen area then whispered to Judy, "Mom, I don't want the rest of my breakfast, what should I do?"

"Tell Becky thank you but you don't want anymore and ask what she wants you to do with it."

He took slow sheepish steps toward Becky. She looked at him with that stern look of hers. "Just put it on the floor for the dog."

Gary looked back at Judy then shrugged his shoulders. He bent down and scraped his food off his plate and onto the floor.

Judy was startled and raised her voice. "Gary why did you do that?"

"Becky told me to!"

Judy looked over at Becky's wide eyes and suddenly her frown turned upside down. Laughter came from deep inside her and she couldn't stop. "I meant to put the plate on the floor, not the food."

She barely managed to get it out for laughing so hard as she ran from the room. "Mom, you'll never guess what just happened."

"Well, I guess our prayers helped her," said Denée. "She's smiling now!"

Certificate of Honor

on This 14 Day of July 1982
Congradulations...
Judy A. Wood for being the winner of the meanest mom award You really deserve this, congradulations Meanie!!!

President Gary Wood
x Gary Wood

Secretary
x Denee Wood

P.S. one of your greatest tasks not letting your kids have cupcakes

# Chapter 19

## Nicole Denée Wood

### Moving to a new school ~ Fall 1980

Denée slipped a few more bracelets over her wrist, glanced in her bedroom mirror, and flipped her hair. So short, it looked *dorky*. Too bad, a girl couldn't grow it out in less than an hour. Another closer look in the mirror assured her she had a sense of style when it came to the rest of her outfit—and she'd need every bit of it today. She was starting seventh grade—alone. All her friends lived in Montana, and as for family—she finally made it to middle school and they moved up to high school. "Why did Mom and Dad pick this year to uproot the family?" She peered over her sunglasses at Grover. "Seriously, that's just cruel!"

Grover stared back with sympathetic eyes and she resisted the urge to stuff him in her backpack. She'd face this by herself. But not alone. She bowed her head and whispered, "God give me a friend."

She was never the girl that stood out in the crowd, but somehow she found her way to the crowd and truly enjoyed being around others. After school, she dropped her books on the dresser, scooped up Grover, and flopped onto her bed. "You know what they say about girls? We travel in herds and I'm doing just that." She hugged her furry friend to her chest. "I found a friend, Jessica, and she took me to her crowd. Her people are my people…well, kind of. You see, I have this other friend I met, Kerry, but she's from Washington and just a little different than the others. I want her to be a part of my *new* people, but she's reluctant."

Over the next few months, no matter how Denée tried to get her two friends to connect, they each seemed resistant, so she tried to balance both, because Kerry needed her and, frankly, she needed Jessica. So Denée tried her best to hang on to Jessica while keeping Kerry in her life. Kerry didn't really have anyone. She lived with her grandparents and her mom, who had recently divorced Kerry's father and worked late afternoons and into the night as a nurse. Denée understood divorce. Her mom had been married three times and even though her current step-dad, Jerry, was a good dad, she often felt like she missed out on the traditional family unit. Whereas, Jessica had two parents, a nice house, nice things, nice friends and lots of them. *She even has a dog!* Yes. Jessica embodied the American Dream.

Denée carried on this wrestling match with herself—she could hang out with Kerry, who had very little supervision, lots of soda, and tons of freedom—or pursue her friendship with Jessica and her fashionable, popular crowd. And she was fashionable herself, hadn't Jessica complimented her on her style? Which of course, made Denée like her instantly! She carried on like that for almost a year, receiving a lot of grief from Kerry for being friends with Jessica, but Jessica was nothing but nice—never rude to anyone. *So why does Kerry have a problem with Jessica?*

Toward the end of seventh grade her friendship with Kerry was falling apart and she was very sad. She liked Kerry and knew her family life wasn't the best. She believed God put her in Kerry's life for a reason and would pray for her friend, but Kerry didn't want her prayers. Over the summer before eighth grade Denée discovered why—Kerry was beginning to do drugs. Denée didn't want to believe it! She confronted her friend and Kerry denied it, but she was changing not just on the inside, but on the outside, as well. Kerry didn't seem as happy and she began to dress differently, not just a change in style, but it was almost like she didn't care. Denée finally took a stand and told her that even though she cared for her so much, she didn't want to be a part of Kerry's new lifestyle. "Kerry, please." Tears streamed down Denée's cheeks as she tried to loop her arm through her friend's arm. "You need to get some help."

"I'm not doing drugs and I don't need help." Kerry pushed her away. "I don't need you."

"I've seen you take pills at school. Everyone's seen you. Maybe your grandparents—"

"No. Grandma is oblivious..." Kerry's face drained of color. "And Grandpa only takes. You don't know anything about living in a nightmare. I'll find my own way out." She spun and stormed off, leaving Denée to walk home alone.

When Denée got home, even the smell of Mom's spaghetti sauce couldn't lift her spirits. Losing Kerry was hard. "Mom, I miss Kerry's friendship, her great sense of humor, and outgoing personality—it's been slipping away, but now it's really gone. I should have saved her."

Mom shook her head and her eyes looked sad. "You're not responsible for the actions of others. It's not your fault she chose to pull away from you. As much as you want to hold onto all your friendships, you have to know when to let them go."

"It's painful. I don't know why she stopped liking me."

"Maybe she hasn't."

"You mean...she's protecting me? From what?" *It must be something more than drugs.*

Mom shrugged and turned back to stirring the spaghetti.

Kerry's ashen face flitted through Denée's mind. Her friend had nearly fainted when she spoke of her grandpa. Could he be hurting her? Denée shuddered. Impossible. That kind of thing was unheard of.

Even though, Denée could see how God guided her away from those influences, she struggled knowing that Kerry felt she had no way out. After reluctantly letting go, Denée became closer to Jessica and some of her friends and was glad to have been welcomed into their lives. Even though she didn't have the history they had with each other, she felt happy to belong to a crowd. Her heart never stopped breaking for her former friend.

## Her hero, Steve ~ Summer 1982

Transitioning from middle school to high school was exciting and even though Denée would finally be able to be at the same school as her brother, Gary, she would be saying goodbye to her brother, Steve. Being four years apart, he seemed so much older than her and their relationship never felt very strong. The summer before ninth grade, she did some babysitting for her piano teacher and her friend around the corner. Both were from Texas and had that southern drawl, so when a man named Matt called and started asking her questions, she thought it was the father of the Texas family she babysat for.

"What color is your hair?"

"Brown."

"How tall are you, again?

"Uh…" She thought his questions were strange and wondered when he was going to ask her about babysitting, when suddenly, Steve stormed into the room and grabbed the phone out of her hand.

"Listen here, you creep! Stop calling this number and stay away from my sister!" He slammed the phone down and turned to Denée, his eyes were still fuming, but his

*Denée and Steve*

voice was gentle and she knew his anger was not for her. "Denée, from now on, never answer personal questions when you don't know the person really well, especially men."

"Oh, okay!" She gave him a relieved smile. Steve was so wise. He worked long hours and went to school, which meant he was rarely home. Up until then, she felt she was losing her big brother, but now she knew he would look out for her if she ever needed him.

## Running in Gary's footsteps ~ Fall 1982

Finally, she was in the *Big House*, Casa Grande High School, and with her brother, Gary. As Denée walked onto the campus the first day of school, people she didn't even know said hi to her. "Oh, you're Steve and Gary's younger sister. If you need anything let us know," a junior said. Cheerleaders, football players, juniors and seniors singled her out. She knew her brothers were well-liked, because people on campus seemed to like her, too. It felt so good to have older kids greeting her—a puny little freshman—and her friends thought it was pretty cool, as well. The teachers knew her brothers, too! They would call role, make the connection, and smile at her. Middle school was just a blur. The future looked bright and she was happy.

However, living in the shadow of two older and apparently, popular brothers proved to be somewhat challenging for Denée. Why did they have to be so good at everything? Both, Steve and Gary were accomplished athletes. Steve was quite the charmer and Gary was an exceptional student and Denée, well, she was none of those things! She couldn't be a charmer and while her grades were good, they weren't exceptional, so when her family encouraged her to run cross country she considered it. *Well, anyone can run.* During the first week of practice, she learned how hard she would have to work just to finish the race. She struggled with running and unfortunately found out she wasn't going to carry on the tradition of excellent runners in the family. Still, she stuck it out and always tried her hardest. It took her at least a quarter of the way through the season before she wasn't finishing dead last! She started to improve her time and running came a little easier for her, but still it was never truly easy.

By the time the season finished up, she was so disappointed that she wasn't a *good* runner and, yes, she felt defeated. However, the coach didn't think so and he awarded her The Most Improved Runner for which she was grateful. As the applause died down Gary received The Most *Valuable* Runner. Now, the focus was off her for which she was relieved and as everyone clapped for Gary, she felt a sense of family pride. *Wow, my brother's really great.*

## Cheerleader tryouts ~ Spring 1983

Denée's friends encouraged her to try out for cheerleading, *Me, a cheerleader? Only popular girls are cheerleaders.* She knew most of the cheerleaders, including her good friend, Jessica, but Denée wasn't super good friends with the others and she felt very insecure. *There's no way I'm going to make the team.* But, for some reason being a cheerleader was all she could think of on the way home. "Hey Mom," Denée burst through the door. "Can I try out for cheerleading?"

The look on Mom's face said she wasn't thrilled. As usual, her mom would be worried about the cost and well, she probably didn't have the best view of cheerleaders. "I tried out for song girl when I was your age and came in seventh place."

"Wow, how many were on the team?"

"Six." Mom turned back to folding laundry and her voice grew quiet. "I cried for weeks."

Denée slowly nodded. "Yeah, and I'm afraid I won't make it anyway, so I'm fine with not giving it a try."

Mom's head popped back up and she looked Denée straight in the eyes. "Don't ever not try something because you're afraid of failure."

Denée thought about that and honestly, she did fear failure. Her brothers seemed to succeed at everything they put their hands to—at least that's the way they're little sister saw it. It really was an important moment for her. She needed to stop comparing herself to her brothers and try out anyway. *If I fail, I fail and I can always try again.* These were not easy words to live by and honestly, she may always struggle with that concept.

Well, she made up her mind—she was going to give it a try. She prepared the best she could, practiced the cheers they taught at cheer clinic, teamed up with another girl trying out, and practiced every weekend leading up to the tryouts. The day finally came and it seemed like at least a hundred girls wanted to be cheerleaders. Denée's stomach was in knots and deep down inside, she just knew she wasn't going to make it, but she still wanted to try. The judges sat behind the tables and each girl went up on their own. Some girls were so relaxed, while others were anxious and unsure. She was the latter! Her turn was about to come up and she just said a little prayer asking God to help her get through it—but she forgot to mention to Him to help her make the team. Honestly, she just wanted to get it over with! As her turn came up, she noticed a familiar face. Her brother's friend, Gunther, the senior vice president was a judge. *Oh, no, not him.* He kept smiling at her and he was super cute, too! The butterflies got worse at that point, but there was no turning back. "Ready, okay…" She did the best she could under these circumstances. Her eye contact wasn't the best and her voice cracked a few times and she probably should have been louder. She just kept telling herself, "It's almost over."

Well, it was over and she was so relieved. The contestants were told the list of those who made it would be posted the next day by the Multi-Purpose Room. *Oh, goody, now everyone in the entire school can see who didn't make it. This ought to be interesting.* Only eight girls would make the team. That would leave a lot of broken hearts, for sure. The night after the tryouts, Mom served a nice dinner. "Whether you make it or not, I'm proud of you for trying."

Gary grinned at her from across the table. "If you don't make it, they're stupid and I'm going to be ticked off."

Denée hid her smile. *Yay, I think he's definitely cheering for me!* Of course, Mom was preparing her for either outcome, but Denée mostly prepared herself for the worst. Even her step-dad, Jerry, was certain she would make it! Sadly, Steve, wasn't there that night, but she was sure he would have threatened to beat someone up if need be!

After a restless night's sleep, she reluctantly got ready for school wanting to get there a little early so she wouldn't be completely humiliated, but lucky for her, everyone else had the same idea. As she walked the *green mile* up to the window, which was plastered with the lists of names of those lucky enough to have been chosen as part of next year's cheer squad, she took a big breath and continued her walk toward the list. After finding the JV Cheer list, she examined it thoroughly, not once, but twice and her name was nowhere to be found. So many others like her walked away with their heads held low, while other girls screamed for joy. *Ugh, the agony of defeat.* It only confirmed what she already knew, she wasn't good enough. She did her best to be gracious and happy for the few who made it. A couple of her really good friends made it and she didn't want them to feel bad. They should be proud and excited. They probably wanted it more than her, anyways, and she was happy for them. She didn't even shed a tear, although her pride was wounded— she wouldn't lie—it hurt. She went home feeling like it was all for the best and it wasn't the end of the world—*but it still would've been nice. Maybe God has other plans for me.* She did find comfort in God, knowing that He doesn't really care who makes the cheer squad. He loves everyone just the same.

Mom was home waiting for her and Denée was sure she'd been praying for her all day. Mom's prayer would have been something like, "God, please help my daughter accept the outcome with dignity and grace." Mom always told Denee that grace was her gift. But what on earth did that mean? It must have something to do with being able to accept the outcome of things without throwing a fit, because Mom usually told her about this marvelous gift when she didn't get what she'd been hoping for. Denée greeted Mom with a downcast look, but told her it was fine and she was glad she'd tried out. She really wasn't glad she'd tried out, but that's what Mom would want to hear. That afternoon they went to Gary's track meet, which was a nice distraction. She had come to terms with the whole cheerleading thing and was already thinking she should consider cross country, again. *Maybe torture is the answer!*

The next day Gary drove her to school like usual, but this time there was a lot of commotion over by the dreaded Multi-Purpose Room. She really didn't want to go over there again, but kids were gathering by the multitudes and she could hear things like… "Can you believe that?" or "I've never heard of that happening." Well, her curiosity got the better of her, so she headed over there herself. As she got closer, some of the girls smiled at her and said congratulations. *Congratulations for what?! Oh my gosh, what are those lists still doing up?* Those girls must have confused her with someone else, but as she got closer, she noticed that someone had added two more names to the JV Cheer squad and her heart starting beating faster when she noticed one of the names was hers. "Someone's playing a cruel joke." She started to turn away.

*Denée Wood*

"No, look." Jessica pointed to the words at the bottom of the list. "We have decided to increase the JV Squad by two more girls. Congratulations to everyone. There will be a mandatory meeting after school in the gym."

She was not quite sure how big the smile on her face was, but others seemed to notice it and they were very happy for her.

*Denée with Casa Grande Cheerleaders*

Now, I realize that cheerleading isn't the end all, but I learned a valuable lesson here. I learned to give something a try even if you think failure is inevitable. Maybe it is, but we learn from each failure in our lives. It really isn't how many times you fail, but rather, how many times you get up, brush yourself off, and try again or even try something else.

My sophomore year would be the last year that I would enjoy the freedoms that come with being young and carefree, because little did I know, my life would be turned upside down by divorce, brokenness, and having to grow up faster than I had ever imagined. I am not bitter about my upbringing. I would have loved the outcome to be different, but I am who I am because of the experiences I've been through. I've always had the best Father—my heavenly Father. I am so grateful that my faith only grew from here and now, I pass that same faith on to my three beautiful daughters, who will have lessons of their own.

~ Nicole Larson

# Chapter 20

## Judy Wood

As I look back, I can now see clearly that God held me in the palm of His hand, just like I asked Him to. In some ways, moving around a lot kept our family close. We finally settled where we could make a more permanent home.

Sadly, Jerry and I were growing apart. This would be the beginning of the end for my third failed marriage. Maybe Jerry got bored with me, but in the end, it was my bitterness that drove him away.

In the meantime, my children grew stronger in the Lord with a few bumps along the way.

### Petaluma, California ~ 1983

Judy took a deep breath. If she didn't open up now, she might never confess this to her husband. And, like it or not, something had to change. "Jerry, something is missing in our marriage and I'm not all that satisfied. Could we go to counseling together?" She held her breath.

He actually looked up from the paper. "No way, you know I don't believe in that stuff."

She couldn't quite read the emotions on his face. He popped the paper back into place and mumbled from behind it. "Tell you what, we'll take a second out on the house and use it to go on a trip and maybe fix up the house a little."

"Are you sure we should do that?" *I hate having more bills.*

"Yes, it'll be fine, you'll see. And Jude, I think you should get a job." He pulled out the page with the want ads and handed it to her.

"Really? I don't want to but if you think I should, then I'll check it out." One glance at the help wanted section and her heart sank. "There's not much here. I'm going to have a hard time getting back into the job market."

Judy searched for several weeks to find a position, but without a second car, she couldn't apply to the across-town jobs that fit her skill set.

"Jude, I don't think you're trying hard enough." Jerry raised his voice.

She screamed back at him. "What do you want me to do?"

His jaw went all tight. "Just take anything to get some experience!"

On foot, Judy begrudgingly left her chores undone to see what she could find at the strip mall on McDowell Avenue. It was exactly one mile from her house at 1032 Catalpa Way. *I don't want to do retail but I have to get Jerry off my back.*

BURGER KING—Help Wanted. *Hummm, I think I'll apply just so I can say I did. They only hire teenagers anyway. How old am I? Oh yea, forty-one.* She waltzed in, asked for an application, filled it out, and got the job! *Oh, brother!*

## That evening

It was dinner as usual. Judy set the table, put the spaghetti and garlic bread in the center, then set out a pitcher of water and milk. Most of the time, she did everything with no help. She didn't want her kids burdened with things like she was. And besides, she loved serving her family. "Who's turn to say blessing?"

"I'll say it, Mom."

"Thank you, Steve."

*I'm so happy Steve is serving the Lord again.* After the blessing was said and everyone got served, Judy made her announcement between chews. "I have good news, guys. I got a job today and I start tomorrow."

All wide smiles around the table. "Congratulations." Jerry nodded his head as if to say *I knew you could find a job.*

"That's great, Mom." The kids said one by one.

"Where will you be working?" Gary grabbed another piece of garlic bread.

Judy reached around for the bag lying next to her and pulled out her brown and yellow uniform with the floppy orange collar. "What, no more smiles?"

Jerry's face went cold and the boys' eyes went wide. Denée was the only one still smiling.

"Mom, that's embarrassing." Gary threw his head back and sighed.

Steve looked horrified. "Mom, please don't tell any of my friends you work there."

"Hey Mom, can we get free hamburgers?" Denée's smile got even bigger.

Jerry slammed his fork down. "I agree with Gary. It's embarrassing, especially since I'm V.P. of my company."

"Oh well, it's too late now. I accepted the job but I promise I won't tell your friends where I work, Steve."


## The next day


"One Whopper, one Whaler, two fries, and two cokes. Here's your receipt. It'll be right up."

"Hi, Mrs.Wood. I didn't know you worked here!"

*Oh brother! So much for not telling their friends.* "Hi there—hey don't tell Steve or Gary you saw me, okay?"

"Oh, I'll tell them alright. Ha-ha!"

## ~ **January 1984** ~

Judy and Jerry never went on a trip. They never did any remodeling. Who knows what happened to the money from the second mortgage they took out on the house. Judy became a bitter woman. After working all day, cooking and cleaning at night gave her no time to relax or be with her family. But, that's not what bothered her. While she was doing dishes or whatever, she could hear the family laughing at something on television and no one missed her. She felt so insignificant.

"It's late, Mom, where's Dad?"

"I really don't know, but I have to get to bed, morning comes early. You guys better hit the hay." Judy went to bed but couldn't get to sleep. About an hour later, the front door opened. Then, her bedroom door. She sat up in bed. "Jerry, why are you so late?"

"I was procrastinating." He looked like he had a dark cloud over him. "Judy, I've made a decision. I'm moving out."

Her head hung without permission. Her dry eyes went wet. Her mouth found it hard to speak. "Are you sure?"

"Once I make a decision, I don't look back. I'll go tell the kids."

One by one, Judy listened—soft whimpers came from brave Gary, then wailing from her darling, Denée, but nothing from her sensitive Steve. *Lord, don't let him hold onto bitterness like I do.*

"Jerry left me, Donna. I suppose I had it coming. I was bitter and didn't try to hide it."

"Jude, I've watched you come to church alone for years now. It reminds me of a line in a movie." She reached across the table and patted Judy's hand. "If you are going to be alone, you might as well be by yourself."

The words rang with truth and Judy struggled to keep her voice steady. "I don't know how to mend a broken heart, Donna, but this I do know: God has a purpose for my pain, a reason for my struggles, and He has always been faithful even when I wasn't."

*Us four and no more*

# Chapter 21

## Gary Wood

### Disqualified ~ Spring 1984

Gary threw his gym bag over his shoulder and headed into the locker room. The day had finally arrived for the California North Coast Track and Field Championships—his chance for self-vindication. This journey started six months earlier, at the conclusion of a disappointing senior cross-country season. Having lost only one race the entire year in Sonoma County dual meets he'd barely finished fifth at the county championships and try as he might, he could not stop the memories from arresting his focus.

*Gary Wood*

He had shown up that afternoon at Spring Lake Park in Santa Rosa feeling a bit queasy, but still confident. He could win this race. When the gun sounded, he darted out in his signature way to get out ahead of the pack. He came by the mile mark in 5:10 with his nemesis, Roy of Healdsburg, in close pursuit. Within only a few seconds, he went from feeling like he could continue pushing himself to a more painful level of labored breathing and burning muscles to a feeling of complete surrender. His energy was immediately sapped and he felt that he had involuntarily shifted from overdrive to second gear. Roy passed him in the next twenty yards as they rounded the west side of the lake. Gary followed him into the narrow trail that cut through a forest of trees over the next mile. As Roy pulled away, Gary felt the rhythmic breathing of two runners that had caught him from behind but were unable to pass because of the trail. When he finally exited the dirt trail to the open bike path that would take the runners through the last mile to the finish, runners two and three flew past, leaving Gary in fourth place. As the only Varsity runner from his high school, he needed to finish fifth in order to qualify for the next meet. He could hear two more runners closing in fast—threatening to put him into a season-ending sixth place. As number four passed, Gary was startled by a hand pushing in his middle back as he struggled intensely with every step hoping just to finish the race. He turned to see Eric, a runner from Analy High School, yelling at him to sprint to the finish. There were three more runners closing in with only a few hundred yards to go. Eric seemed to do the math and more surprising seemed hell bent on making sure Gary finished fifth. The last minute was a fog, but Gary somehow finished fifth, with Eric allowing him to cross the line just ahead of him. Gary was not even five yards past the line when the vomit starting coming in rapid-fire spurts. In his mind, Gary counted one, two, three…eleven—the number of times he puked at the feet of Eric and his coach. The local paper had been there to snap some very becoming pictures of him for the next day's sports page.

But that was six months ago. From the week after a very disappointing ninth place finish at the North Coast Cross-Country Championship, Gary began training for track season. He averaged over forty-five miles per week between November and February in order to reach the lofty goal of winning both the mile and two-mile races at the Sonoma County League Championships.

When track season started, his coach looked to him and a few others as leaders to motivate the team and perform beyond their capabilities in order to have a shot of a team championship.

He tossed his gym bag on the locker room bench and pulled out his uniform. He remembered very clearly standing in line on that unusually warm February afternoon to receive it. These school-issued uniforms were in their eighth year of service and the shorts were of a thick, dark green polyester material that emitted a faint, foul odor reminiscent of the bathroom at the old Jack In The Box in downtown Petaluma. Thankfully, the singlet was fairly new and smelled of detergent with the words CASA GRANDE in bold green pasted on a gold background. The shorts had been tight and not made for distance running so he'd shoved them in the back of his gym bag determined to wear his favorite, red, Sub 4® shorts for the season.

He pulled on his red shorts and zipped his bag closed—no need adding to the locker room smells—and headed out to the field. Over the course of the past few months he managed to go undefeated in both the mile and two-mile at all the county dual meets. He'd run a 4:31 mile and 9:58 two-mile during the regular season, and according to his distance coach the workouts he was completing had him in shape to run close to a 4:20 mile which was his ultimate goal. Today, he felt good.

Gary toed the line for the two-mile, right next to Roy, and looked over at his main competition. How was it the guy suddenly looked older? Roy was all muscle and more intense than Gary remembered. He glanced down at his own skinny legs and was embarrassed that his calves looked like strings hanging off the knees of his 117-pound frame. It was late afternoon and the sun stared him directly in the eyes. The gun rang out, taking him by surprise. Having made the mistake of going out too fast in the past, he took his brother's advice and let Roy have the lead. Steve was a great runner in his own right and in fact had been the two-mile school record holder before Gary broke it. He settled into second place as

*Competition*

Roy took off like a rocket leaving Gary almost a hundred yards behind at the mile mark. *Shoot! I'm going to have to settle for second place.* On lap five, he gained a few yards and started closing the gap ever so. He worked lap six as if it were his last and started reeling Roy in fast. The thought of catching him seemed to shoot adrenaline into his veins like an addict with a needle. He caught and passed Roy at the end of lap seven with only a lap remaining. Gary fully expected Roy to fall in to his strides and challenge him all the way to the finish so he put it in overdrive and started his sprint early. He crossed the line in first and only then realized that he'd outkicked Roy by nearly thirty yards with a time of 9:42 and a 63-second last lap—faster than he'd even run a last lap in the mile races. Finally, he'd avenged the cross-country season. The great disappointment in Roy's eyes proved it.

He enjoyed the moment for about five minutes before waking up to the cold fact that he had to run the mile in about an hour against a guy that would be thirsty for revenge. After being congratulated by cheerleaders in short yellow skirts that would normally pay him no attention, he walked over and sat under the shade of the oak tree that lived on the north end of the track. He must have sat too long because when he stood up he felt as though he were an old man reaching for his walker. He slowly stretched his thighs, hamstrings, and calves back to mobility and began warming up for the final race of the day. The mile was the race that everyone came out to see because it was the most popular race and would determine the team champions, or so Gary's coach told him.

The stands were full of parents and kids Gary had not seen at a track meet all year. A crowd lined both sides of the track anxiously awaiting the start. The race started and that 63-second, last lap of his two-mile race haunted him. His legs were heavy like a hollowed tree full of cement and his lungs burned with each expanding breath. He fell behind Roy and struggled just to maintain second place. Roy got smaller and smaller as he pulled away over the next two laps. Gary had at this point already determined that a second place league finish in the mile combined with his first place two-mile finish was very respectable. As he started the third lap, he saw his brother's face turning beat red as he screamed at Gary to get his ass moving. Instinctively, he pushed a little harder over the next hundred yards to appease Steve that he was giving it his full effort. He quickly realized that he gained just a little on Roy although he was still more than fifty yards behind as they came to the straight away before the final lap. Roy had this race won and his posture showed it. The crowd screamed and leaned into the lanes as Gary sprinted by, now digging as deep as he could to try to close the gap between himself and Roy. He felt as though he were reeling in a fish that wasn't putting up a fight as Roy seemed to come closer and closer into view over the next three-hundred yards. With only a hundred yards to go and still more than ten yards behind, the screams were deafening. Gary was closing in and Roy didn't even seem to be aware of the danger behind him. When they hit the finish tape it was Gary the officials awarded first place as he barely out leaned Roy. This was not his best mile time by far but still the best race of his running career.

The next Saturday at the exact same venue, Gary was entered

into the North Coast Section mile championship race. The top four finishers would move on to the Northern California Meet of Champions at Berkeley Stadium. Given the performance of his competition, he was certain he would need to run under 4:22 to finish top four and as nervous as he was, he was equally confident that his body could complete that task. This was what he'd trained for over the last six months. This was why he dragged himself out of his warm bed every morning at 6:00 a.m. before school to run an extra three miles before track practice. This was why he ran a lonely ten miles every Saturday along Adobe Road, past the cow pastures on the outskirts of Petaluma. This was why he didn't stay up late with his brother to watch *The Twilight Zone*. This was why he endured the ridicule at school for being a *goody two-shoes* and the nickname *Goody Woody* given to him by his good friend Kyle.

The stands were full of people from all over Northern California that Gary did not know. There were only a few runners he recognized from his league in the crowds of athletes readying themselves for their races and events. This was a meet for the elite and he felt pretty special. The race was a blur, but the finish was like no other. His bright yellow spikes and red shorts crossed the line in fourth place snatching the last spot to move on to the Meet of Champions. Before he was even fully across the line, a bitter voice coming from only two feet away yelled, "disqualified!"

He looked to his left to see one of the judges staring at him with disdain. He yelled at Gary in a voice louder than it needed to be, because he obviously wanted the world to hear his authoritative call. "You are disqualified for wearing red shorts which is not your school uniform." His upper lip curled as he turned and walked away.

*What? I didn't even know there was such a rule. I'm a 17 year old, 117-pound kid that's sacrificed a lot just to be at this race.* He decided right there, at that moment, that adults were stupid and petty. He walked away from the finish line, through a crowd of runners awaiting the next race, as nobody seemed to even know he was crushed.

Gary's head coach ran up. "Great race, Wood. Hey, fourth place isn't anything to be bummed about."

"I was disqualified for a non-uniform violation."

Coach looked down and seemed to notice the red shorts for the first time. "Well this isn't a beauty pageant, like *some* coaches want to make it." He smiled and clapped Gary on the shoulder. "Don't worry about it. I will take care of this."

Gary sank down onto the grass. *Coach was the most hated entity in Sonoma County among head track coaches. Some petty coach must have noticed at my league championships that I wear red shorts, and in an effort to get at Coach found, in the official high school track rule book, that every runner must wear a school issued uniform. Knowing that my school colors are green and gold it's obvious my shorts aren't school issued.* He punched the ground. *God, I hate adults! And, just what am I going to do next weekend now that my high school track career is over?*

Coach ran back. "It's settled, Gary, you've been awarded fourth place. You'll be going to the Meet of Champions after all."

"How, what, why?"

"Don't worry about it." He walked away with a smile.

Gary jumped to his feet. His racing career was still on track. He'd train that much harder.


He opened the sports page first thing the next morning, which had been his day-after-the-race ritual since he first saw his name in big print. The *Press Democrat* had a large story covering that Saturday's meet and to Gary's surprise, there was a portion dedicated to his disqualification fiasco. As he intently read the reporter's prose, he realized how he'd become re-qualified, which confused him. It turned out, as reported in the paper, his head coach explained to the Rules Committee that the shorts Gary wore were school issued, and they were red to signify his role as team captain. This untruth seemed to satisfy the committee and he was back in the running.

Gary, however, was now in turmoil. He knew it was wrong that he'd been disqualified—this little lie was completely justified to right the wrong. He'd worked incredibly hard to get here and felt God must have protected him from those petty adults that would have seen him miss his next meet due to some vendetta that other coach had with his head coach. But as the day wore on, Gary felt extremely guilty that a lie had saved him from disqualification. He caught his mom as soon as she got off work and explained the situation, fighting to override his guilt. "There's nothing I can do about it now. I wouldn't even know who to talk to about this."

His mom was not a well-educated woman, but she was smart enough in things of the heart and spirit to say what he needed to hear. "Gary, if you want to make this right, I know you can figure out who you need to talk to about this." She didn't say he should run. She didn't say he shouldn't run. She just bluntly said that he needed to do what he knew was right.

He grabbed the large phone book and started looking for the name he knew he had to find—the distance coach of his school's biggest rival, Piner High School. Despite the intense competition amongst the head coaches, Gary knew this coach respected him as a runner. He was a good man cheering on his own runners as well as other teams during the races. This was a good adult. Gary told him about his situation and asked him if he knew any members of the Rules Committee that would have made the decision to allow him to be *qualified* for the next race. The man did, and he gave Gary the phone number of the man in charge.

Gary dialed the number and tried to swallow his nervousness as he silently counted the rings. When the man picked up, he must have thought there was some kind of emergency, because Gary spoke so quickly. The man asked him to slow down and start over. Gary told him that his red shorts were not school issued and he felt the Rules Committee needed to know the truth. In a deep baritone voice, the man asked if Gary really wanted to share this information—giving him a chance to leave things as they were. "You know this means you will not be running in the Meet of Champions."

"Yes." Gary's voice was less than confident.

The man asked for Gary's number, thanked him, and hung up. Gary was sad, but felt very strong for some reason. He had just accomplished something even harder than running a 4:20 mile. He did the right thing when it cost him something big—a pride-worthy feat.

The next day at school, Gary broke the news to his head coach. He told him what he'd done and that he would not be running the MOC race on Saturday.

"Why did you do that without talking to me?" Coach's face whitened and he ran his fingers through his hair. "Your little self-righteous confession puts me in a tricky spot. Why in hell didn't you come to me first?"

Gary shrugged, not quite sure how to answer. He felt bad all over again.

*School record in the 3200 meters*

Late Monday night the phone rang and Steve handed Gary the receiver. The baritone voice was again on the other end. The man told him he had just come from a meeting of the head coaches in Sonoma County and they discussed Gary's disqualification from the MOC. The man congratulated him on coming forward with the truth and informed him that the coaches unanimously voted to let him run on Saturday. Gary was a little taken aback, but thanked him and quietly hung up the phone.

His season wasn't over.

# Chapter 22


# Judy Wood


I loved my mother one moment in time. But to this day, I don't miss her.


## ~ Spring 1984 ~

Judy's mother, Autumn, had been bedridden with Emphysema for many years. She was in and out of St. Luke's Hospital in San Francisco. One time in particular she was in a coma and wasn't expected to pull out of it. Judy visited Mother as often as possible. She prayed for her—and over her—and drew on a Scripture that proved to work on another occasion. "Lord, by Your stripes my mother is healed." No sooner did she say that, Mother's pinkie finger moved. "Nurse, my mother just moved her finger!" The nurse walked slowly to Mother's bed and checked her vitals.

"Sorry honey, but those reflexes just happen sometimes. It doesn't look good." She gave Judy a weak smile and padded back out of the room.

Judy hated to leave, because for the first time, she could ever remember, she wasn't afraid of her mother. *She can't hurt me with her words or snarling looks.* Judy prayed for her again and, for the first time in her memory, she felt love for her mother like a daughter should. For once, she actually wanted to stay. Unfortunately, she had a ninety-minute bus ride back to Petaluma and had a family to care for.

Autumn pulled out of her coma the next day. It would be awhile before she could talk so visits were quite pleasant. Judy read to her mother and tenderly put lotion on her. It was the only time she felt close to her mother. Until…

"Hi, Cissy," the familiar voice croaked.

"Mother, you got your voice back."

"Yeah— now you don't have to read to me anymore. You're not a good reader anyway."

## ~ July 1984 ~

Autumn gave up the ghost. After the ten-year battle, her lungs finally shut down. It was a scene of sadness in the hospital with her children and grandchildren at her bedside. They came to say good-bye, knowing the end was near at hand. She didn't appear conscious of them being there. Although the grandchildren had compassion for her, they felt disconnected. Autumn never seemed that interested in them. They stood by solemnly, bravely, quietly.

Judy walked over to her mother and timidly laid a hand on her shoulder. In the quiet place under her breath, so no one could hear her, she said, "Mother, I forgive you for all the hurt you caused me." The next day, her mother was gone. Judy shed no tears when Mother died. It made her sad that she couldn't, but she actually felt free. For years, it had been odd to be afraid of someone who didn't have the strength to get out of bed. *I guess it was just the control and emotional tortures that took place when I was in her presence.*

After the funeral, Bob pulled Judy aside. "Cissy, I feel bad telling you this, but your mother told me she didn't want you to have any of her things. Your sisters have already gone through what they wanted. I want you to have something, so I saved an old trunk, if you'd like it."

"Thank you, Daddy. I'll give it to one of my kids."

Denée was enrolled in Outside Work Experience in high school, and Fireman's Fund employed her in their HR department. With her influence, Judy got her first real job since being a stay-at-home mom.

*A day off for mom and daughter*

For the first time Judy understood the meaning of being persecuted for her faith. At break time, she asked to use the telephone. Permission given, she called the eyeglass store and got an answering machine. "Hello, my name is Judy and I'd like some prices on your frames and lens. Please call me at 555-0134. In Jesus name." *Uh-oh.*

The supervisor looked up at Judy and rolled her eyes. "A definite Born Again."

Judy strolled back to her desk, slunk into her chair, and with red ears, went back to work.

Mariann, a coworker, marched over to her desk cussing and yelling. "How can you make so many stupid mistakes?" Humiliation covered Judy's whole being. The other girls went so quiet you could hear a pin drop. Judy just looked up at Mariann with shock in her eyes, then looked away and stared at the papers in front of her that were thrown on her desk. When Mariann finally walked away, Judy slowly slid off her chair, walked into the bathroom, and into an empty stall to hide the tears running down her face. She prayed, "Lord, why is it I have such a hard time learning what is really an easy job, just like I had such a hard time in school."

That evening Judy shared her ordeal with the kids. As she went to bed that night she prayed again. "Why Lord, what is wrong with me?" He showed her in an instant: He didn't make anyone *stupid.* Everyone learns differently and Judy certainly didn't learn like most others. He also showed her the strengths she did have. The

Signs of dyslexia in adults include difficulty reading or interpreting written words, spelling problems and difficulty learning a new language. Even math can pose a problem for adults with dyslexia, as the numbers can be difficult to read. Dyslexic adults may also notice that they have trouble retaining information that they read, particularly any lengthy reading material. Handwriting may also be messy, and dyslexic adults may find that they are easily distracted and have trouble concentrating.

ability to discern what wasn't true or good. He also showed her that everyone has different gifts that complete the body of Christ. With new information, Judy drifted off in a peaceful, sound sleep.

Judy's friend Tenny encouraged her to get tested for dyslexia. The truth would set her free from thinking she was stupid.

"Tenny, thank you for your support and telling me about the testing. I learned that I can do anything anyone else can, I just have to work harder, and it might take me longer. I feel relieved that I'm not stupid after all."

"That's right, Jude. In your weakness, He is strong."

"Oh, I love that Scripture. You know, that experience I had at work prompted my son, Steve, to write me a poem. Let me get it and read it to you." She walked over to her little wooden box where she kept treasured letters from her children. "Here it is, I hope I can get through it without crying."

"She's unimportant," she heard them say
Then they ignored her, just walked away.
"She's not attractive, nor unique"
"There is no beauty in her speech."
Her heart was broken—needed a mend
"Who would have her or be her friend?"
She thought she was plain and even bland
Thought she had no skill in either hand.
There were those whom she did not count
Who admired and loved her without a doubt.
The Lord who was always, forever her guide,
Two sons and a daughter, who'd die by her side.
The quality of love is really what matters
Even so, all the love is in four people gathered.
In God whose love is so very great
And in her three children who are only second rate.

## ~ November 1984 ~

It was a pleasant evening in Petaluma, clear but not too cold yet. Judy was preparing dinner for whoever would come home to eat that day. Everyone had different schedules, but she was surprised to see Steve walk in the door sooner than expected. One look at his sweet, yet serious face and she knew something was up. He looked her straight in the eyes. "Mom, I joined the Army."

She felt all weak inside and the blood left her face. Not, that she wasn't proud

*Best Buds*

of him, but all she could think of was *there goes my baby*. The cord would be torn for the second time and it would be more painful than the first. She took a shaky breath. "I don't know what to say, Steve. I love you and will always hope God's best for you."

Gary stormed up behind Steve. "Oh brother! Steve! Don't do it. Don't be an idiot. Let's go to college together."

"Sorry little brother, what's done is done. I need to get some discipline in my life and a way to pay for college." He put his hand on Gary's shoulder, and then they embraced.

Denée, standing by, just listened with hurt on her face. She didn't say anything but walked down the hall to her bedroom and closed the door behind her. She was keeping her thoughts to herself. *One by one, the men in her life are leaving her. I feel her pain*. The Army wasted no time. Just a couple of evenings later their little family drove Steve to a hotel in a Richmond Marina, where he would be transported to the Oakland Airport, and from there to Boot Camp at Ft. McClellan, Alabama.

The forty-five minute drive from Petaluma to Richmond was hauntingly quiet. Judy could almost hear everyone deep in their own thoughts. She had no words—wisdom or otherwise. She blinked back the tears that were trying to show up on her face. *It's hard to let him go, Lord*. Physically, Steve was sicker than he'd ever been with some kind of virus. Her heart ached for him, but her body was numb. They reached their destination with not much time for drawn-out good-byes. Steve's big blue tired eyes gazed at his family one last time, then he walked away and didn't look back. *Our lives will never ever be the same!*

Judy cried for two weeks. Those feelings were as intense as everything about her firstborn had been. Because Christmas was in the middle of Boot Camp, Steve was allowed to come home

*Steve the soldier*

*Steve on leave*

for the holidays. This time he was in uniform with a shaved head. He was still handsome with those big blue innocent eyes. The family held on to each moment they shared, listening to Steve's stories. He knew how to add such humor to each line. And then, he was off again. *Time goes way to quick when I don't want it to.*

This time mother and son drove to the airport alone. *I will miss his energy, his humor, and his care.* Steve was the most affectionate of all her children. He would come up and kiss her right in front of all his friends, male or female.

As they sat in the airport, waiting for Steve's plane to board, there were no words to express what was on her heart. There she sat, next to her boy—a man—a soldier in his uniform. *My soldier!* "Steve, I want you to know that you are a joy to my soul. I'm so going to miss our togetherness. Remember when we prayed together at the graveyard? You are so unique. I'm going to miss our little conversations, and the way you wrap your arms around me. I'm even going to miss how you make me laugh when I'm supposed to be mad at you. But most of all, I want you to know, I will always pray for you. I will always love you."

Steve wasn't looking at her but bravely staring straight ahead. The single tear, he had been struggling so hard to hold back, rolled down his cheek. "I love you, Mom. Thank you for all you've done. I'll miss you." His voice cracked.

The rest was a blur. Once again, he was gone and it would be a long time before Judy could wrap her arms around him. Her heart was heavy with sorrow, filled with tears as she managed to fight the traffic through San Francisco, over the Golden Gate and all the way home, with tear-stained cheeks.

So much loss happened that year: husband, mother, son. Only one truly broke her heart.

## ~ 1985 ~

Other than her children, Judy's first priority had been Jerry when they were still together. Sitting in church, alone as usual, she checked the bulletin for things to do. Things she hadn't been able to get involved with before. She had spent time learning sign language so she could interpret for the deaf during church services. It would be used for a dynamic ministry much later down the road. For now though, Judy felt a need to be more involved in helping others.

*Jail Ministry* was on the top of her list. She spent the next five years on Friday nights in the Marin County Jail teaching Bible studies—loving every minute of it. The first time she walked the line, not really sure of herself, she clung to her Bible. There were some who really didn't want her there. As she passed the cell of one inmate, her ears picked up a sarcastic voice. "Oh, brother, here comes *Thou shalt not steal*."

Continuing to walk the line, Judy invited other women to join the Bible study. The team met in one of the cells for the study. There were five takers. One girl had killed her baby, three were in for drug charges, and one for embezzlement. At times, Judy had to use their metal, no lid, toilet.

"That a girl, Judy. Now you're one of us." Chuckles spread throughout the cold cell. *Yes. I'm just like them, only we took different paths.* Many girls came to the Lord through that ministry.

On one occasion, Judy met a newcomer to the jail. Before Marjorie's arrest, she'd tried to take her life. She went on her boat in the Delta, swallowed sleeping pills, slept for two weeks, then woke up. What a miracle—the human body wouldn't normally wake up after two weeks, but, God had other plans for her. She'd lost her faith and came to the Bible study, for the sole purpose of bringing someone else. The message Judy gave was on forgiveness.

It ministered to Marjorie. At first there were angry tears in her eyes, but when they prayed, her heart was softened and with a shaky voice, she recommitted her life to the Lord. She would go to prison and on her release stayed in Judy's home till she got back on her feet. She's in ministry today.

*Street Witnessing* was another—every Saturday night with a group called SOS. Judy would meet the team at a small basement church to sing and pray before going out onto the streets. Her heart raced with excitement and even while praying, she couldn't wipe the smile off her face. Each week they went to one of six districts: Fisherman's Wharf, Castro District, Polk Street, Tenderloin District, Broadway, and Haight-Ashbury. At times she was cursed at, spat at, and almost hit in the face. She learned something doing this. Many who once served the Lord and went off the path, never lost their love for Him. They were often willing to return to Him, after someone from this ministry shared His love. At the end of one night, in a not so good neighborhood, Judy nervously walked back to her car alone. Some young adults were gathered on the street corner smoking pot. Still feeling jazzed from all the people she'd talked to about the Lord, she bravely walked up to the kids. "Hi guys, can I talk to you about the love of God?"

One of the girls, with ratty hair was sitting on the curb. She looked up with her dark eyes. "Ha ha! We don't need God. We've got all we want right here. You want to get high with us?" A couple of the guys started walking toward Judy—both scary looking with painted eyebrows and chains hanging from nose to toes.

She felt the color drain from her face. "Uh, no thanks. I'm high on Jesus."

"Yeah, right. I think you better be on your way, lady," one of the boys said.

"Okay, then. Just know that Jesus loves you." She started towards her car, when someone came up behind her. Startled, she turned and saw one of the scary looking guys standing face to face with her.

"Lady, I…I knew the Lord, but I kinda walked away from all that. But, I…I really think I want to come back to God. Will you pray for me? My name is Roger.

"I can pray for you right now, Roger." And so she did and gave the young man her phone number. A couple of weeks later, he called to let her know he was in church and serving the Lord.

## ~ 1986 ~

Judy snapped a few pictures while Denée posed in front of the fireplace, looking so beautiful in her lace, royal blue, tea-length dress with matching heels. It was her senior prom and she was going with her very first boyfriend. As he gazed at her with adoring eyes, he took her hand and slipped a corsage onto her wrist. Judy felt a tug at her heart and wished her daughter had others there to share this special time in her life. However, Denée always handled everything so gracefully. Womanhood, disappointments, everything. Judy really admired her for that. At the same time, it left Judy feeling sad and alone. She didn't take things as graceful as her daughter.

*Denée's prom*

The nest was getting smaller. After attending a junior college for two years, Gary left for Cal Poly. Oh, how Judy missed him and looked forward to the weekends he would come home for a visit. But when the house on Catalpa sold and Judy moved, Gary wouldn't have a room to put his things in—no place to hang his clothes when he came home on school break. That broke Judy's heart. Silent tears rolled down her cheeks as she packed up his things. It was like putting her son in a box.

# Chapter 23

# Judy Charbonneau

ONE BY ONE, my children went out on their own. They were always my life—my confidence in life. Now I will have to find my own way as they find theirs.

My children reclaimed their birth name and asked me to change mine as well.

## Divorce final ~ House sold

With the house sold, the day came to move out. After the movers left, Judy scrubbed the empty house, feeling more alone than ever. *This is the last place my family was under one roof.* It was a hot day and strength was leaving her body. She slowly moved around the house, one last time, with sorrowful eyes and memories flooding her tired mind. Deep in thought, she was about to crumble when... *ding dong.* She opened the door to find her neighbor and Christian sister, standing there.

Debbie stepped in, finding her friend in despair, she gently told her, "Judy, it's time to go. You've done all you could." She put her arms around Judy and let her friend's tears fall on her shoulder. She gathered up Judy's things and guided her out the door, then closed it, shutting away the pain and sorrow.

# Gary's Healing
## ~ October 1987 ~

The stinker didn't tell Judy what he was going through. It wasn't till he was ready to go into surgery that she received the news at work. The boss walked over, "Judy, your son's on the line. It sounds important. You can use the phone on my desk."

"Hello, Mom." My coach made me call you. I'm about to go under the knife."

"What?" Judy sank into her boss's chair." What is it? Why haven't you called me sooner?"

"I didn't want to worry you. It's going to be okay. I'm at peace."

"Should I come down there?"

"No, Mom, you better stay at work. I'll call you when I get out."

Judy called his brother and sister and they all took the five-hour drive to San Luis Obispo to be with Gary when he got out of the hospital. Although they didn't know all the details, they knew it was serious.

During the drive, Judy planned Gary's funeral in her mind. She couldn't wait to hold her son in her arms. Quietly she walked into his hospital room. "We're here, Gar Bear."

"Who's we?"

Steve and Denée, came into the room. "Surprise!"

"Do you feel like talking, Gar?"

"Yes, Mom. I can see you're worried and I was too, although I had so much peace. It started with a routine physical for Cal Poly SLO cross-country. I had just completed the regular season and was chosen as one of the top seven runners to complete in the post-season. I still can't believe what a huge accomplishment that was for me, a marginal high school runner compared to these nationally ranked Cal Poly runners."

"Stick to the story." Steve gave his brother a grim smile.

"During the physical, the doctor asked me if I noticed a lump on my left testicle. I told him I wasn't in the habit of playing with my testicles."

"Gary David!" Judy's face turned hot. How could he joke about such a life-threatening event?

"The doctor didn't laugh either. He told me I needed to see a specialist. I asked him when I should make the appointment and he replied flatly, 'You need to see him today.'"

"Oh, Gary, I wished you had told me. You went through this all alone! Don't ever do that again."

"Go on, Gary." Steve wrapped his arm around Judy and guided her to the seat nearest the bed.

"Well, I was told I had a malignant testicular tumor."

Denée sank into the other chair. "What does that mean?"

"The doctor said I'd have to start chemotherapy after surgery. He told me I had a great chance of survival but may not be able to have children."

Steve moaned. "Bummer."

"Anyway, Coach Tom, drove me to my apartment to pick up some extra clothes for this little adventure. While driving me, he looked over and asked, 'Gary, you are a religious guy so you can handle this, right?'"

"I realized God opened an opportunity right then to share with him the difference between religion and relationship. I said, 'Yes, with God I can handle this.' When we arrived at the hospital, I was taken in for X-rays of my chest to see if the cancer had spread to my lungs. Sure enough, the verdict was traces of small nodules on the ribs—not good. That's when Coach insisted I call you."

"Thank God for your coach. Before we left home, my brother Chip prayed with us for you, and I felt some kind of electricity go through me. No, matter what happens, Gar Bear, we will be by your side."

"Well, that might explain the rest of my story. Soon after calling home, I was wheeled into surgery. I remember telling the nurses that I was still awake, as they began to cut me open. Then

I was out. I had a dream that a nurse came to my side, slightly shaking my shoulder, and whispering that I was okay and that I did not have cancer."

Hope surged through Judy. Words failed her. She squeezed Gary's hand and watched the expressions of concern vanish from Denée and Steve. Gary seemed to notice as well. "It was a dream, guys, but then I began to emerge from my drug induced sleep. As I was struggling to open my eyes, I tried to speak. The drugs would not let me become completely conscious."

Steve chuckled. "Gary, that's the first time you had drugs in your life!"

"Yeah, and hopefully the last. Anyway, I then saw the nurse from my dream and hoarsely called her." She came and asked what I needed, so I told her about the dream where she said I didn't have cancer. She smiled and said it wasn't a dream, then I drifted back to sleep."

"Thank God! Is it true, Gary?" Tears pricked Judy's eyes.

"Well, four more times I called that nurse over explaining, 'I'm sorry, but did you really say I didn't have cancer?' Each time she gave me a resounding *yes!* in an understanding way."

"Nurses know the effort it takes, coming out of surgery," Steve said.

"What about your lungs?"

"When the doctor discovered there was no cancer, he checked my X-rays again and realized it was only 'boney' nodules."

Wide-eyed, Denée leaned forward and asked in a soft voice. "What did they do with your testicle, Gary?"

*Celebrating Gary's Healing*

Gary's face lit up as he smiled. "I got to keep them both. I'll miss my chance to run at Nationals, but I'll be able to get back into running. Imagine the testimony I have to share the Lord with my teammates now."

## ~Spring 1989 ~

*Ring…* "Oooo." Judy retrieved the phone after she knocked it off the nightstand. "Hel..hello."

"Hi, Mom. Did I wake you?"

"Uh, it's midnight. What do you think?"

"Sorry Mom, but I just had the best Bible study and had to share it with you."

"Then it's worth being woke up, Gar Bear. Who was there?"

"There were about nine of us. Can you write these names down and pray for these guys?"

Judy sat up and grabbed her pen and pad. "Sure, just a sec… okay, I'm ready."

"Steve N., Jim, John, Bob, Mike, Mark, Scott, Dave, and Daveed. Oh, and Mom, I'm bringing Scott home this weekend so make your good spaghetti, okay?"

"Can't wait to see you Gar. Good night. Love you."

"Thanks Mom, love you too."


Judy stirred the spaghetti sauce, while listening to Gary and his friend's running stories. Gary got out his scrapbook, flipped it open and tapped a newspaper clipping. "I remember this cross-country race. Some guy in the race before mine took a wrong turn and I had to chase him down to let him know, because none of my teammates would do it."

Judy started setting the table. *Hmm, I remember that story.* The next thing she knew, Gary and Scott pointed their fingers at each other. "Hey—you're that guy." They said at the same time.

Scott slapped Gary on the back. "Only the top six guys got to go on to the next round. Good thing you turned me around when you did, I came in sixth."

"I guess that makes twice I got you on the right path." Gary chuckled. "Once in the physical, and once in spiritual."

Judy got goosebumps as she looked up at the boys. "What are the chances you guys would become friends, without knowing that before tonight, and discover that coincidence in my little apartment?" Scott would go on to be an awesome believer. Gary had many instances like that.

## ~ June 1989 ~

Judy dialed Gary's number by heart. He would be graduating from Cal Poly in just a few weeks. She'd been saving to get him just the right gift, but she didn't know what to get him. Too bad it wouldn't be a surprise.

"Hello?" Gary answered on the second ring.

"Hi, Gar. It's Mom."

"Hey, Mom. Is everything okay?"

"Of course. Why do you ask?"

He laughed. "You seem to call when I find myself in need of prayer, and today I'm feeling confident in my classes and work's going well. But you're welcome to make something up to talk to God about me."

"Oh, I talk to God about you every day, even when there isn't anything interesting to say." Judy joined in his laughter. "I actually called to find out what you'd like for graduation."

"I've been thinking and if it's

*Gary's graduation*

not too much to ask, I'd like a family vacation—just the four of us. Who knows when we'll ever get the chance to be together again."

"All my children together for a week? That sounds more like a present for me."

"It'll be a gift to all of us, but let's make it camping at Trinity Lake. That way you won't have to feel like it's for you and not me." His laughter rang through the phone. "I'll let you work out the details. I've got to run to class. Love you." The line went dead.

Judy set the phone down. She could put up with camping as long as she had her kids with her again. Gary had called it a gift to them all. His words always seemed to warm her heart. She spied her Bible on the table where she'd been reading that morning. "He's kind of like Jeremiah, with words of fire. Right, God?" She flipped her Bible open to that passage.

"How about we write him a special blessing for his graduation. With Your help, I'll write a blessing for each of my children."

*Trinity Lake, California*

# STEVE DARWIN CHARBONNEAU

## "YOU ARE MY FIRST BORN, MY MIGHT, AND THE BEGINNING OF MY STRENGTH" Gen. 49:3a

*Steve—just as when Moses saw the Lord face to face—the glory of the Lord is upon you.*

The Lord is with you and by God's standard you will be considered a successful man. May God cause you to prosper, Steve. You will find favor in the sight of God and man, and God will bless your house. It shall come to pass—every mountain in your life will be brought down and every valley raised. (Gen. 39:1-6, Is. 49:11)

The Lord is to be your strength and your song. How precious are His thoughts to you—if you were to count them they would outnumber the grains of sand. Thus saith the Lord of Hosts, "My thoughts of you are so pure that nothing can touch you that isn't filtered through My hands of love." (Ex. 15:2, Ps. 139:17-18)

Steve—Our Lord will enable you to be a watchman and make the rounds in the city He calls you to be a part of. "God is showing me a picture in my mind's eye—you are walking in a hurting city, town or country, just praying and treading in the enemy's camp—stomping on his head with every step. You will say to the captives, "come out" and to those in darkness, "be free." (Song of Sol. 3:3, Is. 49:9)

Because the Spirit of the Lord is upon you and the Lord has anointed you to bring Good News to the afflicted; He has sent you to bind up the broken hearted, to proclaim liberty to captives and freedom to prisoners—to proclaim the favorable Year of the Lord. (Is. 61:1-2)

God will give you His compassion for them to guide them to springs of living water. Thus saith the Lord—I know the plans I have for you, plans of welfare and not calamity, to give you a future and a hope—which will not be cut off. (Jer. 29:11)

May God show you how to sustain the weary one with a word. For the Lord God will be your help. Therefore you will not be disgraced—therefore He will enable you to set your face like flint and you will know that you shall never be ashamed. When you honor Him, He will honor you. (Is. 50:4, 1 Sam. 2:30)

Your life is not your own and your steps are not
for you to direct, but because you are one who is humble
and contrite in spirit, the Lord will esteem you.
(Jer. 10:23, Is. 66:2)

## GARY DAVID CHARBONNEAU
### "BEFORE THE LORD FORMED YOU IN MY WOMB— HE KNEW YOU." ~JER. 1:5

***Gary—before you were born, He set you apart. He has appointed you to be His spokesman. He will give you strength to perform the task and will honor you for doing it.***

May God bless you in the city and bless you in the country. Blessed shall be the fruit of your body. Blessed shall you be when you come in and blessed shall you be when you go out. May the Lord cause your enemies who rise against you to be defeated before your face. May the Lord command the blessing on you in your storehouses and in all to which you set your hand. And, He will bless you in the land which the Lord your God is now giving you. (Deut. 28:3-13)

The Lord will establish you as a holy people to Himself. He will open to you His good treasure, the heavens, to give the rain to your land in the season and to bless the work of your hands. You will be the head and not the tail.

Your ears shall hear a word behind you saying "this is the way, walk in it," heard by the one who is so surrendered to the will of God that he makes contact with the heart of God, which will bring you peace. Your testimony shall be—you have walked before Him with a perfect heart and have done that which is good in His sight. Since you were precious in My sight, saith the Lord—you have been honored and I have loved you, therefore I will give you students and people for your life and inheritance." You are my witness and my servant whom I have chosen. Who has grown up before the Lord as a tender shoot. Wisdom and knowledge shall enter your soul. (Is. 30:21, Is. 38:3, Is. 43:4, Is. 53:2, Prov. 24:14)

May the Lord put forth His hand and touch your mouth and put His words in your mouth—and because you speak His words, He will make His words in your mouth as fire! (Jer. 1:9)

God will give you knowledge and skill in all literature and wisdom and understanding in all visions and dreams. He will reveal deep and secret things. (Dan. 1:17, Dan. 2:22)

Man shall find no charge against you unless they find it against you concerning the Law of your God. (Dan. 6:5)

He will keep His covenant and mercy with you who are wise and you shall shine and turn many to righteousness. (Dan. 9:4, 12:3)

He shall show you great and mighty things, unsearchable things you do not know. ~Jer. 33:3

# NICOLE DENÉE CHARBONNEAU

## "HOW LOVELY ON THE MOUNTAINS ARE THE FEET OF HER WHO BRINGS GOOD NEWS"

***Denée—arise and shine.***

The eternal God is your refuge and underneath are His everlasting arms. (Deut. 33:27)

Denée—whoever touches you, touches the apple of His eye. (He told me that) no matter what. The Lord called you before your birth; from within my womb He named you. He has made your words like a sharp sword. In the shadow of His hand, He has concealed you and He has also made you a select arrow. He has hidden you in the quiver until an appointed time. You are His servant and with the Lord, you will bring God glory. (Is. 49)

In returning and waiting on the Lord—quietness and confidence shall be your strength. God wants to bring you to a place of worship you have yet to experience. "I can see you sitting at the feet of Jesus with your alabaster box"—in the meantime, the Lord will wait for you. He longs to be gracious to you and He rises to show you compassion. (Is. 30:15, 18)

Denée—The Lord has a veil over you until it is time. He is preparing you to be a bride without spot or wrinkle, so you will stand pure before Him.

The Lord Jesus wants to court you and bring you into the wilderness and speak to you tenderly there. He will give you back your vineyards and transform your *valley of troubles* into a *door of hope.* May you respond to Him there in singing with joy as in days long ago in your youth—and you will call Him Husband as well as Master. Then you will lie down in peace and safety, unafraid—no more insecurity. He will bind you to Himself. He will bind you to Him in faithfulness and love and then you will really know Him as you never have before. (Hosea 2:15-20)

After that you will win favor of everyone who sees you. (Est. 2:15)

Christ has turned your hopelessness into rejoicing and clothed you with gladness.

# Chapter 24

## Scattered

My baby turned twenty-one and moved out. I was left all alone—empty. Not only did my family scatter—my church family was shattered, leaving me with more decisions to make.

### ~ August 1989 ~

Without enough income to pay the raised lease, Judy was forced to rent a master bedroom from a woman and her daughter. Now, she had no place to hold the Charbonneau family gatherings.

With her babies all adults, all she could do was pray for her children. They would make their own choices and have to live by them and Judy would hit her knees. God revealed to Judy through dreams what was going on in her children's lives. *Lord, when my children hurt, I hurt.* And, there was a period when Judy's children were all hurting at the same time, all for different reasons. It was at times like that Judy wished her children were small enough to hold close. Her heart ached to hold them again, like when they were babies—to comfort her kids.

## Christmas ~ 1989

Judy thanked God for the friends who loaned her their home for an evening so the Charbonneau's could have their Christmas gathering—their traditional family dinner and a time of sharing the Lord's blessing. She set out the double-baked potatoes and a nice salad. Oil bubbled in the fondue pot at the center of the table. Steve grabbed the blue skewer he always used, Gary took the red one, Denée the green, and Judy the yellow. Everyone forked steak cubes, fried them and dipping them in the various sauces. When they couldn't eat another bite, they retired to the living room and sat around their friend's Christmas tree. Steve handed Judy and Denée each a lumpy present. He tossed one at Gary.

Judy pulled the wrapping paper from a seashell. The corner of a note peeped out of the shell's opening. "Oh Naomi with rod and staff—sojourner for your Lord's namesake—with your children's children you will laugh. With elders you will sit at the gate! Your Shell: Oh how the simple are the beautiful says the Lord— polished and pure." Her voice broke as she read the last words. "Union of love."

Denée gracefully peeled the tape off the wrapping paper. "I got a shell, too." She unrolled the message, smiled up at Steve with eyes that sparkled her thanks, and tucked the note into her pocket.

"It's true," he said. "It's beautiful like you and perfect in God's love."

Denée's cheeks turned a pretty pink. "No man ever called me beautiful before," she whispered.

Judy's eyes misted. She felt her daughter's pain as intensely as her own.

Gary cleared his voice and stared at his note. "Hey, I got one, too."

"What does yours say?" Judy gave him an encouraging smile.

"It says, 'This shell is empty, just like your head.'" He tried to hide his laughter. "Steve, I'm crushed. Now, I'll cry every time I go to the beach and see a shell."

Steve chuckled. "You write your own fortunes, little brother."

"Really?" Judy snatched the paper from Gary's hand. "It says that shells are filled with chambers we can't see from the outside and God wants every part of us—even the secret and hidden parts we don't want Him to see."

"Wow… God wants a lot of me."

Steve jumped up. "These aren't your only presents. Wait here." He jogged from the room and returned a moment later with a dish tub in his hands and a towel thrown over his shoulder. He prayed a blessing over the family members as he washed their feet.

Judy's heart swelled with pride watching the humility of her firstborn son, as he took on the role of God's Firstborn. With all the loss she'd experienced, he found a way to make this her best Christmas ever.

This was also an emotional time in the church Judy's family had attended for nine years. The members were being controlled or wounded by a pastor they had put on a pedestal. Judy felt God's call to leave this church. Many who left were ostracized, and it pained her to think she might become an outcast with her church family.

Journal Entry on February 26, 1990—*Lord thank you for keeping me thus far. These are heavy times, Lord. Did you feel those prayer meetings were a little off? What did you think? I know they were just a symptom of what's going on in our church.*

Journal Entry on March 1, 1990—*Lord you know the struggles I've had over the years at our church. So many have been devastated, slandered, and cut off. The prayer meetings last week were the last straw. I believe in my heart and spirit You are calling me out of there. I wanted to stay a little longer but I better not. Please lead me and guide me, Lord. Show me your way.*

With a heavy heart, Judy felt she had no choice but to leave her church home. It would be a long time before she felt brave enough to walk into a place of worship with a heart open for ministry.

## Fresno, California ~ May 1990

Steve, attending Fresno State, talked Judy into moving there, too. "Mom, if you come to Fresno, you could buy a little condo and have your own place again." So, she made the decision to follow Steve. And then, Gary followed suit. Finally, her baby girl, Denée joined the family in the San Joaquin Valley.

Thinking she needed a fresh start and new identity, Judy decided to change her name to Jacy—for JC. She went to work at a balloon company and was let go after only five weeks on the job. Well, that name didn't bring her much luck, so she went back to using Judy.

The family got a reputation for playing *musical apartments*. Steve found his mom an apartment next door to his complex, so they were neighbors. Steve lived with his friend Aood. Judy had an international student for a roommate, until Denée came and moved in with her. But, Gary started putting pressure on Denée, to move into a new apartment with him. He told her they were going to have so much fun, it would be so great, etc. So, she left Judy and moved in with her brother. After only one month, he kicked her out so he could move in with Steve. This left Denée with no place to sleep so she moved back into Judy's apartment. Then Gary's college friend came to Fresno, so Gary moved out of the nice, large, and more expensive apartment, rented by Steve and Aood, and in with his friend. In the meantime, Judy, attained another job and bought a condo. Gary's buddy moved into a shared bachelor house when their six-month lease was up, so Gary moved into Judy's condo. After a short time, Gary decided to join his friend again at the bachelor house. Denée moved to San Jose to live with her father and attend San Jose State.

*Aah*, for once, it was nice to have an uncommon last name. Even after the kids moved to Fresno, she'd get calls from people who'd found CHARBONNEAU in the white pages. *What fun to reconnect my kids with their friends.*

Judy's condo continued to have a revolving door for the next fifteen years. Her two future daughters-in-law, and her sons' friends' sisters, and over thirty Fresno State students, mostly international, lived with her at one time or another. One of these students was a girl from San Francisco. Maria lived with Judy during her last year at Fresno State. Judy planned on giving her a graduation breakfast, since her family was coming from out of town. At the mailbox one afternoon, Judy retrieved the mail for her and her roommates. One envelope was addressed from a Dr. Alvin Jacobs. That so happened to be her little brothers and sisters' pediatrician, thirty-some years earlier. *But, why was this coming to Fresno. Dr. Jacobs has to be retired by now.* The letter was addressed to Maria, and Judy couldn't wait to get back to the house and ask about it. She jogged through the door. "Maria, are you home?"

"I'm upstairs, Judy. Be right there." She bounced down the steps like usual. "Hi, what's up?

"Maria, what is your mother's maiden name?"

"Jacobs, why?"

"Is her first name, Annette?"

"Yes, why?"

"Maria, I went to Aptos Junior High School with an Annette Jacobs and her father just happened to be my brothers and sisters' pediatrician."

"Oh my God. We've lived together all this time and are just finding out you knew my mother. I have goose bumps."

"Me, too! What are the chances of that happening? So, your graduation breakfast will also be a reunion for your mom and me. Let's call her.

# Chapter 25

# In the Heart of Darkness

Wrongs and mistakes that have marred my being from the beginning would *slap me in the face*. The repercussions from my earliest sins would have their way. Life hadn't turned out the way I'd planned. My dreams were shattered—and I was the only one to blame. But where would I be, without the love from His nail-scarred hands.

## ~ 1992 ~

She fell into a black, empty hole. Empty Nest Syndrome does not even begin to describe the void left in her heart that would be there for a number of years. Her children were her life and there were no words to express what they meant to her. Within one year, there were three weddings. Hoping the best for her beloved children, she resided in the background.

How many times had she and her children talked about the day their family would grow. They'd looked forward to having more people to pray for, serve, and share the Lord with. Somehow, her vision didn't turn out the way she'd hoped it would. Painful as it was, she knew she needed to let go of her dreams.

The phone stopped ringing. She spent most holidays by herself and scarcely saw her sons. *I haven't given my family one reason to respect me.* Her kids had turned out great, but still she felt like a failure as a mother. Why else would she be in this position?

*Lord, I am reminded that I once was fatherless, then You came into my heart and now I can say, "Abba Father." When my boys took their wives I lost my sons, but you have given me Your Son, Jesus Christ. For many years now I've been without a companion, but then You have become my Husband. I don't have many close friends, but your Holy Spirit does not let me down. Thank You for not giving up on me—the least of all the saints.*

♥ ♥ ♥

*Only the Lonely*

The phone rang at 3:00 a.m. Judy picked it up on the first ring, hoping it didn't wake up her roommates. She wasn't sleeping anyway. She whispered a hello around the tears clogging her throat.

"Judy…this is Chris."

*Chris…an old acquaintance from the church where I got saved eighteen years ago?* "Where are you?"

"I'm in Montana! We moved here two years ago after Dick retired. Judy, are you okay?"

"I guess so. Why are you calling at this hour?"

"God woke me up to tell me that you were really sad and I felt I had to call you."

"Oh Chris… I cried so hard last night that I thought I would die of a broken heart. I can't really share with you why, but I can tell you, this is like a phone call from God."

After more tears and a little laughter, Judy hang up the phone.

Morning came up, with body and soul exhausted from a night of heartache. Her roommate, Pia, met her in the hallway. "Judy, are you okay?" A sympathetic smile broke through her Thai accent. "I heard you crying all night long and if you need anyting, just let me know."

"Pia, I can't share with you, but thank you so much for your concern."

With tears in her eyes, she placed her hand lovingly on Judy's face. "I worry about you. I tink you my mom."

"Pia, you touch my aching heart. I love you, too."

And so it went, in every hour of need, God would give Judy such a token. Even so, the hurt continued with each new blow, until Judy didn't think she could go on. *I know what I'll do, sell my condo, my car and leave the area where no one can find me or miss me. I'll become a bag lady!.* She's sorta adventurous in that way, so it kind of excited her. *I'm going to spell my name Judy with an "i" for my new independence.* Judi called a realtor and put her condo on the market. She made plans for after it sold. *I always wanted to go to New York, so that might be where I'll end up.* Through her situation, old feelings of being insignificant crept in—she was becoming bitter instead of better!

> My eyes are dry, my faith is old.
> My heart is hard, my prayers are cold.
> And I know how I ought to be,
> Alive to You and dead to me.
> Oh, what can be done for an old heart like mine?
> Soften it up with oil and wine.
> The oil is You, Your Spirit of love,
> Please wash me anew in the wine of Your blood.
> ~Keith Green

In the meantime, Judi started attending a Bible study at Peoples Church. Mary Lou was the teacher, encourager, and the example Judi needed in her life. God spoke specific truths through Mary Lou and the Bible study: 1) Stop feeling sorry for herself. 2) Stop centering her life around a family she couldn't attain. 3) Concentrate on regaining control over her life and take responsibility for her own actions. 4) Her obligation was to live the life God gave her in a healthy, constructive manner before Him.

*Lord, I ask you to help free my doubtful mind and melt my cold, cold heart.*

In my anguish I cried to the Lord and He answered by setting me free. ~Ps. 118:5 He lifted me out of the pit of despair and set me on a firm path. He has given me a new song, now many will hear of the glorious things He did for me. ~Ps. 40

Working on the patio, Judi ran to pick up the phone before it went to the answering machine, she forgot the screen door was closed and practically ran through it, leaving the screen all bent out of shape. Feeling a little dingy, she grabbed the phone off the receiver. "Hello."

"Hey Jude, it's Chris."

"Oh—hey Chris! How ya doing?"

"I'm good. Just checking up on you. It's been awhile since our middle-of-the-night talk. Are you doing okay now?"

"Well yeah, except I just ran through my screen door and now I know what a fly must feel like when he gets smashed."

"Ha, that's funny girlfriend. Some things never change with you. How's life treating you these days?"

"You know what? I can't say I'm exactly happy...or sad anymore. Just, content to go forward with the Lord."

"I'm glad to hear it," she said with a smile in her voice. "Do you have any plans of how you're going to do that?"

"You bet. I've started a bucket list and in the meantime, God

*In His Hands*

is using me in a ministry I call, *In His Hands*. I put drama to music. It's quite unique and I've been performing at church, retreats, parties, funerals and more. Chris, thanks so much for your prayers."

"Anytime my friend, anytime you need it, I'm a phone call away."

Children begin by loving their parents; as they grow older they judge them; sometimes they forgive them. ~Oscar Wilde

# Chapter 26

# Sidetracked

So now I am Judi Charbonneau. My son teased me about that for years. There have been many seasons in my life and although I so want to be a good daughter to my heavenly Father, I am still a work in progress.

Judi enjoyed the company of her friends, neighbors, and co-workers, even so, she would get very lonely. Nights were the worst. God should be all she needed, but she yearned to have someone with skin attached. She checked the classified ads and found a dating site. Well, why not? It had a go-between phone number for interested men to call and leave a message that would be forwarded to her phone. If she was interested, she could call them back. She signed up and created her ad.

"Hello, my name is Judi. I'm looking for someone who is committed to God. I love to run, hike, and go out to dinner. I am fifty-four, petite, and semi-attractive. Please call if you want to meet."

Returning home from work every day, Judi rushed into her condo, ran up the stairs into her bedroom, and looked for the blinking red light on her answering machine. This was a daily ritual, but sadly, the light never blinked. *Humm, it worked for others I know. Guess God has something else for me.*

## ~ June 1996 ~

Ten laps in the pool…two more to go! Minding her own business, Judi noticed him watching her. *Hmm…I've never seen that guy before.* He was tall—handsome with a storm of blond hair and sky-blue eyes. Smiling, he jumped into the pool. Judi jumped out, but he followed. A deep voice came up behind her, "Refreshing, isn't it?"

"I agree." She hazard a second glance. *I better leave!*

She started to walk by him, but he stopped her with a charming grin. "My name is Doug, would you like to have dinner with me tonight?"

"I'm Judi and no thank you! How old are you, Doug?"

"Thirty-eight Why?"

"Well, I'm old enough to be your mother. I'm fifty-four." She went on to share the Lord with him and he seemed open. They conversed for a few more minutes.

"Judi, I'm real interested in hearing more. Are you sure you won't join me for dinner?"

His words were harmless, and how long had it been since she'd gone out to dinner? "Uh, okay." They went to a nice steak house that evening. He treated her really nice and afterward, back at their condo complex, he walked her to her door and thanked her for a pleasant evening.

The next morning Judi found flowers with a card on her doorstep. *Oh no!* When it was time to do her laps in the pool, she snuck out the long way, not wanting to walk by his place. She tried to hide her pink swimming noodle under her towel, but it stuck out on both ends. *Oh well, maybe it won't give me away.* Apparently she was wrong. He showed up in the pool area within minutes. "Hey,

Judi, I just came to say hello and see if you'll join me in the hot tub tonight."

"Doug, you need to know that we can never be more than friends."

"Of course, Judi, but I would like to be your friend. I could learn a lot from you."

*He's so sweet, what can it hurt to be his friend?* That week, while he was working out of town, he sent her another card and phoned twice. Friday night he called and invited her to go to the Manhattan, a very nice dinner place. At that, Judi started to like him. The next day they went to breakfast and then to the pool. In the evening Doug bar-b-qued steaks for her. Again, they went to the hot tub. That's when he kissed Judi and she kissed him right back. *Lord, please protect me and keep me in the palm of Your hand.*

The next day she found another card on her doorstep from Doug. She closed the door and leaned against it. She opened the envelope with trembling fingers and read. "I think I'm falling in love with you…fast."

Now her fingers really shook. Then the doorbell rang and she jumped, catching the doorknob in the small of her back. She took several deep breaths, and peeked out the window, before opening the door. "Hi Doug, come on in. I'm glad you came by so we can talk."

He strutted in with no shirt, exposing his strong muscular upper body, skimpy shorts showed off his tanned legs. "That's why I came by, Judi." They sat down on the love seat. "Judi, I want you to know that I think you are beautiful and I don't think you are too old for me, but you are too young for guys your age." He leaned forward and pressed his

*Old enough to know better*

lips against hers. She went all weak inside. Feelings that had been dormant bubbled up in her being. Doug pulled her close to him, then lifted her onto his lap. Too close for comfort, Judi squirmed. There was a battle going on inside her spirit—tears came to her eyes. Her heart and flesh wanted him with everything she had, but her mind and spirit screamed NO! Doug, seeing her reaction, jumped up with a confused expression on his face. "I think I better go." Walking to the door, he looked back at Judi, shaking his head, "I'll call you later."

"Okay Doug, sorry about that." Disappointed and relieved at the same time, Scriptures flooded her mind. John 4:7 "Resist the devil and he shall flee." 1 John 4:4 "Greater is He that is in you than he that is in the world." And 2 Corinthians 12:9 "In my weakness He is strong."

Still, she found herself infatuated with the man. But, Doug didn't call like he said he would, so Judi walked four doors down to his place. Again, he said, he wanted to be her friend and more. "I love you, Judi. Let's go out tomorrow night and we'll talk about how to do this *friend thing*.

Friday night—no show. Her stomach was in knots. She called her son, Steve, to tell him her dilemma of having a crush on this guy. He said, "Mom, you must sever the relationship."

"I know you're right, Steve." Her voice came out muffled through her tears. "I started getting used to all the attention and not being lonely."

Steve prayed for her. "Lord, please end this situation for my mom. She is too weak to walk away. Comfort her from Your Word and in her spirit. In Your Name!"

"Thank you, Steve, I think I'll work on my new song "Forgiven, by David Meece." Judi, hung up the phone, turned on the music, and let the flowing movements of her pantomime speak for her. She felt better, but it still hurt her stomach that Doug hadn't called all weekend.

*Ring…Ring.* Judi rushed to the phone. *Maybe that's him.* "Hello?"

"Hey, Jude. It's Teresa. You wanna come over for some iced tea?"

Judi had been keeping her friend posted on the Doug drama, and she lived right by the pool. "Sure. Be there in a few." Judi wasted no time. *It'll help to talk to someone.* She walked down the courtyard and past Doug's place. As Judi reached the tennis courts, which was right next to the pool, she saw Doug—it was like watching a re-run. A girl was in the pool and Doug was checking her out. He jumped in and she got out, followed by Doug. Judi turned and walked another way so he wouldn't spot her. But, as she was approaching Teresa's place, he did. At first, the blood seemed to drain from her head while her legs went weak. Then, boldly, she said, "Hi, Doug."

Teresa opened her door by this time. "Hi, Jude. You okay? Come in and sit down. Hey, you're smiling!"

"It's so funny, but after all the stomach aches and throbbing heart, suddenly I feel at peace again. I think God just rescued me."

"Well, maybe you'll be much wiser next time."

"No next time. Last time I was fixed up with a blind date, he turned out to really be blind. I thought he was nice till he tried to use braille on me!"

Teresa laughed until tears shown in her eyes.

"But seriously, God seems even more real to me right now. I'm going to share this with the girls at the Evangel Home. They can relate to things like that, with all they've gone through. I know the perfect title for my talk: I Am Exhibit A of What *Not* to Do When a Womanizer Flirts with You."

Teresa got a bang out of that as they both busted out laughing again. "Will you perform a song for them too, Jude?"

"Yes, I have just the one that says it all."

There are voices on the road of life
And I've made choices that I knew weren't right.
And they brought me to my knees
At the end of a lonely street.
I am standing here today,
I want to say,
God gave me back my tomorrow,
I threw tomorrow away.
He took this life full of sorrow,
Suddenly everything changed.
The moment it happened,
It was the moment I knew,
It was like walking in the darkness,
When the light came shining through,
I said that God gave me back tomorrow.
~Ray Boltz

# Chapter 27

## Mission to Romania

In the autumn of my life, I became Judi with an "I". The name no longer represented my independence but rather, me becoming who I am in Christ. I ceased being the child my mother told me I was, the woman my ex-husbands wanted me to be, and the mother my children expected me to be. When I decided to live my heart, I began to find God's heart.

### ~ 2000 ~

I met my daughter for Sunday brunch at our favorite, Mimi's Cafe.

"Happy Mother's Day!" Nicole held out the brightly wrapped present. "Thought you could use this for your trip to Romania."

"A journal… Perfect." I hugged my daughter. "Thank you so much, Denée…I mean Nicole. I'm not used to using your first name again, but I'm glad you returned to it. Pastor Scott said we have to write in our journals everyday while we're on our mission trip. I'm so grateful—this is going to be a trip of a lifetime. I never dreamed I'd have this opportunity. "

"What do you hope to get out of this, Mom?"

"Well, aside from wanting to impart something to the lost children of the world, I want to find God's heart.

"You'll be in our prayers, Mom."

With a heart full of excitement and anticipation, I looked forward to this life changing experience. I'd turned in all my money, plus an extra $200.00 to help others fulfill their commitments. Several people sponsored me, but the biggest donation came from Dave and Kylie. Originally the trip was planned for 1999 but a war broke out in Kosovo so our mission was delayed a year. Now the trip was only two weeks away. Since I started planning this trip, I'd experienced struggles emotionally, physically, mentally, financially, and spiritually. For four months, I battled a bacterial infection—it passed just in time. I hoped I'd be a blessing to God and His people in Romania. *I am so weak, but He is so strong.*

## ~ June 18, 2000 ~

As class leader of my singles group at Peoples Church, I spoke in Sunday school the day before leaving. "Good morning! Thanks to all of you who have contributed to my trip to Romania. My desire to go on a mission trip started about twenty-five years ago when I was only thirty-three and a new Christian. I would hear the young people give testimonies about their mission trips and I was envious. I never dreamed I'd have the opportunity, yet here I am a young fifty-eight-year-old grandma preparing for a life-long dream. Why do I want this so much? Aside from wanting to impart something to the lost children of the world, I want to find God's heart. I'm going with Pastor Scott, who is drawn to the Romanian people. There will be nineteen students from his youth group, five adults, and me.

"I have to confess to you, class. I've been secretly happy that I would be staying in hotels while most of you are going on the camping trip. I only like camping in 5-star hotels." Everyone laughed. "I want to do a song for you called *Stand* by Susan Ashton. Again, thanks for all your support, standing by with me, and most of all your prayers." One hundred fifty class members prayed for me that morning. I was in good hands.

## ~ June 19, 2000 ~

*Judi and Carol Holck*

My house was in order and bed made. Carol arrived at 8:20 a.m. to take me to get my favorite coffee at McDonalds. "Who knows when I'll be able to enjoy a cup of coffee like this again?"

"I've heard that Scott brings his own coffee, Jude. Maybe he'll share it with you."

Entering the church parking lot, I could see everyone arriving on time, ready and excited. We gathered to get our last minute instructions from Pastor Scott, then held hands and prayed before getting on a big bus that would take us to the LAX airport. We played games and shared testimonies along the way. Alisha, one of the chaperones, had quite a testimony and I was drawn to her spirit.

It was quite an ordeal checking twenty-five people onto two different flights. I struggled to stay with the group, bumping into the crowd of people. Pastor Scott and half the team got on the first flight. I waited two hours with the remaining ten for flight 604, due to take off at 6:25 p.m. Finally, with baggage checked, names punched into the computer, and passports held close, we sauntered through security to board the KLM Royal Dutch Airlines. Andrew was team leader for our group. *I am so hungry. Hope these peanuts hold me over till dinner on the plane.* I stayed close to Alisha, who would be my roommate, and Jolinda, my flight takeoff buddy. Jolinda, Jo for short, and I held hands and prayed at every takeoff and sometimes for the landings—our least favorite parts of traveling. "I'll never understand how these big planes get off the ground," I said. Jo gripped my hand and nodded fiercely.

## ~ June 20, 2000 ~

The plane arrived in Amsterdam around 2:45 p.m., that was 5:45 a.m. Fresno time, which meant we'd been up for 24 hours. When my group came out of the airplane, Pastor Scott waved us over. "You guys have three hours before our next flight, so you can do a little sightseeing, but stay close together."

I joined the group headed toward the Anne Frank House, competing for space on the bike-filled streets. "Andrew, look how dirty the canal water is. You know, Holland is a city of bikes and dikes."

"You got that right. I wonder how many canals and dikes there are. We should ask. I can't imagine riding to work in a business suit every day. It's obviously their main mode of transportation."

"It's so warm and humid. Everyone sweats and you can smell it. Otherwise it has its charm with the old buildings and waterways." I tried to hold my nose and keep my eyes wide open.

After our little sightseeing tour, it was time for our flight to Budapest, Hungary. "Hey Jo, ready for another two-hour flight?"

"I'm okay with the two hours, just not the takeoffs."

"Ditto, but we've got each other, right?"

"You bet." Jo smiled with her big beautiful eyes. Her strong hands gripped mine. She and Andrew competed in weightlifting together and their defined muscles provided the proof.

Like the others, I was beat when we arrived in Budapest. It was a scary place. We were greeted by a huge police presence, guns in hand. Pastor Scott looked stressed while keeping his cool. He had a fixed smile on his face as if to keep the rest of us from worrying. He told us to keep quiet and calm, but watch each other's back. Our group lined up to board the charter bus. Being so unorganized in their search, the police put our things in and out of the bus compartment about a dozen times before they were satisfied. In an unfriendly manor, the officials finally allowed our group to board the bus. The six-hour trip would transport us to Oradea, Romania. Getting across the border was a *trip*. I was so tired but couldn't sleep. It was such a bumpy ride. We passed over a hundred trucks trying to get across the border. "And, why do the police stop us every few miles to check our passports? This is crazy!" Hours later we were still lined up waiting to get the go ahead.

## ~ June 21, 2000 ~

Finally, we arrive at, what? A minus-two-star hotel? Our rooms were on the tenth floor. I got in the elevator with Dan, Alisha, and a couple others with all our luggage. When it stopped with a jolt, the elevator was stuck between floors so we had to climb out, dragging our luggage. For the rest of our stay we took the ten flights of stairs up and down. I cringed at all the dead rats on the stairway.

Disillusioned, I followed Alisha into our room. She looked around and noted all the faults. "Judi, look at that hole in the wall."

"No way." I looked around to find something to plug it up with. Finding nothing, I settled on getting my dirty socks out of my suitcase. As I bent down by the hole, I could see into the next room. "*Shhh*," I whispered to Alisha. "There are two Romanian men in there."

"*Humm*, well at least we have our own bathroom, speaking of which, I better use it now! *Uhh*, Judi, the water comes out orange. The toilet tank is above and to flush, you have to pull the chain… and, it leaks."

I looked into the small bathroom. "Great, so you can sit and shower all at the same time. But, where are the shower curtains?"

Alisha's eyes grew bigger by the minute. "Did you notice the drain is on the outside of the shower? And, the towels aren't much bigger than hand towels."

"Yeah, they look like rags to me. We'll use them to clean up the wet floor after our showers." And that's what we did till the maids yelled at us. They only changed the *rags* every other day! I discovered there was

*Hotel bathroom*

only one outlet in each room. Ours didn't work. Well, it sparked! I sighed and tried to find a positive. We did have a balcony, but I didn't dare step out there because it was tilted and looked like it was about to break off. *Oh brother!*

## Our week in Oradea and Băile Felix

Exhausted, my roommate and I got to bed about 6:00 a.m. While we were still sleeping, some locals from the village marched right into our room without knocking, trying to sell us some doilies! They scared me silly, as they jabbered in their native tongue. What an experience. Oh—so much for getting out of camping with my singles group! The joke was on me!

I didn't get much sleep because we had to meet with Save the Nations ministry, who was in charge of our first week in Romania. That brought our combined forces up to fifty foreigners. We met every morning and were bused to different areas for a variety of work. We were invited to different churches, too. At the first church we went to, the nationals put on a service for our benefit. Halfway through the program, I stifled a yawn and whispered, "Oh, we're a sorry bunch. Still jetlagged, everyone's trying so hard, but failing to stay awake." Wes and Candace were the only ones who managed. Heads were all bobbing at different times. On a couple occasions, we were standing for prayer and I almost fell, dozing off. I'd never fallen asleep standing before.

Our group usually didn't eat dinner till about 10:00 at night, maybe because it was still light at that time. Although I never did fast food in the States, McDonald's became a luxury for me. One evening we ate at a nice hotel. However, we were never served butter. We always had to ask for it and then, after a long wait, the waiter could only find one little pat. The food wasn't very good, but the ice cream for dessert tasted grand!

Back at our hotel, after the long days, I used a walkman to listen to my music and drown out the noise from the holes in the wall. Sleep took over, at last.

## ~June 22, 2000 ~

I stumbled out of bed and into the shower, letting the orange water flow over my body and splash onto the floor. Considering all the obstacles, it felt pretty good. Walking back into the room, I discovered two disgusting beetles on the wall above my bed, just waiting to greet me. Covering my mouth, I let out a loud scream.

Alisha jumped up and came to my rescue. She took it upon herself to kill them. "Don't worry, Jude. I'm used to this job. My big, burly husband is afraid of spiders, so it's my role to get rid of all critters." Now there were beetles stuck on my wall. *Yuk.*

I was really looking forward to breakfast and coffee this morning. Per hotel regulations: Come to breakfast at 9:00 a.m.— and don't be late. Well, the group and I got to the hotel restaurant and were told we couldn't come in till 9:30 a.m. The hotel staff was very rude! When we finally got in, the tables were set with bread—no butter—cheese and some kind of orange drink. Waiters came around and put two hot dogs on each plate. We each got a 2" x 2" napkin. To top it all off, we got no coffee. When I asked for some, the waiter gave me something that was much stronger—too strong—and tasted like pee. So much for a nice breakfast. After that experience hardly anyone went the following morning. That made the hotel manager so angry that Pastor Scott said breakfast was mandatory. He said, "People here are used to communist rule and until someone in authority says we don't have to show up, we are expected to do so." *So there!*

After our morning meeting, I watched the teens practice their skit, in which they acted like puppets that the devil could control. It was a beautiful message of how God cuts the strings and frees us.

Different churches hosted our group for lunch—those were the best meals. That particular day, the church I was bused to had a bright pink unisex bathroom. There were four sinks but only one worked with only cold water. Of course—no toilet paper. *They really have a paper shortage in this country.*

Later we got bused to a Christian orphanage. Some of our group played volleyball with the kids. Not I! I sat on the ground watching, when a nine-year-old girl and a ten-year-old boy came over to me with dirty, sticky hands. They started playing with my hair and the next thing I knew, they braided my hair in three places. It didn't look good, but felt so much cooler in the hot and humid weather. When they finished, I sat on some gum, which made me even stickier. That didn't help my phobia of stickiness.


### ~ June 23, 2000 ~

"Hey, Jude. You snored last night." Alisha gave me a sleepy smile.

"I knew I was exhausted. I guess I'll start my day with another rusty shower." There was a nice surprise waiting for me when I came out of the bathroom.

"You had room service this morning, Judi. Pastor Scott brought you a cup of real coffee."

"I haven't had a good cup of coffee since we left the States. He makes it in his room with Starbucks coffee from home." I savored my first sip. "Hey Alisha, can I borrow your curling iron, mine's dead? I look like a wild woman."

"Oh, sorry, mine burned up."

"What else is new? Come on, let's go to breakfast."

This morning the hotel served us a bell pepper, an orange, cheese and bread—no butter. After breakfast, Dan did the devotion on the greatest commandment, which inspired me. We went to another orphanage and got to work. One of the buildings recently burned down and a lot of bricks were still hot. We made a bucket brigade and handed off the bricks till they were all removed from the debris. The sun was hot on my tired sore body, and from the looks of the others, they felt the same discomfort.

When we finished, we went back home. Did I say *home*? I can't believe I called a minus-two-star-hotel home. The curtains were probably fifty years old. The only thing the maid did as far as I could tell was empty the waste basket. *Probably looking for goodies.* Anyway, I only had about fifteen minutes to get ready for our first outside rally.

We walked to the village and set up the sound system. Close to two hundred people came to see what was happening. A few from our group dressed as clowns and played with the kids. The crowd stayed for the whole rally. From the moment it started, and as I looked around to pray for those watching, I got very emotional and couldn't stop tears from splashing on my cheeks. The teens did every skit and drama so well. I was proud of them and so touched. Andrew, my team leader, gave the message. He did such a good job. He gave an alter call and half the crowd came forward. It was a very emotional experience for me. About 10:00 p.m. we had dinner— late as usual—then I did my devotions and went to bed.

## ~ June 24, 2000 ~

Pastor Scott brought me coffee again in the morning. The hotel served hot dogs for breakfast again but I didn't eat them. They also served bananas. I ate two! The maids didn't work on the weekend so our trash didn't get emptied. We had the same *towels* for four days, and some of us were actually accused of stealing these rags. I bought some ice cream for 5,000 lei and later a candy bar for 12,500 lei. The stores were much smaller than my bedroom. We did an outreach in the square where the statue of the famous hero, Mihai Pătrascu stood. He reigned from 1593-1601 and was better known as *Mihai Viteazul*—Michael the Brave. It went well but at the end an orthodox priest started yelling at us to leave.

*Michael the Brave*

## ~ June 25, 2000 ~

On our last day in Băile Felix, Romania, my team went to the English service at 3:00 p.m. and we were in charge. I performed *The Hammer* by Ray Boltz. After church, before leaving for Bucharest, we were transported to eat at—you guessed it—McDonalds. For our big group it was such an ordeal, however nothing could top the experience at the train station. I must mention that when Pastor Scott first told me we would be traveling to Bucharest by train overnight, I was ecstatic. I pictured it being like in the movies with the sleeping compartments, etc. The joke was on me, again. At the train station, our group got separated for a moment and it was scary. There were throngs of people. Once our train stopped, we only had fifteen minutes to board with our load of luggage. Some guy grabbed my bag and darted off with it, so I started yelling at him. One of the guys in my group grabbed it for me. Well, nothing could have prepared me for the train trip we were about to encounter. These trains had to be more than two hundred years old and in need of some repairs. Seven of us girls were put in one sleeping compartment that only had room to sleep four. Besides three bodies too many, we also had to put our suitcases in with us. It was hot and stuffy, so everyone hung out in the two and a half foot hallway. Men walked through with cigs hanging out of their mouths. The grossest thing was the bathroom. I can hardly describe it but there was urine all over the floor because every time the train stopped, everything sloshed out. And of course—*no toilet paper!* The girls and I stayed up as late as our eyes and legs would hold us, and then tried to squeeze into our bunks. Pastor Scott told us to be sure we locked the doors. But of course, our door was broken and we couldn't even shut it all the way. It was past midnight before things quieted down.

## In the middle of the night

I couldn't hold it any longer, so I made my way to the *covered-with-pee* bathroom, my Kleenex in hand. On the way back to my compartment, I evidently dropped a clean piece of Kleenex in the dirty hallway that was covered with cigarette butts. Back in my compartment, I managed to climb over suitcases, working my way to the bunk. It took several minutes to get adjusted before I finally dozed off to sleep. Sometime later, the conductor barged through the door, knocking over our belongings and started barking at us with a cigarette butt hanging out of his mouth. He waved my *clean* piece of Kleenex at us, which he had picked off of his dirty floor. All the girls woke horrified. I couldn't believe how rude he was. I explained to the girls what he was trying to communicate to us. After the shock was over, we all started laughing and digging for snacks. Once again, we settled down. The train was so stifling and hot that we had to rig the window with straps to keep it open. Lightning lit up the sky for about four hours. Rain came down on my head half the night till I got the bright idea to turn the opposite way. Then my feet got wet. I was grateful that the girls let me have the bottom bunk, which I shared with two suitcases and two duffle bags. I bet no one slept more than ten minutes at any given time while on the train. Even so, a loud snore startled me out of a sound sleep. I realized it was tired old me! I sat up and looked out the window, surprised to see some pretty countryside.

At 7:40 a.m. we reached our destination at Bucharest, with another chore ahead—getting everyone off the train. Angie's people from City of Hope, *Save the Children,* were there to greet us and walk us to the Hotel Astoria. There were no lanes on the streets and cars got as close as five inches from each other. I couldn't understand how they managed to escape hitting one another. Luckily we didn't get run over on our way to the two-star hotel—by Romanian standards—a real step up from the one in Băile Felix. The drain was still on the outside of the tub/shower but at least there was a shower curtain and the towels didn't look like rags. I was so tired and feeling carsick, it felt like I was still on the train. I took a nap and barely woke up in time for orientation. I looked terrible, but as it turned out I looked worse as the day went on.

After orientation, we headed for the metro, and Pastor Scott carried our burden. He put all our passports in a duffle bag and wore it backwards to protect them. More than once someone tried to grab his bag. God's angels were covering us. We got off the metro and had lunch at KFC. It had been eighteen hours since any of us had a meal. After lunch, we split into two teams. One group went to the girls' home run by City of Hope and our team went to the boys' home. The boys on our team played soccer with the kids. I just talked to some of the boys and then we got caught in a thunder storm.

Looking gross, we met up again and headed for Pastor Scott's favorite Italian restaurant. It was the best meal so far, but nothing like home. I got a big meal, dessert and *apa plata*, bottled water, for only $5.00. As the cooks made our salads, cigarettes hung out of their mouths. The server told Andrew he could try the different flavored ice creams. One by one, he tried them and the server dipped the same spoon that was in his mouth back into the ice cream. We gave Andrew a bad time and said we would skip eating the ice cream treat.

We had a wrap-up meeting and at 10:45 p.m. I was in charge of room check. I was given a room to myself so I felt like a VIP. I wrote in my journal before turning in and fell asleep with pen in hand. Even though the windows were shut, I woke up to barking dogs at 4:30 a.m., then drifted back to sleep.


## ~ June 27, 2000 ~

Today's breakfast was probably the best so far. I ate all my omelet and toast, leaving the cheese and tomatoes untouched. Smoke was everywhere and made us all appreciate the smoke-free restaurants in California. We had devotions after breakfast and left at 9:30 a.m. for ministry. My group went to the girls' home this time. I wasn't as good with the kids as the students were. We played games and watched a movie, *Parent Trap*. The kids picked their nose a lot. One girl wiped her boogers on her leg and then gave me a big hug and then played with my hair. *Eeew.* I also had a flea on my face. The home was clean but there were so many kids to keep clean. At the end of the day, both teams met at Pizza Hut. I rarely eat pizza but here it's a treat.


## ~ June 28, 2000 ~

I enjoyed the luxury of being able to dry and curl my hair this morning. So, the day started out pretty good. And, what a day it was. *One I feel I've waited for my whole life.* The group's escorts arrived at 10:30 a.m. to take my team to the Rescue Center run by City of Hope. There, we prayed, sang songs, and shared. Larissa, one of the volunteers, was Dutch and had been there since February.

She seemed like a pro as my team followed her to the square by the train station to talk to the street people—adults and children, alike. They were starved for affection. Everyone had a bag of glue or paint that they breathed constantly. I witnessed some of them cut themselves on the arm or other

*Judi and the Romanian Street Team*

places, with broken glass, to escape the emotional pain. "Sometimes the police do it to them!" Larissa explained. One of the street kids, Daniel, was so sweet and hung around with the group. He called me, Mama.

"Daniel, how is it you speak such good English?"

"I stayed at the City of Hope but leaved because the rules too hard for me. I do whatever I want."

"Daniel, please keep talking to Jesus."

Our team then went shopping for bread and lunchmeat to make a hundred fifty sandwiches. First we walked along the train tracks and found families in shacks made of cardboard or tin. One mother had seven children. Her little boy brought me a box to sit on while I visited them. I was impressed with this lady, trying to make the best of nothing and being grateful for what little she had. I felt an immediate connection when I gazed into her face. "Maria, you are a beautiful lady."

When our visit was over, she kissed my hand. And there it was—the heart of God—shining through her eyes. I lifted her hand to return the kindness, but she tried to pull it away. "*Nu, nu!* My hands dirty." I kissed her anyway. She bit her lip and tears brimmed her eyes. I lowered my eyes so she wouldn't see the water in mine—through her, God touched the bottom of my heart. I will never forget this amazing woman.

Our group went back to the train station, the square, and the park to hand out more sandwiches. My little helper, Daniel, led us to a place I'd never forget. "Come, Mama!" Other street people followed. We squeezed through a small, narrow opening between two buildings that led into a dilapidated and condemned building. It was once a hotel. The place stunk and was nothing more than a filthy rattrap. However, the people in there were so proud to have a roof over their heads, even though they were constantly afraid the police would drag them out. A young lady grabbed me—pulled me through the debris and up a decaying stairway. It was the only time I got a little scared. I called for my team member. "Wes!" He ran behind me and the woman pulling me, and into her *room*. It was obvious the woman tried to make this gutted out room into a home for herself. A piece of cloth, which she had managed to tie into a bow, decorated the shabby wall. She had placed a door on the floor that she made into a pallet for a bed. Fleas were jumping on it. She wanted me to sit on it—so I did. This really blessed the woman because she felt honored I sat on her bed, fleas and all. She kissed my hand. It seemed like this adventure only lasted a breath of time. I wished we could do this every day.

## ~ June 29, 2000 ~

*Oh no! My alarm clock overslept, so I overslept. I still can't believe yesterday and pray I get a chance to go back to the streets.* However, today we were divided into four different teams. My team was picked to paint the stairway in the girls' home. The top part of the wall was painted a lime green and the bottom part was orange sherbet. There were three flights to paint with an oil-based paint that was very sticky. We got into some funny and sticky situations. While trying to paint, kids kept running up and down the stairs and their handprints are all over the wall. One thing that bothered me was that the downstairs door was always locked and one needed a key to get out. I hated to think of what would happen if a fire broke out.

## ~ June 30, 2000 ~

I woke up thinking of my kids. *Lord, please bless them and my whole family.* I prepared for a day with a lot of fun and a lot of hard work. There were nine people on my team that went to the warehouse to clean and purge. We found a lot of outdated, donated food items and clothes full of holes. We made an assembly line to pass cases of jarred food to be tossed. That was back breaking and I got more fleabites for souvenirs. Let's see, where did we have lunch? Oh yeah, McDonalds. At the end of the day, instead of asking all four teams *where* they went for lunch, we would ask each other, "Which McDonalds did you go to?" Yes, McDonalds became my new best friend. And, since I didn't usually drink coke, I had enough to last me ten years. I praised God for it, too.

Tonight was our last meeting in Romania and Pastor Scott said some nice things about me. He said that my coming on this trip with a bunch of teenagers, showed something of my character. *Or, did he say I was a character?*

## ~ July 1, 2000 ~

My last day in Bucharest was also the sightseeing/shopping day. As usual, our group took the metro to our first site. Pastor Scott continued to carry all our passports. Since we'd been there, four of our members had been pick pocketed. We had to be extra careful on the metro and wear our backpacks in front of us. We kinda looked like twenty-five pregnant people. While we were on the metro, a lady knelt down with hands folded in a prayer-like manner as she shoved her son into the aisle to beg for money. It hurt my heart to watch.

We went to see the Palace of Nicolae Ceaușescu, an egotistical Communist ruler. Nicolae Ceaușescu fled Bucharest by helicopter on December 22, 1989. Our group couldn't go inside because some government officials were there. So, we took the long walk back down the mall and went to lunch—to, guess where? We then went shopping. I got some souvenirs for my family. Some of the group got accused of stealing, even though they had receipts.

Back at the hotel, I saw Daniel again. "Hi, Mama."

"Hey, Daniel. You want an ice cream?"

"Sure." We walked around awhile then I prayed with him. He gave me a big hug.

"Good bye, Daniel, please keep talking to Jesus."

## Leaving Bucharest
## ~ July 2, 2000 ~

*It's July 1ˢᵗ in Fresno. This is the day the Lord has made and it's early to rise to head for home.* I checked out of the hotel about 4:45 a.m. but the manager said I needed to pay for a telephone bill, even though I never touched the phone. Pastor Scott paid it for me. We were all ready with our luggage and were greeted once more by our Romanian friends. For the last time we heard our new friends say, "We go now." *I love that phrase and hope we continue to use it every time we leave for an outing.* We had a convoy of four vans to transport us to the airport.

KLM Royal Dutch Airlines—flight 1358 left Bucharest about 7:00 a.m. and arrived in Amsterdam at 9:00 a.m., however, the clock on the wall showed we'd gained an hour. This was where we bid farewell to Dan Baker and his daughter, Whitney.

"I'll miss you guys. Especially your teasing me, Dan." My voice cracked, knowing I might never see them again this side of Heaven. I said my goodbyes with a little hug and a huge lump in my throat.

Hmm…I wonder why people call it 'good' bye, if you really don't want to see someone go!

Now for another five-hour wait for our next flight, back to the states.

We boarded Northwest Airlines, flight 8617 and left at 2:20 p.m. It was a nine-hour flight and we arrived in Detroit at 4:45 p.m. What a hassle going through customs at this ugly airport. We had time to get a bite to eat. I was looking forward to getting a decaf Mocha Frappuccino® at Starbucks. As luck would have it, they didn't have decaf and they didn't have mocha.

## United States
## ~ July 2, 2000 ~

As we boarded the plane to California there were two other teams just leaving for mission trips. One was a Christian team going to Mexico and the other group, People to People, was going to Australia. I thought to myself, "This is going to be a bumpy ride." Our team had been up for twenty-four hours now and this was a miserable five-hour flight. While we were tired and at the end of our venture, the other teams were full of excitement to start their journey and were not at all quiet. It was over-the-top uncomfortable and I couldn't sleep over all the noise.

We arrived in L.A. at 9:17 p.m. and my luggage didn't show up there. I had put my luggage on the belt with everyone else's in Detroit for the L.A. destination, but mine went right back off because someone tagged it Detroit. *Huh? I had every stitch of underwear in my suitcase.* Jeff picked us up with the church bus. It had a bathroom, too. And, toilet paper, yea!

As the bus drove into Fresno I thought, "This is a *beautiful* city." We arrived at the church at 2:00 a.m. Everyone dispersed so fast. Alisha and her husband Ashley, drove me home. I hadn't seen a bed in thirty-two hours. After a nice shower, I got to bed about 3:30 a.m. I was in my home, safe and sound.

The next morning I couldn't find my keys. I'd left them on the outside in the door lock. So much for safety measures.

## ~ **July 4, 2000** ~

I went into work the day after coming home to clean up my desk. All I could think of was going on another mission trip. My singles group was planning a mission trip to Mexico in the near future. After Romania, a mission trip this close to home just didn't seem as exciting, but I realized that God would always have something special for those who heed His call to do and experience. Excitement started mounting in my heart once more. *I'll follow wherever He leads!*

# Chapter 28

# Mexico Mission Trip



IF I'VE LEARNED ANYTHING ABOUT MY GOD IT'S THIS: His heart is everywhere and it's His heart I want to satisfy most.

## Campos de Sueños
## ~ 2001 ~

The sun was barely up when I climbed into the van. Another adventure—another means of finding God's heart—and the dust hadn't fully settled on my previous journal entries. Early to rise and shine.

Two vans and one trailer pulled out of the parking lot at 5:45 a.m., accompanying Pastor Mick and his group of single adults to Ensenada, Mexico to build a house in two days. The church in Mexico chose the families in need. Sitting right behind the driver, Kylie and I prayed, sang and shared testimonies on the long ride. I was in charge of the walkie-talkie our van used to communicate with the other van. *Lord, get us across the border with no problems.*

Arriving at Campos de Sueños compound, our vans were

greeted by the missionaries waiting and ready for us. The helpers cooked and served a great spaghetti dinner to our team of hungry mouths. We were shown to our dorms to settle in. I picked the bed next to the sink so I could use the mirror. However, with fourteen girls, I hardly ever got to it. We couldn't put toilet paper down the toilet due to bad plumbing. It was hard to remember that at first, but after awhile, the smell from the wastebasket reminded me. It was rough sleeping the first night because we had three snorers in our dorm. I borrowed earplugs the next night.

The following morning I took an early walk to the beach with some of the volunteers before devotions. Somehow, I accidently got on the wrong side of a barbed wire fence. If the soldiers caught me, I would be shot. One of the guys helped me find my way back to the right side. I ran back to the compound for fear of a soldier seeing me.

Being on the construction team, I put my work boots on and grabbed my gloves. Our team went to the site where the family who had been picked to receive this blessing lived. The family looked anxious and excited as they stood waiting for us, beside their present cardboard house and the rock stove they cooked on. One of the little boys had just hurt himself, and I was able to doctor his cut and make friends with his family. In return, they made us some tortillas. *Yum!*

After a morning of hard work, the girls were in charge of making sandwiches for the lunch. We forgot to bring utensils so I rolled up a paper plate and used that to spread the peanut butter. One mentally-challenged teenager from the village walked around us all day. Pastor Mick told me to invite him to eat with us. However, I said his name a little backwards when I called to him. "Hey-hor, como eat luncho."

Pastor Mick turned around, his eyes set on me—a perplexed look froze on his face. "Judi, his name is Jorge, pronounced hor-hey, not *hey whore*." Then everyone that heard me started laughing, and my ears turned red.

*A sticky situation*

I must mention again, that I have a phobia of being sticky, so I wasn't happy when one of the guys told me to make another sandwich for a little Mexican kid that looked hungry. Obediently, I made a sandwich and when done, another kid came up behind me, tapped me on the shoulder—his eyes begging for one. I made another sandwich. Then another tapped on my shoulder. I looked behind me and, to my surprise, it looked like a whole village of kids were coming for sandwiches. God really has a sense of humor.

The next day our tired bodies set out to finish the house. The partner I was working with that day was about my age. We were painting the wood along the foundation. He was struggling getting on his knees for the job. I had no problem getting on my knees, but getting back up was a problem. I had to admit to him that I felt I was getting too old for this job. At that point, I took a break and walked over to the field next to us to help shuck little green tomatillos with the field ladies. This was easier than building a house. Without understanding what the ladies were saying, they taught me what to do. We gathered around the wash barrels and somehow I kept splashing myself and my new friends with water. They seemed to get a kick out of a gringo just walking up to them wanting to help. Somehow we were able to communicate enough to laugh at each other.

Break time over, I walked back to the house that was almost finished. I was looking forward to when we would turn the keys over to the designated family. Finished with my part, I headed to the van where Alice sat. She was too tired to do anything else. There was a boy standing by the van and he kept looking at my boots. He had no shoes. I gave him a smile. "*Quieres mis zapatos?*"

He grinned back. "*Sí, sí.*" He took them as soon as I got them off my feet, put them on, and off he went.

The crew was now getting ready to pray and hand over the keys to the family. I didn't want to miss that, so I turned to Alice and asked if I could borrow her shoes.

She gave an infectious laugh. "I knew that was coming."

I slipped on her shoes, which were way too big for me, and ran over to the house for the ceremony. I got blessed out of my socks, as we prayed for the family and handed them the keys. It was a real *Kumbaya* moment. When we finished, I noticed a yard sale across the field. I grabbed a couple of friends, headed over there, and bought a pair of shoes for only 50 cents! They fit perfectly. The family that sold them to me was so happy. Now I could return Alice's and still have shoes to walk in.

Although it was a huge blessing to do God's work there, when it was time to go home, I was anxious to get back to the States. No more putting my *used, soiled* toilet paper in the trashcan. No more worrying about food poisoning. But, getting to the border was always a concern, especially with two vans full of gringos! From Ensenada to the border, we were stopped by *policia* several times. We had to get out of the van each time while the police searched it and gave each of us the look over. We managed to keep our cool and got to the border safe and sound and homeward bound.

# Chapter 29

## Rock 'n' Roll Marathon

I DIDN'T REALLY RUN ALL THE WAY—I jogged and walked off and on. I guess you could say I *jalked*.

## ~ June 2, 2002 ~

I trained for an upcoming 26.2 mile marathon to be held in San Diego. In the midst of my training, I fractured my right shoulder, which was the second year in a row that I damaged my shoulder. Up at 4:30 a.m. every morning to meet the running group and train. Then off to work every day. Since I was up so early, I was eating lunch about 9:30 a.m. My co-workers enjoyed teasing me about that.

It was important, as marathon participants, we got to a certain point in a specific amount of time or we wouldn't be allowed to continue. Reason being, the race committee couldn't close the freeways beyond a reasonable time. I stopped at every port-a-potty while others went in the bushes! That was evidently a tradition. I even stopped to get a ten-minute massage because my hip was screaming at me. Then there were the bands. I got up on stage and danced with every band along the way! I also joined the cheerleaders and did a cheer. I always wanted to be a cheerleader, and couldn't pass up my childhood dream. I met a lot of people and *jalked* with one or another along the way. Near the end, I could only walk, but when I heard the crowd, I jogged the last two-tenths of a mile. When I crossed the finish line, my head was pounding and it kind of scared me. Someone put a medal on me, another person gave me an energy bar—which I gladly ate—and a bottle of water—that I was in much need of. I was the last one in my group to cross the finish line—

# 20821

then again, I was also the oldest in my group!

| Race | Rock 'n' Roll Marathon |
|---|---|
| Last Name, First Name | Charbonneau, Judi |
| Sex/Age | F/60 |
| Time | 6:29:58 |
| Over All Place | 13569 |
| Sex Place / Div Place | 6789 / 26 |
| DIV | F 60-64 |
| Net Time | 6:25:30 |
| City, State | Fresno, CA |

After the race, I retrieved my belongings from UPS Truck #5. These people were so organized. It took me awhile to hobble around looking for my group. I gave up and decided to limp the long road back to my motel with a hurting hip and blistered feet. I asked the Bike and Buggy man for directions. He asked if I wanted a ride. First, I said no because I thought it was strange and not safe to accept a ride from a stranger, as I was taught. However, the more I thought about it and how sore my body was, I finally asked, "You'd really give me a ride?"

He grinned. "Yes, for a price."

*Oh, Duh!* We agreed on ten dollars, which would be worth it and kinda fun having something to *write home about*. It was a little scary moving through the traffic, and I didn't think we'd make it up the hill. It was more fun passing up my jealous friends along the way. When we got to the motel, the guy asked if I wanted him to carry me up the stairs! Of course I said, "No, the buck stops here."

# Chapter 30


## My Climb


M Y  FIRST-BORN,  STEVE,  TURNED  THIRTY-SEVEN
TODAY. I don't know what he did on his birthday, but I
hiked twenty miles.


### ~ June 2002 ~

I learned a long time ago I don't like to camp out, so while my
hiking friends pitched their tents last night, I stayed with my friend,
Carol, in her quaint little cottage that looks out into the meadow,
with Half Dome peaking beyond it.

"Thanks for keeping me last night, Carol. Visits with you are
always the best."

"My pleasure, Jude. Here, let me have your backpack." Carol
tossed it in the trunk of her car. "Hope you have plenty of water,
it's supposed to reach ninety degrees today."

The scene was gorgeous this time of morning, with the moon
still crowning the cobalt sky, suspended between the towering walls
that made up Yosemite Valley. Carol pulled into a space at Curry
Village and as I got out, I breathed in the cool fresh air.

My colleagues at work spent the last two and a half months

planning this venture. And, I'd hiked more miles than I could count this decade to prepare for it. After a quick breakfast, we'd be on our way. Destination: Half Dome.

The sun had yet to make an appearance, though it was officially up when we set out at 6:00 a.m. The shuttle busses didn't run that early, so we had to walk an extra mile and a half to the trailhead. The first part of the trail was paved, but quite steep. Don, the leader of our group, passed me on one of the few down hills. "Stay on the Mist Trail, it's the shortcut to Half Dome."

"Anything to save a step." I was already feeling the altitude.

Kathy laughed. "That means it's the hard way up."

"As if this isn't?" In order to keep going I put my head down and watched the trail directly in front of me. *If I keep looking at my feet I don't see the beauty before me. If I look too far ahead, I stumble and fall. I think the Lord is teaching me something here!*

Each time I looked up, I found myself farther than I imagined. I rounded another corner and got my first glimpse of Vernal Falls. *Now I'm really making headway.*

"It's breath taking." A stranger whispered as I passed him on the bridge.

"In more ways than one." I was still gasping for air, but paused to look up-river and watch the light play on the cliffs. It danced in the spray of the waterfall. Tearing my gaze away from the beauty of creation, I realized I was no longer with my group. Kathy and Tom were the pros, they must have gotten way out ahead of me, so I didn't linger. Up and up the series of stone steps I trudged to the top of Vernal Falls. I was drenched by the time I reached the plateau, whether from the mist or sweat, I didn't care to know. I hadn't caught up with anyone I recognized, so I pushed myself harder climbing up to Nevada Falls. Still no one from my office.

Carol was right. It was warmer than usual up there and oh so beautiful. There weren't any real strangers when I was out hiking. Something about a shared journey linked me to those around me, even if we didn't speak the same language—and I heard a lot of different countries represented that day. At one point, the trail got too quiet. I didn't see anyone in front of me or behind for that matter. *Do bears make a warning sound before they charge?* My feet wouldn't wait for my brain to figure it out. I jogged until I caught up with another group of people. We shared a smile and a nod—they might have been Swedish.

The population on the trail picked up, and hikers started passing me more frequently. *Who filled this pack with rocks?* My back screamed at me, because I knew water and snacks couldn't weigh that much. More footsteps crunched up behind me and I edged to the side of the trail to let another hiker pass.

"Judi." Kathy's voice sounded breathless in my left ear. "We thought we'd never catch up with you."

I spun around so fast I almost knocked myself over.

Tom caught my arm and steadied me. "Think we can catch Don? He's the only one ahead of us now."

I nodded dumbly and forced my feet to start moving again. "Whew. I thought I was way behind."

"How about we exchange loads?" Tom held his one bottle of water out to me. "I'll wear your backpack for a ways."

*What a deal—I couldn't pass it up.* He slipped the pack off my back and I discovered a new joy in the verse about bearing one another's burdens. Chatting with friends was the perfect distraction. But once my back stopped hurting, my legs started to give out. "Go on without me." I sounded just like some mortally wounded explorer.

"Are you sure, Jude?" Kathy looked concerned.

"Really, I'll be fine here." When they left, I

*Trail to Half Dome*

plunked down on the perfect sized rock at the side of the trail. I dug an orange out of my bag and savored every juicy bite. I let my head droop and eyes close for a moment. Then I prayed. *"Lord, I think I will just see how far I can get on my own again."*

I hit the trail once more, rejuvenated and within a half-hour, I spotted Don up ahead of me. He was at the last stop before the stretch that leads to the steps that go up to the cables of Half Dome. He patted the rock next to him. "Take a rest. I'll wait for you."

"Thanks, but I don't think I'll go much farther." I lowered myself gingerly and pulled a snack from my backpack.

"You've got to at least go to the steps, Judi."

With a little more fuel in me, I was revived again. I changed my socks and Don pulled me to my feet. As we got closer to the steps, Don's encouragement started to make me believe I could actually climb the steps and conquer that mountain, except for one thing. "I'm afraid of heights, Don."

"You can do it." We came to the steps and began our ascent. "Don't look down."

*How can I climb without looking where my feet are going, and my feet are in the down region.* One, two, three…eighteen, nineteen. My peripheral vision was working too weak at that point and I started to get queasy. Then I froze completely. There were two way's off the mountain at that point—three if you count the drop-off on the other side. I forced my gaze up to see how much farther I had to go, and everything started to spin. I knew, without a doubt, my children and grandchildren were the only bragging rights I needed.

Leaving Don to continue on without me, I turned around, sat down, and inched my way down the steps on my butt. Once back on safe ground, fear and disappointment gradually gave way to a new sensation. I'd made it farther than most of the younger people in our group. "I really accomplished something." Every step I took, I knew God was watching me—smiling.

On the way down, I met up with some of my friends that were

still climbing. They were surprised I'd gotten so far ahead of them. "Good job, Jude."

"Thanks, I need to get back to catch my ride home."

One of the guys told me to look for Debbie. Her hip was hurting and she couldn't make it the rest of the way. When I found her, we had a bite to eat before starting back down the mountain. "Jude, both my knees are giving out. It's very painful."

"Okay, Deb. We'll take the easier trail, although longer, we have no choice"

"Whatever you think best, Jude."

I loved Debbie and thought she was a real trooper—hardly complained even though she was in so much pain. I found a stick for her to lean on and I supported her on the other side. "Hey, Deb—there's Merced River. Let's take a rest and put our feet in."

"That sounds so refreshing!"

Refreshing it was, but it couldn't last. We had to get back to our slow descent. Even coming down the mountain, there are hills to climb. We were running out of water and Debbie really needed some, so I gave her mine. *What a martyr huh?*

"Gee, Jude. I feel like a sixty-year-old woman."

"Hey! That's my age and I feel like a 37 year old." *Which was Debbie's age.*

"Oops! Then I guess I feel like a ninety-year-old woman."

Since we were taking so long to hike down, our friends caught up with us. "Hey guys! You're a sight for sore eyes. Can you take over taking care of Debbie? I have to get to my ride."

"Sure, will do. You go on."

I gave Debbie a hug and promised I'd pray for her. I really enjoyed our talks and time together. Then I took off jogging almost all the rest of the way down the mountain trail—after hiking for eleven hours! I had another two miles to go. When I got to the road, I realized I didn't know how to get to Curry Village. There were two groups, but I didn't know which one to follow. *Good thing I'm not a guy, 'cause I'm not too proud to ask for directions.*

Jeff and Diana were waiting for me and ready to hit the road. We stopped at Oakhurst to eat dinner. One by one we wobbled into the restaurant. As people stared at us, we would turn and say, "Half Dome." When one guy started clapping, the whole restaurant exploded in applause.

It was a great experience, but I think next time we should take a trip on a houseboat. It would be easier on the younger folks.

# Chapter 31

## Black and White Days



I THINK I'VE ALWAYS BEEN A COP WANT-TO-BE. I'm too old for that now but I was able to attend the academy to become a Citizen on Patrol and drive a real police car.

## ~ 2004-2009 ~

I graduated from Citizens on Patrol academy. Now, as a C.O.P., I can wear a uniform, drive a patrol car, and assist the real cops. Fun, fun, fun! Everyone was given a detail number to use while on duty. As a volunteer, ours started with the letter V. However, in law enforcement, to avoid confusion or miscommunication, a Phonetic Alphabet Scheme is used in dispatching and routine communication. It works by using specific words to represent each letter of the alphabet. Thus, Victor

*C.O.P Graduation*

represents the letter V. The first time I heard the dispatcher call my detail on the radio, I really flubbed up.

"Victor 227 what is your location?"

"Victor 22 uh 7 we err can uh." My partner had to take over. I was so embarrassed because every cop on duty heard me over the radio. It took awhile, but I eventually got the hang of it.

I always went with a partner. Most of our calls were to do a tow sheet when someone was being arrested. While getting ready for the tow, we did inventory of the vehicle. Looking for drugs, we often found some. My partner took a picture of me and the cop with a bag of drugs. Then the cop looked inside and said, "Oh, crap." There was a bomb inside the bag of drugs.

He put it on the hood of his car, drove to the nearest open field, and put it in the middle of the area. We were then dispatched to that field. "Victor 227—I'm sending you an event." The event showed up on the computer in our patrol car.

"Victor 227— copy." We were sent to secure the scene while the robot secured the

*Bomb scare*

bomb. Watching with eyes wide, we crouched behind our vehicle until it was safe. Eventually a special police truck came to take the robot to some remote place, where the bomb could be detonated safely.

Another call that should have been a simple tow, almost turned out to be deadly for me. While filling out the tow sheet, little did I know, a police chase was going on a few blocks away. The suspect blew a light at the corner I was on and hit a car, which sent the suspect flying into another car that started rolling toward me. At the last second, I managed to move just in time, so as not to be squashed between the runaway car and my patrol car. One of the cops later told me when he saw that happening, he prayed that God would keep me safe. God's angels are everywhere!

"Victor 227, are you available for a call?" The dispatcher's voice crackled over our radio.

"Victor 227, affirmative."

An event came up on the computer to transport a citizen from one location to another. We followed the GPS and arrived at an apartment complex to meet the officers that needed us. There had been a dispute between a mother, about sixty-five years old and her daughter. We were assigned to take the mother to a friend's place. It took awhile to get her large body in the back, plastic seat of our patrol car.

The lady pressed her face up to the bars that separate the front from the back seat. "I just had a baby today."

"Really? Where's your baby?"

"Oh, I left him in Oregon."

My eyes met my partner's with raised eyebrows! When we reached our destination, the lady wouldn't get out of the car. We called her friend's phone number and she informed us that she didn't want this lady in her apartment. Then the lady in the backseat started yelling at us. I was so glad there was a cage between us. We called the sergeant and he sent an ambulance to take her off. My partner was pretty freaked out, but I told her it was just another story for us to tell.

I was surprised at how many cops actually try to help people. They try to counsel them when needed. They are often lenient when they can be. We are all out here to be a service to citizens all over the city. On duty one evening, my partner and I tried to wave a car over to tell him to turn his lights on. When he noticed us, he started speeding.

"Victor 227 to dispatch."

"Yes, Victor 227."

"Please run license number Adam Baker Charles one two three. He is driving recklessly, heading south on Lincoln Avenue."

"Copy." At that point, officers on that beat pursued the driver. When he was stopped, he was arrested for having weapons, and in violation of his parole. That made us look good.

*Cop Judi*

I learned a lot from my sergeant, Eddie Barrios, and had a blast working with the cops.

The saddest part was securing a scene when someone had died. We weren't allowed to tell the family until the coroners finished their job and then the chaplain's role was to notify the family. In the meantime, we just had to stand there, watching parents, spouses, and children crying and waiting to be told.

I think my favorite part was looking for and finding lost children. Fortunately, for me, my calls always had a happy ending. I think that was my specialty.

# Chapter 32

## New Best Friend

### ~ August 2009 ~

My baby turned forty-one, so I took her to breakfast and shopping for her present. After I dropped her off, thoughts of returning to an empty house drove me to the animal shelter. I'd wanted a dog for more than five years and had been diligently looking for the past two. Just couldn't find the right one. I had my heart set on a yellow lab or one close to it. On the adoption side of the shelter I could take the dogs out to see how they responded to me. One little guy looked at me imploringly, so I took him out. He tricked me. All he wanted was to pee and be free. He wanted nothing to do with me. Other dogs were either too shy or too hyper. Some were just too strong for me to handle.

"Why don't you look on the other side of the shelter," one of the volunteers advised. "That's where we keep the strays, hoping to be rescued by their owners. If you like an animal, you can't take it out until the fifth day it's been here, but you just might find the dog that's perfect for you."

I walked the line not seeing anything I wanted, but one dog kept sticking his arm out for me to pet. It was a black dog with white trim. Not the color I was looking for but he was real sweet.

I tried to talk other visitors into looking at him, but there were no takers.

Day 2—I came back looking for my blondish-labish dog. I wanted an adult dog that would be mellow like me. No luck, but that black dog with white trim was still there, sticking his arm through the wire fence for me to pet. He looked so sad.

Day 3—That same dog was there with a roommate. He came over and put his arm out but his roommate growled at him and pushed him over. With a sigh and discouraged look, the black dog moved to the corner and looked at me with those gentle, chocolate-brown eyes.

Day 4—I walked both sides of the shelter, the adoption side and the stray side. *No! No! No! There's that dog again, sticking his arm out for me to pet.* I looked at his card and it said ADULT. *Hmmm. Not exactly what I'm looking for, but he's an adult. Not sure.*

Day 5—*He's still here. You know, even though I don't want that dog, I think I'll take him out to give him a break.* The worker put him on a leash and led us out to the front. There were men, women, and children. He liked everyone. Outside, he stopped at the first tree and peed for a good minute. He'd been holding it forever. I then took him to their enclosed training area, which was about fifty square yards. Once inside and gate closed, I let him off his leash and he took off running. I sat on the bench and watched him enjoy his freedom. Suddenly, he ran back to me and jumped up on the bench next to me and put his head on my lap. *Oh boy, what's happening here?* "We better go back buddy."

*One smart dog*

Back in the office, the worker was waiting. "Do you like the dog?"

"Well, yeah! He's real nice."

"Okay—I'll just fill out the papers. He has to be neutered and given his rabies shots, etc. It comes to $189.00."

"Oh, okay then." I wrote a check and was told I could pick him up on Friday. That gave me two days to think of a name for him. *Did I just buy me a dog?* I took Friday off work, to pick up Henri and he hasn't left my side since. Oh, the vet said he was about a year old, i.e. still at the puppy stage. So much for getting an adult dog.

I know he must have had a family with kids because when I first got him, he cried every time he saw children. Not anymore. He's so attached to me that he only cries when I cry. He's a handsome guy being a lab/pointer mix, but when people ask what kind he is, I say; "He ain't nothin' but a pound dog."

# Chapter 33


## Redeemed Regrets


"Be still and know that i am god." What else is a girl to do when she can't do anything anyway? It might be time to take inventory of my life. I lost my job of eighteen years and had another bad fall.


### ~ 2011 ~


"Help… Help… Somebody help!" A car drove by, but it didn't stop. Henri never left my side. "Is this how I'm going to die, Lord? Just walking my dog on this windy day and end up like this." I couldn't move. *How did this happen?* Finally, someone stopped and called 911.

"Don't move ma'am, help is on the way. Do you want me to call someone for you?

"Yes, my daughter's number is in my phone. Nicole."

"No answer, anyone else?

"My son-in-law, Michael."

He looked in my phone and touched the number. "No answer."

"My best friend, Robyn."

For the third time, he left a message and shook his head. "No answer."

Within minutes, the firemen and EMTs were there. "We need to cut your jacket off, ma'am." *Why are these guys always so young and CUTE?* It was my only Jason Meyers racing jacket. Well, Robyn's been asking me to get rid of it, being it's so old now.

The fireman holding Henri's leash bent down and scratched his ears. "If you don't have anyone to take your dog, we'll have to put him in the pound."

"Oh no! He'll freak out. Please put him in my house and I'll have someone get him later." So that's what they did, and sent me on my way to the hospital. A fractured shoulder on one side and broken leg on the other—would keep me from a trip to Dubai to visit my son, Steve, and his family. I seem to have a talent for falling. This was my fourth bad one. There was one while running, one exiting the treadmill—I forgot to turn it off, one on an easy hike, and now this—just walking my dog.

And, as I'm being loaded into an ambulance, life suddenly seems fleeting.

I think I'll write a book. Why do I want to write a book of my life? Maybe it will help me feel significant. Yet, my existance holds little value apart from the work God does in and through me. He has revealed things in my heart that I never knew before my journey with Him. Things I want to share with my children. Things that will touch the *heart of my seed.*

I've experienced His faithful forgiveness, yet bear the scars of sin, which remind me each day of His abundant grace. Even though redeemed, I still have some regrets. Number one—I regret I never joined the service. But then, since it was during the Viet Nam war, I might not be here today. Number two—I regret I ever married Norrell to escape my mother. But then, I wouldn't have my three treasures in Steve, Gary and Nicole and my eight grandchildren. Number three—I regret I didn't nurse my babies, but at least they were nourished through God's word at an early age.

Number four—I regret I ever divorced Norrell. But then, I might not have come to know my Lord and Savior!

Have I accomplished everything I wanted to? Have children. ✓ Jail ministry. ✓ Street ministry. ✓ Dramatic Music Interpretation. ✓ Go to New York. ✓ Mission trips. ✓ Marathon. ✓ Half Dome hike. ✓ C.O.P. ✓ Get a dog. ✓ Move into a brand new house. ✓ Have someone to grow old with and always have my back. ✘ Close-knit family. ✘ Overcome all my inequities. ✘ Write a book. ✓

---

People are often unreasonable and self-centered.
Forgive them anyway.

If you are kind, people may accuse you of ulterior motives.
Be kind anyway.

If you are honest, people may cheat you.
Be honest anyway.

If you find happiness, people may be jealous.
Be happy anyway.

The good you do today may be forgotten tomorrow.
Do good anyway.

Give the world the best you have and it may never be enough.
Give your best anyway.

For you see, in the end, it is between you and God.
It was never between you and them anyway.

~Dr. Kent M. Keith

---

I've tried to live by this—not always successfully.

# Heart of My Seed

*Steve, Chyna, and Khanh*

*Rebecca, Chase, Gary, Sheila, Natalie, Storm*

*Paige, Michael, Morgan, Madeline, and Nicole*

# Afterword

## Steve Charbonneau

I write the following pages to contribute to my mother's work. She has asked me to write and contribute to her project—her effort to document our family's history. I do so, somewhat reluctantly, in order to honor her. Who would be interested in reading about my past? Perhaps not even me. Nevertheless, I write on.

At the center of my personal history, is an effort to follow Jesus. If there is an award in Heaven for *hanging in there*, I might be a candidate. However, at present I am afraid I am not in the running for anything more than that when my time comes. This statement does not come from a place of self-deprecation or even false humility. In fact, I can say that I have genuinely stayed in love with Jesus for most of my life. Nevertheless, that love has ebbed and flowed over the years, in a cyclical pattern, with fits of passion, at times followed by seasons of tepidness.

Nevertheless, I am happy to report that I sense no condemnation from Jesus. In fact, I do sense His satisfaction that I remain a follower of His. I also feel his patient encouragement for me to give more of myself to Him. I am continually working on that. I establish this aspect of my spiritual life here, because it has a great impact on how I now see my past. Indeed, Jesus has been better to me than I have been to Him. I am very grateful for that!

My relationship with Jesus began at the age of eight, a few years after my mother divorced my father. My mother took her three children—I was five at the time—away from our average middle-class suburban existence and initially relocated us to a low income neighborhood in Milpitas, California, which is just north of San Jose. Three years later and still struggling financially, we moved to *the projects*, a low-income government housing, in a sketchy San Jose neighborhood and were there for a number of years. To be honest, during this time I had no idea we were poor. I do remember a sense of feeling less secure and lacking self-assurance.

While living in this San Jose neighborhood, my mother was approached by some *church people* who offered to take us kids, along with others in our neighborhood, to church every Sunday. Those church people ended up being Baptists and drove a bus to our neighborhood to deliver us to and from their church. I do not remember much about my experience at that Baptist church. I do remember that we often received little gifts and tokens on our way back home from church each Sunday—a happy meal, gold fish, a toy. It was on one of those Sundays that I asked Jesus *into my heart*. Honestly, I am not sure why we call making a commitment to Jesus, asking him into your heart. Nevertheless, that is what I did. I believe He is still there today.

The years following my parent's divorce are somewhat of a blur to me. I do recall that my mother re-married and had several boyfriends enter the picture—I am not sure what order all this romance happened. My father rarely spent time with us kids. I do fault him, and yet forgive him, for allowing the broken heart he received from the divorce with my mother to get in the way of a relationship with his children. Life was a bit chaotic during those years and my mother's relationship choices were not all that beneficial to her or her children. And yet, she consistently instilled good values in her children and showed us a mother's love.

From time-to-time my mother asks me if the choices she made and the life we led with her in those days scarred or hurt me. While I am certain I bare scars, they are scars I have earned myself from choices I made during my life. Even those scars fade away over time, as I turn to my Maker and ask for grace and healing. He never denies me. As for my mother, I can honestly say that her *sins* were committed when she was a young mom. Looking back, it is easy to see that her life was on a slow upward climb. Her trajectory in life began to change when she became a Christian at the encouragement of her children, who learned about Jesus from Baptists who helped us escape from an impoverished and dangerous San Jose neighborhood for a few hours each Sunday.

Things got dramatically better for all of us, when my mother married her third husband. Jerry Wood brought solid Midwestern American values and consistency to the family, but after ten years of marriage my mother and Jerry also divorced. I was just out of high school at that time. Although that divorce was devastating, I do see now how Jerry was a godsend to us. As God blessed Jerry and his career took off after his marriage to my mother, our socioeconomic status also improved. That meant we could move away from neighborhoods like the one in San Jose and have a better life.

I recently read an article in Medical News Today that summed up a ten-year study on the marriage habits of children who are a product of divorce. While children of divorce want to avoid putting themselves and their own children through the pain that comes from the dissolution of a marriage, they face unfavorable odds. In fact, Barna Research Group states that if your parents were divorced, you're at least forty percent more likely to get divorced than if they weren't. If your parents married others after divorcing, you're ninety-one percent more likely to get divorced. Yikes!

My mother is herself a child of divorce—and then re-marriage. However, I believe she helped break the cycle of divorce in our family by standing against it just in time to make a difference in the lives of her children. How did she do this? During her marriage to Jerry Wood, she had her own true conversion to Christianity. Consequently, my mother began to pray for the long-term spiritual well-being of her children. This included prayers for our future spouses and for successful marriages. Ironically, her newfound faith would be a big part of the reason she and Jerry eventually grew apart. Her marriage to Jerry was her last marriage—at least at the time I am writing this. My mother has since lived as a single woman for the past thirty years.

I had always suffered from a short attention span at school. We moved around a lot during my formative years. In fact, I attended at least eleven different schools during my kinder through high school years. While that transitory existence did not help my academic development, it was not the sole reason I did poorly at school. Now that I am older, I realize that I am wired a bit different than others. I enjoy learning, trying, and doing many, many things. I get bored easily if I am not able to take on some new adventure. That is how God made me. Unfortunately, a conventional education did not foster this spastic and creative brain of mine.

I was attending junior college, when Jerry and my mother separated. At that time, I went from a less than average student, to a failing student. By the age of twenty and still living with Mother and siblings, I decided to join the Army. This shocked everyone, as I went from visiting an Army recruiter to being shipped off to boot camp in just three days. My sister would tell me years later, she felt at that time I had abandoned her like so many other men in her life had done. I regret having caused her to feel that way and always will.

I disliked every moment I was in the Army. I have often said that a minute in the Army seemed like a day, a day like a month, and a month like a year. It truly felt that way. I suffered greatly while in the Army, by making poor choices and just being young and stupid. However, I have always been too stubborn to quit anything and so I did achieve success while in the Army and earned a few official military accolades as a result. On the day of my release from the Army, I drove on an adrenaline high for twenty hours straight back to California.

As a full grown, mature, and balding man, I now know the secret of attracting women. It's a secret that does not benefit me at all now, as I have been happily married for many years and am no longer interested in attracting women, save my own beautiful wife. The secret? Self-confidence! Unfortunately, I had zero self-confidence until I was twenty-five or twenty-six years old. Growing up, I watched my younger brother establish himself as a *chick magnet*. Even as an underdeveloped high school freshman, girls my age found my brother irresistible. For a man, self-confidence works like a powerful love potion. Unfortunately, until I was in my mid-twenties, I attempted to engage the female species with a moderately effective love potion that worked only intermittently.

After a few serious, but ultimately not-meant-to-be relationships and toward the end of my bachelor's degree program at university, I finally began to feel comfortable in my own skin. I had an easier time relating with women and was not interested in dating anyone casually. Timing is everything and I thank God for his perfect timing! In 1992, after a few series of events and seemingly random circumstances, I met my wife, Khanh. Had I met her any earlier, I am certain I would not have been ready for my destiny—our destiny. Khanh and I started out as long distance pen pals, writing letters to each other with paper and pencil, the old-fashioned way as email was not an option then. After a few months of romantic letter writing, we met in person and have rarely been apart since.

I do not regret a single day of my marriage to Khanh. I look forward to spending what is left of my life with her. By the grace of God, we have beaten the statistical odds and have a healthy, long-term relationship that only gets better each year. I often say that there is nothing sexier than history. That is history with someone you love. A few years ago, I went back to university to earn my doctorate. I wrote the following preamble for my dissertation that sums up how important my marriage—my family—is to me:

"It is in the concept of family that I find purpose and meaning. I did not find true joy in life until my wife and daughter entered the picture. I consider them to be gifts from God. Without their support, I could not have completed this research. My wife is my equal in every way. I have benefited from her counsel and encouragement during my doctoral studies. The love I have for my daughter is what inspires me to try to make a difference in the lives of other peoples' daughters and sons. I thank both my wife and daughter for making my life complete."

Khanh and I had our first and only child, Chyna, after three years of marriage. I have always felt so unworthy to be Chyna's father. In part, not having a consistent father-figure in my life to model what being a good father is all about, left me feeling unprepared. I pray every day that God will help me be the kind of father that Chyna needs. While I put a lot of passion and good intentions into being Chyna's father, I always wish I was better at being a father. Nevertheless, I have pledged to remain actively engaged in my daughter's life as long as I breathe. That is a pledge I intend to keep. It has been an honor and pure joy to be her father. I often feel sorry for my father when reflecting on how amazing it is to be a parent.

Being a Christian is something that should be natural and organic, not cold and religious. I have tried hard to model having a rubber-meets-the-road relationship with Jesus for my daughter. A meaningful relationship with Jesus is something that can only happen when we are unpretentious with God. It means being faithful to him, trusting Him whether we understand our circumstances or the world around us or not. I had the opportunity to write a song with my daughter. It is a simple and short song, but says so much. I pray she will make these lyrics an important part of her approach to life.

# Summer and Winter

*By: Steve Charbonneau and Chyna Charbonneau*

*Verse 1*
*God, please be there when I'm doing great*
*and be there when I make mistakes.*
*I need You in good times and bad times too.*
*I need You in summer and winter, oooh.*

*Chorus*
*Lord I'm trusting in You,*
*know You'll see me through.*
*I'm trusting in You.*

*Verse 2*
*Sometimes it's hard to believe in You,*
*but Lord I promise I am going to.*
*Even when it's hard to do,*
*Jesus we put all our trust in You.*

*Steve and Chyna*

# Author's Note

Whew! I have spent hundreds of hours and dollars on this project. What am I going to do with my time now? Well, look for a new job of course. Like I tell my dog, Henri, "If you want to eat, you gotta work." That's biblical. Since I got in the job market late in life, I wasn't able to accumulate enough savings to live comfortably when I reached retirement age—seems I like a higher standard of living than my pension allows—and since I'm dyslexic, it's difficult learning any new job. When I do find one, my friends call me a miracle worker. They say it's a miracle I'm working. Seventy-one now and not liking it one bit. What was God thinking?

But, after all is said and done, I have absolutely NOTHING to complain about. God has always been good to me. I've never had so little that I had to steal, or had so much that I was ungrateful. On the mountain top or in the valley, nothing has touched me that wasn't filtered through the love of His nail-scared hands. Besides, why should I question God when there is always someone walking on a harder path. My one desire is that I won't be a burden to my children, since I have never been able to give them all they deserve. However, God has given us all more than we deserve and I hope one day I will hear Him say, "Well done, my good and faithful servant." I'm looking forward to that day! And, like Job said, "Though He slay me, yet I will trust Him."

Jesus truly fulfills my heart!

As I look back, I'm amazed that God has brought me through so much. Maybe I'm not standing on the best road He would have chosen, but, He's held me close when I needed Him most. I know everyone has a story and I hope you enjoyed mine. Don't you wonder what God has in store for you and me? I've heard it said that every ending is also a beginning. I'd like to believe that's true.

# Photo Credits